CONFRONTATION . . .

The constraints of quiet widowhood have become too much for Lady Caroline Pearson to bear—especially now that her brother-in-law has idiotically, and illegally, gambled away her house. Boldly, she confronts the new owner in person. But not only does the dashing rogue, James Ferrington, refuse to return Caroline's deed, he tries to take scandalous advantage of her as well.

. . . AND CAPTURE

Sheepish and repentant, James arrives on Caroline's doorstep to make amends—unaware that the young widow and her eccentric aunt are intent on retaliation. James merely meant to seduce a bewitching minx and have done with it—and, suddenly, he's a kidnapped prisoner in Caroline's cellar. But most shocking of all, James realizes that he has no desire whatsoever to be free—for the audacious Caroline has inflamed his senses, destroyed his reason . . . and completely captured his heart.

CATHY MAXWELL

"A bright new star who zooms into orbit with a luminescent radiance that happens only rarely."

Affaire de Coeur

If You've Enjoyed This Book,
Be Sure to Read These Other
AVON ROMANTIC TREASURES

CATHY MAXWELL

YOU AND NO OTHER

An Avon Romantic Treasure

AVON BOOKS ◆ NEW YORK

YOU AND NO OTHER is an original publication of Avon Books. This
work has never before appeared in book form. This work is a novel. Any
similarity to actual persons or events is purely coincidental.

AVON BOOKS
A division of
The Hearst Corporation
1350 Avenue of the Americas
New York, New York 10019

Copyright © 1996 by Catherine Maxwell
Inside cover author photo courtesy of Glamour Shots
Published by arrangement with the author
Library of Congress Catalog Card Number: 96-96079
ISBN: 0-380-78716-4

First Avon Books Printing: September 1996

AVON TRADEMARK REG. U.S. PAT. OFF. AND IN OTHER COUNTRIES, MARCA
REGISTRADA, HECHO EN U.S.A.

Printed in the U.S.A.

RA 10 9 8 7 6 5 4 3 2 1

For Ned and Pat Maxwell, with love

Prologue

London, 1813

Widowhood suited Lady Caroline Pearson just fine.

Her late husband Trumbull had recognized no difference between his wife and his horses, although Caroline suspected the horses had fared better than she. She and Trumbull had been the match of the Season, but Caroline considered the marriage a failure.

When Trumbull had choked on a chicken bone at the age of thirty-four while attending a cockfight with some of his sporting-mad cronies, Caroline had gladly wrapped herself up in widow's black . . . and hard-earned peace.

To that end, for the past three years since her husband's death, she'd avoided his family like the plague, lived within the meager allowance they provided, supplementing it with a small stipend she earned teaching at Miss Elmhart's School for Young Gentlewomen, and kept her existence

1

respectfully discreet, as was expected of a Lady of Quality. And if occasionally she grew restless with the sameness of her days, well, then, that could be expected from a woman widowed so young. She'd told herself years ago that life rarely lived up to one's expectations.

However, today, the day she turned thirty, the futility of her life hit her with the force of a slam against a stone wall.

Thirty marked the end of her youth, the halfway point between birth and death—and what did she have to show for it? Drab respectability, loneliness . . . and a sense of being incomplete.

Of course, children might have filled the void, but Caroline was barren. In seven years of marriage, she'd failed to conceive. After the second year of their marriage, not a day had gone by without Trumbull complaining bitterly of her worthlessness. It didn't matter to him that his wife had been presented at Court, knew all the expected social graces along with French and Latin, could manage his household and see to his capricious whims. What mattered was whether or not she could breed—and making sure his family and acquaintances knew that the failure to produce an heir was hers, not his.

Sane, sensible Caroline, who always played by the rules, had lost the game.

That night, lying alone in her bed, Caroline cried herself to sleep. Great sobbing cries of anger, disappointment, and sorrow. Not since her sham of a marriage had she indulged herself in such a manner.

Consequently, she overslept and woke up late

the next day, heavy-lidded, tired, and cranky—
which was unfortunate, because her whole world
was about to change. . . .

Chapter 1

What do you mean you've lost the deed to my house?" Caroline stopped in the act of pulling off her gloves, and stared at Lord Freddie Pearson, Trumbull's brother and heir to his estate, uncertain she had heard him correctly.

She had returned home from teaching her class at Miss Elmhart's Academy for Young Gentlewomen only a few moments ago, to find Freddie waiting impatiently for her in the parlor and anxious to speak to her concerning a "grave and urgent" matter. She was not surprised. Freddie rarely paid her a call unless he wished to criticize her conduct or report a death in the extensive Pearson family.

However, not in her wildest dreams could she have imagined he planned to evict her from her home!

Freddie shifted uncomfortably, unaccustomed to being challenged so directly. Caroline didn't care. "It was an affair of honor," he said at last, as

5

though such a statement explained his foolish actions.

But not to Caroline. Not today. "An affair of honor?" she repeated in disbelief. She placed her gloves on the writing table and confronted her foppish brother-in-law. "Taking a pistol and shooting someone is an 'affair of honor.' Gambling away a sizable fortune, including my house, is sheer stupidity!"

Freddie blustered. "Now see here, Caroline. You don't understand these things." He tugged on his green-and-white-striped waistcoat, which was a half size too small for him. "They are matters between men.

"What's to understand?" She took a step toward him. To her satisfaction, he sidestepped gingerly in the opposite direction, but Caroline wasn't about to let him get away. She stalked him step for step around the parlor's bare wood floors, the volume of her voice increasing with each sentence. "I understand that Trumbull left this house to me. And I understand that between you and the Pearson's incompetent solicitor, the deed to this house has been tangled up in your affairs—in spite of my repeated requests for the matter to be settled cleanly, openly, and honestly, *for almost three years.* Furthermore, I understand that not only have you ruined yourself on the turn of one single card, but you've also lost the roof over my head! Is that enough *understanding* for you?"

Freddie backed away from her until he bumped into the wall. The action made him realize his own retreat. He straightened his shoulders, his color high. He was a handsome man, much like Trumbull, with blond curls and light blue eyes. And he was just as vain and difficult as Trumbull.

He spoke, his tone indignant. "I didn't come here to explain myself to you. The reason for this call is that Mother and I have long thought you should not be living on your own. Now, with this change in my circumstances, we have decided that you will move in with her. She needs a companion, and the two of you are of suitable temperament."

"Suitable temperament! Freddie, your mother and I can barely abide to stay fifteen minutes in each other's company." Caroline gave a shiver at the memory of Lucinda Pearson's world of overheated rooms, medicinals, and quacks.

Freddie started moving along the wall, heading for the door. Caroline blocked his path. "And what about Minerva?" she asked, referring to Trumbull's maiden aunt who lived with her.

"You know you are the only one in the family who recognizes her," he said stiffly. "She was disowned years ago by the rest of us. She should never have come back from Italy."

"But she's your aunt. You can't mean to throw her out in the street."

"She can't stay with Mother. Mother still hasn't forgiven her for spilling wine on her Court dress."

"Freddie, that happened thirty-some years ago."

"Mother has a long memory."

Caroline knew that firsthand—and she also knew she'd rather be subjected to a life in the poorhouse than to serve as companion to Lady Lucinda Pearson.

Freddie, taking advantage of her moment of thought, stepped around her and reached for the door handle. Quickly, Caroline pressed her body against the door, her hand over his, preventing his easy escape. "Freddie"—she tried to make her voice almost friendly—"I think I have a solution. You must go visit the man you lost your fortune to—" She paused. "What was his name?"

"Ferrington. James Ferrington."

"I've never heard of him."

"New in town. A nabob from the Indies and wealthy beyond belief," he added with a great deal of bitterness. "He just purchased one of Nash's new houses around Park Square. He's set himself up in Society, and they all slobber over him as if they're his lapdogs. Why, do you know, Caroline, that he's already a member of the Four-in-Hand Club?" he said, referring to the prestigious driving club.

"I've been petitioning them for membership for years. I can't tell you how much money I've spent, not just on my cattle and my equipment, but also buying suppers for that whole crowd so they will give me a look. But do they care? No. They drink themselves blind and turn a deaf ear to my requests. Then Ferrington, who's little more than an adventurer, shows his face in London, and, within two weeks, they're letting him in on the first ride of the year to Salt Hill. Oh, his family is good enough, I suppose, although he is really nothing more than some upstart squire's son from Kent. And too arrogant by half about his abominable wealth. I hear the blighter spent a thousand guineas to get his driving coat and striped vest ready in time. Drops the money just like that!" He snapped his fingers. "Doesn't think twice of throwing money away."

Caroline felt a burst of confidence. "All the

better. This Mr. Ferrington doesn't need your fortune then, or my house. Freddie, you must pay him a call, explain the mistake, and ask for my house back."

His eyebrows rose to his hairline in a look of complete horror. "Caroline, what are you suggesting?"

"Oh, don't look at me as if I'm ordering you to dig up graves! The house wasn't yours to lose." In her opinion, the majority of the fortune he'd lost hadn't been his either.

After her parents had died, she'd been deeply hurt to learn her father had failed to entail a portion of his estate to his only child, but left it all to her husband. Freddie had then inherited it upon her husband's death. The thought that such a sizable estate had slipped through Freddie's fingers made her want to shout in vexation.

She used her most reasonable voice. "Freddie, if you go to Mr. Ferrington and explain the situation, I'm sure he'll give me my house back."

"I will do no such thing."

"Whyever not?" she demanded.

"Because it's not honorable." Freddie bit each word out in that curt, determined manner of his that set Caroline's teeth on edge. "A gentleman doesn't welch on a gambling debt. Or air family business in public."

"No," Caroline said bitterly, "a gentleman throws his widowed sister-in-law and his aunt into the street on the turn of a card."

That remark hit its target. Freddie's mouth began working with the speechless motions of a fish gasping for air. Caroline lifted her chin, ready to brave the storm. She didn't care if her head ached or her eyes felt scratchy from lack of sleep. In fact, she was glad of them. Maybe it was time she had it out with one of her overbearing relations on her husband's side.

But instead of giving her the fight she craved, Freddie stepped back. He took several seconds gathering his composure before he turned to her, his manner as stiff and correct as if they were strangers at a garden party. "I'm sorry you feel that way, Caroline." He tugged at his vest.

Caroline recognized the Pearson tactic: formality, withdrawal, deadlock. Trumbull had stalled her with this same approach for years. "You aren't going to talk to him, are you?" Freddie didn't answer, but he didn't need to. The first wave of shock at her new situation was slowly receding, and in its place came angry disappointment. She pushed away from the door, feeling a need to distance herself from him.

That was a mistake.

Without a moment's hesitation, Freddie bolted to the door, turned the handle, and slipped across the threshold before she could gather her wits. Caroline charged the door and tried to turn the handle to follow him. It wouldn't budge. There was no lock on the door! Then she realized he was holding the door shut.

She pounded on it with her fist. "Freddie, open up! Do you hear me? Open the door."

"I'll be by in three days' time, Caroline, to remove you to Mother's," came the muffled reply from the other side. "I'd advise you to start packing this afternoon."

Caroline slammed her palm against the door. "I

don't want to move! Do you hear me? I don't want to live with your mother."

"You know, you are still an attractive woman, Caroline, even if you are growing a bit long of tooth. Mother might even manage to find a husband for you."

That thought almost sent Caroline spinning like a top! "I don't want a husband." She pounded the door to emphasize each word. "I-want-my-house-back!"

No answer.

"Freddie!" she cried, wishing she wasn't a lady and could say exactly what she thought. Violent, vivid anger at Freddie, his stupidity, and the Society that let men like him hold all the power welled up inside her. Well, she didn't have to be a lady. Not anymore. She was over thirty. Caroline lifted her chin toward the door and said what she really thought, "Damn you, Freddie. Do you hear me? Damn you!"

Still no answer came from the other side.

Suddenly suspicious, Caroline reached down to the handle. It turned easily. He'd escaped!

She flung the door open. Freddie was gone. Two steps away from the parlor, the front door to the house stood wide open. Caroline caught sight of her cowardly brother-in-law jumping up into his phaeton. She dashed after him, but her own skirts tripped her up on the front steps, and she had to stop before she tumbled down them.

With a snap of his whip, and barely giving his tiger a chance to hop on board, Freddie drove his matched set of bays down the street—and out of her life.

At least, he'd better be out of her life because so

help her, she promised, if he showed his face in three days' time, she'd . . . she'd . . .

She didn't know what she would do. Or could do.

The realization deflated all her pride, her carefully nurtured sense of peace. Her self-esteem.

One thing she wouldn't do is pack. There had to be a way to keep her house.

"Lady Pearson, is something wrong?"

Caroline quickly blinked back the bitter, angry tears of frustration and turned to her servant, Jasper, who held Freddie's hat. He looked at her with mild confusion. "Lord Pearson left without his hat," he said. His wig moved slightly on his bald head, and he reached up to shift it back into place.

Jasper had come to her with her husband's aunt Minerva. Decades ago, when Trumbull's grandfather had disowned Minerva, his only daughter, Jasper had gone with his then young mistress. He'd served her as butler, footman, chef, and protector. Now he performed those same services for Caroline, although she could barely afford his wages. She'd grown as protective of him as she was of Minerva. They were her family.

"Yes, Jasper, something has gone terribly wrong." She shut the front door, letting her fingers linger on the smooth painted wood. Her door. Her house.

Damn Freddie!

"Is there something I can do to help?"

Caroline smiled at the elderly man, touched by his offer. Reaching out a hand, she waited until he tentatively followed her silent command and placed his hand in hers. What was going to become of him and Minerva once Freddie forced her to move out? She squeezed his hand, wanting reassurance from his aged strength.

Instead, he watched her with trusting brown eyes, his wig slightly askew, waiting for her to make a decision or give a command. With a heavy sigh of resignation, Caroline let go of his hand. "No, I don't think so. I don't think there is anything anyone can do—except for Mr. Ferrington." She said his name with heartfelt derisiveness— and it was in that moment that she experienced a flash of insight.

She took a step and repeated to herself, "Except Mr. Ferrington," testing the words and the idea forming in her head.

Caroline shook her head. She couldn't.

Hope teased the edge of her mind . . . but no. It was too bold, too daring. Still . . .

Leaning against the newel-post anchoring the stairs that led to the second floor, Caroline traced the pattern carved into the wood with her fingers. She knew and loved every square foot of her home.

If Trumbull had been alive, he would have dismissed it as a "hovel." Perhaps for that reason Caroline took so much pride in the small house.

She'd decorated it with the Pearson family's castoffs. In the parlor, two sturdy Elizabethan chairs were arranged alongside an elaborate Baroque writing desk. The large, feather-stuffed armchair in front of the fireplace had been a purchase of Lucinda Pearson's, who'd quickly grown tired of the figured fabric's pattern. Across from the armchair was Caroline's favorite piece, a graceful Queen Anne settee with cabriole legs. Surprisingly, the mixture of furniture styles worked, giving the room a comfortable, pleasant feeling, especially when the morning sun streaming through the bow window gave the room a golden glow.

Upstairs were three small bedrooms: one for a guest, should they ever have one; one for Minerva; and one for Caroline.

Caroline adored her bedroom. The single window in the room looked into the branches of a magnificent old elm tree. Every year, she knew when spring had arrived by the first light green buds appearing on the tree. During the summer, she enjoyed the cool shade of the tree's lush green leaves. Autumn saw the tree's glory, the leaves turning yellow as gold . . . and in the winter, she watched the moon rise and cross the sky, her room sheltered by the elm's stark branches.

But could she confront Mr. Ferrington herself to save her home?

"Yes!"

Jasper jumped at her sudden exclamation.

She didn't need Freddie. She'd ask for the deed back herself! Caroline took several excited steps into the parlor. "Jasper, where's Minerva?" She snapped her fingers in sudden memory. "She is with the Baroness."

Minerva spent almost every day with her friends—cronies, Caroline called them. Each had an independent and eccentric personality, and their friendships had existed over a span of years—and numerous scandals, if one believed the gossip.

Caroline gave little credit to the rumors. Minerva was well-bred, sophisticated, and intelligent, even though, by her own admission, she'd lived as the mistress of an Italian nobleman for years. It had been after his death, and finding herself practically penniless, that Minerva had ended her self-exile and returned to England—but that was where her confidences stopped.

Three years ago, when Trumbull had died and she'd invited Minerva to live with her, Caroline had been too buried in the guilt and failure of her marriage to open herself to others. As if sensing Caroline's need for privacy, Minerva had neither asked questions nor passed judgment. Gratefully, Caroline had returned the same courtesy, and in this manner they'd dealt very well with each other over the years.

Of course, Caroline was curious about the scandal in Minerva's youth that had caused her to be disowned, but the time for asking such questions was past. The Pearsons never discussed it, not even Lucinda.

Not that the scandal mattered. Caroline cared for and admired Minerva. There were many times when she wished she had Minerva's self-confidence and daring.

Caroline looked at the hall clock. A quarter past five. Minerva was due home sometime in the next hour—or later, if she was caught up in her friends' gossip. Maybe it was a good thing that Minerva wasn't here.

Caroline reached a decision. "Jasper, call a hack. I want to go out. And I need you to find an address for me. Mr. James Ferrington. He lives somewhere around Park Square. A new residence."

"You're going calling, Lady Pearson? Now? Alone?"

His questions made her pause. Caroline rarely went anywhere other than St. Martin's Church, where she was active in charity work, or Miss

Elmhart's Academy for Young Gentlewomen, where she taught French. She never went calling.

Especially not to visit a gentleman's home. Alone.

The clock on the mantel ticked. Through the open windows, she could hear a neighbor woman chat with the butcher's boy, who must have just made a delivery. A horse whinnied. A bird chirped outside the parlor window. Everything was so completely, everyday ordinary.

So, why did she feel as if she were taking a tumultuous step?

Because she was making a huge decision, an inner voice whispered. Perhaps debutantes didn't visit men's private residences, but she was no longer a debutante. She was a woman of thirty. A woman in charge of her own life, just like Minerva. No more tears. No more regrets. No more escorts. A woman of thirty could call on a gentleman to conduct business.

Minerva would.

Besides, Caroline thought with wry self-deprecation, it wasn't as if she were planning to become a *fille de joie*, the path Minerva had chosen decades ago, to the Pearsons' shocked dismay.

The thought of becoming a courtesan almost sent Caroline into a swoon of laughter. First, her mother would rise from the dead at the thought of her only child stepping over that line; second, Caroline was not the great beauty that Minerva had been; and third, Caroline didn't have the temperament for such a life. Certainly, for a woman to choose the life of a mistress, she must harbor grand passion.

Caroline had thought she'd known what passion was. She'd thought she'd felt it for Trumbull, years ago, before they'd married. Perhaps if she hadn't married Trumbull . . .

Caroline pushed the sudden unhappy memories aside.

"Yes, alone," she said to Jasper. "I'm making a business call." The words made her feel better. "Now hurry. It is of the utmost importance."

Jasper lifted his bushy gray eyebrows in surprise but shuffled off to do her bidding.

Caroline watched him as he left the house to hail a hack. She knew nothing about Mr. Ferrington. If he was anything like Trumbull or Freddie, he'd think it was his right to keep her house. Well, she wouldn't let him. Perhaps Mr. Ferrington had a wife who would sympathize with her plight. Yes, she would plead her case to his wife and avoid meeting Mr. Ferrington entirely.

"Coward," she called herself. If ever there was a time to be bold, it was now, when the threat of spending the rest of her life as Lucinda Pearson's companion hung over her head. Throwing caution to the wind, Caroline climbed the stairs to her room to change quickly into her best dress, a black Empire cut gown with a discreet white collar, her good black kid slippers, and the black poke bonnet she wore for special occasions.

And a veil. A long, heavy black veil.

A woman never could be too cautious.

James Ferrington drummed his fingers impatiently on the polished desk in front of him, his mind furiously engaged on the problems of shipping schedules, fund rates, and market opportunities. He and his business partner, Daniel Harvey, sat in their shirtsleeves. They'd been behind the closed doors of his study working on answers to these problems for most of the day.

He was determined that in a week's time, his fleet would set sail on his largest venture yet. But he was no closer to receiving a license from Parliament's Board of Control than he'd been ten months ago, when he'd decided to challenge the East India Company for a share of the silk and spice trade. He'd gambled a large stake of his fortune, as well as the money of a good number of well-placed investors, on this expedition.

Money he had no intention of losing.

Looking across his desk at Daniel, he asked, "So, do you think we've been blocked?" The officers of the East India Company had been working diligently to protect their monopoly—but they couldn't protect it forever. Granted they had money, influence, and power, but so did he. The question was: did he have enough influence to challenge their charter?

"It would help our cause if Lavenham would finally make up his mind and throw in his lot with us," Daniel said. "He could easily swing the Board of Control over to our side."

James pushed away from the desk and stood, feeling the need to stretch his long legs. Lavenham. The very influential Lord Harold Stanbury, Earl of Lavenham. James walked around his desk, thinking.

"I take it your meeting didn't go well this morning?" Daniel said.

James sat on the edge of his desk before answering, "No." He preferred to be out riding than cooped up in his study. In fact, maybe that was what he needed, a good ride. "I saw Lavenham this morning. He has no response yet."

Daniel asked the next question somewhat delicately. "About which? Your difficulties with the House of Lords, or your marriage proposal?"

"Both." James picked up a ledger and flicked through its pages, working the problem through his head. One problem was tied to the other. He tossed the ledger back on the desk. "Lavenham isn't going to use his influence in any direction unless there is money in it for him."

"So, let's pay him for his influence and you can forget this ridiculous notion of marrying his daughter."

"And here I thought you were a romantic, Daniel," James said dryly.

"No more than you are. Furthermore, if a man has to marry, why marry someone as flighty as Lena Stanbury? James, she's barely out of the schoolroom. And her voice . . ." He gave a mock shudder. "She'd drive me to madness with that incessant lisp."

James crossed his arm over his chest. They'd had this conversation more than once. In fact, since Daniel had started complaining about Lena's lisp, James could barely stand to be in the room for more than three minutes before it irritated him enough to drive him from her presence. "The marriage is a sound one. Besides, Lena is attractive."

Daniel rolled his eyes. "Not even with her mouth shut."

"There's nothing wrong with her—"

"Her eyes bulge out like one of those dogs her mother carries everywhere."

"All right." James stood. "She's not perfect, but neither am I. After all, I'm thirty-four years old and set in my ways."

"Another good point," Daniel agreed amicably. "You are too old for her."

James ignored that comment. Instead, he ran down his own list. "I'm arrogant, overbearing, extremely ambitious—"

"How do these faults compare to a 'lisp'?" Daniel asked irreverently.

"And I snore," James finished.

"Ah, yes. You do that."

"You're impertinent, Mr. Harvey."

"But efficient, Mr. Ferrington, very efficient—and if I had my way, we'd both be leaving with those ships for India. It's too bloody cold here."

James moved restlessly. "No. I like it here. Even the drizzle. London is my next step, Daniel. My next world to conquer. You can go back to India if you wish, but this is where I want to be."

"We've fought pirates together, made sultans kowtow to us, and chased women as if the fairer sex was a new religion. Now, you're telling me you want to conquer London, and what do you use for this grand adventure? Marriage." Daniel said the last word as if it left a bad taste in his mouth. "I'm disappointed in you."

"We all have to grow up."

"Not me."

"Well, my time is coming. If it makes you feel better, marriage was Lavenham's idea. He may be an earl, but he's cash poor. He's made bad investments. Lena is his youngest and only chance to fatten his coffers through marriage."

Daniel started to swear under his breath at that statement, but James cut him off with a wave of his hand. "I'm committed, Daniel, and influence like Lavenham's doesn't come cheaply. An alliance with the earl will make Ferrington and Harvey one of the most powerful trading companies in England. We'll end up ruling the China trade—and will be very wealthy men. Remember when we used to dream of this day, back when we had barely two halfpennies between us to scrape together?"

"I never dreamed of you having a wife who lisps."

"Most of the young women on the Marriage Mart lisp," James reminded him gently. "It's fashionable."

"So why hasn't Lavenham snapped up your proposal?"

"Because his wife refuses to speak of it. She wants a title for Lena."

In the way of a loyal friend, Daniel immediately took James's side. "You come from a good family. Even without a title, you could match Lena bloodline for bloodline."

"The countess thinks I'm an adventurer." James said the last word with mock horror.

Daniel shot him an easy lopsided grin. "Well, she has you there."

"Yes, but it won't matter. Lavenham won't receive a better offer for his daughter than mine."

"Don't underestimate the power of a society

matron, James. If the countess doesn't think you're good enough, nothing will make her change her mind."

"Would you like to place a wager on it?"

Daniel pursed his lips together as if he tasted something sour. "No, damn your eyes. Every time we bet, you win, and this is one wager I don't want to lose."

James laughed. James had saved Daniel from being sold into the slave trade during a skirmish with a Bedouin sheik. Since that moment, the two of them had been together. Side by side, they'd fought, struggled, and worked to build the business into what it was today. James valued Daniel's advice on everything except this one issue.

Daniel was a confirmed bachelor who enjoyed a different actress every night and admired their easy virtue. At one time, James had been equally self-indulgent. But since arriving in London, he had found he yearned for something more. Returning to England meant returning home. And what he'd said about himself was true. He'd reached the age when a man should settle down. Should set up a household with a wife and children—children who would ensure the succession of the business he was building.

James voiced his thoughts aloud. "Lena may be hopelessly silly in her manners, but she's no different from most women I've met among the *ton*. Furthermore, she is young and strong and, if she is anything like her mother, she should be able to give me many children. The countess carried nine children and all but one lives. She bore Lena when she was in her late thirties. Not many women can do that."

"Are we discussing horse breeding or marriage?" Daniel leaned forward in his chair. "James, I realize I'm not an expert, but there has to be more to marriage than that. You will be with this woman for the rest of your life, looking at her face every single morning over the breakfast table and seeing her head beside yours every night on the pillow." He raised a hand for emphasis. "England isn't like the East, where you can set a wife aside. Here, if you marry her, she's yours. Forever and ever. World without end. Amen."

James moved back around his desk to his chair before correcting him. "In England, once you've made the offer, my friend, she's yours whether the banns have been announced or not. So that bridge has already been burned. She's mine—unless she rejects the offer, which is not likely if the earl gets his way." He sat down. "And if a man must be married, let it be a wise business decision. Ferrington's Law, not God's," he added with a smile.

"So if she's yours, and this marriage is such a good business opportunity, why aren't you dining with her tonight? You were scheduled to." Daniel crossed his arms, skeptically sitting in judgment.

James felt his smile freeze into place. He turned his attention to the ledger on his desk. "I'm tired of waiting while he reasons with her. We must have Lavenham's assistance at the Board of Control meeting Friday. So I informed him that I would not be dining with his family tonight. Perhaps if I appear to lose interest, the countess will come to her senses."

"Good. Let them stew about all that money slipping through their fingers."

"Or let me stew about how we're going to

convince the Board of Control and the bankers without his support," James countered.

A knock sounded on the door. "Enter," James said.

The heavy paneled door swung open on well-oiled hinges and a regal Indian manservant entered, dressed in a turban and the black-and-white formal wear James preferred for his servants. He gave a low bow. "There is a woman to see you, *Sahib* James. She waits in the receiving room."

"A woman?"

"She asked first for your wife, *Sahib*. When I told her there is no mistress of this house, she asked for you. She says it is most urgent she talk to you."

James shut his eyes for a moment, summoning his patience. He could almost feel Daniel grinning at him. "Is she alone, Calleo, or does she have an escort?"

"She is alone, *Sahib*, and she is dressed like a widow."

"Ah, another widow," Daniel said in mock surprise.

Since James had come to London, there had been an endless succession of willing and available women knocking on his door. Some were actresses attracted to his wealth. Others were women of rank and privilege searching for a new lover and a break from boredom. All of them never ceased to surprise him by the forwardness of their advances. One opera dancer had had herself delivered in a carpet and rolled out before him by two footmen dressed in Eastern garb. The bored young wife of an aged duke had bribed his servants and waited for him naked in his bed. And more than a few had adopted the guise of a "widow."

"The attraction of looks and money," Daniel said with a sigh.

"You sound jealous, Daniel."

"I am. Think of the success I could have if *I* was over six feet tall with a full head of hair." He ran a hand over his thinning locks. "Hair is wasted on you. All you think about is building your empire. It pains me to see nubile young women turned away at your doorstep."

"Then why don't you go meet her?"

"Because you need a distraction. Put aside the ledgers for one night and relax."

James didn't want to argue. Instead, he nodded to Calleo. "Tell the woman that unfortunately, I am occupied at the moment. Offer her hack fare and send her on her way."

He started to turn his attention back to his reports when he noticed that the servant didn't instantly move to obey his command. James regarded him expectantly.

Calleo bowed again, his manner completely subservient. "I beg your pardon, *Sahib*, but I think perhaps you should honor this woman's request."

"Something special to look at, hmmm, Calleo?" Daniel asked with a sly glance.

"I do not know. She wears a heavy dark veil."

Daniel frowned. "Then what makes her so special?"

"Karma," the manservant answered.

His eyebrows coming up in surprise, Daniel turned and looked at James. Calleo rarely expressed an opinion. He had walked out of the jungle one day in India and into their camp, a dirty ragamuffin with the straight-backed pride of a king and the clothes of a beggar. Because of his clearly spoken English, some speculated that he was a banished nobleman's son. James never had discovered his story. From that first day they'd met, Calleo had latched himself onto James, seeming to want nothing more than to serve.

One thing James had learned during his years in the East was a very healthy respect for the mysterious religions of the Orient. A man did not argue with karma. Hearing the word said in the civilized center of London gave it even more mystic meaning.

James frowned. He didn't need this interruption. As it was, he would have to work past midnight to prepare for Friday's meeting with the Board of Control. "I'll be with you momentarily," he said, letting his irritation show.

The servant didn't so much as blink. "I will wait, *Sahib*."

James studied Calleo for a moment. It was unlike him to press an issue. He turned to Daniel. "Care to dine with me this evening?"

Daniel pretended to make a great study of his fingernails as he answered, "Sorry, but I've already made plans with a certain actress."

"Lucky bastard," James said mildly.

"You're not married yet," Daniel pointed out. "Accept the widow's offer. Put Lady Lena," he said her name with a shiver, "out of your mind for one night and enjoy yourself with a woman who doesn't lisp."

To James's surprise, Calleo said, "I think it would be most wise, *Sahib*." He held the door open expectantly.

Daniel laughed. "There, it's settled. You go meet your widow, and I will pursue that redhead who has the crowds clapping and shouting for more at the Drury every night." He rose to his feet. "I will see you tomorrow then? At our regular hour?"

James shook his head, curious now about this "widow." "Let's make it an hour later." His eyes met Daniel's. "After all, we both might have a busy night."

"It's my fervent desire," Daniel vowed, as he began placing ledger volumes in their place on the study's shelves. "Challenging the East India Company is interesting, but women are far better sport."

James agreed, and it would be pleasant for once to be with a woman who knew how to play the game instead of an indifferent debutante who had yet to see her twentieth birthday. He closed the report file in front of him, got up, and reached for his jacket. Pulling the jacket on, he headed toward the door.

"Happy hunting," Daniel called softly, his good-natured laughter following James as he walked down the black and white marble floor of the hallway, following Calleo to the receiving room.

James was proud of this house, just as he was proud of the business he'd built. He'd chosen every color, every drape, every stick of furniture himself. The truth was, the Countess of Lavenham's objection to his marrying her daughter didn't sit well. He had no use for aristocratic snobbery, and his years in the Orient had taught him that a man should be judged by who he was and not by his rank and title. However, now the game was to make Lady Lavenham accept him.

And he would win. He always did.

Calleo stood waiting by the ornate double doors

of the receiving room located off the front foyer. "She waits for you inside, *Sahib*," he said, and opened the door with the solemn ceremony of a eunuch presenting a harem.

James entered. The receiving room faced the street and, other than the grand ballroom, was the largest room in the house. Paneled in polished teakwood with a thick patterned carpet in red and gold covering the entire floor, this room was designed to impress visitors with James's power and wealth. He intended to rule London, and this room declared his intentions.

It was so large that it took him a second to find "the widow."

She sat on the edge of one of the gilded wood sofas—and Calleo was right. Dressed in a long, heavy veil, she looked more like a black haystack than a woman.

This was what Calleo found so special? James tossed an irritated look in the direction of his manservant.

She came to her feet. "Mr. Ferrington?" she asked, and the well-modulated tones of her low voice sent a shaft of sweet, wild desire straight through him.

He gave a curt nod, suddenly wary.

Her gloved hands slowly lifted the veil and let it fall gracefully from the crown of her hat down her back. James stopped dead in his tracks.

She was beautiful.

She personified his image of British womanhood, with her porcelain-perfect skin and clear, gray eyes the color of a lake beneath a summer storm, framed by long, sooty eyelashes. Beautiful.

The black of her widow's weeds only emphasized the trim perfection of her figure and the gentle roundness of her curves. Wonderful, full and lush curves. The wide brim of her hat made her oval face stand out, while its heavy veil drifted regally behind her. He wished she would remove the hat. He wanted to know the color of her hair.

God in Heaven, she'd fit very nicely next to him in bed. Very nicely.

"Yes, I am James Ferrington," he answered, his voice taking on a huskiness, a sign that he was in full, hot-blooded pursuit. He pulled the door shut firmly behind him.

Chapter 2

The door clicking into place sounded ominous. For the first time in Caroline's life, she was alone with a man who wasn't a member of her family.

Furthermore, James Ferrington was a far cry from what she'd expected. Here was no pampered Englishman. He brought to mind men who were explorers, adventurers, raiders. Men who knew what they wanted and were bold enough to take it. Every inch of Mr. Ferrington radiated power, self-assurance, wealth.

Only with a great deal of money could a man purchase and maintain this house. Quality was stamped on everything from the ornate carving of the divan legs and ceiling medallions to the perfect cut of the bottle green jacket stretched across his broad shoulders. He probably paid more than her annual teaching stipend for his mirror-shined boots or to get his buff-colored breeches to hug his thighs so closely that it was almost indecent.

Reminding herself that she was here on

business—important business—Caroline searched
her mind for the speech she'd mentally rehearsed
during the hack ride. She'd planned on being
straightforward and to the point, the way she imagined a cleric's wife would handle a difficult matter.
She'd also prayed that she could appeal to the
sensibilities of his wife and not to him directly.

But he had no wife.

Caroline raised her eyes to his face, her cheeks
flaming at the direction of her thoughts, and found
herself staring into a pair of the most sparkling,
beautiful eyes she'd ever seen on a man. They were
green, with flecks of gold. Eyes made for laughter—and they were all but undressing her.

The huge, spacious receiving room suddenly felt
too close.

Caroline struggled for the cool authority she'd
practiced. "I am Caroline Pearson. Lord Freddie
Pearson's sister-in-law."

"Freddie Pearson?" He appeared to test the
name as he pushed away from the door and
stepped into the room. It took all of Caroline's
control not to sidestep in the opposite direction.
"I'm sorry, I don't recall the acquaintance." He had
a deep, rolling baritone, the kind Caroline admired
in a man.

"You played cards with him recently." At his still
blank expression, Caroline's intimidation evaporated into exasperation. "You won," she reminded
him.

James Ferrington appeared to search his memory
for a brief second and then shook his head in
apology. "I'm sorry . . . Lady Pearson." He said
her name as if he questioned the title for correct-
ness.

She gave a curt nod of her head. He smiled, a disarming smile. Caroline found herself thinking almost crossly that it should be a crime for a man to have such a charming smile.

He continued, "I don't recall playing cards with a Lord Freddie Pearson." He added, almost apologetically, "I often win at cards."

His words knocked all thought of his winsome smile or rugged masculinity out of her mind. "You don't remember?" she said in open disbelief. "How could you not remember winning an absolute fortune?"

He shrugged. "I play to enjoy the game, Lady Pearson, not for the winnings."

Caroline stared at him, struck dumb by the idea of his having so much wealth that he didn't care if he won or lost. Obviously he'd never worried about where to find a coin to put in the basket for the poor at church or haggled with the butcher over a cut of meat.

She gathered her scattered wits. "My visit has to do with Freddie's game of cards with you." She drew in a deep breath, sobering herself—and couldn't help noticing the way his eyes discreetly, but avidly, followed the movement of her bosom. Could he be as aware of her as she was of him? The thought set her senses swimming with new and not-altogether-unpleasant responses.

"Is something the matter, Lady Pearson?" he asked politely—but with that voice, that rolling masculine voice—and again, he shot a discreet, appreciative glance at her breasts.

Sudden heat rushed to her cheeks. She struggled for command over herself. She was a woman. *Over thirty*. Not some giddy schoolgirl. "Mr. Ferrington, when you won Freddie's fortune, you also won the deed to my house, which was not his to lose. It was left to me as my widow's portion, and I wish it back." She didn't pause to take a breath until she'd spoken the last word, which seemed to hang in the air between them. She squeezed her thumb in a tight handclasp.

"Why, certainly," he said.

It took Caroline a full minute to realize that he'd agreed to her request, and then she almost laughed with joy. She could keep her house! She and Minerva wouldn't be dependent on relatives. She could almost dance a jig, she was so happy—

"Provided you join me for supper," he added.

Caroline's joy vanished. "I beg your pardon?"

"No, don't be alarmed." He took a step toward her. Caroline discovered that in spite of being a tall woman, she had to lean back to look up into his face. "And don't stop smiling. You're lovely when you smile."

His words startled her. She wiped the smile off her face.

"No, please," he said. "I don't mean to alarm you." The warm timbre of his voice was almost hypnotic, and she could swear his look of contrite anxiety was real. "You're not accustomed to compliments, are you?"

That was an understatement! Caroline almost laughed—but instantly sobered. No matter how tempting, his request was out of the question. She shook her head, casting a worried look at the door. "I'm sorry, I couldn't. It wouldn't be right—"

He held up a hand to stop her words. "No, let me start again." He took a step back, and Caroline was amazed how much easier she breathed when there was a little space between them. He straightened his shoulders, gathering himself up like an actor performing a part. Making a great pretense of raising an imaginary quizzing glass, he said with bored hauteur, "Lady Pearson, I find myself dining alone this evening. Would you do me the very great honor of joining me?" He made an elaborate bow that would have done a cavalier proud.

His game was foolish, but fun. Caroline caught herself smiling at him.

"Please," he added in his own voice and held out his hand.

Caroline looked down at it. She looked up into his eyes, which were dancing with laughter.

"Now, when I hold out my hand, you're supposed to place the very tips of your fingers on mine," he prompted. "At least, that's the way we snobbish sticklers for decorum handle matters."

Caroline shook her head. "You don't strike me as snobbish or a stickler. If anything, I have a feeling you enjoy breaking the rules."

The merry gleam in his eyes was infectious. "Absolutely," he agreed. "And what about you? Do you enjoy breaking rules?"

For one long minute, Caroline was tempted to answer "yes"—but she didn't. She shouldn't.

He read her indecision. "Lady Pearson, I mean no offense. I hate to dine alone. It's the loneliest thing to do in the world, but I understand . . . after all, you are in mourning."

Caroline pulled back, alarmed to think that he might believe her disrespectful of Trumbull's memory. "My husband died years ago. I mean, I'm past the official mourning period. That is, I still wear black, but I'm not actually in mourning . . .'' Her voice trailed off.

He didn't miss a beat. "I'm delighted to hear that. Then you can officially join me for supper?"

"Mr. Ferrington," she said, shaking her head, "I can't possibly—"

"Yes, you can."

Caroline looked down at his offered hand and back up to his all-too-handsome face. "It would be very forward of me." But oh, how she wanted to do it.

"I would never think that of you, Lady Pearson."

She looked again at his hand. It would be pleasant to eat with someone besides Jasper or Minerva for once. Often Minerva wasn't home for dinner, and Caroline would eat off a tray in her room while she worked on tallying the charitable accounts for Reverend Tilton. Actually, it had been years since she'd gone out, since Trumbull didn't like to dine out often—at least, not with his wife.

The blood pounded in her ears as she reached a decision. "And will you give me the deed afterward?"

"My word of honor." He smiled at her. "Besides, no one will know except you and me. What harm can it do?"

He was right. It didn't seem such a wicked thing. Tentatively, Caroline reached out, placing the tips of her fingers lightly on the tips of his.

To her surprise, Mr. Ferrington lifted her hand to his lips, the action pulling her closer to him, and lightly brushed his lips against her gloved fingertips.

A tingling sensation as bright and sparkling as

shooting stars raced down her arm, and made everything inside her tingle in response. Caroline almost didn't recognize her own voice as she whispered, "Yes, I'll join you."

His eyes blazed with bright happiness and she felt ridiculously pleased with herself that she could make him feel this way.

Nor did he give her time to reconsider her decision. He pulled her gently toward the door, opened it and called, "Calleo, Lady Pearson will be joining me for dinner this evening. Inform the chef."

"Immediately, *Sahib*," the servant said with a quick bow. He clapped his hands, and two footmen in dark blue livery appeared to do his bidding.

The sound of clapping snapped Caroline out of the haze James Ferrington had created. Their fingers broke contact. Suddenly, she realized she'd agreed to dine—unchaperoned—with a man she barely knew.

Panic . . . which immediately evaporated when he turned from the doorway and shot her a lazy good-natured grin. He was stunning. Absolutely the most masculine, handsome man she'd ever met. The pull she felt toward him was almost overwhelming . . . undeniable. After all, it was a business call, she reminded herself. And she was no longer a green girl. She could handle herself.

James leaned against the doorframe. Looking at her gave him pleasure. He saw her indecision, her hesitancy in the shadows of her incredible eyes. If she was an adventuress, she was either a timid one or an excellent actress. It had taken all of his prowess to bring her to this point, and he'd been surprised at how important it was to him that she accept his invitation.

For the first time in his life, a woman offered a challenge to him.

"Do you like curry?" he asked.

"I don't think I've ever had it."

"I'm addicted to it, from all my years living in the East. My chef makes a wonderful curry. You must try it."

"I'm sure that I must," she said, and then smiled at him, that wonderful, tentative smile that made his heart do strange things.

Catching himself staring at her like a slack-jawed fool, James straightened and pushed away from the door. "I hope you don't mind eating early. I usually eat at half past six or at seven. I've never gotten into the habit of Town Hours when I eat alone."

"That is perfectly acceptable to me. I'm often in bed by nine." She blushed when she realized what she'd said. Not a practiced blush, it was the gentle shade of pink clouds before dusk, and James found he wanted to believe her.

Sudden, fierce pride filled him. This beautiful, refined woman was his discovery, and he thanked whatever gods had sent her to him. He would woo her, win her, protect her. Lady Pearson would be his.

No, not Lady Pearson. Caroline, he reminded himself. The syllables of her name rolled through his mind. Car-o-line. He wondered what color her hair was.

"Would you like to remove your hat?"

"My what?" she asked, and then seemed startled

to realize she still wore it. "Oh, yes, I should do that." She untied the ribbons and started to lift off the bonnet, but the weight of the veil made it difficult.

"Here, let me help," he offered. In two steps he crossed over to her and reached around to try to lift the veil. He wanted to see her hair. Every fiber of his being tightened in anticipation.

Unfortunately, the black netting appeared to get hopelessly tangled with the black brim and ribbons, and by the time they'd removed the veil, they were both chuckling over the silliness, until James realized how close he was standing next to her.

But not as close as he would like.

He looked down in the gray depths of her eyes and felt a pull as old as time. *Kiss her*, something inside him ordered. And he wanted to. Right now.

But it would be a rash thing to do.

As if feeling the tension of the moment, she took a step back, raised her hands, turning slightly away from him, and lifted the bonnet from her head. James held his breath and then almost gave a sigh of satisfaction. Her hair, braided and pinned in a heavy chignon, was the rich, warm color of mahogany or the most expensive cinnamon. The style emphasized the graceful column of her throat, her genteel femininity.

James ached to touch her hair, to see if her hair was as silky as it looked. And to pull out the pins, one by one, letting it spill down around her shoulders so he could see it in all its glory. See where it reached on her body and how it would cover her. He imagined her naked beneath her hair, the image in his mind turning so erotic, the air around him fairly crackled with desire.

"Champagne, *Sahib?*" Calleo's voice brought James back to his senses. He stood in the doorway holding a tray with a wine bottle and glasses.

"Did I ask for that?" James said, feeling in something of a daze.

"No, I asked for it," Daniel Harvey said, coming through the door around Calleo and grabbing the wine bottle. He picked up a glass and was ready to help himself when his gaze fell on Lady Pearson still holding her hat. His movements froze as he stared at her with open appreciation. "What have we here? Calleo, we need to take the hat from this woman to make sure she stays."

Calleo calmly set the tray on the table in the center of the room and took Lady Pearson's hat, before quietly leaving.

Aware that Daniel's interest had been aroused, James stepped between them, taking the glass and wine bottle from his friend's hands. He poured a glass of the sparkling wine and offered it to Lady Pearson. "This gentleman, Lady Pearson, is my business partner, Daniel Harvey." He reached for the other glass on the tray. "But be wary of him. He is not only a scoundrel but also a notorious liar. A wise woman would avoid him at all costs."

Daniel feigned hurt. "I ask you, Lady Pearson, do I look like a scoundrel, or the most honest gentleman in the room? After all, I am short and rather round, whereas James is dark and swarthy like a pirate." He gave a mock shiver. "There are times when he frightens even me."

Laughter lit up Lady Pearson's eyes and James relaxed a bit. She'd been so skittish earlier, as if looking for an excuse to leave, that her enjoyment of their banter pleased him. She further delighted him when she said, "I can't be a good judge of that, Mr. Harvey. My mother told me years ago that all men lie, and a wise woman should remember it."

"All!" Daniel moved toward her. "Don't wound me so," he said, his voice all injured innocence. "Perhaps James and all the others lie, but I am a man of honor—"

"Who has a previous engagement for this evening," James pointedly reminded him.

"I can break it."

"I don't think that would be wise."

"I'd rather hear why Lady Pearson believes that all men lie," Daniel said. He reached for the champagne glass in James's hand, but James held it out of his reach.

The sound of her laughter made both men turn and stare.

James looked down at Daniel. "She's laughing at us."

He shrugged. "It won't be the first time a woman has laughed at us."

"Speak for yourself," James said, and took a sip of champagne. He looked at Lady Pearson. "So explain yourself, Lady Pearson. Why do you think men lie?"

Her eyes opened innocently wide. "Oh, it's not that they want to. It's that it is easiest. Ask a man a direct question and he will first ask himself, what is it she wants to hear? If it is the truth, he answers with the truth. But if it's not the truth, then he gives her the answer he thinks she wants. You can see it on a man's face. His eyes move to the side and the corner of his mouth tenses just a bit—and you know he's asking himself that very important question."

"And if he is any man at all," Daniel said easily, "he'll tell her what she wants to hear." He turned to James. "I see nothing wrong with that."

"You wouldn't," James retorted. "But what about women? Don't they lie from time to time?"

"Women never lie," she replied, her eyes sparkling.

"Not ever?" James asked.

"Never," she confirmed.

"Hmmm," Daniel said, "I can see that it is time for me to wander off and keep my appointment with a woman who is definitely more gullible and will believe all the lies I tell her." He gave Lady Pearson a bow. "It was a pleasure meeting you."

"Thank you, Mr. Harvey."

She gifted Daniel with a smile so lovely that for a second James feared Daniel would forgo his plans for the evening and stay right where he was, staring at her. James gave Daniel a shove toward the door.

"Oh, yes. James, have a good evening. I'll see you tomorrow."

"Good night, Daniel."

"Yes, good night," Daniel said again, catching one more glimpse at the lovely Lady Pearson before he finally slipped out the door.

James turned to her. She hadn't yet touched her champagne. He raised his glass. "To England," he said dryly. A toast she couldn't resist.

She acknowledged the toast with a slight lift of her glass and sipped the wine, then laughed.

"What's so funny?" he asked.

"The bubbles. I'd forgotten how they feel."

James grinned at her, experiencing an inner effervescence as bubbly as the champagne. He wanted to know everything about her. Everything, from how she had ended up dependent upon a fool like Freddie Pearson to how she enjoyed her eggs at breakfast.

She was right that men lied, and he'd already told her one. He did remember Freddie Pearson, a pompous young gentleman with the looks of an Adonis and the brains of a goat. Everyone knew Pearson had already gambled away a good portion of his inheritance. Whatever James had won at the card table was a pittance of what the young man had once owned, although it could quite possibly have included the deed to Lady Pearson's house. He hadn't misled her. James had every intention of seeing that she received that deed—and his protection.

"Do you have children?" he asked abruptly.

The teasing, relaxed look in her eyes disappeared. He didn't regret the impulsive question, just his timing. "Why do you ask?"

Her question caught him off guard. There was so much grace and dignity in her manner that he felt slightly ashamed, as though he'd touched something very close and personal. But he wanted to know the answer.

"I'm curious," he said noncommittally. "I don't mean to pry."

She took another sip of champagne before answering quietly. "No. No children."

James almost grinned with happiness. Children always made an affair tricky. Not impossible but slightly more difficult. He preferred fewer encumbrances.

At that moment, the front door knocker sounded. Through the open doorway, he saw one of his footmen move to answer it. Lady Pearson made a small strangled sound.

He turned to find her staring out into the hallway at the opening front door with a morbid fascination. Her eyes, storm gray and troubled, met his. "I shouldn't be here," she whispered. "I shouldn't."

Setting his champagne glass down on the tray, James moved to the open double doors of the receiving room. He closed one and partially closed the other, just as, to James's surprise, Lord Dimhurst, one of the few members of the Board of Control who stoutly supported him, slipped past the footman and entered the grand foyer. The footman opened the door wider and Lady Dimhurst bustled in behind her husband.

"Lord Dimhurst," James said in greeting as he walked out to meet him. "This is an unexpected surprise."

Lord Dimhurst shook his head, refusing Calleo's offer to take his hat. "You've met Lady Dimhurst, haven't you, Ferrington?" He nodded toward the attractive older woman standing beside him in a purple velvet wrap with ostrich plumes of the same color in her silver hair. "We were on our way to her sister's for dinner this evening when she learned I had a message for you. She insisted we stop."

James gave a short, wary bow to the woman whom many in London considered a pillar of Society and a notorious gossip. Lady Pearson's original alarm at being caught here alone appeared to be well-placed. He resisted sliding a guilty glance toward the receiving room door. "I'm sorry, I was just on my way out."

Lady Dimhurst didn't take the hint. She moved

around the large entrance hall, her eyes avidly searching out every detail.

Lord Dimhurst shook his head, frowning at his wife. "She's been after me for months to get an invitation from you. Meddlesome woman. Wouldn't let me alone when she found I needed to stop here. Otherwise, I would have taken my own carriage." His confession done, he brought his mind to business. "The Board needs five copies of that lading statement your man prepared for us last Thursday. Tomorrow, if possible."

"Certainly," James said, conscious that Lady Dimhurst was appraising the vase on the foyer table, her eyebrows raised in appreciation.

Just then, James realized Lady Pearson's hat had been set on the table beside the receiving room door. Lady Dimhurst saw the hat. Like a child inspecting a new toy, she moved over to it.

James forced himself to remain calm, nodding his head in feigned interest at Dimhurst, who was warming to his subject. "I don't need to tell you that those buggers with the East India Company are fighting this with everything they've got. Only yesterday, Burton and I entered into a rather heated discussion about the Mysore Treaty. I thought the Company acted completely beyond the bounds of their authority."

"And I greatly appreciate your support, Lord Dimhurst," James said. His focus on Lady Dimhurst, he barely heard a word the man was saying. His diligence was rewarded.

"What a lovely room," Lady Dimhurst said, cocking her head to peep though the half-open door of the receiving room.

"Thank you," James murmured, moving to reach the door before she did and shut it tight.

He was too late. "May I see it?" Her voice sang out even as she pushed the door open and walked right in.

"Millie, stop poking your nose in other people's business," Lord Dimhurst barked out. He gave James a beleaguered look. "She embarrasses me." He chased his wife into the room.

James tensed, waiting for Lady Dimhurst to discover Lady Pearson, almost afraid to enter the room behind her. He heard nothing. Not a sound other than Lady Dimhurst "ooohing" over the ornate design on the silver candlesticks and Dimhurst grumbling to his wife that they should leave.

Puzzled, James moved toward the receiving room door—just in time to hear Lady Dimhurst's carrying voice say, "Why, Lady Pearson, what a surprise!"

Chapter 3

⌒◯◯⌒

With fascinated horror, Caroline had watched as Lady Dimhurst walked around the room, too busy appraising the value of the furnishings to notice her standing right in front of her. It took all of Caroline's self-control to say, "Good evening, Lady Dimhurst. It's a pleasure to see you again."

"Do you two know each other?" James said from the doorway.

Caroline forced herself to smile and act as if being caught in a bachelor's private residence, alone, was commonplace. "Lady Dimhurst is the president of St. Mark's Ladies Charity League." And also an influential patroness of Miss Elmhart's School for Young Gentlewomen, she might have added. Now that Freddie had lost everything, the stipend she received from the school was all that stood between her and penury.

Caroline drained her glass of champagne.

At that moment, James's smooth voice cut in. "Caroline," he began, shocking her with his bold use of her Christian name, "have you met Lord

Dimhurst then? My lord, this is my cousin, Lady Pearson."

Cousin? Caroline thought.

"Cousin!" Lady Dimhurst said, delighted with this snippet of news. "I wonder why you've never told us, Lady Pearson."

"Because I—" Caroline could think of no plausible reason.

James came to her rescue. "Because we thought everyone was already aware of our connection," he said smoothly, walking over to where the women stood. "Tell me, Lady Dimhurst, in what way are you involved with the charity?"

"I'm the president," Lady Dimhurst said. "Lady Pearson is one of my soldiers in accomplishing our Lord's work. Tell me, are you two close cousins?"

Caroline marveled at how easily the lies rolled off Mr. Ferrington's tongue as he answered, "On our mothers' sides of the family. Not close, yet close enough."

Lady Dimhurst's mouth formed a small circle as she tried to make sense out of that statement. "But I thought you didn't have any family living, Lady Pearson—"

"Lord Dimhurst, would you care for some champagne?" James interrupted. He signaled his butler to bring more glasses.

Lord Dimhurst, who had been listening to the conversation with vague interest, his hands in his pockets, snapped to attention. "Champagne? Frightfully expensive what with the frogs hoarding it all for themselves. I'll be damned glad to see Napoleon's head on a pike, I will."

"Does that mean you'd care for a glass?" James asked.

"Yes. Love a glass. Been ages since I've had good frog juice," Lord Dimhurst said. He tossed his hat to a footman, prepared to stay.

"Dimhurst," his lady said, her eyes still on Caroline as if she feared she'd disappear, "we can't stay. We're promised to my sister Bernice for dinner."

"But your sister won't be serving champagne." Lord Dimhurst licked his lips in anticipation.

"Then I have a better suggestion," Mr. Ferrington said. "Why don't you and Lady Dimhurst dine with us this evening."

Caroline stared at him as if he'd gone mad.

He wasn't paying any attention to her. Instead he was turning his considerable charm on Lady Dimhurst. "Of course, I realize that this is spur of the moment and you can't change your plans suddenly—"

"Yes, we can," Lord Dimhurst said. "Bernice bores me silly, and her husband is twenty years older than we are. You can imagine how entertaining and lively he is."

"Dimhurst!" his wife chastised, but the butler had arrived with a tray of glasses and another bottle of champagne, and her husband cut her off.

"Tell her I've taken ill," Lord Dimhurst said, holding out his hand for the first glass.

"Please," James echoed, picking up a glass and offering it to Lady Dimhurst. "I wasn't planning anything formal. Just a simple meal with family. Tell me, do you enjoy curry?"

Caroline listened with a sense of wonder at how easily Mr. Ferrington wove the web of small deceits.

"Love curry," Lord Dimhurst said. He drained

his glass of champagne, smacking his lips. "I say, Ferrington, this is fine brew. I haven't tasted anything so fine in years. You wouldn't happen to have a good brandy in your cellar, too?"

"Several," Mr. Ferrington said, refilling Lord Dimhurst's glass.

"Millie, we can go to your sister's anytime and eat that boiled mutton her chef passes off as food. Write her a note and tell her I'm suffering a bout of heartburn."

"Which you will have if you eat curry," she informed him.

Lord Dimhurst sipped more champagne before saying, "It will be worth it."

Lady Dimhurst chewed on her lip, undecided, until her shrewd, speculative gaze fell on Caroline. She looked to Mr. Ferrington and back to Caroline again. "Well, perhaps we can miss dinner with Bernice this once."

"Thank the gods," Lord Dimhurst said, draining his glass.

"Excellent," Mr. Ferrington said. "Calleo will escort you to a desk and paper and see that your message is sent immediately. Perhaps both of you would like to freshen up before we eat?"

"Why, that would be lovely," Lady Dimhurst said.

"I don't want to freshen up," Lord Dimhurst said. "I want another glass of that champagne."

"Dimhurst," his wife said. "Come with me to write the note. Now."

Reluctantly Lord Dimhurst set his empty glass on the tray. He looked at James and rolled his eyes. "At least I may be able to stop her from snooping in your drawers and closets."

"Dimhurst! I would never do that."

"I was only teasing, m'dear." He followed his wife out the door like a well-trained lapdog.

They were gone.

Caroline's knees went weak. She sank down on the settee. "I'm astonished that you told her we were cousins."

"Would you rather I told her that we weren't?"

"No!" Caroline could easily imagine what the self-important Lady Dimhurst would do with that piece of information.

He sat down beside her and refilled the glass she held loosely in her hand. "Buck up, Cousin Caroline."

She cringed at his familiarity, while his eyes danced with laughter. "Besides, I was only thinking of you. If Lady Dimhurst says anything about seeing you here this evening, it will be to reveal that she served as our chaperone." He laughed into his glass as he lifted it to his lips and added, "It's been a deuced long time since I've been chaperoned."

"But the lies you told." Caroline's head ached at the thought.

"Yes. It seems your theory is correct."

"Which theory?"

"That men lie. Wasn't that what you were telling me earlier?" He frowned in pensive reflection. "However, in my defense, I did not ask myself what Lady Dimhurst wanted to hear. I could tell by the look on her face that she would definitely have preferred the truth. She looked disappointed to learn that she hadn't stumbled into an illicit meeting."

"Our meeting was not illicit! I came on business, Mr. Ferrington—

"James."

"What?"

"If we are going to masquerade as cousins, you should call me James." He added, his voice intimate, "I can't wait to hear my given name on your lips."

Caroline groaned with frustration. "Stop flirting with me. If she finds out the truth, I could be ruined and find myself living with my mother-in-law." That thought alone made Caroline take another sip of champagne. "Lady Dimhurst lives for gossip. She'll pry until she knows our bloodlines back to the Conqueror. In fact, she probably knows mine already. It is you she will investigate."

"England is a small country. She might discover that we really are related. Now, that has charming possibilities." He grinned at her, his gaze drifting downward again to the region of her bustline.

With the tips of her fingers, Caroline raised his chin and looked him in the eye. "I'm up here, Mr. Ferrington, not down there. And this is serious. If Lady Dimhurst discovers we're not related . . ." She didn't want to put the consequences into words.

He took her glass from her hand and set it on the table. Slowly, fully absorbed in what he was doing, he started removing the glove from her hand. She closed her fist. His eyes came up to meet hers. "You can't live your life being afraid. If she says something, then we must brazen it out. So, you might as well stay and be bold. I like to think that I have enough credit in some quarters to see us both clear of any scandal."

"Trust you?" she repeated, her hand relaxing. He removed the glove. "After watching you smoothly charm Lady Dimhurst?"

He laughed, the sound warm and appreciative before he started taking off the glove on her other hand. He had long tapered fingers, strong and capable. "If I embellished a bit, I did so to protect you," he said.

"Protect me?"

"It's obvious that what this woman thinks is important to you . . . and if she carries that much weight with you, then she is equally of interest to me."

Caroline looked into his face, at the strong lines of his nose and jaw, the sensual curve of his mouth lightened by laugh lines, the shadow of whiskers along his jaw. This man lived life to its fullest.

Her heart compressed with uneasy excitement. New feelings . . . old feelings. She sat so close to him that she could catch the clean, bold scent of his shaving soap. The feelings swirling around her were hot. Like the red hot tip of a poker pulled from the fire—

"Lady Pearson, Mr. Ferrington, what are you doing?"

Caroline jumped at the sound of Lady Dimhurst's voice coming from the doorway. She would have yanked her hand back but Mr. Ferrington held it firmly.

"I'm reading Caroline's palm," he said easily. Caroline rolled her eyes toward the ceiling, praying for deliverance.

"Oh, really?" Lady Dimhurst's eyes turned bright with interest. "Do you know anything about palmistry?"

He raised his hands, palms open. "It's one of the mysteries of the Orient."

"Read mine," she demanded. She turned to Caroline. "I've always wanted to have my palm read."

"Why, certainly," James said. "Caroline, please make room for Lady Dimhurst."

Caroline rose from the settee to give Lady Dimhurst her place. One of the ever-present footmen offered her another glass of champagne, and she took it. Brazen it out, he'd said. She didn't know if she had the skill to go point for point with Lady Dimhurst. The woman truly was the terror of the Ladies Charity League. No one crossed her, not even Reverend Tilton, and Miss Elmhart literally quaked in her shoes whenever Lady Dimhurst sent a message that she planned to visit the school.

No, few people stood up to this *grande dame* of society—except Caroline. She and Lady Dimhurst had long held sharp differences of opinion on what the girls at Miss Elmhart's should be taught. Caroline favored a curriculum of rigorous academics, much like what young gentlemen studied. Lady Dimhurst believed that such intelligent pursuits were wasted on young women. She endorsed a program of instruction on needlework, watercolor, and dancing, with the most challenging class being the conjugation of French verbs.

The two women had clashed bitterly at the beginning of the present school term. Miss Elmhart agreed in private that Caroline was right. However, for financial reasons, she'd been forced to side with Lady Dimhurst.

Furthermore, Lady Dimhurst was not a graceful winner. She'd gone so far as to question whether or not Caroline, who taught history and French, was necessary to the school's staff. Afraid of offending her leading patroness, Miss Elmhart had cut back Caroline's classes to only one class a week on Monday mornings. That was all the time Lady Dimhurst felt was necessary for the study of French verbs. Caroline still received the same stipend . . . but how long would that last?

Lady Dimhurst seemed tame enough now, with Mr. Ferrington holding her hand. He flirted outrageously with her and told her nonsense about her past, present, and future while the woman blushed and giggled like a debutante.

"No, I'm not going to have more children," Lady Dimhurst said.

"But it is here," he protested. "Your palm says you are going to have seven children." He drew several lines across her right wrist.

"Mr. Ferrington, I'm too old to have more children, and I already have six."

"Ah, but the palm doesn't lie. Besides, I don't think you are very old at all." He said it with such warm regard, Lady Dimhurst practically melted into the settee.

"And I see money in your future," Mr. Ferrington said, his index finger tracing a line across Lady Dimhurst's palm.

"Money?" Lady Dimhurst squinted down at her hand to see what he was seeing. "How can you tell?"

"It's here," he assured her. "In fact, I think it looks like a draft coming from my bank."

Lady Dimhurst's eyes opened wide. "Where is the money going?"

Mr. Ferrington frowned in concentration. "It looks as if . . . it might be going . . ."

"To St. Mark's Ladies Charity League?" she supplied helpfully.

He raised his gaze to meet hers. "Do you think that would be a wise choice?"

"Oh very wise," Lady Dimhurst assured him, and Caroline knew why. It pleased Lady Dimhurst to know that her influence, or actually her husband's, led to money being donated to the League's activities. It gave her power and made her the envy of other matrons, who wished they could flaunt their prestige by bringing in pounds and shillings.

Caroline was also aware that Mr. Ferrington was discreetly bribing Lady Dimhurst.

"Damn me, Ferrington, what are you doing? Making love to my wife?" Lord Dimhurst entered the room, chuckling at his own joke, and headed straight for the champagne bottle.

"Dimhurst, Mr. Ferrington has just donated one thousand pounds to the Ladies Charity League."

Caroline almost choked on the champagne she'd been sipping. It was a staggering amount.

"He has, has he?" Lord Dimhurst said. "Well, he's got the blunt. Should have doubled it."

"Perhaps I will after Friday's meeting, my lord," Mr. Ferrington said.

Lord Dimhurst shot him a conspirator's smile. "Then let's drink to your success," he said, raising his wineglass.

"Thank you, my lord."

At that moment, the turbaned butler entered the room. "Dinner is served."

Mr. Ferrington looked up at Caroline. "Dimhurst, will you escort my cousin in to dinner?"

"I'd be honored." Lord Dimhurst offered Caroline his arm.

Mr. Ferrington bowed over Lady Dimhurst's hand and offered his arm. "My lady?"

He led them to a large dining room of cream-colored walls, burgundy velvet drapes, and plush burgundy carpet. The table could easily seat twenty. The fire burning in the huge marble hearth added warmth to the room. Brightly burning wax candles filled wall sconces and candlestick holders. At one end of the table four places were set for dinner. Footmen stood near a sideboard laden with food—and more bottles of wine.

Mr. Ferrington seated Lady Dimhurst and Caroline on either side of him while he took the seat at the head of the table. "This is a simple dinner?" Caroline said to him.

"The kitchen staff can work miracles," he said, lightly touching her hand. Startled by the intimacy of the innocent gesture, Caroline jerked her hand back and shot a glance at Lady Dimhurst to see if she had noticed.

Fortunately, she'd been watching the butler with avid curiosity. "Does he always wear that turban?" Lady Dimhurst asked, not bothering to keep her voice low. Lord Dimhurst motioned for one of the footmen to fill his wineglass.

"Ever since I've known him," James answered serenely, as if the brief body contact with Caroline hadn't affected him at all. "But then, there is a story to that." And he proceeded to tell them of how Calleo had come out of the jungle and joined his expedition in India. That tale led to another and another. He described places Caroline had only read about. Madras. Sumatra. Macao.

Several times he called Caroline "cousin," his twinkling eyes inviting her to join in the jest. She couldn't do it, although she found that she could relax and enjoy the dinner.

To her surprise, she liked curry, although it set her mouth on fire, a fire she quenched with wine. Lord Dimhurst enjoyed it too, complaining about his heartburn all the while. As the wine flowed, Caroline found her own reserve evaporating. At one point she reached out to stop Calleo from refilling her glass. The wine splashed on her fingers.

Mr. Ferrington wiped her fingers off gently, teasing her that she was a "clumsy coz." It sounded so natural for him, as if he'd teased and cajoled people this way for years. Without thinking she asked, "Do you have a large family?"

It was the wrong thing to say.

"You mean you don't know?" Lady Dimhurst looked up, her eyes a touch unfocused from the wine, but her mind still sharp.

Caroline froze, her brain refusing to operate.

Mr. Ferrington rescued her. "Our families did not know each other well, but my mother ordered me to look up Cousin Caroline and see to her welfare once I arrived in London. I was only too happy to do so."

"Truly?" Lady Dimhurst said. "Then maybe you can convince her to accept Reverend Tilton's proposal of marriage." She motioned to Caroline with her dinner fork. "The dear man asks her at least once a week, but so far she's refused him. You know, don't you, Caroline, that all of us in the

Ladies Charity League believe it would be an excellent match, and you wouldn't need to teach at Miss Elmhart's any longer."

"A match made in heaven," her husband said, chuckling into his wineglass.

Mr. Ferrington raised an eyebrow in mock concern. "You hadn't told me this, Caroline." He rolled the syllables of her name, his smile lazy and good-natured.

"It isn't important," she said curtly, wishing she hadn't imbibed so much wine and could think with a clearer head. "Lady Dimhurst, I don't think Reverend Tilton and I would suit."

"You'd be a wonderful match," she insisted enthusiastically. She set her elbow on the table and made to set her chin on her hand, but missed and almost tumbled off the chair. Her husband roared with laughter.

"Be quiet, Dimhurst," she said, her attention completely diverted from Reverend Tilton's marriage proposal.

He shut up and reached for his wineglass. "I say, Ferrington, didn't you say you had French brandy?"

"The best."

"Well, where is it, man?"

Mr. Ferrington nodded and the ever-present Calleo motioned to the footman to clear the table. Lady Dimhurst stood, her dignity restored. "Come along, Caroline. Let us leave the men to their cigars and brandy."

Caroline had no choice but to go with her. Lord Dimhurst had already started in on a rather drunken tirade about the state of Parliament, and her

presence would be unwelcome. Her feet feeling
like lead weights, she followed Lady Dimhurst out
of the room.

Calleo escorted them to a very pretty sitting
room across the hall. The room faced the east, with
two huge bay windows, and Caroline could imagine it was a lovely room in the morning. Here
again, everything was new and in the latest style. A
cheery fire beckoned them to two chairs placed
right before it. A footman carried in a large, ornate
silver tea service and set it on a tray between the
ladies.

"I shall pour," Lady Dimhurst said. She picked
up a china cup and turned it over. "Limoges. Can
you imagine? Even with the war going on. And this
teapot." She lifted it, tapping her finger against the
silver. "Eight pounds and not a penny less." She
looked around the room. "I've heard about him,
but I didn't believe any of it until now that I see it
with my own eyes. And just think, according to
Dimhurst, he's gambling everything to take on the
East India Company. I wonder why a man would
waste his money that way."

"I'm sure I don't know," Caroline said, wishing
that Mr. Ferrington would hurry and drink his
brandy. He was smoother at fabricating truth than
she was.

"You don't? All of London is talking about it. I
would have thought you would know the facts."

"I don't see Cousin James often."

James. It was the first time she'd said his name,
too aware of the number of proprieties they'd
already tread upon to be so bold. James. She liked
the sound of it.

"And what is this nonsense about not accepting Reverend Tilton's proposal?" Lady Dimhurst said, handing Caroline her tea. "Lady Pearson, I'm not the only one who's concerned about your welfare."

"I'm not certain what you mean," Caroline replied cautiously.

"I'm talking about 'that woman' you live with. I've heard some rather distressing rumors about her."

"You mean Aunt Minerva?"

"She is not your aunt."

"She certainly is," Caroline said and almost added, "More than Mr. Ferrington is my cousin," but caught herself in time. "By marriage."

"The Pearson family disowned her." Lady Dimhurst sat back in her chair with her own cup and saucer. "You are under no obligation to her."

"Minerva has been living with me for three years. I consider her part of my family."

"Lady Pearson," Lady Dimhurst began in the frosty tone she saved for talking to subordinates, "one of my responsibilities as president of the Ladies Charity League and as a patroness of Miss Elmhart's School is to consider the moral character of those entrusted to fulfill its good works."

Caroline set her cup on the tray. "There is nothing wrong with my moral character."

Lady Dimhurst set her own cup aside and crossed her hands primly in front of her. "Living with a known courtesan is not a sign of good moral judgment. Furthermore, you've been widowed for three years. It is time you accepted Reverend Tilton's proposal and remarried."

"I'm not ready to marry."

"It's not natural for a woman to live alone."

"It is what I choose to do."

"You should make other choices, and begin by changing your live-in companion!"

Caroline was livid. Her relationship with Minerva was the one bright spot in her life. Without her, she would never have been able to face down the Pearsons that first year after Trumbull's death. She rose to her feet. "Minerva is an intelligent, sophisticated woman—"

Rising from her own chair, Lady Dimhurst said, "She's a scandal! Her reputation is in shambles!"

"I'm surprised, my lady, that you would listen to vicious gossip!"

"I'm surprised you defend her so—"

"Millie, what are you caterwauling about?" Lord Dimhurst shouted out.

Both woman turned to see the men standing in the doorway. Lord Dimhurst listed drunkenly, but Mr. Ferrington appeared not to feel the wine's effects. Mortified to be caught arguing with Lady Dimhurst, Caroline wondered how much he'd heard.

Lady Dimhurst straightened her shoulders. "I was just advising Lady Pearson that she should marry Reverend Tilton."

"It sounded to me as if you were pounding her over the head. Now, come. We must go home while I can still stand; otherwise, one of these big brutes"—he nodded toward a footman—"will have to carry me home."

Lady Dimhurst turned to Caroline. "May we offer you a ride home, Lady Pearson?" she asked with stiff formality.

Caroline wouldn't walk across the street with the woman after what she'd said about Minerva, and she had enough wine in her system to say so. Fortunately, James interceded. "I will see Caroline home."

"Yes, Cousin James will see me home." Caroline took a step closer to him.

Lady Dimhurst frowned, her expression that of a malevolent toad. Caroline almost laughed at the image.

"Well, then. I will see you at the next Ladies Charity League meeting," Lady Dimhurst said. With a swish of her skirts, she walked an unsteady line toward the door. "Come, Dimhurst. We must be going."

At the door, she stopped and turned to Caroline. "Aren't you coming, Lady Pearson?"

Caroline wanted to snap, "No, I'm going to stay right here, and drain another bottle of wine." But she didn't dare. Once the bravado fueled by wine dissipated, she feared that she might regret having crossed verbal swords with Lady Dimhurst.

But she wasn't about to let the woman say whatever she wished about Minerva! "Yes, I'm coming," Caroline responded in a polite but equally frigid voice.

Mr. Ferrington nodded to his butler. "My coach."

"Which one, *Sahib?*"

"The burled wood with the bay team this time."

Lady Dimhurst's eyes widened with new respect. "You have more than one coach?" Mr. Ferrington took her arm and escorted her up the hallway toward the front door.

"I have three."

"Three?" Lady Dimhurst said, almost giddy with the thought of such wealth.

Caroline felt a stab of jealousy for the way Lady Dimhurst fawned all over Mr. Ferrington. Lady Dimhurst wouldn't think of questioning his character or make inpertinent demands concerning his personal life. His charm was based on more than good looks and money. Mr. Ferrington watched people, analyzed them, and then played them as sweetly as a musician played an instrument.

Caroline wondered how he was playing her.

"He won't have a shilling if he doesn't win his bid for that license Friday," Lord Dimhurst said, taking his hat from the footman and shoving it on his head. He poked James in the chest with one finger. "I'll do my best for you with the Board of Control, young man, but you'd best remember who it is you are taking on. The East India Company has more power than the monarchy. Make sure you have others coming through, like Lavenham. Now there's a man who can deliver a block of votes."

"I'll remember that, my lord, and thank you for your patronage."

"Ha! My five percent of the profits will make me happy enough. Come, Millie. I'm ready for bed. Tomorrow, Ferrington," he tossed over his shoulder. "I must have those lading reports tomorrow!"

Lady Dimhurst had put on her velvet wrap and now pulled on her gloves. "Thank you for your hospitality, Mr. Ferrington. I've had a wonderful evening." She smiled warmly at him before casting a decidedly chilly smile in Caroline's direction. "Are you sure we can't see you home, Lady Pearson?"

"Thank you, but I will be fine with Cousin James," Caroline said, tying the ribbons on her own bonnet.

Lady Dimhurst leaned toward her. "You really should come out of black, dear. It doesn't do a thing for your complexion."

Caroline smiled serenely. She would not answer the woman's cattiness in kind, no matter how much she wished to!

"Come, Millie!" Lord Dimhurst barked. One of the footmen opened the door for him.

"We must wait for Lady Pearson to leave," his wife said.

Lord Dimhurst frowned and then his frown turned into a smile as he looked out the door. "Ferrington's coach is already here. Good stable lads you have there, Ferrington."

"The best," their host agreed. "Caroline?" He offered his arm.

Lady Dimhurst had no choice but to follow her husband out the door, with Caroline and Mr. Ferrington right behind them. The Dimhurst coachman hopped down from his perch and held open the door. Finally, the duo was gone.

Caroline let out a long sigh of relief.

James chuckled. "She's a challenge."

"By tomorrow noon, everyone in London will know she dined here tonight, what you served, what you said, what I said, what she said." Caroline waved her hand back and forth, and then joined him in laughter.

"I'd hoped you and I would have time for one last glass of wine."

Caroline stopped laughing.

Need, yearning, desire—feelings she hadn't felt since her wedding night—rose inside her. She must move away from him. Now. Before she took him up on his outrageous suggestion and made a complete fool of herself. She was already flirting with the boundaries of propriety—and she didn't want to step too far over the line.

She turned away, but he caught her arm and pulled her back. "I'd never do anything to harm you."

He looked so intent, so sincere standing in the flickering golden light of the porch lamps . . . and so tempting. Caroline shifted and he released her arm, his hand sliding down to take her hand.

"Do you believe me?" he asked.

Caroline felt the calluses on his palm which told her that for all his aristocratic airs, he wasn't a stranger to manual labor. She forced herself to keep her voice light. "How can I not, considering we are related?"

He laughed, as she'd intended.

She squeezed his fingers. "Thank you. Your quick thinking saved my reputation this night." She pulled on her hand and he released it.

"Ah, so now 'male lying' has become quick thinking?" He placed his hands in his pockets. There was a decided nip in the air, and wisps of fog were already drifting along the drive and across the lawn of his estate. "I'll see you home, but I'm not ready to let you go. I'd like you to stay."

Caroline stepped back. "I can't," she said, even though there was a strong part of her that wanted to stay.

She drew a deep breath. "This has been a special

evening, but I must go home. If I know Lady Dimhurst, she's ordered her coachman to pull over and is waiting for me to drive past."

James watched the way the lamplight caught and highlighted the red-gold in her auburn hair. Before she'd said the words, he'd known she wouldn't stay. He'd seen the flash of vulnerability in her eyes, and he found himself proud that she wasn't an easy conquest. If anything, her refusal only whetted his appetite for more.

"Then let's go," he said, taking charge.

"It's not necessary for you to see me home. I'll be safe with the coachman."

"Don't be ridiculous. I want to escort you. You can't refuse me that honor, not after tonight."

"No," she agreed with a slight smile.

"Good," James said, and offered his arm.

She turned to take it, and then gave a gasp of surprise. "The coach is beautiful."

James grinned. Made of burled wood with brass trimmings, and pulled by a perfectly matched set of bays with black markings, he'd designed the coach himself, and it was his pride and joy. He usually drove it when he took it out, but tonight he was anticipating the ride inside with Caroline.

He proudly walked her to the waiting coach. "What is your address?"

She gave him the name of a street he was unfamiliar with before he helped her up into the coach's plush darkness. Fortunately, his coachman knew the address and James quietly encouraged him to take the very long route to get there. The man nodded his understanding.

James smiled. The advantage of being wealthy

was having intelligent servants. He climbed into the coach.

Heated bricks had been placed on the floor and a heavy wool blanket offered comfort and heat from the night chill. The coach windows were up, but the lamps on either side of the exterior provided a measure of dim flickering light. In her widow's black, Caroline blended in with the deep shadowy darkness of the interior, leaving only the line of one cheek and the curve of her lips visible to him. James shook out the blanket to cover them, then knocked on the roof, signaling the coachman to go.

Only the slightest jerk signified they were moving. Caroline placed her hands on either side of the seat. "I barely feel a thing. This is the most incredible coach I've ever ridden in. It's as if . . ." She paused, searching for words. "As if we are riding in a giant soap bubble. I feel as if we're floating."

The idea pleased James. He could think of nothing better than to float around London with Caroline Pearson. Looking out the window, he noticed that Caroline had indeed been right. Lord and Lady Dimhurst's coach was parked on a side street within a few feet of his front gate. Lady Dimhurst had been waiting for Caroline to leave! They both burst into laughter.

Caroline sank back against the plush leather seat, turning to look out the window so that the long, graceful column of her neck was highlighted by the flicker light of the coach lamp. "This evening has been magic, almost a dream. Despite Lady Dimhurst." She paused a moment before whispering, "Thank you."

James didn't answer. He couldn't. His whole being focused on the little hollow where her throat met her chin, where a tiny pulse point beat.

She turned to look at him in the darkness. Her lips curved into a lovely smile and the coach light caught the soft glow of her eyes. She lightly touched his hand beside her on the seat. She wore her gloves, but gloves or not, her slightest touch had the power to inflame his senses. He wanted her, now, and with a passion he hadn't felt in years.

Slowly, almost reverently, James lowered his head and kissed that sweet pulse point at the curve of her throat.

Chapter 4

C aroline had been so intensely aware of him all night that when his lips brushed her neck, she thought she must be dreaming.

For one wild minute, she relaxed, enjoying his lips against her skin, his hand on her waist, pulling her closer toward the warmth of his body.

And then, when he had her nestled against him, his hand moved upward and cupped her breast.

Caroline almost moaned aloud with the sheer joy of being touched. Her breast grew fuller, tighter, as if to fill his hand. She shouldn't let him touch her this way. She should stop him, had to stop him, couldn't stop him—and then, his fingers stroked the nipple.

She didn't want to stop him.

Her breath caught and then released in a deep, satisfied sigh when his lips found hers. He kissed her slowly, deeply, expertly . . . and she melted into the pleasure of it.

How long had it been since anyone had even touched her this way, let alone inspired these deep, swirling needs inside her? How long had it been since she'd felt passion?

A wiser woman would push him away, but Caroline no longer wanted to be temperate and wise. She wanted to be kissed, and James was a very good kisser. Wine coursed through her veins, mixing with the easy sway of the coach and the buttery softness of the coach cushions. She could let him kiss her like this all the way home.

He liked kissing her, too. She could tell by the tautness of his muscles beneath her hands and the way he stroked and gentled her.

For one crystal moment, the world faded into oblivion, and there was nothing but the two of them traveling forever in his coach and four.

Then the watch cried the hour.

Caroline struggled for sensibility. "We mustn't—I shouldn't." She forced herself to push away from him and leaned against the corner of the coach, her heart beating as if she'd run up three flights of stairs.

"Car-o-line." He rolled each syllable in his low, baritone voice, making her name sound like music. "I'm tired of your 'shouldn'ts.' The time has come to say 'we should.'"

She shook her head, almost not trusting her voice to speak. "We shouldn't," she repeated inanely.

He reached across her and braced his hand on the coach wall beside her so that they faced each other, his lips only inches from hers. "Yes. We should," he said slowly, as if teaching her a foreign language. The intensity in his eyes held her mesmerized. "I like kissing you. And I think you like kissing me."

Her mouth went dry. She swallowed, the movement bringing his attention to her throat.

He whispered, "I like kissing you here." He gently placed a kiss underneath her chin. The soft warmth of his lips tickled compared to the rough texture of his cheek against hers. Caroline squirmed, her movements bringing their bodies closer. "And here," he said, kissing the corner of her mouth where her dimple was. "And here." He began intently kissing his way up to her ear. Nuzzling her bonnet aside, he playfully traced her ear with his tongue . . . and then kissed her.

Caroline arched up into his arms, the brush of his lips sending her straight to heaven. No one had ever kissed her ear before.

"But where I'd really like to kiss you . . ." his deep voice said softly in her ear. And he whispered a suggestion, so bold, so shocking—so erotic—she thought she would burst into flame from the combined heat of embarrassment and lust.

Caroline struggled for sanity. "I think—"

"We should," he finished for her, and then silenced her by claiming her mouth.

His kiss was magic, like dragonfly wings and lily pads under a warm summer sun, and sweeter-tasting than honey cakes, even when it turned more demanding.

With a sigh, Caroline surrendered to her own desire, her arms coming up around him. She didn't know that kissing could feel this good. He shifted his weight slightly, pulled down the shades over the coach windows, and then drew her close so that she fit against him better.

The intimacy of darkness relaxed her. How marvelous it was to have a man's hands caress her, to feel his warmth and taste his skin, to hear his soft sounds of pleasure. James Ferrington was so handsome, so strong and hard—and when he did the unthinkable and kissed her with his tongue, Caroline's toes curled in her black kid leather slippers. She barely heard them drop to the floor, her senses singing.

No one had ever kissed her like this. She almost purred with satisfaction. Tentatively, she stroked him with her own tongue.

His reaction was immediate. He crushed her to his chest, his arms around her body, and his kisses became more possessive, more passionate. It was as if he wanted to devour her, and she was kissing him back with equal intensity. She met him kiss for kiss, her hands pulling him closer, her fingers curling in his dark hair. She could lay all night stretched out along the seat, her breasts crushed against his chest, her legs along his.

"Have you ever made love in a coach, Caroline?" he asked in a voice hoarse with desire. The sound of it flowed through her as evenly and sweet as her own blood. "Can you imagine the rocking of the coach and me deep inside you?" He ran his hand up her leg. "I want to be inside you, Caroline. Now. This minute."

Caroline moaned at the image his words created, of riding in this heavenly coach with James Ferrington making mad, passionate love—

Her thoughts broke off abruptly.

What could she be thinking? What was she doing?

What was he doing? She felt his hand stroke the curve of her buttock, pressing her closer to him while his voice whispered how beautiful she was,

how much he wanted her. She also felt the cool-
ness of night air—against her thighs.

The alarm sounded in her head like a church bell
on Sunday morning.

Caroline pushed with both hands against his
chest and sat up straight, pushing Ferrington off in
the process. He started to slide to the floor and
struggled to get up, grabbing hold of the seat next
to her for balance just as she hurried to push her
skirts down. Startled, she lifted her knee to fend
him off and accidentally kicked him right between
the legs.

Immediately, he doubled over, the sound of the
air leaving his body anything but loverlike, and slid
onto the coach floor between the seats.

"I'm sorry." The words burst out of Caroline,
who was deeply embarrassed not only to have
come in contact with such an intimate place on his
anatomy, but also at the size and state of his
arousal. The cut of his breeches left nothing to the
imagination.

She thanked the Lord he still had them on!

Caroline whisked open the coach shade on the
window nearest her, then realized her own disheveled state. Her hat hung down her back, hopelessly
crushed. The pins had disappeared from her hair.
And her face burned with mortification.

How could she have gotten herself into this
shocking situation?

"Mr. Ferrington," she began, but he shot her a
look so pained and angry, the apology died in her
throat. Obviously he hadn't yet recovered.

Caroline curled up next to the coach door and
wished she were home. They should be. She didn't
know how much time had passed, but certainly it

shouldn't be taking this long to travel home. Looking out the coach window, she noticed that the passing scenery looked familiar. They were only a block from her home.

Thank the Lord, she would be safe and sound and out of James Ferrington's irritated presence in a few minutes.

Then to her surprise, the coach, moving at the pace of a slow tortoise, turned in the opposite direction of her address. How could the coachman make such a mistake?

Understanding slowly dawned on her. James Ferrington had planned her seduction. Probably before he'd offered her the first glass of champagne.

Shame and humiliation made her angry. "I trusted you!" She practically spit the words at him. He'd played her for a fool, and she, like some silly milkmaid, had almost allowed him to throw her skirts up over her head and tumble her.

White-hot anger surged through her. Without even thinking, she doubled up her fist and punched him, hitting him square in the nose.

"What the bloody—" he started, the words ending in a groan.

Caroline didn't wait to hear more. She turned the door handle, stood poised for a moment in the doorway until she caught her balance, then jumped to the ground, wincing as her right foot hit a rock.

She'd left her shoes on the floor of the coach.

Caroline didn't waste time worrying about them. Instead, she hobbled toward the pavement and away from the coach as fast as she could manage. The only light on the street burned from the windows of a few houses and the receding coach's lamps. Wisps of fog drifted along the ground and the bumpy cobblestones felt hard and cold against her stockinged toes.

She shoved her hat back up on her head and prayed that no one who knew her would happen to look out their front door at this moment. She had to get home.

Caroline had just reached the pavement when James apparently recovered enough to shout for the coach to stop. She hurried her pace. Her left foot encountered another small rock. This one hurt, and she accepted the pain as a penance for her folly.

"Caroline!"

Lifting her skirts, Caroline hobbled faster in the dark. Behind her, she heard the jangling of traces and impatient stamping of horse hooves. One of the coachmen said something to Mr. Ferrington. He ordered the servant to wait for him, his deep melodic voice carrying clearly to her in the night.

He was so close! And she didn't want to confront him. Not now. Not like this. She recognized an alley that led from this street to her own. If she followed it, she'd be home in a minute and a half. Silently, she slipped down the alley, praying that he would pass it by.

Caroline reached out a hand, searching for the brick wall of the house bordering the alley, then following it. This alley joined another that ran behind the houses on this block. She stayed close to the deepest shadows, thankful for her widow's black.

While she kept her right hand against the wall, she held her left out, searching for anything that might trip her in the darkness. For precious seconds the only sound was her own heavy breathing. Cooking smells came from the house across from her. Her left hand hit some bins leaning against the wall of the house. Her right hand told her there was a gate leading into a garden. She safely negotiated her way around the bins and kept moving.

The sound of the door opening and closing on the other side of the gate wall made her pause. A woman spoke to a man about the schedule for the morrow. Servants. Caroline waited, wondering what she would do if one of the servants emerged from the side gate and discovered her. Again, James called out her Christian name. He wasn't far from the alley's entrance. "It's Lady Pearson," she muttered under her breath. The maid said something angry to the man. The door opened and closed with a slam. A second later, the door opened and shut again quietly.

Caroline didn't dare waste any more time. Like a thief in the night, she ducked low and made her way to the back alley. She'd just rounded the corner and thought she would reach safety when she startled a cat.

The animal hissed. Frightened, Caroline jumped, missed her step, and fell to the hard ground.

James heard the sound. From the street, she heard him running back to the entrance of the alley. "Caroline? Wait." He started moving down the alley toward her, his steps cautious.

Caroline wasn't about to let him find her sprawled in the dirt. In the ink black darkness, he'd probably trip over her. She scrambled to her feet, tearing her hem in the process. Her bonnet had slipped forward over her face with her fall. She pushed it back and hugged the garden wall.

She heard Mr. Ferrington let out a loud grunt, followed by the sound of crashing trash bins. He was so very near. Certainly he could hear the hammering of her heart—and she was so close to being home!

Caroline looked up the alley in the direction she had to travel. She could make out the lines of a large box one of her neighbors used for storage. Holding her skirts close, she raced on tiptoe to where the box met her neighbor's back garden wall. Arranging her veil to hide her face, she crouched into the deepest shadows beside the box and waited.

A heartbeat later, she heard him. He was more cautious now. Who could believe that such a big man could move so quietly? He came to the point where the two alleys met. "Caroline." His voice held an edge of temper.

For an icy second, she feared that he'd found her cowering in her hiding place. She wanted to shout, "Go away. Leave me alone." Instead, she held her breath.

He started walking in her direction. His feet made a crunching sound on some broken glass. "Caroline, I know you're here."

Caroline scrunched down lower in her corner.

"You don't have to play this game." He walked by her as he said this, the shadow of his tall form moving right in front of her. If she'd dared, she could have reached out and touched his boot.

He stopped, not more than five feet from her, and didn't say a word. Caroline feared he could hear her breathing. *Oh, please, God,* she prayed.

"All I want to do is escort you home, Caroline."

His continued use of her Christian name grated on her nerves. She doubled her fist.

"Now, come out from wherever you are hiding and let's end this nonsense."

Caroline frowned. Who did he think he was, dictating to her in this manner?

"Caroline," he said again, as if she were a lapdog that should jump to his command. He took a few steps farther down the alley. "Caroline, this is ridiculous. Come out and let me take you home."

When she still didn't answer, he walked back toward her. For a second she feared he'd seen her, especially when he stopped right in front of the storage box, but he hadn't. Instead, he addressed the alley as if addressing Parliament. "Lady Pearson, I'm sorry if I alarmed you, but please understand that it is safe for you to come out from wherever you are." He paused a moment before tagging on, "If you are still here and not somewhere else." He turned slightly as if waiting for her response. "I feel like a bloody fool," he shouted, sounding genuinely angry now.

"If you're worried about being debauched, forget it. After the way you kneed me, I'll be lucky to sire children, let alone debauch another widow." He waited. The minutes stretched out, and then he started talking to himself, as if he'd determined that she was no longer in the alley. "Although how one can debauch a widow, I don't know. It's a slice off an already-cut loaf—"

A voice interrupted his soliloquy. "Who's making that racket? Get out of my alley or I'll call the Watch."

Caroline ducked her head and leaned against the

rough wooden storage box. The voice belonged to the cranky textile merchant who owned the house on the opposite side of the alley. For once, she was thankful for the man's ill humor. Her cheeks burned with humiliation . . . "a slice off an already-cut loaf." If she had a pistol in her hand, she would aim it at him—but not at his heart. She'd make sure he wouldn't ever be able to sire children!

Mr. Ferrington muttered a soft oath. People probably didn't disobey him often. She was fiercely proud she had done so.

"Did you hear me?" the merchant growled again. "I'll call the Watch."

Under his breath, he said, "She's probably not here anyway." Caroline watched as his shadow moved past her. He was leaving. She lowered her head onto her knees, stifling a sigh of sweet relief.

Waiting until she couldn't hear him any longer, Caroline rose to her feet and, using her hand to feel her way along the wall, found her neighbor's gate. Mr. Hendley valued his flowers more than his wife, but Caroline wasn't going to stop and ask permission to trespass. This was a crisis.

Her fingers felt the rusted metal hasp of the gate lock. Sure of her surroundings now, she lifted the hasp and let herself inside. She skirted Mr. Hendley's prized rose garden and followed the walkway to the front gate, which led onto her street. Her front door was only three houses away.

Caroline didn't waste a minute. Thankful for the light of a slim quarter moon, she quickly made her way to her doorstep and knocked softly, knowing that Jasper would be waiting to let her in.

She looked up and down the street, searching for

a sign of Mr. Ferrington's coach, half-afraid that he would follow her. All was quiet—and then her heart dropped.

Waiting patiently for his mistress was the coachman in the service of the Baroness de Severin-Fortier, which meant that Minerva had returned home with all her card party cronies. Caroline prayed she could sneak past them.

Just when she was about to pound on the door again, Jasper opened it. She almost whacked him on the face.

Instead, she slipped through the door and grabbed the lapels of his faded jacket. "Jasper, lock the door immediately. And don't answer it for anyone, not even the King."

She'd never seen Jasper look so startled, but Caroline didn't pause to give explanations. She shut the door herself and fumbled to slide the bolt in place.

Now, she had to make it the few feet from the front door to the stairs without Minerva seeing her. She turned to tiptoe and froze.

Minerva and her card party friends stood in the parlor doorway watching her actions with avid interest.

Caroline decided the best response was the brazen one. Painfully aware of the picture she must present, with her crushed and crooked bonnet and her hair falling in wanton tangles around her shoulders, Caroline forced a smile to her lips. "Good evening, Minerva," she said, as if she'd just come in from a meeting of the Ladies Charity League. Thankfully, she still wore her gloves.

"Good evening," Minerva countered. Age hadn't diminished Minerva's petite beauty. Silvery gray now mingled with the golden blond hair of her youth, but the effect was arresting. Furthermore, although she shared the Pearsons' light blue eyes, experience and good humor had added intelligence to her expression.

Caroline knew she couldn't fool the sharp-witted lady. Or the women crowding the door behind her, including the Baroness Charlotte de Severin-Fortier. With her elaborately styled silver-gray hair, she stood almost a foot taller than Minerva. Tall, thin, and with striking good looks, the Baroness had escaped the French Revolution with her head intact, and for years she and Minerva were rumored to have shared the favors of George III during his better days. Caroline didn't believe the rumors. No woman could share something as intimate as a lover and still maintain a friendship—and the two women were great friends.

Behind them was Mrs. Violetta Mills. The former vicar's wife had scandalized society twenty-five years ago by leaving her husband in the middle of his Sunday service—with a Russian count. Rumor had it that the count had charged into the church on a white horse, swept her up in his arms in front of the entire congregation, and run away with her to St. Petersburg.

Caroline found it hard to believe that such a mousy, nondescript woman, with her love of flowers and shy, thoughtful ways, could inspire such grand passion. Still, the story was tragically true. That Sunday in church had been the last time Mrs. Mills had seen her children, a loss she felt keenly to this day.

A loud, gasping snore came from the parlor and

Caroline peeked beyond the doorway to the source of the sound. As she suspected, Lady Mary Dorchester, the oldest of the four friends, slept comfortably in a huge armchair by the fireplace, her high powdered wig pushed forward on her head.

Lady Mary, as she loved to be called, had been the wife of the late "Mad William" Dorchester, a great British leader in the Colonial Rebellion. Minerva had known both of them for decades. Whenever she had a touch too much wine, Minerva loved to reminisce about the Dorchesters' parties. Wicked parties, Minerva said, where everyone had the most ribald of good times. Looking at the heavyset Lady Mary snoring in the armchair, Caroline couldn't imagine her hosting a single party, let alone wickedly wild ones.

One thing Caroline did know to be true. It was going to be very difficult to bluff her way past this group. They were taking in every detail of her appearance.

She tried anyway. "If you'll excuse me, I must be off to bed," she managed to croak out in some semblance of her normal voice. "I have a bit of the headache." That last was true. Her mad dash through the night had dissipated the happy glow caused by the champagne. Now all she longed for was bed.

"Caroline." Minerva's voice stopped her just as she reached the staircase. "You look like you've been tussled."

Hot flames of embarrassment practically consumed Caroline from the top of her head to the tips of her stockinged toes. She had no idea what "tussled" looked like, but it certainly was an apt description for what had almost happened in Mr. Ferrington's coach.

Caroline shook her head. "I'm all right. I was at the, ah . . ." She searched for someplace she could have been and grabbed the first one that struck her, "the church doing some work. Quite a bit of work, actually."

The Baroness's shrewd gaze swept Caroline before she commented lightly, "You appear to have been most rigorous in your prayers, *chérie*."

Minerva limped forward, leaning heavily on her ivory-handled walking stick, a sign her arthritis was acting up again. The expression on her face was one of loving concern. "Are you sure you aren't feverish, dear? Your cheeks look as if you are burning up."

"That's not fever," the Baroness said with an all-too-knowledgeable lift of one dark eyebrow. "That's whisker burn."

"Whisker burn?" Minerva said with a surprised look at her companions.

"Oh, my yes," Mrs. Mills chimed in. "It looks like whisker burn to me."

At that moment, a heavy hand pounded on the door. Caroline's heart almost leaped in fright.

It was him! It had to be.

"No!" Caroline cried. "Don't open it." Jasper gaped at her, and then, with a small shrug of his shoulders, obeyed her command.

Minerva wasn't so accommodating. She stepped past Jasper and opened the door. As the heavy portal swung wide, Caroline's last protest died on her lips.

James Ferrington stood on the doorstep. His

broad shoulders and impressive height filled the doorframe—and no one could miss the fact that he looked slightly "tussled" too. Or that his eyes blazed with bright, green-eyed fury. Without so much as a passing glance to Minerva, his gaze shot straight to Caroline.

Lifting her chin, Caroline met him proud, indignant glare for proud, indignant glare until she thought her eyes would water. Why should she feel ashamed? She'd done nothing wrong. He was the one who should apologize. He was little better than a rake, the kind of man who knows he is irresistibly attractive to women and is shameless enough to take advantage of it.

And he was attractive, very attractive. She didn't need to hear Mrs. Mills's soft, "Oh, my heavens," or see the stirring of interest in the Baroness's eyes to know that he impressed them.

Minerva broke the stalemate. "May I help you?" she demanded in a voice that would have done the Queen proud.

Mr. Ferrington broke eye contact first. His expression closed and tense, he looked down at Minerva standing boldly in front of him. "I'm here to assure myself that Lady Pearson"—he placed a soft emphasis on the stiff formality of her title—"arrived home safely."

"And who are you?"

He glared at Minerva as if he were unaccustomed to being challenged. "Ferrington. Mr. James Ferrington."

"Then, as you can see, Mr. Ferrington, she *is* safely home," Minerva answered, her own voice formal and expressionless.

Ferrington bowed his head. "Yes, I can see that,"

he said, and his eyes rested for a moment on Caroline before he finished. "And would you please see that these are returned to her." He placed a pair of black kid slippers in Minerva's hands. "Good evening to you, madam." Without looking again at Caroline, he turned on one expensively shod heel and disappeared into the darkness.

Speechless, Minerva stared at the shoes. Mrs. Mills and the Baroness appeared to be turned to stone, their mouths comically open in surprise. Lady Dorchester snored.

With expressionless aplomb, Caroline strode forward on stockinged feet and took her shoes from Minerva's hands. "Good night," she whispered, before turning toward the stairs leading up to her bedroom. Halfway up the stairs, Minerva's voice stopped her.

"Caroline, are you all right?"

Caroline looked down at her companion standing at the foot of the staircase, her eyes bright with curiosity and concern.

Caroline forced a smile. "I'm fine. Nothing happened. Really."

Except that everything she'd previously thought about herself had been turned inside out!

Afraid that her thoughts could be read on her face, Caroline didn't wait for a response. She lifted the front hem of her skirt and made for her bed. In the safe haven of her room, she took a moment to gaze in her mirror.

Trumbull had never kissed her the way James Ferrington had kissed her . . . and, God help her, she'd kissed him back!

She brushed her fingers lightly against her

cheek. She didn't remember getting whisker burn when she was kissing him. Kissing him had seemed to be the most natural and pleasurable of acts. Now, she felt he'd branded her with his passion.

One thing she could be thankful for was that Lady Dimhurst hadn't seen her in this state!

What she needed was a good night's sleep and a chance to forget the whole unfortunate incident. It was an experience, she told herself, something that she had better not catch herself doing again.

To her surprise, she fell asleep the minute her head hit the pillow, but it was a restless sleep, full of deep, vivid dreams. She woke in the wee hours before dawn, sweating and hugging her pillow. She'd never had such dreams—and then she realized they were dreams about him, Mr. James Ferrington . . . and deep, soul-reaching kisses.

Just the thought of him sent all her senses spiraling in a swirl of emotions that left her achy and full of need. Caroline rolled onto her back, pulling her pillow protectively against her chest. Like Pandora's box, his kisses had opened her up to memories that were best forgotten. Memories of her late husband, of edgy, unsatisfied desires, and dreams left unfulfilled . . . of never ever having had her ear kissed.

Caroline stared at the ceiling, willing the feelings to go away. She would not give in to them. She had to redirect her thoughts toward practical matters such as what she would buy for dinner or the lesson she needed to prepare for next Monday's class. And she'd be fine—just as long as she never had to lay eyes on Mr. High-and-Mighty Ferrington ever again.

Immediately, the turn of her thoughts conjured his face in her mind. It wasn't just that he was handsome; he was also extremely male, and entertaining, and thoughtful—at least over dinner. How was she to know he would leap on her *after* dinner? Or that she would let him?

Fearing where this line of thinking would take her, Caroline closed her eyes and prayed for common sense. A heartbeat later, her eyes popped wide open. Her skin broke out into a sweat and her heart started with an irregular and rapid pace.

He hadn't given her the deed to her house.

Before the day was out, she would have to confront him once more.

But no games this time, she promised herself. She'd have her guard up. No dinners. No coach rides. And definitely, no kisses.

Please, Lord, no kisses.

Chapter 5

"Caroline, is something the matter with your hearing?"

Startled by Minerva's sharp question, Caroline jumped and turned, almost knocking over the ink bottle with her elbow. She caught the container before it spilled across the sheets of paper over which she'd painstakingly spent her morning.

"Minerva, you surprised me," she squeaked out before thinking that she needed to hide what was on the paper from her aunt's prying eyes. She laid her arm over the words she'd written.

"I can't imagine how. I've been calling your name for the last three minutes. What have you been up to? For more than an hour you've been spread out at that desk laboring like a pupil practicing in a copybook." She used her walking stick as she crossed the parlor to the small writing desk set in the light of the room's only window. "Do you realize the ink on that paper wasn't dry before you placed your arm on it? You'll get it all over the sleeve of your dress."

Alarmed, Caroline lifted her arm off the paper. The words *Mr. Ferrington* were smeared but legible. Immediately she realized her mistake. The stain of black ink wouldn't show on the black bombazine of her dress, but Minerva could see the words on the paper.

"You're writing to Mr. Ferrington? Wasn't he the gentleman you were with last night?" She picked up another sheet of paper. "And what is this? Row after row of F's?"

Caroline's face flooded with hot color. She hadn't liked the curve of her "F's" when she wrote out "Mr. Ferrington," so she *had* been practicing her penmanship. Then there were the sheets of stationery on the desk all starting with different salutations: Mr. Ferrington, Dear Mr. Ferrington (with the "Dear" crossed out. She feared after last night, he'd misinterpret the "Dear"!), To Mr. Ferrington, and so forth. And the sheets where she'd mulled over the details of their next meeting. She wasn't going to march over to his house again. That was a fact. This time, he'd come to her—and she'd have all her defenses up.

Caroline snatched the incriminating piece of stationery out of Minerva's hands and made an elaborate pretense of stacking the writing paper.

Minerva sat down in the chair beside the desk. "Caroline, you're blushing."

"That's ridiculous!" Caroline felt her cheeks burn hotter still.

Struggling for composure, Caroline set the stack of paper on the upper corner of the desk, away from Minerva. She folded her hands on the desk in front of her and forced herself to face her aunt. "I have business with Mr. Ferrington."

Minerva's eyebrows shot up with surprise. "Business?"

"Yes," Caroline said, and didn't elaborate.

Minerva's eyes narrowed in concern. "You know, if you need anything . . . advice . . . or a shoulder to lean on . . . you can come to me. I still have a little money."

Caroline reached out and took her aunt's hand. "I know—and if I didn't think I had matters under control, I would turn to you first."

"There are times when I believe you are too independent."

Caroline pulled her hand back. "The pot calling the kettle black?"

Minerva nodded her head, acknowledging Caroline's point. Even though they had lived together for three years, the two women had too much respect for each other—and too many secrets of their own—to pry. Caroline never offered an opinion on the way of life Minerva had chosen. In return, the older woman didn't press on issues that Caroline did not wish to discuss.

Except for today . . .

"Jasper tells me Freddie paid a call yesterday. Did he have anything important to say?"

"No," Caroline answered too quickly, and then forced a smile and added lightly, "But then, does he ever?" She wasn't about to let Minerva know they could be evicted—because she wasn't going to let it happen.

"Not that I've noticed. In fact, we so rarely see him that I was surprised he had come by." Minerva started pulling on her gloves.

Caroline realized her aunt was dressed for going out. "Do you have plans today?"

"Charlotte's invited me to lunch. Would you care to join us?"

Caroline shot a glance at the clock on the mantel and realized she'd been fussing with the letter to Mr. Ferrington for a good two hours, and still was little farther along than when she had started. She shook her head. "Thank you, but I'm afraid I can't spare the time today."

Minerva tilted her head. "What are your plans?"

"Plans?" Caroline repeated. "Well, I have my lesson to prepare for next week and some work to do for the Ladies Charity League . . . some reports to copy—"

"I think they work you too hard, and those other women involved with the charity treat you unfairly. Why won't any of those other ladies do as much work as you do?"

"Because they contribute money to the charity's work. I contribute my time."

"That pale-faced Reverend Tilton won't be calling, will he? He irritates me with his self-righteous platitudes and weekly marriage proposals. How you put up with him is beyond me."

Caroline smiled. "He really isn't that bad. And every time I refuse his offer, he acts so relieved."

"Then why does he do it?"

It was on the tip of Caroline's tongue to say "Lady Dimhurst," but the name brought back unpleasant memories. There was a good chance Reverend Tilton *wouldn't* be making a marriage offer this week.

When she didn't answer immediately, Minerva gave her an uncomfortably all-too-knowing look. She tapped the desk with the tip of her fingers. "Oh, yes. You have your letter to write."

"And other things," Caroline replied, certain that she didn't fool Minerva at all. However, if Minerva was with the Baroness, she wouldn't be here when Mr. Ferrington arrived, which would be a blessing. For the first time today, Caroline relaxed. "In fact, I'll be so busy today that perhaps you might want to spend the evening with the Baroness. That is, if she doesn't have other plans."

For a brief second, Minerva looked surprised by the suggestion, and then answered, "I might." She rose from the chair, leaning heavily on her walking stick.

Caroline also came to her feet. "Your arthritis?"

Minerva nodded. "It started acting up yesterday. The weather here is so cold and misty." She shivered in spite of the warmth from the parlor fire. "Italy spoiled me."

Caroline put her arm around Minerva's waist and walked with her to the front door. Pierre, the Baroness's huge, hulking coachman, stood talking to Jasper while he waited for her. The Baroness always sent her own coach over for Minerva.

Taking Minerva's bonnet from Jasper, Caroline set it on her aunt's head and tied the ribbons under her chin. "Perhaps you should stay home."

Minerva reached for her heavy wool shawl off the hall table. "And have you fuss over me as if I were a child? No." Handing her walking stick to Pierre, she threw the shawl around her shoulders and would have taken Pierre's offered arm to be escorted to the coach, but stopped. "Caroline, if something is bothering you, I want you to know that you can trust me. We may be of different generations, but I don't think I'm completely out of touch."

Caroline smiled at her aunt and the gentle concern written on the woman's face. "I have no worries that I can't handle. Don't worry about me."

Minerva studied her intently for a second before saying, "I'll see you this evening."

"Enjoy your day." Caroline waited until the front door had closed before she turned back to her desk, and the letter waiting to be written.

Minerva and Violetta Mills had finished their luncheon and were still at the table enjoying a glass of Ratafia. The Baroness, lying amidst pillows on the floor, sucked on a hookah, filling the air with the sweet scent of tobacco, while Lady Mary snored lightly from the chair in front of the fireplace she'd chosen after the meal.

Charlotte wore one of her favorite outfits, a red gauze caftan shot through with gold threads and the white silk trousers of a Turk. She'd adopted the costume years ago during one of her many travels, although now that she lived in London, she wore the outfit only in the privacy of her home. There were few things Charlotte wouldn't do, or hadn't done, but wearing trousers on a London street wasn't going to be one of them. "The English are so staid, I would stop traffic in trousers," she had assured her friends, and they agreed with her.

In contrast, Minerva dressed as elegantly as a duchess. Many of her gowns were ones she had acquired during the years she'd spent in Italy. Bernardo had been a generous man, even though his estate had gone to his wife and not to Minerva, his mistress, upon his death. Minerva didn't begrudge the woman Bernardo's wealth. She had received his love, and to Minerva love was more important than money.

Violetta Mills sat across the table from her, looking every inch the vicar's wife. She'd never embraced the dress of her adopted homeland, Russia, or her role of paramour. Although stylish, the colors she chose were discreet—lavenders, soft blues, beiges, and browns—and the material of her gowns was durable, practical stuff.

Violetta lived with Lady Mary, who hadn't purchased a dress in over three decades. Her William, she'd say, referring to her deceased husband, hadn't admired the current fashions, and she bluntly saw no reason to change her ways, even if he had been dead these past two decades.

She enjoyed wide-brimmed hats with jaunty ostrich plumes, sported black patches on her face, dressed her hair in powder, and wore heavy brocade gowns that she felt showed her generously endowed figure to best advantage. A tall, large-boned woman, she appeared to those first meeting her to be almost larger than life—but then, her husband had been as bold and colorful a character. Minerva knew that the reason Lady Mary slept as much as she did was because she was bored. She'd once confided in Minerva that since her William had died, life had lost its meaning and she was merely waiting for that time when she would be called to join him.

Out of the four women, only Lady Mary enjoyed an excellent standing with Society, but she rarely went out, not even for family obligations. She preferred the warm, easy companionship of Charlotte, Minerva, and Violetta.

Minerva brought up the subject of Caroline. "I've never seen her behave so oddly," she said, finishing the story of Caroline's letter writing.

"To whom was she writing?" Violetta asked.

"Mr. Ferrington. The gentleman from last night."

Charlotte sat up, suddenly interested. "Did you ask her why she was writing to him?"

Minerva shook her head. "Caroline is a very private person . . . and I believe she was afraid I would ask exactly that question."

"Why didn't you?" Charlotte asked in her French-accented English. "I would have." She frowned in response to Minerva's long-suffering sigh. They'd had this argument before. "She's your niece—"

"Only by marriage. Nor does it give me the right to intrude."

"—And younger than you are. Youth should always answer to age. That's my belief. Otherwise, there are absolutely no advantages to growing old." Charlotte popped the pipe back into her mouth.

"Caroline wants to feel independent." Minerva leaned her elbows on the table. "She doesn't ask advice from anyone, including me, since her husband passed on. Sometimes I worry about her."

"What was her marriage like?" Charlotte asked.

Minerva gave a small shrug. "I don't know. Trumbull died in '10, but I never knew him. I'd been living on the Continent since he was born and only returned a few months before his death. No one in the family would receive me, except Caroline—she even went against Trumbull's wishes, although she wouldn't want me to know that. At his funeral she asked me to live with her."

She traced the stem of her wineglass with one finger. "She never talks about her marriage. It's a taboo subject between us—and yes, I have asked her about it," she said in answer to the question she knew Charlotte had opened her mouth to ask. "I asked years ago, right after Trumbull died. I thought it might help her to confide, but Caroline isn't an open person. She grew up an only child, and I understand that her father was very demanding."

"Do you think Trumbull hurt her?" Violetta asked, her eyebrows drawing together in an anxious expression.

Minerva knew the Honorable Reverend Mills had been a pious man with a heavy, often brutal hand. Count Alexei Varvarinski had done more than introduce Violetta to love. He'd saved her life.

"No, I don't think he abused her," Minerva said, "but I don't think she loved him. I know she wasn't happy with him."

"A man doesn't need to hit a woman to abuse her," Charlotte said. She drew on the pipestem of the hookah and released the smoke before adding, "Some Englishmen treat their dogs with more good humor than they do their wives." Her expression grew worldly. "It is the reason that most women are better off playing the mistress than the wife, n'est-ce pas?"

"I did ask Caroline after the birthday dinner we gave her if someday she might wish to marry again," Minerva commented.

"What did she say?" Violetta asked.

"That she has no intention of marrying again.

She said that part of her life is behind her, even if that silly Reverend Tilton proposes to her each week. The man just won't take no for an answer." She frowned. "And his proposals lack any sign of passion."

Violetta frowned. "But why wouldn't she want to marry? She is so young, and so lovely."

"I agree, and I told her she was being silly . . . and then, she told me she couldn't have children." Minerva looked around the table at her friends, watching their expressions change from curiosity to concern as the import of that statement struck home. "She's right. No man wants a barren wife, at least not men of Caroline's rank and station."

"Some men don't care," the romantic Violetta claimed.

"But very few," the practical Charlotte finished.

Minerva placed her palms flat down on the table. "Then she arrived home last night with Mr. Ferrington and it was very obvious that she'd been kissing."

"And she didn't have her shoes on," Violetta added.

"What does that mean?" Charlotte asked, nestling down among the pillows. "That she didn't have her shoes on?"

A new voice interjected. "Perhaps Caroline has decided to take a lover."

The other women turned in surprise toward Lady Mary, who sat up, bright-eyed and apparently well rested. Lady Mary returned their looks of wonder with a sober stare of her own. "Well, you just said the gel can't have children and she don't want to marry. We all know she's too young to consider herself dried-up and put out to pasture. Why shouldn't she take a lover?"

"No, not Caroline," Minerva said with conviction. "She would never think of such a thing!"

"That's what people used to say about me," Violetta said. She heaved a soft sigh. "And then, I met Alexei."

Charlotte blew out a smoke ring. "Perhaps, *mes amies*, Mr. Ferrington is Caroline's *Alexei*, the one man who can slip past her defenses and sweep her off her feet, hmmmm?"

Startled by this new thought, Minerva pushed away from the table and stood up, needing to ease some of the stiffness in her joints. She took several small steps around Charlotte's supper table, considering this new possibility. Could Caroline be interested in taking a lover?

She turned to her friends. "I've never imagined it. Granted, she has been open-minded to the fact that I chose to live outside the dictates of society, but Caroline always struck me as being more conventional. Oh, every once in a while, a man other than the Reverend Tilton will show interest in her, but Caroline cuts him off. She can be very cold when she wants to be. I suppose that is why her behavior last night surprised me. And then this morning, I discovered her writing a letter to him."

"And she did tell you she has plans for this afternoon," Lady Mary said.

"No, she said she had business. She was very specific on that point."

"Business?" Charlotte said, her eyes twinkling. "What other business could a woman have—unless it is with a man?" She sent a sly smile to her companions before adding softly, "And there's only one kind of business that is important between a man and a woman. The kind that gives one the whisker burn. Tell me, Minerva, did she blush when you caught her writing? Not a purple, embarrassed blush, but a bright rosy one—like the flush one feels when one first falls in love?"

For a second, Minerva stared at Charlotte as if struck dumb.

Of course.

Hadn't she noticed this morning how distracted Caroline was? And Jasper had said Caroline had barely touched a bite of breakfast. Then there was the letter, and the pages with Mr. Ferrington's name written over and over that Caroline thought Minerva hadn't seen.

Could Caroline be falling in love? And, if she were determined not to marry again, would she actually entertain the possibility of forming a romantic liaison with James Ferrington?

From her disheveled state last night when she had walked through the door, it appeared as if the liaison had already been established!

"Minerva," Violetta said softly, "what are you thinking?"

Minerva looked at her friends. "I'm thinking that perhaps I'd better pay a call on Mr. Ferrington and find out what manner of man my Caroline is getting herself involved with. I will not let her be hurt."

"Well, I'm going, too," Lady Mary said.

"Oh, yes," Violetta agreed.

"Absolument," Charlotte added, joining the others as they rose to their feet. "We shall all go meet

this Mr. Ferrington, and make sure he is good enough to take care of our Caroline."

James sat at the big mahogany desk in his paneled office and tried to concentrate on the figures Daniel recited off a ledger.

He couldn't remember ever having passed such a restless night. Several times throughout the long hours, he'd rolled over, punched his pillow, and ordered himself to put all thoughts of Caroline Pearson out of his mind. The woman was a tease. Nothing more; nothing less.

There were other women in the world, a good number of them more attractive than *Lady* Pearson. And far more willing. They wouldn't kiss a man until he went mad for wanting her, then kick him in the balls and hop out of his coach.

Bloody hell, the only reason he'd behaved like such a fool over her was that he'd been living like a monk. If he'd enjoyed any form of healthy sexual activity at all, he wouldn't be tossing and turning on his sheets because one woman had worked up his senses.

And then, to top off his foul mood, he'd showed up at his breakfast table and there hadn't been anything decent to eat. Everything, from the rashers of bacon to the coddled eggs, which were usually his favorite, had looked equally unappetizing. He had grumbled something about paying a bloody fortune for a decent cook and not having anything worth eating. Calleo had offered to have the chef prepare something else, but James had discovered he had no appetite, period.

He'd gone for a ride, but it didn't seem to have curbed any of the restlessness—

"James, you haven't heard a word I said," Daniel snapped irritably.

His angry tone broke through James's brooding. "Of course I have."

"So you agree with me on that last point?"

James stared down at the round glass paperweight he'd been turning over and over in his hands, unwilling to admit that he hadn't been listening. He set the paperweight down. "I agree with you completely."

Daniel's eyebrows rose in mild surprise. He shuffled the ledger sheets in front of him as he said, "All right, then I will draft a letter to the Lord High Chamberlain saying that you think we should smear the King's feet with blackberry jam and leave him in the woods for wild forest animals to nibble on."

"What gibberish is that?"

"The gibberish I've been speaking for the last five minutes without so much as a question out of you. Are you quite well, James? You don't look as if you slept soundly."

"I slept fine," James lied. "I'm just edgy." That was the truth.

He wished he hadn't admitted it when Daniel honed in on that single statement. "Edgy, eh? Did you find the widow entertaining last night?"

"What widow?" James asked cautiously.

"The one Calleo said you escorted home last night."

"Go to the devil."

Daniel laughed, making James want to silence him with a fist to the jaw, when Calleo interrupted them. "*Sahib*, you have visitors." He read from four cards. Miss Minerva Pearson, the Baroness de

Severin-Fortier, Mrs. Violetta Mills, and Lady Mary Dorchester.

Pearson. James frowned. What could they want?

"Wait a minute," Daniel said. "Calleo, did you say Mrs. Violetta Mills?"

"Yes, *Sahib.*"

"Amazing," Daniel said, sitting back in his chair.

"What is?" James asked, and then told Calleo, "I'll see them in here." The servant bowed and withdrew, shutting the door behind him.

"Violetta Mills," Daniel said. "I mean, there could be two of them, but the one I've heard of, if she's still alive, is infamous."

"How so?"

"She left her husband, a vicar, in the middle of his church service. Some foreign count charged into the church on horseback and plucked the Reverend Mills's wife right out of the pew. She ran off with him. Scandalized everyone. Remember, my father is a deacon. When he took his training, he studied under the Reverend Mills for a month or two. But this can't be the same woman. Besides, why would she be here?" Daniel shook his head in wonder and added offhandedly, "And you've heard of the Baroness."

"I have?"

"Yes. When we were doing that bit of smuggling in Egypt. I'm sure we heard of her there." He searched his memory before snapping his fingers. "She is the Frenchwoman who rode in the hunt like a man and was rumored to be the mistress of Napoleon."

James frowned. "No! She couldn't be."

Daniel shrugged. "From the talk I overheard, Napoleon claimed she was very special as a lover."

"Do you keep a glossary of women in your head?"

"I can't imagine anything better to keep there," Daniel responded, "unless it is your appointments. By the way, now that I have your complete attention, don't forget that you agreed to dine with the Lavenhams tonight around nine."

"When did I agree to that?"

"This morning when the invitation arrived. I told the messenger you'd be delighted."

"Damn."

"I knew you would be delighted. Besides, we need Lavenham, and his letter was so solicitous and contrite, it would have been boorish to refuse."

"I've got to teach you to stop opening my mail."

"Ah, but your mail is always so interesting," Daniel lightly replied before Calleo's soft knock interrupted them.

"Come in," James said as both men rose to their feet.

The door opened and four attractive older women entered. James recognized three from the previous night's adventure with Caroline Pearson. Leading the group was the petite gentlewoman who had answered the door of Caroline's home and accepted her shoes. She was followed by a tall, regal woman sporting a small black beaver cap trimmed with gold tassels and dressed in the latest fashion *à la militaire*. She wore a dashing white-and-gold cape over one shoulder with all the flair of a hussar, while gold tassels, hanging from very key places on the woman's stylish dress, swung in rhythm with her movements.

In contrast, her companion appeared as sweet and quiet as a wren. She wore a simple straw bonnet and a serviceable brown dress trimmed in blue. James could imagine a prayerbook in her hands.

The fourth woman waited until the doorway cleared before she made her entrance. A good-sized woman, she had to duck and enter the room sideways to accommodate her wide skirts and high powdered wig topped with an elaborate broad-brimmed hat. Once through the door, she straightened and smiled. James blinked, startled to realize the woman sported a patch in the shape of a miniature coach and four at the corner of her mouth.

He frowned. "Daniel, will you give us a moment alone?"

Daniel had been avidly studying the women, obviously searching for the infamous Violetta Mills. "What? Oh, yes." He bowed to the ladies. "If you'll excuse me?"

"Thank you." James waited until his partner left the room and shut the door behind him. He came around his desk.

The petite woman stepped forward to meet him, a walking stick in one hand. The green plumes of her stylish bonnet swayed with feminine grace as she held out her hand. "Mr. Ferrington, I am Miss Minerva Pearson, Caroline Pearson's aunt." He took her hand and made a polite bow, surprised when she squeezed the tips of his fingers slightly.

She turned to the women behind her. "These are my friends. The Baroness de Severin-Fortier." The regal Frenchwoman barely nodded her head to him. He could easily imagine her on Napoleon's arm. "Mrs. Violetta Mills." If this was the infamous

Mrs. Mills, James found it hard to imagine her inspiring such grand passion. She was the most unassuming of the group. "And Lady Mary Dorchester, the wife of the late Colonel Sir William Dorchester," Miss Pearson finished.

Sir William Dorchester was a name James recognized from his boyhood days. He and his brothers had spent hours playing colonial battles and fighting over who would have the opportunity to play their favorite British hero, "Mad William." Usually, the role went to James.

He bowed to the group, intensely curious as to how their business might involve Caroline Pearson. "Would you care to sit?" He indicated a group of chairs near the window overlooking his back garden.

"Yes, thank you," Miss Pearson said for the group. "Although we plan to take only a moment of your time."

As the women moved toward the chairs, the Baroness commented, "I greatly admire your study, Mr. Ferrington. I enjoy the smell of book leather and tobacco. Very masculine." She said the last in such a way, and with just the right tilt of her head, so as to flatter him.

"Thank you, Baroness," he said, keeping his voice neutral and waiting until each woman was seated before taking his own chair. He was conscious that they studied him closely.

He sat back. "How may I be of service?"

Minerva Pearson opened her mouth to speak, but it was Mrs. Mills, sounding exactly like a vicar's wife, who said, "We'd like to know your family background, Mr. Ferrington."

"Violetta!" Minerva Pearson protested.

"It's a fair question," Lady Dorchester said. "If he is going to involve himself with our Caroline, we have a right to know."

James sat up. "Did Caro—Lady Pearson send you to meet with me?" he couldn't stop himself from asking.

All four ladies looked at him, and then at each other. Some private signal seemed to pass among them, and James almost cursed himself because he'd sounded eager, anxious even. He shouldn't have started to use her Christian name. He forced himself to relax.

Minerva Pearson took control. "Mr. Ferrington, Caroline does not know we are here. In fact, I imagine she would be most embarrassed if she learned of our visit. We can trust your discretion?"

"Of course."

She continued, "We are curious about you. We don't know you and felt it was in Caroline's best interest to pay this rather unconventional call."

"And what is it you wish to know?" he asked, his voice cautious.

"Who your family is," Mrs. Mills demanded. The other three women sat waiting for his answer, their expressions expectant.

James felt decidedly uncomfortable. He cleared his throat.

The women didn't move.

Finally, he said, "My father is a squire in Bedford. Very well respected, I believe. My mother is descended from James I, hence my name." He smiled. "A touch of Scots blood is good in every family, but they did name my oldest brother for Charles."

"Charles?" the Baroness asked, giving the word the French pronunciation.

"An English king," Mrs. Mills whispered.

"Yes," Lady Dorchester agreed, "but did they name him for Charles I or Charles II?"

"Does it make a difference?" James asked.

"Of course it makes a difference," Lady Dorchester said. "One Charles was silly enough to lose his head, and one was wise enough to keep it."

James stared at her for a second, wondering if she'd asked the question in jest. The expression on her face was very serious. "Both," he said lightly.

A smile of approval spread across Lady Dorchester's broad face. "Clever! Very clever," she replied, and settled herself more comfortably in her seat.

James leaned forward, placing his arms on the chair. "I have two brothers and two sisters. My oldest brother farms with my father; my other brother is a solicitor and quite well-known in our shire. One sister married a Lord Barnhart, and they reside in Nottingham. The other sister is considering a proposal of marriage, and I am expecting word any day now as to whether or not to wish her happy."

The women didn't move, not even a hair.

James searched his mind before adding, "I graduated Oxford. Left home and worked my way to India with a small stake my uncle lent me." He sat back in his chair. "Built my fortune. Self-made and proud of it." Crossing his arms against his chest, he frowned. "Now, why are you here?"

"Are you very wealthy?" Mrs. Mills asked.

"Violetta, sometimes you are so naive," the Baroness responded. "Of course he is wealthy.

Only money could buy so much good taste, and the cut of his jacket . . ." She slid him a look out of the corner of her eye. "Excellent tailor, *monsieur*. Excellent."

"I'll tell him you approve of his work," James responded tightly. He turned to Minerva Pearson.

"I know we must seem a bit odd to you, Mr. Ferrington, but Caroline and I have no male relations whom we trust to ask these questions for us. Experience has taught me that I can find out more for myself than through an intermediary."

She was interrupted by a snore. Lady Dorchester had nodded off to sleep in the seat beside James. Her chin had dropped down on her chest and all he could see of her was her huge hat. He regarded her with surprise before turning to the others and asking, "Will she be comfortable there? Perhaps we should let her lie down?"

Miss Pearson laughed, the sound as light as goose down. "She's perfectly comfortable, Mr. Ferrington. She enjoys napping wherever she finds herself." She touched him lightly on the arm. "And your patience with us says more about you than any financial statement could."

"What exactly is it you wish to know about me, Miss Pearson?"

"I want to know if you are a kind man, Mr. Ferrington."

"And?"

"I think, perhaps, you are."

"Your point being?"

She looked to her friends for approval. The Baroness closed one eye in assent. Mrs. Mills nodded with a smile. Obviously, he'd passed their test, but what test he wasn't sure until Minerva

Pearson turned back to him and said, "I believe Caroline is going to make a proposition to you."

If the hand of God had come down from heaven and smacked him dead, James could not have been more surprised.

He waited, certain he had misunderstood.

Miss Pearson looked him directly in the eye and said in a firm, clear voice, "Mr. Ferrington, remember that Caroline is a gentlewoman. You will be her first liaison of this type. It is my sincere hope that she does not regret this decision."

He hadn't misheard. Caroline Pearson wanted to become his mistress.

As if to clarify his understanding, the Baroness leaned forward. "We also don't want you to think that Caroline is not without friends, and we understand the rules of this type of arrangement. If you do not take the most precious care of her—"

"If you hurt her," Mrs. Mills interjected.

"—then we will avenge her," the Baroness finished, her French accent making the threat more ominous.

Miss Pearson stood as if to indicate that their business was done, and the others followed suit. James sat dumbfounded.

He'd just been threatened by a group of women who looked like grandmothers. And the only way he could save himself was to be gentle with Caroline Pearson when he made her his mistress.

Mrs. Mills shook Lady Dorchester lightly on the arm. She came instantly awake and looked around expectantly. "Did you tell him?" she asked Mrs. Mills.

"Yes," she replied. "We also told him that he would face serious consequences if he hurt her."

"Good," Lady Dorchester said cheerfully. She pushed herself out of her chair and walked with the others to the door.

Minerva Pearson said, "Good day to you, Mr. Ferrington. It was truly a pleasure to meet you." She paused by the door before adding, "And I truly hope that you and Caroline deal well together."

She left the room, her companions following. For several seconds, James stood exactly where he was, listening to them walk down the hall to his front door. Lady Dorchester and Mrs. Mills were discussing their conversation while the Baroness exclaimed over a Sèvres vase on a table in the hallway.

He heard the front door open and close behind them.

Had the world gone topsy-turvy, and he was the last to know?

Someone knocked on the doorframe. James looked up to see Calleo standing there with a silver salver in his hand. "A message arrived while you were with your visitors, *Sahib*." He offered the salver to James. In the middle of the small tray was an envelope. He didn't recognize the elegant handwriting.

He broke the seal:

Mr. Ferrington

We have unfinished business between us from last night. Please meet with me as soon as possible so that we might settle the matter.

Caroline Pearson

He'd received more romantic love letters from women.

But then, Caroline Pearson wasn't like most women . . . and the presence of this note gave credibility to her aunt's prediction. Perhaps they had been sent to assess his willingness. Thinking, he tapped the note against his palm.

Caroline Pearson, the woman who epitomized his every ideal of English beauty, was a member of the fallen sisterhood. She was going to ask him for *carte blanche*. In fact, if he acted quickly, he might even manage to negotiate their arrangement—she could have anything she wanted—and bed her before he appeared at the Lavenham's for dinner that night.

For a blessed second, he forgot to breathe, every pore in his body burning with lust . . . while in the back of his mind, some niggling doubt questioned whether this turn of events was too good to be true.

But James Ferrington had not built a fortune that spanned four continents by failing to recognize and seize an opportunity. Even if it took every resource available to him, this was one negotiation for which he guaranteed a positive conclusion.

"Calleo," he said, coming to a sudden decision, "direct me toward the nearest flower seller."

Chapter 6

Even though she'd been expecting it, Jasper's knock on her bedroom door and muffled, "Mr. Ferrington is here to see you, ma'am," sent Caroline into a panic.

He was here! His curt written reply to her request for a meeting had indicated he would arrive in one hour's time. An hour couldn't have passed so quickly. It couldn't have!

Jasper knocked again. "Lady Pearson?"

She cleared her throat. "Have him wait in the parlor, Jasper," she said, thankful her voice emerged without any indication of the turmoil James Ferrington's presence in her tiny home had set off.

She stared at her reflection in the looking glass. For the past half hour, she'd been toying with the mobcap of black lace and white ribbons. She should wear the thing, she told herself. It was right and proper. Every matron over a "certain age" wore one.

But the thing looked like one of those new

French soufflé dishes sitting upside down on top of her head, a black monstrosity that wasn't the least bit flattering. She looked incredibly stupid in it, and had no desire to tie the ribbons under her chin. For some reason, the simple act of tying the cap ribbons brought to mind wrinkle-faced dowagers.

And for the first time in years she was weary of black.

Jasper knocked again. "Lady Pearson? Are you coming?"

Caroline paused in the act of fluffing the cap. Jasper sounded almost anxious for her to come immediately. Curious, she walked to the door, making herself tie the ribbons of the cap under her chin, and opened it. Jasper stood there with a grin that stretched from one large ear to the other. "Jasper, what is it?"

"Downstairs. In the parlor. Mr. Ferrington is waiting for you." His eyes danced with excitement.

"I heard your message. Tell Mr. Ferrington I will be down in a moment."

"No," Jasper said, motioning her toward the staircase. "You must see what he's done."

Now he had Caroline's attention. She hurried for the staircase. Jasper followed her so closely down the stairs, he practically stepped on the hem of her dress. She shot him a cross look over her shoulder. He held back after that, but remained only a step behind her until they reached the bottom step.

There he scurried around her to stand by the open parlor door. Cautious, not certain what to expect, Caroline self-consciously untied the cap ribbons as she walked slowly to the parlor door. She peeked in.

Her breath caught in her throat.

Her parlor had been turned into a spring garden. Vases full of lilies, poppies, roses, and peonies, surrounded by greenery filled the tables, the floor beside the chairs, the mantel, and the writing desk. She could barely see the furnishings for the flowers. And in the middle stood the commanding figure of Mr. James Ferrington.

Dressed in a deep marine blue jacket that emphasized his broad shoulders, buff breeches that revealed his muscular thighs, and polished top boots of the highest quality, he appeared every inch the aristocrat. His rugged good looks contrasted with the backdrop of flowers. The effect on her senses was devastating.

"Caroline," he said, and flashed her a radiant smile. A woman could bask in such a smile for a lifetime.

He spread out his hands to indicate the room. "Do you like them?"

"Like what?" Caroline asked dumbly, attempting to make sense of her rioting thoughts. And since when had her heart begun this erratic beating? Certainly she was still too young for heart palpitations . . . ?

"The flowers," he said, and took a step toward her.

The memory of his body pressed against hers blazed through her mind. "They're lovely," she managed to say, and backed away from him, afraid . . . and unprepared for these crazy, whirling emotions that seemed to spring to life whenever she entered his presence. What magic did he wield? What incantations did he say to rob her of all sense and sanity?

The back of her legs bumped into the edge of her writing desk. She wanted to shout with relief, like a drowning man discovering shore. Caroline followed the edge of the desk around to the chair and, with a sigh of relief, sat down in it, feeling a measure of her common sense return.

Now, why had she asked him here . . . ? The deed! She had to ask him for the deed.

Caroline cleared her throat, straightened in the chair—and then stopped. So many bouquets of flowers covered the desk she couldn't see anything else in the room. She felt trapped in a flower box.

Ferrington's head popped over the flower "hedge" as he leaned over the desk. "Caroline, I want you to know how deeply I regret the misunderstanding between us last night."

"You do?"

"I do. And I hope you'll accept my apology."

He smiled down at her, leaning forward over the flowers until there was little more than a hand's distance between their faces. Caroline found herself reflected in the depths of his green eyes. No man should have such wonderful long lashes, or crinkle lines from sun and laughter. . . .

Caroline shot to her feet, almost knocking the chair over. She caught the back in time, steadied it, and had turned to take a step away from the desk when she practically walked right into Mr. Ferrington's chest.

His arm came around her waist and Caroline found herself pulled so close to him that she could feel every line and curve of his body. He looked down at her, his gaze serious and intent.

She recognized the minty scent of shaving soap. He'd shaved. For her. She reached a hand up, wanting to feel one lean cheek, and then stopped, her hand poised in midair. To touch him would be a mistake—

He turned his head and pressed his lips to her fingers. To save her soul, Caroline couldn't have moved. She felt the beat of his heart as deeply and distinctly as her own. His jaw felt smooth and strong beneath her fingers, his lips soft. A dizzy humming started through her, within and around her.

"I can't tell you how many times I've thought of you last night and today," he said, his voice low and slightly hoarse. "Caroline, I want things to be right between us."

"Right?" she asked. Her knees felt weak. She leaned against him for support.

His eyes had darkened to the deep green of the darkest forest. Dark with desire, Caroline realized, and felt an answering call in her own body. She'd never felt such passion, such yearning.

"Yes," he said, "I want us to get along very . . . very well."

"Very well," Caroline echoed, her own voice breathless. *He's going to kiss me*, she thought, and lifted her face even closer to him. Funny, but she'd never noticed how absolutely sensual the curve of a man's lower lip could be. How it stretched and moved as he said—

"But I never want to see you wearing that silly cap again. You look ridiculous."

"What?" Caroline blinked, not certain she'd heard him correctly.

"Your mobcap. You look as if there's a spider sitting on top of your head. I don't want you to wear it ever again." He pulled it off her head and tossed it aside. His expression softened to that of an amorous suitor. "Now, let me kiss you senseless."

But Caroline had recovered her senses. As he leaned down, she ducked out from under his arm. Hands on hips, one toe tapping angrily on the bare wooden floor, she confronted him. "Who do you think you are?"

Her indignation didn't seem to register with him. He smiled, his eyes still dark and full of fire. "I am your keeper. Your master. The man who wants to make love to you until you cry out that you are filled and sated—and then I will love you once more."

Caroline listened to his declaration with a mixture of growing horror and desire. "Have you gone mad?"

"Yes," he declared, and began walking toward her. "If happiness can make a man mad, and you have made me very happy, Caroline."

Caroline backed away, not trusting herself to let him get too close. She stepped around the sofa, almost kicking over a vase of flowers on the floor. "What in the world are you talking about?"

"You," he said, coming around the sofa in hot pursuit. When she doubled back in the opposite direction, he stopped and spread his arms out before adding, "Us."

"Us?"

He laughed, the sound happy and light. "Yes, us. Caroline, I've never felt this way about a woman before. For the first time, I understand how Samson could give in to Delilah, why Paris stole Helen, what Anthony saw in Cleopatra."

Caroline pressed a hand to her forehead, trying to understand his behavior—and then all the air in her body seemed to leave her in one quick "whoosh" when he reached into his jacket pocket and pulled out a black velvet jeweler's case. "What is that?" she asked, fearing the answer.

"It's for you," he said, and flipped open the lid to reveal a strand of perfect pearls. "I purchased them in Persia from the Sultan of Objanii and have been saving them for someone special."

Caroline stared at the creamy pearls. They suited her taste exactly, and must have cost a fortune. She'd never seen such luster and size. She shook her head. "I shouldn't. It's not proper," she added with halfhearted conviction.

"I can't imagine anything more proper than seeing them around your throat," he said. "The heat of your body will bring out their luster. Try them on. You were meant to wear pearls."

Caroline struggled against temptation. The pearls were worth three times the deed to her house. "Why are you doing this? Why do you want me to have these?" She waved to indicate the flowers. "Why all of this?"

"To celebrate."

"What are we celebrating?" Caroline pleaded, needing to know.

"Our arrangement."

"Arrangement? Do you mean our business with the deed?"

"Caroline." He drew the syllables of her name out in a soft, chiding roll. "You may have whatever house your heart desires. You don't have to settle for this one. It's little better than a cottage. I'm a wealthy man and very generous. I'll set you up in style, someplace close by. How about those new town houses in Mayfair? Would you be happy there?"

Caroline felt the first stirrings of uneasiness. "I'm happy here, Mr. Ferrington—"

"James. Call me James."

"I prefer calling you Mr. Ferrington."

His steps were measured and deliberate as he moved toward her. "And I want to call you Caroline. Beautiful Caroline. *Cara mia. Ma belle étoile.*" He stopped when they stood toe to toe, her breasts almost brushing his chest. "I want you, Car-o-line."

Caroline stopped breathing.

And then, slowly, she began to understand exactly what he was saying.

She frowned. "Are you offering me *carte blanche?*"

He smiled. "With all my heart, and anything your heart desires." He leaned toward her, as if preparing to gather her up in his arms.

Caroline was quicker. She braced both hands against his chest, prohibiting him from coming closer. "Whatever made you think I would—" Her voice broke off at the heady memory of their kisses last night. Her own culpability made her face burn. She pushed away from him and stormed to the door before finding her sense of righteous indignation and whirling to face him. "Of all the rude, insulting . . ." She searched for words to describe him—and could find none.

"Rude?" He held the velvet case toward her. "Caroline—"

"And stop calling me Caroline!" In one rash move, she pulled the bouquet out of the vase nearest her and threw it at him. If she hadn't been so angry, his expression as the lilies and roses pelted him and then fell harmlessly to the floor would have been comical.

"What made you think I would even entertain such a dishonorable proposal from you?" she shouted.

"Made me think?" he repeated, sounding genuinely puzzled. He closed the jewelry case. "You're the one who requested this meeting, *Lady Pearson*."

"I didn't request this meeting for you to offer me *carte blanche*."

"The devil you say."

"The devil I do say! I asked you to meet me to hand over the deed to my house—which you promised to give me last night," she added, punching the air with one finger for emphasis.

"The deed to your house?"

"Yes. The one you won from my brother-in-law Freddie Pearson. Don't you remember? I asked you about it last night. You said you'd turn it over to me."

For a second he stared at her, his expression vacant, and then she watched, fascinated, as understanding dawned. His brows came together in a sharp V. "I won the deed to your house from Freddie Pearson at White's last week sometime."

"Yes."

"And you asked me here to talk about the deed to your house? Not to suggest I set you up as my mistress?"

"Your mistress!" The words shot out of her. She stared at him, stunned to think he could even voice such an infamous offer. Slowly, her shock subsided and in its place rose cold, hard indignation. Her palm itched to slap him to avenge her honor.

She took two steps away before turning to him. Her voice tight, she said, "I realize that perhaps my behavior last night may have led you to think—"

"Last night had nothing to do with it," he interrupted almost ruthlessly.

"Then why? What made you think that I would consent to becoming"—she paused slightly before forcing herself to say the word—"your mistress. I've never been so insulted!"

A dull red stain crept up his cheeks, and Caroline realized he was as embarrassed by the turn of events as she was. "Forgive me, Lady Pearson. I meant no insult. I wouldn't have approached the matter unless I had been assured this was what you wished."

Puzzled, Caroline said, "Someone told you I wished you to make an offer?"

"Yes."

"Who?"

His stiff reserve softened her manner toward him, but his terse reply caught her off guard. "Your aunt gave me that impression, Lady Pearson."

"My aunt? Minerva?"

He didn't respond but reached for his hat, which had been placed on the sofa table between two bouquets of lilies. He started for the door when Caroline stepped in his path.

"Mr. Ferrington, I asked you a question. Would you be so kind as to answer?"

He looked as if he'd rather mow her over on his way out the door. An angry muscle worked in his jaw. Caroline didn't care. She wasn't about to move until he answered her. "Mr. Ferrington, this is an awkward situation for both of us. However, I would appreciate your plain speaking. I have recovered from my complete surprise at your offer and am willing to listen without cocking up my toes in a swoon. So, please, may I have a moment more of your time?"

His voice was low and sharp. "Yes. Your aunt and several other women paid me a call this afternoon. They subjected me to a bit of an inquisition. Your aunt explained you wished to be my mistress and they wanted to convince themselves that I would be worthy of you."

"*Minerva* paid a call on you this afternoon and said I was interested in being your *mistress?*"

His eyes were as bright as green shards of glass. "Not in so many words," he answered through clenched teeth.

"Then what words did she use?"

"It doesn't matter—"

"Yes, it does!"

"Very well," he said with an elaborate show of patience. "She said that you were going to make me a proposition."

"A proposition? I wonder what gave her that idea." Suddenly struck by the irony of the situation, she couldn't help laughing. It took her a few minutes to notice he wasn't also laughing.

She spread her hands in exasperation. "Be honest, Mr. Ferrington. There is humor in this. I mean, matters couldn't have stood any farther from the truth between us. If I'd never laid eyes on you again, I would have been very happy."

She'd said the words without little thought, and

once they were in the air found she held her breath, waiting for his reaction.

For a second, he looked as if he was going to disagree with her, and then the lines of his mouth flattened. "Of course, you're right, Lady Pearson. The mistake was all mine. I should have known better than to place any credence in her suggestion. Silly of me."

Caroline sobered completely. She may not have wanted his ardent pursuit, but she hated this stiff formality. "No, please, Mr. Ferrington. I don't know what possessed my aunt but please—"

"Accept my apology, Lady Pearson," he said, cutting her off. He laughed then, the sound bitter. "I don't often make such a bloody fool of myself."

"Mr. Ferrington, you didn't make a fool—"

"I disagree with you," James said, unable to look at her. She was so lovely. So very, very lovely. It almost hurt to stand here, so close to her, after he'd made such a complete and utter ass of himself.

He'd never before tipped his hand before he was certain of the outcome. And he'd never been rejected by a woman. He'd never not gotten what he wanted—and, he realized with alarm, he wanted Caroline Pearson, even now.

Standing in this room, filled with flowers that he'd happily chosen for her, the soft rain against the windowpanes creating a sense of separateness from the outside world, he knew Calleo had been right. Karma, fate, destiny, need, wanting, desire. They all ran together and through him. He spoke, his voice raspy with pent-up emotion. "I can't believe that you don't feel what is between us."

He forced himself to look at her. She appeared

startled by his words, and for a second, he thought she might agree with him. The very beat of his pulse seemed to race at the thought. And then, to his bitter disappointment, he received her rejection, first in her clear gray eyes, then her words. "There can be nothing between us, Mr. Ferrington, except for my request that you return the deed."

You lie! he wanted to shout—but kept the words to himself. He'd already made enough of a fool of himself. Still, he wasn't prepared for the statement that left his mouth. "Unfortunately, I don't think I'll be able to do that."

Her eyes opened wide. "Why not?"

Because it was the only link he had with her, and he wasn't ready to give it up, not yet. "The deed was won in an honorable game of cards. It's mine."

Her anger rose swift and sure, showing him another facet of this woman who was becoming an obsession with him. "You can't do this." She practically choked on the words. "I won't let you."

"Unfortunately, the matter is out of your hands," he said briskly. He started to step around her, wanting, needing to escape and examine the feelings that led him to such an impulsive act.

She refused to let him pass. "And what are you going to do with it? You're rich. What is this tiny town house to you—or are you going to sell it and add more money to your coffers?"

"The deed is not for sale."

Her eyes narrowed. "And neither am I."

James reacted as if she'd slapped him—and it was then that he realized his rash statement might reap consequences he would regret. But once

James Ferrington chose a course, he stuck to it. And he wasn't ready to give up Caroline.

"Then it appears that we have nothing further to say," he said tightly.

She didn't answer but stood defiantly before him, a cold and proud goddess.

He placed his hat on his head, setting the brim at a determined angle. "Good day to you, Lady Pearson." She appeared rooted to the spot, her face a mask of fury as he stepped around her and left the house.

Caroline heard him slam the front door, but it took several minutes before she could move. Slowly, she walked over to her writing desk and in one sudden, angry movement sent the vases of flowers flying off the desk. The sound of dripping water brought her to her senses.

With a soft exclamation, she ran to the kitchen closet where Jasper kept the cleaning rags. The servant quickly picked up a knife and pretended to peel potatoes for dinner when he heard her coming. She wondered how much of her conversation with Mr. Ferrington he'd heard. Hurrying back to the parlor, she quickly mopped up the water to protect the wood of the desk, and then knelt to clean up the floor.

This mess, too, she laid at the door of that "infamous bounder" and a few other choice names she had for James Ferrington. Her anger made her feel better. She was glad he'd turned out to be a blackguard and a devil. It gave her the distance she needed to fight off those aching, swirling needs that she found so hard to control every time she came close to him.

Slowly, Caroline rose to her feet. When she'd first married Trumbull, she'd had these feelings. For a moment she let herself remember how it had been, before their marriage, when he had courted her. She'd let him kiss her once, the night their engagement had been announced. That kiss had promised passion—a passion that had never materialized after they'd married. It was the last and only passionate response Caroline had ever received from him.

A wife had been nothing more than a possession to Trumbull, and his callous, bullying ways had killed whatever desire, care, or concern she had once felt for him.

Years ago, when she'd been a new bride and still naive, she'd asked her mother if it was wrong for a woman to feel such needs. The question had embarrassed her mother. One didn't talk about "intimate matters." Caroline found herself wondering if Minerva might not have a different answer—and then frowned. Minerva was the reason Mr. Ferrington thought Caroline wanton—that is, Minerva's conversation and Caroline's own response to his kisses.

Pacing, Caroline worked herself up into a fury all over again. She'd get the deed. There were courts set up to make sure that widows weren't taken advantage of by blackguards like James Ferrington. James. A good, strong solid name . . .

For an unprincipled rake!

Tomorrow she'd go and see a solicitor. Not the Pearson family solicitor but one she'd select on her own. It is what she should have done years ago, but she'd been unwilling at the time to spare the expense or rock the Pearson family boat. She'd rock it now! And Mr. Ferrington's boat, too!

But first, she must confront Minerva. That task was easy to accomplish. Within the hour, Caroline was at the Baroness's luxurious town house requesting a private audience with her aunt. A few minutes after the Baroness's servant relayed the message, Minerva rushed into the small sitting room.

"Caroline, is something wrong?"

Caroline took hold of her aunt's hand and pulled her down to sit next to her on the room's low sofa. "Minerva, what did you say to Mr. Ferrington?"

Minerva went very still.

"Then it's true. You did tell him I might be interested in being his mistress." She wished she could say the word without a rush of color burning her cheeks, but she couldn't.

"We told him that you might be interested in offering him a proposition."

"We?"

"Charlotte, Violetta, and Lady Mary."

Caroline rocked back in her seat, startled by this information.

As if reading her mind, Minerva said anxiously, "Please don't be upset with them. They think of themselves as your godmothers and only have your best interests in mind."

"But to tell him that I wanted to proposition him?" Caroline shook her head. "Where did they get such an outrageous idea?"

Minerva folded her hands in her lap before confessing, "From me."

"Minerva, whatever gave you the idea that I would ever even imagine such a role for myself?"

"Because of your recent behavior. You told me last week that you had no plans to marry again, but then, you spent an evening with Mr. Ferrington—"

"How do you know I spent the evening?"

"Jasper told me what time you went out. And when you came home . . ." Minerva let her voice trail off before finishing quietly, "You were practically barefoot and had obviously engaged in some rather rigorous kissing."

Caroline burned with embarrassment.

"Then, this morning," Minerva continued, "I caught you writing to Mr. Ferrington, and you acted so guilty—well, I didn't know what to think. It was Lady Mary who suggested you had decided to take a lover."

"A lover?" Caroline repeated with disbelief. She rose from the sofa and moved across the room, needing to regain her composure. "Why does she think I would want a lover?"

Minerva crossed the room and gently massaged Caroline's shoulders. "Here, see? I've upset you and I didn't mean to. You're so tense and tight." Her expression serious, Minerva rested a hand on Caroline's shoulder. "You're too young to go through life alone. It's not natural."

"I don't need a man."

"Caroline, don't judge all men by Trumbull."

"What do you know of it?" Caroline said, moving away from Minerva's comforting hand.

"I know that he hurt you—"

"He never raised a hand to me."

"Perhaps not, but he soured you on marriage, and the notion of love."

Uncomfortable with the direction of the conversation, Caroline said stiffly, "It's interesting that I'm receiving a lecture on love from you."

"Oh, Caroline, set aside your pride and realize that you don't have to carry the weight of the world around on your shoulders. I love you as if you were my own daughter, but there are times when your stubborn refusal to accept help from anyone frustrates me, and you do so need someone to confide in. Even more, you need someone to love."

To Caroline's horror, a tear slid from the corner of her eye and rolled down her cheek. She raised a gloved hand to stop it—then realized that a stream of tears now flowed freely from her eyes. "Am I really so transparent? Can you read me so easily?"

"There isn't a woman on the face of this earth who doesn't need someone to trust and love."

"I don't," Caroline said. She fumbled with her reticule, reaching for her handkerchief to help stem the tide of silent tears. She pressed the cotton cloth against her face, gathering her composure. "And you're wrong, Minerva, I did talk to someone about it once. I talked to my mother."

It hurt to speak, but Caroline suddenly felt a need to bare her soul. "I told her that I was very unhappy with my marriage, that often he was mean to me. Not mean as in he had foul moods or spoke rudely, but vicious as if he enjoyed letting me know how unimportant I was. He killed my pet." She had to pause and take a deep breath. Several seconds passed before she could continue. "Wags was a silly little puppy I'd befriended, just a hound from the village actually, and so ugly . . . but I adored him. Unfortuately, he was clumsy and made little messes because he wasn't very well trained—but that was my fault. Then one day Trumbull stepped in one of Wag's little puddles and grew angry. He picked up the pup and threw him against the stone fireplace and then threw him again, and again, until he'd killed him."

Caroline closed her eyes against the memory, praying for strength. When she spoke, her voice was hard. "Trumbull destroyed everything I enjoyed or cared about. I wasn't allowed to go to town. He forbade my friendships, and kept me in the country as if I were in prison. Of course, I found after several years of marriage that he had a mistress in town and was much happier spending his time with her than with me . . ."

She couldn't go on. Gently, Minerva led her back to the sofa and Caroline gratefully sat down.

Caroline continued, "I told my mother I wanted to leave Trumbull." She closed her eyes, the memories of that day as sharp and clear as if the conversation had happened yesterday. She willed herself to be strong. "Mother said that if I left Trumbull, she and father would disown me. She said that she couldn't live with the shame. It's ironic, isn't it, that you and I have both been threatened by our families? The difference is, you had the courage to face the consequences, whereas I did not."

Caroline shook her head. "My parents and I never talked to each other after that day. I'd disappointed them."

"They'd hurt you, broken your trust."

"No, I broke *their* trust. It's very hard to be an only child. My parents held such great expectations for me, and I sorely disappointed them."

Minerva placed her hand over Caroline's. "My dear, you could never be a disappointment."

Caroline studied the hand covering hers before saying, "They died a year later. We didn't speak, and our relationship had grown coldly cordial . . . but I miss them."

Minerva wrapped her arms around Caroline's shoulders and, for once, Caroline allowed herself to relax in the warmth and comfort of that embrace. Slowly, a sense of peace unraveled the tension that she'd carried inside her for so long. "If I'd known they were going to die in that coach accident, I would have tried harder. I wouldn't have been so angry."

"I'm sure they know that, dear," Minerva said. "They're in heaven now, and I believe they know what is inside your heart for them." She sat back. "But I'm also certain they wouldn't want you to turn your back on living life to its fullest. Caroline, someday you're going to want to open your heart to another man. No, not a man like Trumbull, but a man who is worthy of what you have to offer."

Caroline clenched her fist in her lap. "I will never turn control of my life over to a man again."

"But not all men are like Trumbull. Bernardo wasn't . . . and neither was Robert."

Minerva had never mentioned a Robert before. "Who was Robert?"

"The very love of my life. For him, I gave up my family, my place in society, and everything I'd been taught to believe."

"What happened to him?"

The happy glow in Minerva's eyes faded. "He died." She look up at Caroline. "But I have no regrets. Nor did I stop living. If I'd had your attitude, Caroline, I would never have met Bernardo. He enriched my life in ways that I still feel today . . . just as the memory of Robert's love burns strong and vibrant within me. Please, don't be afraid to love. Open yourself up to life and accept all it offers."

Suddenly, Caroline caught a glimpse of herself through Minerva's eyes. "I must appear very boring to you."

"Not boring, frightened. That is one of the reasons why now that you've decided to start living again, the ladies and I want to make sure the man is deserving of you."

Caroline shot up off the sofa. "I have no interest in Mr. Ferrington. The truth is, Minerva, Freddie lost the deed to my house to Mr. Ferrington in a game of cards. James Ferrington refuses to turn over the deed, even though he knows it wasn't Freddie's deed to lose and he promised me last night that he would do so."

"What is this?" Minerva asked, bewildered, and Caroline told her the whole story, starting from Freddie's call the day before.

"We thought Mr. Ferrington was such a gentleman," Minerva said.

"Well, now you know him for a rake of the worst sort. I would never, repeat never, agree to such a dishonorable liaison as being his mistress. But don't worry, I'm not going to lose my house." She gathered her shawl around her, preparing to take her leave. "Mr. Ferrington is going to discover that women are not without rights in this world."

"What are you going to do?" Minerva asked, rising.

"Engage a solicitor. I should have done it years

ago, when Freddie first refused to turn over the deed." She took a step toward the door. "Are you coming along now, or will you be staying longer?"

A distracted frown marred Minerva's brow. She gave a small wave. "I'll be home later. Charlotte wants to play another hand of cards."

"Very well, then," Caroline said briskly, then paused. "Minerva, thank you for listening to me." But words were not enough. In two quick steps, she crossed the room and wrapped her arms around her aunt. "I hadn't realized how much I'd closed myself off from everyone."

"Please remember that I'm here for you, dear. You can trust me."

Caroline gave her one last squeeze. "I know that now. Thank you." She moved to the door. "I'm on my way. You'll be home for dinner?"

"I should be."

"Till then," Caroline said, and returned home to plot her meeting the next day with a solicitor.

Minerva returned to Charlotte's sitting room, where she shared the details of Mr. Ferrington and the deed with her wide-eyed friends.

"Why, he must have known all along that Caroline wanted the deed," Violetta said.

"And yet he let us continue to talk on and on, almost compromising poor Caroline's virtue," Minerva finished. She closed her eyes for a moment, feeling the ache of tears. "I should have known better. Caroline isn't a woman to give in to passion. She'd never do anything outside the bounds of propriety."

Charlotte leaned toward Minerva. "You are making it sound as if we are not proper. I reject that implication."

"This is England, Charlotte. We aren't proper to the sort of circles Caroline was raised in, and now look what it has gotten her," Minerva said. "I wish I could have saved her from being embarrassed in this manner."

"Embarrassed?" Lady Mary said. "I saw her when she took her leave, and she looked angry and fighting mad to me. In fact, I don't ever think I've seen Caroline's eyes sparkle so. Ever. She seems to enjoy a good fight."

"Lady Mary is right," Charlotte agreed. "However, this Mr. Ferrington has insulted our Caroline. Did we not warn him this afternoon that we expected him to take care of her?"

Violetta chimed in, her voice soft with irony, "I think that's what he was trying to do."

Charlotte dismissed her comment with a wave of the hand. "We cannot promise to defend her and not act upon that promise." She pushed away from the game table, where she and the others had been playing before Caroline's visit, and stood. "Although, Minerva, I wish you and Caroline would move in with me. I have more room than I need. I do not know what Gerald," she said, referring to her last lover, a very wealthy merchant, "was thinking when he left me this huge house and so much money."

"Caroline would never agree to it, dear. She takes so much pride in her independence. And you should have heard her talking to me. She plans on getting the deed back."

"How does she intend to do that?" Lady Mary asked.

"She will retain a solicitor and take the matter to court."

"She'll lose," Lady Mary said emphatically.

"She will not," Minerva answered. "The deed was never Mr. Ferrington's or Freddie's."

"But Mr. Ferrington is a man, and he has not only a man's influence but also the advantage of a heavy purse," Lady Mary said.

The truth of the statement made the women sit in silence.

Charlotte finally spoke. "Then we must get the deed for her. It is what we owe Caroline for placing her in this situation in the first place." So saying, she stretched her arms out to her friends. "Together, we can make this Mr. Ferrington pay for insulting Caroline."

"Yes," Violetta agreed. "Together." She took Charlotte's hand and reached out to Lady Mary.

"You mean we are going to take him on? Do battle? Oh, this is going to be lovely fun," Lady Mary said, and took Violetta's hand. She held her free hand out to Minerva.

Minerva looked at each of her beloved friends' faces before smiling and placing her hands in Charlotte's and Lady Mary's. "Between us, we know enough about men and how to handle them to make Mr. Ferrington wish he'd never crossed our path."

"This is true, *chérie*," Charlotte said, "although I have a feeling Mr. Ferrington will be a particularly challenging opponent."

"We're up to it," Violetta declared stoutly.

"Yes! I haven't felt so excited in years. What do we do first?" Lady Mary asked.

"First?" Charlotte said. "We find out everything we can about Mr. Ferrington. Knowledge is power, and we have many resources. If he has a weakness, we will hunt it out. I will start by asking many of Gerald's friends."

"And I'll talk to my banker," Lady Mary said. "Violetta and Minerva, you follow Mr. Ferrington around whenever he goes out. We need to know whom he sees and what he is doing. Charlotte, may we use your coach? It's smaller than mine."

"No! We must hire a coach. Mr. Ferrington must not suspect anything. But we will use my Pierre. He will be needed for brute strength."

Softly the others agreed with her. Charlotte smiled. "Then here's to our success," she said, and gave Minerva's hand a squeeze.

Minerva in turn squeezed Lady Mary's hand. "To success."

"Yes, success," Lady Mary said. "We'll make him wish he'd never laid eyes on Caroline." She squeezed Violetta's fingers.

Violetta smiled. "Or the deed to her house," she promised, and completed the circle by squeezing Charlotte's hand.

"Now, here's what we will do first," Charlotte announced, and for the next fifteen minutes the women were very busy making plans. Then they broke up their meeting and went to their respective homes to contact their sources for everything they could find out about one Mr. James Ferrington.

Chapter 7

❦

The gloomy afternoon drizzle gave way to a dark, forbidding twilight and the threat of heavy showers. From the shelter of the garden room, James barely registered the change. Alone with his thoughts, he stared out through the open windows, letting the breeze and light rain settle on him as if he were a piece of statuary.

"I have been looking for you everywhere." Daniel entered the room, his footsteps scraping the brick floor. "And why are you sitting in the dark?"

The hiss of a lucifer sounded before there was the bright flare of a light. Daniel lit a set of lamps on two tables. The rain outside raised the garden smells of peat and earth.

James took another sip from the whiskey glass in his hand. The warm bite of malt rolled off his tongue and down his throat.

Sitting in a chair directly opposite him, Daniel studied him for a moment before saying, "Calleo told me you came home three hours ago. We have reports to go over."

James frowned. "Reports?"

"Remember? For Friday's meeting. It's what we were doing before those women interrupted."

At Daniel's reminder, the events of the afternoon returned to James. Daniel sat forward. "James, is something wrong?"

"Why do you think something is wrong?"

"I've fought by your side, man. We've marched across deserts and hacked our way through jungles together. I've battled Turkish renegades and Oriental pirates by your side, wenched and drunk with you. I know you better than I know my own mother."

James set his glass down on the table, lowered his feet to the floor, and stood. Looking out into the dark garden, he confessed, "Daniel, I've done something I'm not very proud of."

Daniel appeared to digest that piece of information. Finally, he said, "I've never known you to behave in a less than honorable manner."

James didn't answer. He couldn't. In the silence, the skies opened, and the rain came down, hard and steady.

Daniel sat forward. "It can't be that bad. Tell me and together we'll solve the problem."

"Solve the problem," James repeated and gave a short, bitter laugh. "I could solve the problem in three seconds if I had a mind. All I need to do is turn over the deed to Caroline Pearson's house." He leaned his arm against the window frame and stared out into the rain before admitting, "But I can't do that."

Silence stretched between them, broken only by the sound of the rain rolling off the roof and hitting the bricks.

"James, are you in love?"

For a moment, James almost didn't believe he'd heard correctly. Startled, he turned on Daniel. "What did you say?"

"I asked if you are in love," Daniel repeated, completely serious.

"Have you gone daft? I've only just met the woman."

"Yes, and since that moment, you've been irritable and edgy—except for a few hours this afternoon when you charged out of the house and bought every flower in London—"

"How do you know that?"

"James, you took ten footmen with you. The Mayor of London should have such a parade . . . and we all know where you went. Even the scrub maid. You're the talk of the house."

James shifted uncomfortably.

"And now, when the most important meeting of your business career is practically upon us, you've spent a good portion of the afternoon with a whiskey bottle for companionship, brooding over a problem that you admit could be handled and dismissed with three seconds of your time. But you won't handle it, will you, James? Because if you do, she might disappear from your life completely."

James slowly sat down on the windowsill, humbled to hear his situation so accurately described. "It doesn't make sense, does it? I've known her less than twenty-four hours, and yet I can't get her off my mind." He pressed suddenly sweaty palms down his thighs.

Daniel sat back in his chair, making the hand motions of shooting an arrow from a bow. "Cupid has found his mark. You're lovesick."

"Don't be dramatic. It's impossible to fall in love so quickly."

"Tell that to Mark Anthony."

"Mark Anthony?"

"Within moments of meeting Cleopatra, he gave up Rome and honor. Arthur destroyed Camelot for Guinevere, Samson turned from God for Delilah, and Adam gave up the Garden of Eden for Eve. History and legend are full of stories documenting what folly awaits a man who falls in love."

"And it's all nonsense. Besides, what do any of those stories have to do with me?"

"It's not all nonsense. Every day in every park in this city, young men duel over beautiful women for no other reason than that they like the turn of her ankle or the tilt of her head. James, there is no rhyme or reason to love. It makes strong men weak and sane men mad. The question I'm asking is, why do you feel you should be any more immune to love than the rest of us foolish male mortals?"

James stood, his mind reeling with a sudden revelation. He took a step and stopped. "I'm not in love." He took another step. "But something pulls me to her." He balled his hands into fists. "She doesn't feel what I feel. She wants nothing to do with me. And I'm not certain I don't blame her."

"Ah," Daniel said sagely, "unrequited love."

James frowned. "The devil with it." Anger, pure and irrational, filled the void left by confusion. "I'm not over the edge yet. In fact, this is for the best. Yes. I don't need Caroline Pearson," he declared, gathering strength from the statement. He picked up the whiskey glass and drained the last of its contents.

Daniel watched him as if he were seeing a strange and unusual sight. "If you say so."

"I say so," James promised solemnly, silently daring Daniel to challenge him. "There are many women in the world, a good number of them more attractive and certainly more willing and entertaining than Caroline Pearson."

"Ummmhummm."

James struggled with the desire to wipe the smug look off Daniel's face. He retreated behind a businesslike attitude. "Let's work on these reports."

"Of course, but *after* your dinner with the Lavenhams this evening."

"What dinner with the Lavenhams?"

"Don't you remember? Lady Lavenham penned the invitation herself. You had me send your acceptance before our meeting was interrupted by those four women." He watched James closely as he added, "We discussed that the invitation is a sign the countess is about to give her blessing to your match with her daughter. You still have enough wits to remember that conversation, don't you?"

No, he didn't remember, but he hid it well—he thought. "Well then, I'd better dress for dinner." He started toward the door, anxious to escape his friend's too knowing eyes, when Daniel's voice stopped him.

"By the way, we received a very angry dressing down from Lord Dimhurst via his personal secretary."

James paused in the doorway. "Whatever for?"

"It seems you promised him copies of lading reports last night."

Damn! "I did." He looked to Daniel. "How upset was he?"

"Upset enough to let us know that if we can't be more responsive, he might pull his investment and not show up at the meeting. I promised him the reports for tomorrow but managed to finish them this evening. They are on their way over to Dimhurst now."

James sighed with relief. "Thank you, Daniel. And I promise, we'll go over the other reports this evening, when I return. From now on, I'll keep my mind on my business."

"Very well," Daniel replied, but James didn't think he fooled him. Furthermore, Daniel's unerring insight had rattled James to the very core of his being.

He took the stairs to his bedroom two at a time. What he needed was to concentrate on business and not on Caroline Pearson. She was too strong-willed for him, too fickle. One second she melted in his arms. The next, she warded him off like an outraged virgin.

He wouldn't think of her again, ever. His resolve firm, James entered the suite of rooms that served as his bedroom and turned himself over to his valet.

But he didn't keep his resolution.

While his valet prepared him for the evening ahead, James studied his reflection in the looking glass. In elegant black evening dress, he looked exactly as he always had, a man in his prime who knew his place in the world.

So, why did he feel changed? Why were this day and this moment different from all the other days and moments that had come before?

Because he might be in love.

The thought caught him off guard. The expression on his face turned to one of stunned uncertainty, that of a man adrift, lost in a world he had never known existed . . . or was sure he wanted to explore.

With sudden decision, James turned on his heel and crossed to his writing desk, his valet tripping behind him with a clothes brush. Waving the man away, he took out paper, pen, and ink and scratched out a quick note:

Lady Pearson, changed my mind. Please accept this deed to your house with my good wishes.

Ferrington

James lifted the paper, impatiently blowing the ink dry, when his glance rested upon his bed. In a flash of his mind's eye, he conjured a picture of Caroline Pearson lying naked on the gold brocade bed covers, her heavy auburn hair spread out over the pillows, her lush body, smooth, white . . . inviting.

His soul turned to fire.

He crushed the letter in his hand.

A knock sounded at the door, startling James out of his reverie. He looked to the door, then back to the bed. The bed remained empty, the cover smooth and undisturbed.

The knock sounded again. "Mr. Ferrington?" the valet said uncertainly.

Not trusting his voice, James nodded and the valet moved to open the door. James opened his fingers and stared down at the letter.

"Sahib, your coach is waiting."

James vaguely registered Calleo's words. He held the letter over the flame of the candle on his desk. The heavy paper turned brown and then caught fire. James let the fire spread until it licked the tips of his fingers. He blew, and the letter disintegrated into black ash.

"I'm not taking the coach tonight, Calleo. Please have a mount brought round. Preferably Trojan," he said, referring to his favorite, a black stallion with a strong spirit.

"But, *Sahib*, it is raining. You'll be drenched before you arrive at your destination."

James rubbed the black ash from the tips of his fingers. "Good."

The ride in the rain didn't improve his humor.

James presented himself, a trifle damp but in reasonable shape, on the Earl of Lavenham's doorstep at the appointed hour. The butler announced him with all the pomp of an honored guest. Lady Lavenham herself met him at the drawing room door with one arm outstretched. Her other arm cradled one of her pampered spaniels to her chest.

For the first time since James had been introduced to her, the woman attempted to smile at him. "I'm so pleased you could join us this evening, Mr. Ferrington. Lena, come here and say hello to Mr. Ferrington."

Lena, charmingly dressed in a frock of yellow tulle in spite of the chilly weather, dutifully broke away from a group of young people to answer her mother's summons. Her blond curls bounced with her movements, and James found himself comparing her to one of his sisters' china dolls—and to

Caroline, who would have presented a more mature and graceful picture. He immediately erased that last thought from his mind and bowed over Lena's hand.

"It's a pleasure to see you again, Mr. Ferrington," Lena lisped, every "s" sounding like a "th."

A shiver ran up his spine. "You look lovely this evening, Lady Lena," he lied smoothly.

She gave a small half smile at the compliment. "Thank you."

She offered nothing else in the way of conversation, and for the first time in his life, James's own mind went blank over small talk . . . because, he discovered, he had nothing to say to her. What would they talk about after they were married? He hadn't quite considered that before.

Lady Lavenham rescued them from the awkward silence. "Lena, take Mr. Ferrington around the room and introduce him to our other guests."

For a brief second an emotion almost like anger flashed in Lena's eyes. She looked at her mother and answered dutifully, "Yes, mother," her "yes" sounding like "yeth." "If you will come with me, Mr. Ferrington."

James followed. He didn't know many of the people present other than Lord and Lady Dimhurst. Dimhurst had apparently recovered from his tantrum over the shipping reports because he introduced James to several gentlemen, all of whom were keenly interested in James's challenge of the East India Company's license.

Dutifully Lena stayed by James's side, but she barely paid attention to the introductions. Instead, she craned her head to better see the group of young people in the corner of the room she'd been forced to abandon upon James's arrival. James noticed that a good number of them were military officers in dress uniforms.

Dinner itself was a tiring affair, with endless courses and insipid small talk. James fought the urge to check his fob watch. Lena joined in an animated conversation with one of the military officers. Lady Lavenham ignored him.

To add insult to injury, his dinner companion on his right, a lively Hungarian noblewoman, became increasingly amorous as the wine flowed. They'd just finished the fish course when James felt something run up and down his leg and realized with a start that it was the woman's foot!

She leaned toward him, placing her hand on his thigh. "Such firm, strong legs," she whispered, and drew a deep breath, like a bloodhound catching scent of its quarry.

"Has anyone heard the news from Freddie Pearson?" a man's voice said from the other end of the table.

James completely forgot the Hungarian and her roving hands. The speaker was a balding young military man, Captain Soane, who was sitting close to Lena.

"Freddie Pearson?" said a plump, attractive matron who had been introduced to James as Lady Elizabeth Andrews. "Is he related to Caroline Pearson?"

James's heart jumped to his throat. Pretending a studied nonchalance he was far from feeling, he said, "Yes." He cleared his throat. "I believe they are related. Do you know her?"

"Caroline and I attended Miss Agatha's Scientific Academy for Young Women together." She blushed prettily. "Of course, that was years ago."

"Well, Freddie is about to seek his fortune," Captain Soane announced.

"I thought he was done up. Lost everything to gambling, including the house his sister-in-law inhabits," the Earl of Lavenham said. "With help from Ferrington here." All eyes at the table turned toward James.

"He did," Captain Soane said. "But now he has a plan to go to America and try his hand at farming. What do you think of that?"

"I think, knowing Pearson, he'll lose his shirt," the earl replied. "The man's a fool."

Lady Lavenham pursed her lips, her face taking on the expression of a dried peach. "The Pearsons were never of the first stare. I'm not surprised he squandered his fortune."

"But what of Caroline?" Lady Andrews asked. "I mean, since her husband's death she must be dependent upon the family. And doesn't Freddie still have a mother living?"

"Yes, Lucinda Pearson," Lady Lavenham said. "I believe she has money of her own." She turned to the gentleman next to her. "Lucinda was a Nevins-Melford before her marriage. Very good family."

"Yes, indeed," the gentleman murmured.

"I don't think Caroline has any family," Lady Andrews said. "Both her parents died sometime after she married Trumbull, and she has no brothers or sisters."

The woman's concern seemed so genuine that James dared to say, "I think that, ah, she has an aunt with her . . . from her husband's side of the family. Minerva Pearson is her name."

"Minerva Pearson!" Lady Lavenham's voice rang through the dining room. "Please tell me I didn't hear you correctly." She pinned James with her gaze.

Conscious that apparently he had offended his hostess, James said cautiously, "Yes, I did say Minerva Pearson."

Lady Lavenham gave a gasp of outrage and flung herself back in her chair as if ready to swoon. Two footmen jumped forward and began fanning her with table napkins. The other guests watched this little drama with openmouthed interest while her husband continued eating.

Finally, when it looked as if Lady Lavenham would recover, a woman who was bolder than the others asked, "Did you know Minerva Pearson?"

Lady Lavenham sat up. "*Everyone* knew her. And no one will receive her." She looked up the table directly at James. "Not if they have any social standing."

Lady Dimhurst nodded her head, the canary yellow plumes of her headdress bobbing up and down. "No one," she echoed.

"Who is Minerva Pearson?" asked portly Lord Grimsley, motioning for a footman to pour more wine.

In a voice that could freeze a man's soul, Lady Lavenham announced, "She was one of us—" She paused for dramatic emphasis. "Until she disgraced her family by running away with a man and causing his death."

Raised eyebrows and discreet murmurs met their hostess's pronouncement.

"The Pearsons disowned her and would have

nothing to do with her," Lady Lavenham said
briskly. "I'd heard that she is not only back in
London, but one of the Pearsons is sheltering her in
our midst." She shot a pointed look at Lady
Dimhurst. "Or is she still?"

"As far as I know, Minerva Pearson is still living
with Caroline Pearson. I talked to her," she assured
Lady Lavenham, "after the conversation we had
over the matter, but Caroline doesn't always listen
to reason. She's very independent. She teaches at
Miss Elmhart's School, where I am a patroness and
never listens to my advice. However, you may want
to talk to Mr. Ferrington, Lady Lavenham. He's her
cousin."

James felt all eyes turn toward him.

"Cousin?" Lady Lavenham said. "I didn't know
you had family in town, sir."

"We're distantly related," he murmured.

"How distant?" Lady Lavenham asked, but before James could think of an answer, Lady Andrews came to Caroline's defense.

"If Caroline has taken such a person of question-
able morals into her home, then I am sure she has a
very good reason. The Caroline Pearson I knew
was a compassionate, caring girl of unquestionable
moral character."

"Really?" Lady Lavenham said, her eyes glowing
with malicious humor. "Then we shouldn't be
surprised to find this paragon of virtue at your ball
tomorrow night, should we?"

Lady Andrews didn't flinch from Lady Lavenham's sarcasm. "If I knew where she lived, I would
invite her."

For one long second the two women took the

measure of each other, and then Lady Lavenham changed the subject by asking a Lord Higgins if his gout still bothered him.

James could barely wait for the dinner to end. The ladies excused themselves to leave the gentlemen to their port and cigars. This time of discussing business was usually James's favorite part of a dinner party. Tonight, anxious to search out Lady Andrews, he waited impatiently for the earl to suggest the gentlemen rejoin the ladies.

Skillfully avoiding the Hungarian, he searched out Lady Andrews, whom he found seated in a corner of the room. "May I join you?"

Lady Andrews smiled. "Are you sure you wish to? I am obviously in Vera's bad graces," she said, referring to Lady Lavenham.

"I'm already there myself," James demurred, sitting in the chair next to her.

Lady Andrews's eyes twinkled with genuine delight. "Yes, you are. You aren't her first choice for a son-in-law."

"How do you know of my offer?"

"We're distantly related . . . and Vera has never learned discretion. She doesn't approve of you, you know."

"She's made her sentiments very clear."

"However, never fear. I believe you will win your suit for Lena's hand. Vera must let some new blood enter the family sooner or later. Of course, as her cousin, I can say that."

James paused a moment before broaching his reason for searching her out. "Actually, I was surprised to hear you knew Caroline Pearson."

"I'm surprised you are a relation of hers. I didn't believe she had any family living."

"We're distant cousins . . . very distant."

"We were very close friends at one time," Lady Andrews said. Her expression changed to one of angry determination. "I'd love to invite her to my ball, just to see the expression on Vera's face. I would have attended Trumbull's funeral, but I was in my confinement for my third child then. Poor Caroline."

"Did you know her husband well?" James couldn't stop himself from asking.

"We all knew Trumbull. He was the catch of the Season, handsome, dashing, clever—and Caroline caught him. She must still be overcome with grief for him."

"Why do you think that?" James asked, experiencing a sudden surge of jealousy.

"Because he was so wonderful," Lady Andrews said simply.

That wasn't the answer James wanted to hear, especially since Caroline still wore black for the man.

Lady Andrews continued, "I'd like to see her again."

James pushed his jealousy aside. "She might even be willing to come to your ball," he suggested tactfully.

"She might." The expression in her eyes grew thoughtful. "We had such a good time in school together, and then during our first Season. She was a much better student than I could ever hope to be. I'm not surprised to learn she is encouraging education for young women. She was so intelligent." She drew a deep breath. "But all of that seems a lifetime ago. Before the demands of children and husbands . . . and household duties."

She reached out and touched James's hand. "She just had a birthday, or did you know that? She's turned thirty. I know because I'm five months older than her to the day, and it seems that now I'm older, I feel a need to visit those good friends who knew me when I was young."

"You're still young," James said, pleased to learn more about Caroline.

"But I'm not getting younger. Do you have her address, Mr. Ferrington? I would like to pay a call on her tomorrow in spite of preparations for my ball. If the rumor is true and Freddie intends to leave the country, Caroline may need a friend."

James was only too happy to comply. "Perhaps you should invite her to your ball," he added after writing down Caroline's address on a slip of paper and handing it to Lady Andrews.

"And set Vera's nose out of joint? I'd love to."

James had another request, one more sensitive than the first. "I don't suppose you'd have still one more invitation to your ball. For me?"

Lady Andrews's eyebrows lifted in surprise. "But you've already received one, Mr. Ferrington. And accepted it. Please don't tell me you've forgotten."

James made a great pretense of the engagement having momentarily slipped his mind, until she was smiling and satisfied, while another part of his mind thought that perhaps he shouldn't give Daniel such free rein to set his social calendar.

Lady Andrews nodded her head in Lena's direction. The young woman stood on the other side of the room talking to a handsome cavalry officer. "Lena is most fortunate to have a gentleman with your understanding ask for her hand. Lavenham will make Vera see the wisdom of this marriage, Mr. Ferrington, and I know that soon we'll all toast your happiness."

"Thank you." Struck by a new and urgent thought, he'd barely heard what she'd been saying. "Lady Andrews, I wouldn't say anything to Caroline about my having given you her address. She might not appreciate the fact that I've been talking about her."

"I understand absolutely," Lady Andrews said. "She was always a very private person. Since you are her cousin, I will warn you in the strictest confidence that the ill will Vera holds for Minerva is of long standing." She leaned closer, dropping her voice almost to a whisper. "Vera and Minerva made their come out together, years ago. According to my mother, there was a bit of a scandal involving a young man who was promised to Vera. He ran off with Minerva Pearson, leaving Vera at the altar. No one talks about it in the family, and I hadn't thought of it until tonight when Minerva's name came up in the dinner conversation."

"What happened?"

Lady Andrews shook her head. "My mother didn't know the details other than to say that Vera's suitor died tragically. It was for that reason, I believe, that Minerva Pearson left the country. Shocking, isn't it? I've never heard of a woman being forced to leave the country. I've heard of gentlemen who have decamped after they've killed someone in a duel or perhaps been guilty of even worse crimes, but never a woman. Poor Caroline. And poor Vera. Look at her, Mr. Ferrington."

He turned toward his hostess. Lady Lavenham's

eyes burned a touch brighter than they had before dinner. Her expressions and hand motions were more animated. Her loud laughter sounded forced.

"I was under the impression that she already knew Minerva Pearson was back in London," he said.

"Perhaps a few people did," Lady Andrews answered, "but I assure you that a good many more are like ourselves and did not know. They are probably all doing exactly what we are doing right now, searching their memories for the reason that Vera would have such a strong dislike of Minerva Pearson. Oh, but there is my sign from my husband that he is ready to return home."

She rose, and James politely came to his feet with her. Lady Andrews offered her hand. "It was a pleasure to talk to you, Mr. Ferrington, and thank you for Caroline's address. It shall be our secret, although someday Caroline will thank us."

James bowed over her hand, thinking that he didn't know about that. However, he argued with himself that whatever happened next was in God's hands. After all, Caroline could turn down the invitation.

Or she might accept it.

He took his leave from his host and hostess shortly after Lord and Lady Andrews left. The rain had stopped and a full moon had emerged from behind the clouds. Moonlight reflected off the city's wet bricks and cobblestones. The air smelled clean and fresh.

He meant to ride directly home. Daniel was waiting and would want to hear all the details from the evening as well as work on the reports that were due Friday. However, almost without realizing it, James discovered himself sitting on his horse in front of Caroline's house. Silver moonlight bathed the house, making it appear separate, sacred, and apart from all the others that lined the street.

Inside, Caroline slept.

Hidden by the night, James understood how Romeo felt waiting outside in Juliet's garden, praying for her to appear. What if Caroline came to stand at her window? Would his heart sing?

The direction of his thoughts caught him by surprise. When had he turned into such a fool?

He kicked his horse into a trot toward home.

From the safety of the hired coach, Minerva watched Mr. Ferrington ride away from the small house she shared with Caroline. This was their first spying mission, and all four of the friends had insisted on coming along.

The coach pulled away from the curb and discreetly followed Mr. Ferrington to the safety of his home. Charlotte watched him dismount and climb the steps to his door before closing with a snap the opera glasses she'd used to observe him.

She turned to her companions in the close confines of the coach. "He sits a horse so well. Rich, handsome. It's almost a pity Caroline won't accept his protection." She tilted her head and gave Minerva a knowing look before adding, "You know what they say about a good horseman."

"Charlotte, keep your mind on the plan," Minerva ordered. She looked at the others. "Well, do you think we will succeed?"

"Wait a moment," Violetta answered, and leaned over to give a shake to Lady Mary, who was snoring softly in the corner.

She came awake with a start. She looked around her, her gaze coming slowly into focus. "Oh, I see. We've moved."

"*Mais oui*," Charlotte said. "Did you think he would stay at the Lavenhams' all night?"

Lady Mary righted her wig and rubbed the small of her back. "This is boring, and the coach is very uncomfortable."

"I'm sorry," Charlotte said. "Next time we'll use my coach with its coat of arms and liveried servants so he'll know exactly who is following him."

"Please, ladies," Violetta said. "Let's keep our tempers under control and our mission in mind."

Minerva took charge. "Do you think we will succeed?" she asked again.

Charlotte smiled at her through the dark. "In kidnapping him? *Absolument.*"

Lady Mary nodded. "According to my banker, Ferrington is gambling everything he owns in his challenge of the East India Company's monopoly of the spice trade. Furthermore, he has a good number of investors who are depending on him to succeed. These investors are important men who will not be happy if he does something irresponsible . . . such as failing to attend the meeting."

"And the meeting is scheduled for Friday?" Minerva said.

"Friday at eleven in the morning sharp," Lady Mary said. "If we kidnap him, I would wager a hundred pounds sterling that Ferrington will be more than happy to hand over the deed in return for his freedom. My dear William would have considered this a capital plan."

Violetta's eyes danced with anticipation. "When are we going to do it?"

Minerva leaned forward. "The sooner, the better."

"Pierre has been busy bribing Ferrington's servants for information about the activities he has planned right up until the meeting," Charlotte said. "He should have all the details by tomorrow morning."

"Right, then," Minerva said. "Let's meet at Charlotte's tomorrow at half past ten. We can finish our plans then." She held out her hand. "To success." Each woman placed her hands in Minerva's.

With a sigh of pleasure, Violetta summed it up. "Isn't this a grand adventure?"

Chapter 8

❧⨀❧

Caroline woke hugging her pillow . . . the memory of vivid dreams of James Ferrington kissing her in secret places making her twist in the bedcovers.

Shocked, she jumped out of bed and threw the pillow across the room. What had come over her? Since when had she begun entertaining such, such—her mind searched for a word—*erotic* thoughts?

Her hands shaking, she poured water from a pitcher into the basin and vigorously scrubbed her face, hoping to inject some sense into her system. Her heartbeat slowed. Caroline sat down on the edge of the bed. Where had such vivid dreams come from?

Certainly not from her marriage to Trumbull. Caroline had grown to dread those nights when her husband had come to her bed. He would climb under the covers beside her and have his way without the slightest touch of affection.

Nor would she have ever conjured the images of

Trumbull that she'd just dreamed of James Ferrington. The passion had seemed so real!

If she hadn't let him touch her that night in the coach, especially in such an intimate way, she wouldn't be having these dreams. Even now, she could recall the heady taste of his kisses and feel the rough texture of his whiskers against her skin. The man was all hard muscle, but his touch was gentle, especially when he'd slipped his hand beneath her garters, searching for her most secret place—

She had to stay away from him.

Her body ached for him, and yesterday, it had been all too easy to yield to his kisses.

Caroline hopped to her feet. How could she think of him this way? She detested James Ferrington. He was arrogant, stubborn, and far too self-possessed for her taste. She had never been so insulted as when he'd offered her *carte blanche.*

Well, he'd discover that she wasn't going to tumble into his arms at a snap of his well-groomed fingers.

No matter what her dreams said!

Caroline dressed quickly, with more energy than she'd shown over the last ten years. The sooner she made the appointment with her solicitor, she told herself, the sooner she would remove Mr. Ferrington's disturbing presence from her life. And she definitely wanted him gone!

She picked up the pillow from the floor and made the bed before marching downstairs for breakfast. Minerva was waiting for her in the dining room across from the parlor. Jasper had heard Caroline coming down the stairs and had poured her morning cup of tea. Caroline gratefully accepted it.

"You have a particular sparkle in your eye this morning, my dear," Minerva noted over the breakfast table. "Did you sleep well?"

Caroline choked on the mouthful of tea she'd just sipped. She was saved from making an answer by the sound of the front door knocker. Jasper had gone to the kitchen so Caroline rose from the table and answered the door herself. There on her doorstep stood a lovely young matron.

"Do you recognize me, Caroline?" the woman asked.

It took only a moment. "Elizabeth Leighton!" Caroline cried, and threw her arms around her childhood friend. "Come in, come in!"

"Except now I'm Lady Andrews," Elizabeth said. "You haven't changed."

"Or you! I can't believe that after all these years, you've come to see me!"

The two women happily embraced again.

"Come, I want you to meet my aunt Minerva." Caroline shut the door and started to lead Elizabeth back to the dining room. "Can you join us for breakfast?"

"Oh, I can't stay, and I shouldn't have come so early, but I have so many things to do today and I'd hoped that you would forgive the early call."

"I'll forgive you anything. Minerva, this is Elizabeth Leighton, a friend of mine from Miss Agatha's, where we went to school together. She's now Lady Andrews. Elizabeth, please sit down and join us for a cup of tea. Or would you prefer coffee?"

Elizabeth sat down, still insisting that she couldn't stay for more than a minute. Minerva said

she didn't care for any more tea. She'd promised
Charlotte that she would call on her at ten o'clock.

"So early?" Caroline asked. "I didn't think Charlotte ever rose before eleven."

"We are working on a project together. She's
sending her coach over." As if on cue, a knock
sounded on the door. This time Jasper opened the
door and Caroline could hear from the conversation in the hallway that it was the Baroness's
coachman. Minerva pulled on her gloves. "It was a
pleasure meeting you, Lady Andrews. I hope you
two have a good visit." She left the room.

"So that's the infamous Minerva Pearson," Elizabeth said in awed tones.

"A far cry from what you would expect from the
stories people tell, isn't she? I love her dearly. She
has been a godsend since Trumbull's death."

"Caroline, I am so sorry I didn't attend his
funeral. I was in the country at the time."

"Having a baby. Yes, I know. I received your
note, and I think you had a perfectly good excuse."
Caroline smiled. "Do you like honey in your tea?"

"Oh, anything. I can't stay long," Elizabeth
repeated. "I just wanted to drop off this invitation
to my ball tonight. It's short notice, Caroline, but I
was afraid that if I didn't deliver it personally, you
wouldn't attend. I only discovered last night that
you still live in town. For some reason, I had
thought you would stay on Trumbull's country
estate after his death. Isn't that where you had
been living?"

"Through most of my marriage," Caroline said
softly. "However, I've always preferred London."

"Yes, that's right, you did. Oh, Caroline, please
say you'll come to my ball. This will be our only

chance to talk. I leave for the country the day after tomorrow and won't be back for months."

"For months?"

Elizabeth blushed. "I'm pregnant again. Douglas likes me to spend my confinement in the country and, in truth, I prefer it as well, although it does grow tedious. But, then, where will I be able to go in town once I start to show?"

"Pregnant again? That's wonderful news, Lizzie. How many children do you have now?"

"Five," Elizabeth answered and rolled her eyes expressively. "All of them lovely, remarkable children, but having them is so hard on my figure."

Caroline didn't try to hide the envy in her voice. "Five children, and another on the way. Girls? Boys?"

"Four girls and one boy, David, who is excessively spoiled. He's the eldest and the image of his father. His sisters have all told me that this next one had better be another boy to even out the family." She set down the spoon she'd used to stir her tea. "Did you and Trumbull have children?"

Caroline took a calming sip of tea before saying quietly, "No, Trumbull and I weren't blessed with children."

Elizabeth placed her hand over Caroline's. "I didn't mean to pry."

With a shake of her head, Caroline said, "To be honest, at first I was disappointed but I've come to accept it."

"Caroline, I'm sorry. I shouldn't—"

"Elizabeth, please, don't apologize," she started, then realized two huge tears had run down her cheeks. "I can't believe this. I never cry and now, over the past few days, I seem to be turning into a watering pot. It must have something to do with turning thirty." She managed a shaky laugh and brushed the tears away before admitting with brutal candor, "I'm lying, Elizabeth. I'm jealous. I wish I'd had children."

Elizabeth rose from her chair and wrapped her arms around her friend—and Caroline let her. How comforting it was to have someone from the past enter her life again. It made her realize how completely she'd been shut away from everyone after marrying Trumbull. First, by his dictate and then later, because she hadn't had the energy to break the pattern.

Caroline confided, "I always wanted children and when I found out that I couldn't . . . "

"Please, darling. I didn't come here to make you unhappy."

"Oh, no, you've made me very happy," Caroline said, wiping fresh tears away with the back of her hand.

Elizabeth had tears in her eyes too. "Yes, I can see that," she said, and the two friends found enough joy in their reunion to laugh. "Please, when I retire to the country, come for a visit. Maybe over the holidays. Don't hide yourself away."

"I haven't been hiding," Caroline lied.

"No, you've been in mourning. You must have loved Trumbull very much."

Guilt welled up. "Perhaps the time has come to put mourning aside," she said noncommittally.

"Then join us this evening. There will be so many people there whom you know. Remember Sarah Daniels?"

Caroline nodded.

"She's a duchess!"

"No!" Caroline said. "Quiet, mousy Sarah?"

"Yes! She's a grand duchess now by her second marriage!"

The thought sent both women into gales of laughter . . . and it felt good to laugh, Caroline realized.

She touched her friend's hand. "I would love to attend the ball."

"I'm so glad. Your presence will make this night special, like one of those fairy stories. Now, don't tell me you are going to come in mourning. You've already admitted that you are ready to set it aside and there will be dancing. I remember you always loved to dance."

Caroline pulled back. "Oh, I can't. I haven't danced since before my marriage."

"Trumbull didn't dance? How odd. I remember standing up with him a time or two when we had our come out."

Then he had been looking for a wife, Caroline thought cynically. There were many things he did to please would-be brides that he wouldn't do for his wife. She hadn't had a new ball gown since before her marriage, because Trumbull considered such expenses frivolous. "I'm afraid I don't have anything to wear. But I want to come."

"You can't come in mourning. You'll find yourself sitting with the dowagers, bored to tears. I must have something you can wear."

"No, I couldn't borrow a dress from you," Caroline demurred. Her poverty embarrassed her slightly. It was too bad that Minerva was four inches shorter or she'd be tempted to borrow a dress from her.

"Don't be ridiculous. I'm sure I have something that would fit you. In fact, I'm certain. I put on weight with each child and must have a dress in every size. Douglas thinks I'm foolish, but I don't have the heart to part with my ball gowns. I'll examine my wardrobe and, if I have something, I'll have a servant run over with it later."

"Elizabeth, I don't know what to say—"

"Don't say anything. It pleases me to do this. Oh, Caroline, we were such good friends in school, as close as sisters. Remember? I need you. I find that the older I grow, the more I need people around me who remember when I was young and pretty."

"Elizabeth, you are still very pretty."

"Do you think so?"

"Yes. And I also know exactly what you are saying. It does feel good to laugh. I've missed laughter, and friendships. I've missed them very much."

The look in Elizabeth's expressive dark eyes grew pensive. "We were all jealous of you when you made a match with Trumbull Pearson."

"You shouldn't have been," Caroline said baldly.

"Yes, I think I realize that now." Elizabeth gathered up her gloves and reticule. "Douglas is good to me, and we share a mutual affection. If it was anything more dramatic, we'd have twice the number of children, and I don't know if I could manage that," she added with good humor.

"Is it enough?" Caroline asked without thinking, remembering a room filled with flowers and the almost-overwhelming presence of James Ferrington.

"Of course," Elizabeth said sensibly. "Whatever

else could there be? Burning desire? Torrid romance? I don't think I could live in such an agitated state. Could you?"

"No," Caroline said quickly. "I assure you I could not." She paused a moment before adding, "But tell me, Elizabeth, do you believe there is a thing called love, not romantic love, but the type of love that lasts forever?"

"Yes," Elizabeth said without hesitation. She leaned her arm on the table. "But it's not what we thought it was when we were girls, and it's not exciting either. Comfortable is the word I would use to describe it, and heartening. When I see Douglas with one of the babies in his arms, I know at that moment that I will love him forever. But there are other times when he is the most infuriating, stubborn man and he makes me so angry . . . but I think I love him in those moments, too, in spite of his faults."

She smiled at Caroline. "Do you know what he said to me the other day? He said he was going to enjoy growing old with me. It sounds like a very silly compliment, but it touched me deeply. You see, Caroline, the truth is, I don't mind growing old so much with someone like Douglas at my side. Perhaps that is what love is. Knowing that someone will always be by your side, and wanting him to be there."

She looked up as if suddenly aware of the time. "I must be going," she said, moving toward the door. "Now, don't forget that you are promised to me for tonight."

"I won't," Caroline assured her as they walked to the front door. "I'll be there even if I have to sit with the dowagers."

"I'll find something for you to wear," Elizabeth promised. "Oh, and why don't you ask your Cousin James and see if he would be willing to escort you tonight?"

"Cousin James?" Caroline repeated blankly, then stopped dead in her tracks as she realized Elizabeth meant James Ferrington. The lie they'd told Lady Dimhurst was already catching up with her.

"Such a charming man, and very handsome, too. You are most fortunate to have him here in London to look after your best interests."

"My best interests!" Caroline practically choked on the words. She took hold of Elizabeth's arm. "Who told you about James and me being cousins?" she asked, immediately realizing how odd the question must sound to Elizabeth. "I mean, we don't discuss it or see each other often. We're not close."

"Oh, dear," Elizabeth said. "I didn't mean to upset you. Actually, it was Lady Dimhurst who told me."

Relieved, Caroline let go of Elizabeth's arm. "I'm sorry I reacted the way I did. You surprised me. Not many people know about our relationship."

Elizabeth frowned. "Caroline, I'm afraid that is no longer true. Lady Dimhurst announced it at the Earl of Lavenham's dinner table last night. There were more than twenty people present. Oh, now see, I've upset you. Please don't worry, Caroline. I'm sure few people at the table placed any value on that bit of information."

Caroline managed a weak smile. "I'm sure what you say is true."

"It is." She gave Caroline a quick kiss on the

cheek and hurried down the front steps before climbing into a handsome open carriage. Last night's rain had given way to clear blue skies and a fresh breeze. It was a good day to be out riding. Elizabeth's coachman snapped the reins, and they were off.

Caroline waved good-bye until Elizabeth's conveyance turned a corner and disappeared from sight. She didn't go back in her house immediately but stood on the doorstep. The street still looked familiar, the sights, sounds, and smells the same— but there was something different. The air around her seemed to hum with excitement, anticipation, a sense of purpose.

Her heart felt lighter than it had for years. Elizabeth's visit was a good omen—and she wasn't going to worry about Lady Dimhurst's telling everyone in London that Caroline was James Ferrington's cousin. As Elizabeth had pointed out, that bit of gossip was of little consequence to anyone of importance.

Dismissing that worry, Caroline went inside to pen a note requesting an appointment with a solicitor who had been recommended to her a year ago, after she'd had one of many fights with Freddie over the deed. She should have spent the money and acted then, she realized, instead of waiting. Well, she wouldn't wait any longer. And, once she had finished the note and given it to Jasper to be delivered, she planned to rummage through her closets and a few trunks in the attic in the hope that there might be something salvageable to wear to Elizabeth's ball.

* * *

From his vantage point in an alley down the street, James Ferrington watched Caroline turn and go inside her house. Once the door closed, he urged his mount to follow Lady Andrews's carriage. He caught up with her a few minutes later.

"Good morning to you, Lady Andrews," he said, tipping his hat.

"Mr. Ferrington, what a surprise! You'll be pleased to hear where I've just come from."

"I can't imagine," James said politely, riding alongside her carriage.

"Why, Caroline Pearson's. I must thank you again for telling me that she is in London. It is so good to have her rejoin my circle of friends."

"I'm glad to be of service, Lady Andrews." James let a few seconds elapse before he boldly asked the question that was most on his mind. "Did you invite her to your ball this evening?"

"Yes," she admitted slowly, "I did." Lady Andrews tilted her head, her expression thoughtful. "I wondered last night after our conversation, Mr. Ferrington, if Caroline was upset with you for winning Freddie's fortune from him."

James felt the full force of his lie. "Did she say anything this morning that made her sound less than pleased with me?"

"When I suggested that she ask you to escort her this evening, she did not like the idea. Nor was she happy that I knew the two of you were cousins."

"You didn't tell her that I was the one who gave you her address, did you?"

"That was our bargain, was it not? She knows nothing of your involvement, but I sense she does not fully approve of something you have done."

"She wasn't pleased over Freddie losing his fortune to me," he admitted. "And Caroline is the most independent woman I've ever met. However, she knows she need not be concerned for her welfare. I plan on taking excellent care of her."

"You might find her more difficult than you think," Lady Andrews said.

He was silent a beat before asking cautiously, "But you were successful in convincing Caroline to come tonight?"

Lady Andrews smiled. "Yes. She might even dance, provided I can find her something to wear besides black."

Caroline might dance? He imagined holding her in his arms and twirling her around the ballroom floor. His horse pranced beneath him in response to the sudden pressure of his legs.

"Of course, I must be careful," Lady Andrews said. "I will not have a scandal ruining my ball, and as you heard last night, Caroline's affection for Minerva Pearson could come down on her head."

"Why is that?"

"Mr. Ferrington, don't underestimate my cousin Vera. She has a cold-blooded hatred for Minerva, and it could be transferred to Caroline."

"I will see that nothing happens to Caroline."

"As will I, sir, as will I." She laughed, the sound light and happy. "At least this evening should be interesting. Good day to you, Mr. Ferrington. I have a list of errands to finish before my ball this evening. I look forward to seeing you there."

"Good day to you too, madam," James said with a tip of his hat. Her carriage pulled away, her horses moving smartly. He reined Trojan to a halt. He would see Caroline that evening. His pulse raced at the prospect. The sunshine seemed brighter, colors more vivid, life more precious.

He had to make Caroline realize the attraction between them—because things couldn't continue as they were. He'd dreamed of her last night, and had woken up this morning hard, aroused, and burning for release.

No one but Caroline could satisfy this mad lust beating through his veins. He'd woo her, win her, and claim her.

Maybe tonight.

If she danced. But Caroline couldn't dance if she wore black.

James pulled out his fob watch and looked at the time. A quarter to ten. Daniel expected him back to work on more financial figures for Friday's meeting.

However, James suddenly had more pressing business to attend to. He had to make sure that Caroline had a dress to wear to the ball. The more he considered the matter, the more his imagination caught fire. He had little notion of women's fashions, but he knew what color he wanted her to wear. Blue, the rich color of sapphires or the clear autumn sky. A color that would bring out the red in her auburn hair.

He guided his horse toward the shops of the most fashionable milliners. He knew these shops because they were located around the Exchange. Certainly, the milliners would know where he should go to purchase a dress.

Three hours later, he was still at it, giving little thought to Daniel or bankers.

There was so much to consider when choosing a woman's hat. He visited three milliners until he found one with a velvet cap the color of Egyptian lapis sporting a diamond stickpin and soft, plumy feathers. The milliner assured him it was perfect for a ball. James quite liked it. It would look wonderful on Caroline.

Following the milliner's advice, he shopped for gloves, shoes, and finally found himself, hatbox and packages in hand, entering the salon of Madame Bertrand, the best dressmaker in London. The milliner had warned him that finding a dress already made would be very difficult, so when he entered Madame Bertrand's shop, James insisted on being presented to her.

Madame Bertrand was a thin, imposing woman with brown hair piled high on her head and eyebrows penciled in over each eye in an expression of permanent disdain. Passing her a few folded pound notes, James stated his business.

"But, *monsieur*," she protested in French-accented English, "it is impossible to have a dress ready by this evening."

"Oh, I need it sooner than that," James said reasonably, handing her several more pound notes. "I want the dress by four o'clock this afternoon."

The dressmaker's eyes grew as round as saucers. *"C'est impossible!"*

"Nonsense. Nothing is impossible," James said, holding out a small leather purse, heavy with coins.

Madame Bertrand took the purse in her palm and weighed it before practically purring, "Sometimes miracles can be performed."

"That's right. I want a miracle," James said, "and I'd like it in blue."

"Bleu?"

"To match this hat." He pulled the velvet cap from its hatbox."

Madame Bertrand's eyebrows rose in disbelief. "Are you saying, *monsieur*, that you have bought the hat first, and now you want me to make a dress to exactly match the hat? And you want it all by four o'clock *this* afternoon?"

"Yes," James said simply.

"What you ask will be expensive," she warned.

"Expense does not concern me."

Madame Bertrand ran a practiced eye over the cut of his coat and the quality of his boots before her fingers closed around the money bag. *"Tiens!* I shall perform a miracle."

"I had faith that you would," James said, confident in his own power.

Madame spun around and, after giving sharply worded orders to her assistants, soon had James comfortably seated in a private curtained fitting room, sipping a glass of wine while she turned her shop upside down to fulfill his request. Ten minutes later, she stuck her head inside the room. "The exact color of the hat, *monsieur?"*

"That is my first choice."

"And her size?"

"I don't know."

Madame Bertrand's mouth flattened and James could almost imagine her counting to ten in an attempt to control her temper. However, her tone was patiently polite. "Is she this size?" she asked, pulling one of her seamstresses forward from the outside room.

"Oh, no. Caroline is taller . . . and thinner."

Madame went behind the curtains and emerged

with another seamstress. James shook his head. "Too tall and not enough—" He made a gesture with his hands, one holding the wineglass, to demonstrate Caroline's full-sized breasts.

"More bosom?" Madame interpreted. "And mid-sized?"

James nodded.

Madame's head disappeared behind the curtain. "Where is Suzanne? I need Suzanne."

A few minutes later, Suzanne, a pretty young seamstress, was pushed forward by Madame. "Like this, *Monsieur* Ferrington?"

James smiled. "Yes. Very much so. But then, still a little, how do I say it? Heavier on top?"

"I understand," Madame answered.

"And narrower at the hips."

"We see," Madame said, wisely pushing a now-pouting Suzanne out of the room with her.

James sipped his wine happily. He'd never shopped for a woman before. This was fun.

"Mr. Ferrington, I thought I heard your voice."

Startled, James turned to see Lady Lavenham wearing a dressing gown standing in the curtained doorway. He rose to his feet and gave a short bow. "My lady?"

For a long moment, the two of them took the measure of the other. Lady Lavenham broke the silence first. "You can't be any more surprised to see me than I am to see you in the fitting rooms of Madame Bertrand's, Mr. Ferrington." Her gaze fell on the hatbox and wrapped packages piled beside his chair. "I never imagined you were interested in the purchase of women's fashions."

James said nothing. He could claim he was

shopping for his mother or one of his sisters, but suddenly he didn't want to fabricate the truth, not in something that involved Caroline. It was enough that he'd claimed to be her cousin!

Furthermore, Lady Lavenham's manner alarmed him. She held herself tightly erect, her light blue eyes cold and angry. "Aren't you going to say something?" she demanded. "Make up some excuse? You men always have easy lies ready at your disposal. I'd like to hear what you have to say."

At that moment, Madame Bertrand hustled Suzanne and a small army of seamstresses into the room. "*Voilà, Monsieur* Ferrington! We have worked magic."

Lady Lavenham practically hissed at the intrusion. Madame Bertrand skidded to a halt. "I have come at a bad time?"

"No," James said with genuine relief.

The French dressmaker looked from the scowling society matron in one of the dressing gowns she used for fittings to Mr. Ferrington. "Perhaps it will be better, *monsieur*, if we return in a moment." She motioned for her seamstresses to follow her, but Lady Lavenham stopped her.

"No, please do not leave on my account. I'm sorry to have interrupted you, Mr. Ferrington."

Watching Lady Lavenham with the caution one saves for dealing with a cobra, James responded cordially, "Your visit was not an intrusion at all, madam."

Lady Lavenham smiled, her expression almost pleasant. "Will we see you this evening at Lord and Lady Andrews's ball?"

"I plan on attending," James answered.

"Very good," Lady Lavenham said. She slid a look toward the dress. "I'm sure Lena looks forward to seeing you."

"As I do her," James responded gallantly.

"Until this evening then," Lady Lavenham said, and left the room.

James frowned. He should have handled Lady Lavenham with more finesse but her unexpected presence had caught him off guard. Now she might use this incident as an excuse to reject his marriage offer to her daughter.

He took a thoughtful sip of wine. The idea of her withholding her approval of the match no longer worried him. In fact, he might even welcome the opportunity to be free of the obligation . . .

Madame's voice brought his attention to the dress. "This dress was commissioned for the Duchess of Bedford, but we can add the little pearls, like this"—she held up a sting of seed pearls across the dress's bodice—"and like this to make it more evening wear."'

"The color is perfect," James said.

Madame pointed out that the sleeves would be removed and new ones sewn on, trimmed in a white water satin another seamstress was holding. Pulling pins from a pin cushion, Madame showed James how it would look. It took her little time to convince him that the simple day dress could be turned into an elegant ball gown.

Caroline would look beautiful.

Lady Lavenham turned to her abigail. "When Madame leaves Mr. Ferrington's fitting room, send her to me." She returned to her own curtained private room to wait—and simmer.

She'd been having James Ferrington watched ever since Lavenham had proposed him as a match for their youngest child. Her sources said that he kept no mistresses.

Now it looked as if he'd chosen one. No man spent this much time choosing a dress for his mother.

Not that she was surprised with this new tidbit of information. Lavenham had kept a mistress for years.

Bitterness, as thick and sour as bile, welled up inside her. She would never have married Lavenham if the one man she had loved more than her own life hadn't died.

She felt the pain of Robert's death, sharp and fresh, as if it had happened yesterday instead of thirty years ago. Tears stung her eyes. Her hands began to shake. Vera sat down on a cushioned chair in the fitting room. The grief never went away for long, and she suffered moments such as this when all she could do was give in to the anguish.

Over the years, one thought alone had given her the courage to go on—that the woman responsible for Robert's death, Minerva Pearson, had suffered for what she'd done.

But then, Minerva hadn't truly paid for her crime, had she? She was back in London now, and appeared younger-looking and happier than most women their age.

The need for vengeance replaced Vera's grief, and gave her renewed strength. The day would come when she would destroy Minerva.

A light rap on the outside of the fitting room and Madame Bertrand's voice interrupted her dark thoughts. "I am so sorry to have kept you waiting, my lady." She entered the fitting room, followed by Lady Lavenham's abigail. "You wished to see me?"

Lady Lavenham's smile could chill wine. "Who did Mr. Ferrington order that dress for?"

Madame raised her chin. "I am sorry, my lady, but it would be indiscreet to answer your question."

Lady Lavenham raised her fingers. She held several pound notes. "I want to know. Everything."

Madame smiled, the soul of discretion. "But of course, my lady, for you I will tell everything I know." She pocketed the pound notes before admitting she knew nothing.

Lady Lavenham wanted to box the woman's ears. Some of her terrible temper must have shown because Madame hastened to tell her what little she could. Mr. Ferrington had asked that the dress and the other purchases he had made be delivered to a certain address and that the recipient be told that it was a present from Lady Andrews. No, he hadn't included a note.

"How curious," Lady Lavenham said to herself. "Did he say what the dress was for?" she asked.

Madame's eyes narrowed shrewdly, and she gave a shrug of her shoulders.

"You're not getting any more," Lady Lavenham said, "and I advise you to cooperate or there might be some very unpleasant rumors started, such as the fact that you just sold a dress commissioned by the Duchess of Bedford to another woman. What excuse will you give for not having it ready on time? One of your seamstresses took ill? The fabric didn't arrive?"

Madame Bertrand's whole demeanor changed. "The woman is wearing it to a ball tonight. All I have is the address where the packages are to be delivered."

A ball tonight? Everything fell into place. There was only one such event scheduled for that evening—the Andrews's rout. The mystery was why James had had the dress sent in Elizabeth Andrews's name.

"Let me have that address," Lady Lavenham said smoothly. "I have a sudden desire to take a ride."

Chapter 9

I didn't think you'd ever come home!" Caroline said, confronting Minerva and the Baroness in the hallway outside her bedroom.

"Why, it's only a little after four—" Minerva stopped in mid-sentence. "Caroline? You're not wearing black."

"Yes! Don't you think it's time?" She laughed happily, pleased at Minerva's surprise. In truth, she'd barely recognized herself when she'd first put on the dress Elizabeth had sent over. Performing a little pirouette, she danced back into the room. Minerva and the Baroness followed.

Caroline stopped in front of her looking glass, giving herself another critical glance. "What do you think? Do you truly like it?"

"I've never seen you in anything but black," Minerva said, as if she were unable to adjust to the change.

"That pale yellow washes you out completely. The dress is five to seven years out-of-date, and the

180

lace train is silly," the Baroness said without ceremony.

"Charlotte!" Minerva said with exasperation.

The Baroness looked at Minerva as if surprised
by her disapproval. "She requested my opinion."

"But do you have to be so French about it?"
Minerva countered.

The Baroness opened her mouth to comment
when Caroline stepped between them. "The Baroness is right," she said to Minerva. "But it's either
this dress or my black. I have nothing else. Not
even something in gray or lavender. I even checked
the trunks up in the attic. There's nothing suitable
for a ball gown."

"Where are you going?" Minerva asked.

"Elizabeth Andrews, my friend from school
whom you met this morning, has invited me to her
ball! But it's tonight! This evening. Oh! I almost
forgot. Will you come with me?"

Minerva made a small sound of distress. "Oh no,
I'm sorry. I've made other plans."

"That is not good news," Caroline said, meaning
the words. For a moment she debated whether she
should accept the invitation at all.

As if reading her mind, Minerva said, "But you
must go. It is time you came out of mourning. High
time."

"Of course she should go," the Baroness agreed.
"What is to stop her?"

"She needs a chaperone."

"A chaperone?" the Baroness asked, as if the
idea was foreign to her. "Caroline is a woman, not
a child."

"Charlotte, in England no gentlewoman of any
age goes out at night without some sort of escort,"

Minerva explained. "After all the years you've lived here, you should understand that fact by now."

"Bah! What use do I have for your silly English customs?" She considered Caroline thoughtfully a moment. "Is it possible for a maid to serve as an escort?"

"It's possible," Minerva said, "if the servant is of a certain age and demeanor."

"Would my assistant Mirabelle be considered a suitable escort? She is close to my age and has a virtuous disposition. Too virtuous sometimes," the Baroness added. "She never hesitates to let me know when she disapproves of something I do!"

"She'd be perfect," Minerva said, clapping her hands together. "Thank you, Charlotte."

"Yes, thank you," Caroline echoed, deeply touched by the Baroness's generosity. For the first time, she understood what Minerva had meant yesterday. The Baroness, Mrs. Mills, and Lady Mary were like godmothers of sorts. The knowledge filled Caroline with a security she hadn't known since before her ill-fated wedding day. Impulsively, she leaned over and gave the Baroness's cheek a quick kiss.

The look in the Baroness's eyes softened. "I am only too happy to help, *ma petite*."

Caroline turned her attention back to her reflection. "Lizzie loaned me this dress. She had others, but the moths got to them, and this is the only one that survived." She frowned at her reflection. "If I don't wear this one, I'll have to wear my black . . . and I'd almost rather not go if I have to sit out the dancing." She lifted the hem and let it fall. The Baroness was right. The dress had seen better days, and the lace edging around the bodice was too tight.

"Not go!" the Baroness exclaimed. "You must go. I can't tell you how long I have waited for you to leave this silly mourning behind. Perhaps I have something you could wear."

Minerva and Caroline both turned at the same time and took in the Baroness's daringly low-cut dress of bright yellow velvet trimmed in cherry red satin. Minerva put Caroline's doubts into words by saying, "It is very generous of you to offer, Charlotte dear, but your taste is a bit too extravagant for an English ballroom."

"So? What is wrong with that?" the Baroness asked. "Everyone will notice her and say, 'there is a beautiful woman.'" She tilted Caroline's chin up with the tip of one finger. "All the men will want to dance with you and the women will be eaten up with jealousy."

"Yes, but since this is her first social engagement in years, Caroline might not want to be so—" Minerva searched for an appropriate word. "Bold."

"Ah, the English," the Baroness said, rolling her eyes. "You are right. We don't want our Caroline to look too worldly." Her attention focused on the dress, the Baroness turned Caroline by the shoulders. "Let us see. There must be something we can do."

Minerva sat down on the small chair beside Caroline's bed and rubbed the joints of her knees. "Imagine, you're going out again, Caroline. What is this now? The second evening out in three days? You haven't spent two evenings out over the last six months."

"Then it is about time she went out, no?" the

Baroness asked, flipping the train up and over Caroline's head so that she could see the construction of the back bodice.

"Yes, it is time she went out," Minerva agreed. "It's just such a sudden change."

Caroline pulled the train off her head, and pushed away a lock of her hair that had come loose from her neat chignon. "You make me sound like a recluse. I go places, do things."

"Yes, my dear," Minerva said. "You go to the lending library and the school—

"And church," the Baroness reminded them. "She might as well marry that priest for all the time she spends in church."

"He's a vicar," Caroline said, "not a priest."

"*Quelle différence*? He is single and pious."

Minerva continued as if neither of them had spoken, "I'm fifty-three, and I have a more exciting existence than you have, Caroline. But from the moment you've met Mr. Ferrington—"

Caroline interrupted her with an angry snap of her fingers. "Please do not mention his name in my presence." The Baroness turned her around to face the mirror. In the glass, Caroline caught the two women exchanging pointed glances.

"What name?" the Baroness asked, her voice deceptively innocent.

"You know exactly *what* name," Caroline said. "He's a rake and a scoundrel, but just wait. I'll settle my business with him yet. He'll discover he can't trifle with a woman just because she lives alone—"

A knock sounded on the door. The Baroness answered it. In came Jasper juggling a hatbox, what looked to be a dress under the protection of a cherry-and-white-striped dress cover, and a letter. "This dress and box were just delivered for you, madam. The servant said he'd been sent by Lady Andrews, and this letter arrived by messenger from Mr. Ashworth."

Ashworth was the name of the solicitor she'd contacted that morning. Caroline waved for Jasper to set the box and dress on the bed and took the letter. As Jasper left the room, she broke open the wax seal and read the note three times.

Minerva rose from the chair. "Is something amiss?"

Caroline frowned, her disappointment leaving a bitter taste in her mouth. "Mr. Ashworth will be unable to meet with me until sometime next week." She drew a deep breath, trying to steady her anger. "I told him it was urgent." She walked toward the window before she whirled around and threw the letter to the floor. "I'd lay a wager that if Mr. Ferrington requested an appointment, Mr. Ashworth would bow and scrape to meet his needs. Whereas I, a widow—!" She couldn't even finish the thought, she was so furious.

Minerva took a step toward her. "Caroline, don't give up hope. There are ways of getting your deed back."

"Oh, yes!" she agreed bitterly. "I'm sure if I agree to accept *carte blanche* from Mr. Ferrington, he'll turn the deed over in a trice."

"If you become his mistress, *chérie*, you should receive a good deal more than just the deed to one house," the Baroness said readily.

"Charlotte," Minerva chided, while Caroline turned on her in anger.

The Baroness shrugged her shoulders. "You have

already accused me of being too practical. Can a leopard change her spots? Men have been very generous to me."

"But it does not mean that Caroline should follow the path we chose."

"*Oui*," came the noncommittal reply.

It made Caroline even more angry to realize that she was somewhat tempted. She might profess to follow the high road, but Caroline knew how many times during the day her mind drifted to Mr. Ferrington and, heaven help her, to those shared kisses in the rolling coach.

As if to deny such feelings, she ground the letter into the bare wooden floor. The devil take Mr. Ferrington—and her own confused senses. She faced the other women, lifting her chin with determination. "I'm not giving up. If it takes a week, a month, or a year, I will win on my terms."

Minerva took Caroline's hands in hers. "Charlotte and I will do everything we can to help. And I'll promise you this. You won't have to wait a week for satisfaction."

"Apparently I must if I'm to enlist the help of Solicitor Ashworth."

Minerva looked as if she was about to say something, when the Baroness nudged her arm. Minerva's mouth closed abruptly. For the briefest of moments, their gazes met, and Caroline had the distinct feeling some sort of silent communication passed between them. Her every ounce of common sense sounded a warning. "Is something amiss?"

Minerva's eyes opened wide in feigned surprise. "Amiss, good heavens no." She turned to the Baroness. "Charlotte?"

"*Rien*. Nothing that I know of," the Baroness

said with a lift of her shoulders, "except for my extreme curiosity over this dress that Lady Andrews sent over. I can only hope the color is more suitable than the first one."

"She's kind to lend it to me," Caroline murmured, still puzzled by Minerva's strangely worded promise to help.

"Wouldn't it be nice if the style were more modern." Without waiting for an invitation, the Baroness opened the hatbox. Her exclamation of delight made Caroline's uneasiness over Minerva's behavior flee her mind. "*C'est magnifique!*" She pulled out a soft blue velvet cap sporting a graceful white plume held in place by a diamond pin. "Is it real?" the Baroness asked, eyeing the jewel.

"It's too large to be real," Caroline said.

The Baroness gave her a look of superiority. "*Chérie*, nothing is too large to be real." She held the pin up to the light, letting the late afternoon sun catch the flash and fire of the gem. "This stone is perfect, and genuine," she pronounced with a slow smile of satisfaction.

"Charlotte, let me see it," Minerva said, reaching to take the cap from her. She traced the velvet nap with her fingertips. "It's beautiful. So rich and fine. Caroline, try it on."

"Oh, no, I couldn't."

"Why not?" the Baroness asked. "She sent it for you to wear." Without waiting for a response, she untied the ribbons on the dress cover and gave a soft cry of pleasure.

Minerva dropped the hat on the bed and reached for the dress. It was made of silk so fine, the shimmering deep blue material pooled like water on the floor. Tiny seed pearls edged the deep Vnecked bodice and formed a belt around the high waist. Moving slowly, as if in a dream, Caroline touched the small puffed sleeves. The material was clean and fresh, just like new. "It's beautiful."

"Try it on," Minerva urged, breaking the spell.

"I can't," Caroline said.

"Yes, you can." Minerva held the dress up to her. "Look in the mirror. You're lovely."

Caroline dared to look, and caught her breath. She'd never worn anything so elegant. The Baroness lifted the hem of the dress Caroline was wearing. Before Caroline knew what was happening, the Baroness had pulled off one dress and Minerva had dropped the blue silk over her head. The silk skirt shimmered to the floor.

"You look like a princess," the Baroness whispered, slipping the velvet cap up and over Caroline's heavy chignon. "A hairpin here and here and you will be ready to go."

"The fit is nearly perfect," Minerva agreed.

Reverently, Caroline lifted her fingers and lightly touched the pearl beads across the bodice. The pearls Mr. Ferrington had offered her the day before would have finished the ensemble off to perfection.

Realizing the direction of her thoughts, she forced Mr. Ferrington from her mind. She pinched the bodice material. "It fits perfectly everywhere but here."

"A few darts will eliminate the extra fullness," the Baroness said with a dismissive wave.

"I found these in the bottom of the hatbox," Minerva said, pulling out a pair of long, cream-colored kid gloves. "See if they fit."

"If you have needle and thread, *chérie,* I will take care of the darts," the Baroness offered.

"You?" Caroline asked. She slipped her hand into one of the luxuriously soft gloves.

"But of course. I was a seamstress until the Baron swept me off my feet." The Baroness's eyes sparkled at the memory. "Come. We have much to do and little time to do it."

"I'll find the thread and order Jasper to start heating water for your bath," Minerva volunteered, moving toward the door.

"*Bon,*" the Baroness said, "and tonight, you will use my coach."

Minerva skidded to a halt "Your coach, Charlotte? But I thought—well, Pierre . . ." Her voice trailed off and she shot Caroline a decidedly guilty look.

"I have many coachmen. Pierre can be with us and we will use Lady Mary's coach or hire one. We will manage," the Baroness assured her.

"You've been riding around in a hired coach? Why?" Caroline asked.

"It's a game we've been playing," the Baroness said smoothly. "But don't worry about us. Instead think of the charming picture you will make when you walk into the ballroom. You must arrive late and make a grand entrance. The men will grovel at your feet. They will fight for your attention. Perhaps you will even inspire a duel." She smiled before adding, "It is too bad Mr. Ferrington will not be there to see it."

Her words replaced Caroline's unease over what the women were planning with a new source of anxiety. "He will be there. Worse, Elizabeth Andrews thinks we are cousins. She suggested he escort me tonight."

"Cousins!" Minerva said. "Why would she believe you are related to him?"

Caroline groaned her frustration aloud. "Because he said I was! Oh, Minerva, ever since I've met that man my life has been tied up in impossible knots! I can't wait to be rid of him!"

But the Baroness wasn't listening. In the looking glass, Caroline saw her give Minerva another playful nudge. "The ball . . . " the Baroness said quietly. "He's going to the ball tonight." Minerva lifted her eyebrows in surprised understanding, then both women started laughing.

"What is so funny?" Caroline demanded.

"It is a private jest," Minerva hastily assured her. "One you need not worry your head over."

The Baroness practically purred with pleasure. "No, do not worry your head." She turned Caroline back to face the mirror. The blue silk rippled with her movements. "Instead, think of this night, and remember . . . at a ball, anything can happen. Even magic."

Studying her reflection, Caroline's anticipation began to build. Yes, tonight, she would set her worries aside and pretend the Baroness was right. Anything could happen at a ball.

Vera, Lady Lavenham, surprised her cousin Elizabeth Andrews by being the first guest to arrive for the ball. Her husband and daughter accompanied her, both complaining bitterly about being forced to arrive at an unfashionably early hour.

Vera ignored them. She had come on a mission:

to find the lady wearing the blue silk dress from Madame Bertrand's.

That afternoon, she'd driven by the house at the address Madame had given her earlier, but had learned nothing about the occupants. The house was located in a shabby but genteel neighborhood, not exactly the place for a love nest.

Shortly after she'd arrived home from her excursion, Vera had demanded an audience with her husband and informed him she had very firm doubts about a match between Lena and Mr. Ferrington. She and Lavenham had argued bitterly. He said he'd given Ferrington his word of honor. Vera repeated that she wanted a title for Lena. That's when Lavenham informed her that they were near financial destitution. He'd squandered his fortune on bad investments.

Vera had snapped back that his fears were ungrounded. When her father died, they would inherit his fortune. Furthermore, what value was money without a title? That argument had made him so angry, Lavenham had stormed out of the room and had barely spoken two words to her for the rest of the day.

Vera wasn't concerned. Her husband might not love her, but he was a weak man. He would do as she said, or she would make his life miserable.

Lena had acted overjoyed that her mother had rejected the match. In fact, for the first time since Lena had declared she was in love with the Duke of Allvery's youngest son, some six months ago, mother and daughter had actually spent a pleasant half hour together, without recriminations or tears.

Lena's avowal of love had been one of the

reasons the earl had become so interested in seeing his youngest daughter settled as quickly as possible. The Lavenhams and Allverys had feuded for generations, and Lavenham would rather plunge a dagger into his own heart than see his daughter married to one of them. Vera wasn't interested in the feud. Her major objection was that as the youngest of six sons, Lena's choice had slim prospects, other than what he earned for himself. He served as a mere Captain of the Guard.

A flurry of activity at the front door brought Vera's attention back to the present. The first guests were arriving.

Since the night was pleasant, Elizabeth had positioned the receiving line in the grand foyer. Guests entered the house, paid their addresses to the host, hostess, and two maiden aunts who were houseguests, then climbed the stairs to the ballroom on the second floor.

Vera positioned herself at the top of the staircase so she would have a clear view of everyone's arrival. She searched for a dark blue dress with puffed sleeves and pearl beadwork. Or James Ferrington, since her intuition told her that he would lead her to the woman.

Several guests looked at her with curiosity as they made their way to the ballroom. She nodded to those she knew and ignored the others. From the ballroom, located behind her, she could hear the musicians tuning up. Hundreds of candles lit the room to almost daylight brightness, while the smell of burning wax hung in the air. Laughter mixed with the growing hum of conversation. This party would be a crush. Everyone of importance was attending . . . but Vera was interested in only one woman.

At last the receiving line broke up and Lord and Lady Andrews moved up the stairs to join their party, leaving the servants to watch the door for late arrivals. Stifling a yawn, Vera remained at her post.

A goodly number of latecomers streamed in now. The musicians struck up the first dance. A group of handsome young military officers dressed in red, gold, and white uniforms arrived and marched up the stairs, their dress swords and fastenings jangling at their sides.

Vera turned from the front door and searched the milling crowd around the ballroom door for a sign of her daughter. Just as she'd thought, Lena had noticed the arrival of the young officers and soon stood in the center of their group, her eyes shining with laughter, her cheeks glowing from the attention. Her daughter's obvious happiness only reinforced Vera's decision to have Lavenham reject Ferrington's offer. She had seen her older children wed reasonably well. It shouldn't be too hard to find a titled husband for Lena. After all, the family name was good, and Lena was healthy and strong.

"Good evening, Lady Lavenham."

Vera turned in surprise to see that James Ferrington had arrived and climbed the stairs without her noticing his presence.

She kept her voice deliberately cool. "Mr. Ferrington." She looked away.

James wasn't insulted by Lady Lavenham's direct cut. If anything, he was slightly amused, and very pleased. Apparently their short conversation at Madame Bertrand's was going to reap the now anticipated results. James almost couldn't wait for Lord Lavenham to inform him that he'd decided to refuse the marriage offer.

Moving smoothly past the haughty matron, James searched the crowd for Caroline. He saw Lena surrounded by military men. He didn't see Caroline.

A few minutes later, a very anxious Earl of Lavenham appeared by his elbow. "Ferrington, I need to talk to you."

"Why certainly, my lord. Perhaps we can find a private room down the hall."

"No, no, not here. This isn't the sort of thing to discuss at a ball. Call on me tomorrow, at my home. Let's say around four."

"I will be there."

"Good," Lavenham said gruffly, and then turned on his heel and charged into the crowd as if he feared James might engage him in further conversation. James did not need to hear the words to conclude that Lavenham was going to reject his marriage offer. He was free of his obligation to Lady Lena.

James almost did a jig right there on the ballroom floor.

"Mr. Ferrington!"

James turned toward Lady Andrews's voice and bowed over the hand she held out to him. "I believe your party is a success, madam. Everyone in London seems to be here."

"Except your cousin," she said. "Where is she? In fact, I had assumed you would escort her tonight."

"She's very independent," he said truthfully.

At that moment, Lady Lavenham walked past them. Lady Andrews caught her attention. "Vera, are you having a good time? I saw you waiting at the top of the stairs for the longest time."

"I was, but I've grown tired of waiting. I've decided to pass some time in the card room."

"Let me know if there is anything I can provide for you," Lady Andrews responded in her best hostess voice.

Lady Lavenham nodded to Lady Andrews but looked straight through James as she started toward a chamber off the ballroom, where card tables had been set up.

Lady Andrews frowned at her cousin's retreating figure before saying, "I apologize, Mr. Ferrington. Vera's rudeness is legendary, but I regret that you've been subjected to it while under my roof."

"Please think nothing of it, Lady Andrews. Lady Lavenham has never been enchanted with me."

"Well, she's being silly. You would be an excellent match for her daughter."

"Perhaps," James hedged, and said no more. As a gentleman, he could not announce that his proposal had been rejected until after Lord Lavenham formally gave him the word. Nor could he ever add that he welcomed the news.

"I hope nothing has gone wrong, and Caroline still plans to attend," Lady Andrews repeated to fill the void left by his silence. "Do you care for some wine?" She nodded to a servant carrying a tray laden with full glasses. The servant offered the tray to James.

James took a glass, his movements perfunctory. "Thank you."

"Oh, I see my good friend Sarah. Will you

excuse me, Mr. Ferrington, or may I introduce you?''

"Perhaps later this evening," he answered.

Murmuring her excuses, Lady Andrews went off in search of her friend, leaving James to his own thoughts.

He strolled the length of the ballroom, waiting. At last, he took a position by the dance floor and watched the dancing, feeling disappointed. Caroline should have been here by now.

Perhaps, she wasn't coming.

Out of the corner of his eye, James noticed Lord Dimhurst motioning for him to join a group of gentlemen in a heated conversation. Placing his untouched wineglass on the tray of a passing servant, James started to join the men, and then stopped.

Caroline was here! He could feel her presence even without seeing her.

Slowly, he turned toward the door, and there, across the crowded ballroom, standing in the doorway—there was Caroline.

Wearing his dress.

Dear Lord, she looked beautiful. The lapis blue silk worked magic with her hair and clear gray eyes. The diamond from the velvet evening cap flashed in the candlelight while the curving white feather swayed gracefully with her movements— and the dress fit just as he'd imagined it would. She was the most beautiful woman in the room.

There was a sparkle in her eyes that he'd never seen before, a look he recognized as anticipation and excitement. Color bloomed in her cheeks, and everything about her glowed with vitality.

Lady Andrews crossed over to her, her arms out

in welcome. A woman James had never seen before stood behind Caroline and said something in her ear. A second later, the woman moved to a corner of the room, which had been set up with chairs for the chaperones.

Lady Andrews had greeted Caroline and now shepherded her into the ballroom. Heads turned in Caroline's direction and with a start, James realized that other men were seeing her for the first time as he saw her. The air filled with a sudden energy, a stirring of masculine interest, and the accompanying flutter of fans as women assessed new competition.

A woman let out a cry of surprise. James recognized her as the mousy little duchess he'd been introduced to on a previous occasion. The duchess's stiff pretense to formality dropped away like leaves falling in the wind. "Caroline!"

"Sarah," Caroline said back, and the women kissed each other on the cheek in a sign of genuine friendship.

Several other people came up to greet her then, many just now recognizing Lady Pearson . . . many more of them men begging for an introduction.

While Caroline greeted old friends and was introduced to new ones, Lady Andrews scanned the crowd as if looking for someone. Her gaze landed on him and she smiled. With a wave of her fingers, she urged him to join them.

But James didn't move. He couldn't.

For the first time in his life, he realized he was scared. He'd challenged man-eating tigers, sliced his way through pirate hordes, and laughed in the face of typhoons—but all these dangers paled compared to the simple act of crossing the room and paying his respects to Caroline Pearson.

Seeing her now as she was welcomed by all the best families in London, he realized how deeply he had insulted her by offering her *carte blanche*. She might be so angry that she would have nothing to do with him.

Suddenly unsure of himself, he took a step back and bumped into a turbaned dowager in the act of lifting a glass of wine to rouged lips. The woman gave a gasp of surprise as champagne trickled down the front of her dress.

Deeply embarrassed, James murmured apologies to the woman while offering his own handkerchief to repair the damage. The dowager declared him a "clumsy oaf" and waved him away.

James was only too happy to retreat. He withdrew to a safe place, the company of men, joining Lord Dimhurst and his banking friends. From the shelter of masculine society, James barely listened to the conversation around him as he watched a tall, handsome man named Lord Wamsley bow low over Caroline's hand. Apparently, he'd asked for a dance because a second later the two of them stepped onto the dance floor and took their places for the next set.

Jealousy, hot and blazing, shot through James at the sight of Caroline tilting her head to laugh at something her partner said. He'd never experienced such a strong, uncontrolled emotion over a woman. But then Caroline wasn't just any woman. She was *his* woman.

His woman.

The words settled deep inside him.

His feelings ran deeper than just wanting her in his bed. He wanted her in his life.

No longer apprehensive about what she might say or do when they met, James waited for the dance to end. At last the musicians played the last chord. Wamsley bowed over Caroline's hand again and offered his arm to lead her back to the group of people standing with Lady Andrews.

James made his excuses to Lord Dimhurst and the others. His focus on Caroline, he skirted the crowd around the dance floor and came up behind her. "Hello, Cousin Caroline."

She released Wamsley's arm and turned to face him, her clear, gray eyes opened wide with surprise. Was it his imagination, or did she almost seem pleased to see him?

For a second the air around them went still, charged with the same energy, the same sense of expectancy, as the moments just before a violent storm. As if from a distance, James heard himself say, "Would you honor me with this next dance?"

He held out his hand to her.

Chapter 10

From the moment Caroline had entered the ballroom, she had known James Ferrington was there. The room seemed to vibrate with his presence . . . and she cautioned herself to harden her resolve against him. She should not acknowledge him in any way. To do so would be to encourage the insults and outrageous behavior he'd exhibited during the last two days.

Now he stood in front of her, tall, broad-shouldered, handsome, and unsure of himself.

She could see the anxiety in his eyes and in the tense set of his mouth. His vulnerability slipped past her defenses and melted her resolve.

For the first time, Caroline saw James Ferrington not as a domineering male intent on bullying her, but as a man full of the same self-doubts, weaknesses, and, yes, ambition she found in herself.

As if caught in a dream, Caroline placed her gloved hand in his.

His lips curved into a huge, triumphant grin, and she felt an answering surge in her own heart that she could make him so ridiculously pleased. The pressure of his hand tightened around her fingers, and he would have led her to the dance floor, except for the interruption of a man's voice.

"I beg your pardon, Lady Pearson, but I believe you've promised this next dance to me."

Caroline turned to the speaker, a balding middle-aged man who had been introduced to her only a moment earlier. He was right! She had promised him the next dance. Embarrassed, she said to Mr. Ferrington, "I'm so sorry, he's correct. I did promise this dance to—" She paused, unable to recall his name.

"Lord Kenyon," the gentleman supplied for her.

"Yes, Lord Kenyon. I'm so sorry. Your name slipped my mind for a moment. I'm very sorry." She pulled on the hand Mr. Ferrington held in his palm.

He didn't release it.

Lord Kenyon tapped his foot impatiently. "The dance set is about to begin," he said. He offered his arm.

"Yes, I know," Caroline replied. She gently tried to slip her hand from Mr. Ferrington's while placing her other hand on Lord Kenyon's arm.

Mr. Ferrington tightened his hold.

In an awkward position, she pleaded with him for understanding. "Mr. Ferrington—"

"Cousin James," he whispered.

"What?" Caroline asked in confusion before remembering the lie he'd told Lady Dimhurst, which seemed to be haunting her. She tugged on her hand, but still he wouldn't release it.

Caroline managed a strained smile to the impatient Lord Kenyon. "Cousin *James*, please release my hand."

James gave up her hand, but took a step to block Lord Kenyon's path to the dance floor. "Promise me the next dance," he urged her.

"I beg pardon, sir," another gentleman said, "but after Lord Kenyon, Lady Pearson is promised to me."

James frowned at the interloper. Before Lord Kenyon could lead her away, he said, "Then I'll claim the next one."

"That's mine," said a red-haired gentleman called Lord Givens.

"And I believe that I'm leading her in the last dance before supper," Lord Wamsley added smoothly.

"But you've already stood up with her," James protested. "You can't stand up with her twice."

Wamsley's eyebrows rose to his hairline. He was a crack shot with a hot temper, and few people dared to cross him. "I can, and I will. The lady is promised to me."

Anger flooded through James, warring with his common sense. It wouldn't do any good to lose his temper here. Furthermore, it would embarrass Caroline. "Very well," he said to Wamsley before asking Caroline, "Perhaps I may lead you to supper?"

"I would like that—" Caroline started to say, but Wamsley interrupted her.

"She'll be going to supper with me."

The two men stared at each other, the air between them taut with challenge. Caroline placed her hand on his arm, and James felt her silent plea for him not to create a scene. He stepped back.

Lady Andrews let out an audible sigh of relief as she moved to James's side. Watching Lord Kenyon lead Caroline to their places in the next dance set, she said, "It's your own fault, Mr. Ferrington. Every eligible man in the room swarmed around her begging for introductions the minute she made her appearance." She tapped James's arm with her fan. "However, since you are available for this set, allow me to pair you with a partner."

Before the music started, Lady Andrews had introduced James to Lady Martha, a debutante from Yorkshire, and had them both in their places for the set.

James danced with Lady Martha, then with a Miss McKay, and after that with a Lady Alana, but his gaze was on Caroline the whole time. She danced well, gracefully covering for the clumsiness of some of her partners. Whenever she left the floor, Lady Andrews was waiting for her, surrounded by more gentlemen begging introductions.

James began to wish he'd never arranged for Caroline to attend the ball. By the time Wamsley led her onto the floor for the second time, for a lively country dance, James had had quite enough of ballrooms, good manners, and sharing. His frustration reached the breaking point when Wamsley dared to shoot him a look of superiority as he positioned himself across from Caroline.

The man deserved to be put in his place.

Partnerless for this set, James stood at the edge of the dance floor, watching. Of all Caroline's partners, Wamsley took the most liberties. Small intimacies the man made began to irritate James. Wamsley danced too close to Caroline. He flirted with her and tried to make her laugh. At one point in the dance, when the gentlemen circled with the ladies, Wamsley's hand slipped down to Caroline's waist and squeezed her.

The second time James heard Caroline laugh, he'd had enough. Wamsley was not going to take Caroline down to supper.

He waited until the dance's movements brought Wamsley and Caroline even with him, and then he made his move. With all the grace of a gentleman, James stepped onto the floor, tapped Wamsley on the shoulder, and before the surprised man could make comment, cut in on his partner.

Finally, he held Caroline in his arms. James didn't stop there. He was tired of stuffy ballrooms, polite society, and lines of men waiting for introductions. With the boldness of a corsair, he danced Caroline off the floor and pirated her out a set of French doors that opened onto a small stone balcony overlooking the garden.

He stopped dancing the second they were outside, released her from his arms, and shut the doors firmly behind them.

Her eyes opened wide in astonishment. "Mr. Ferrington, you shouldn't have done that."

"The dance is over," he answered, and shot a glance at Wamsley through the glass panes. Wamsley was searching the dance floor, looking for her. When he couldn't find her, he scratched his head, then stormed off in Lady Andrews's direction. James turned his attention back to Caroline. "The musicians are taking their break. Everyone is going to supper."

"I was promised to Lord Wamsley for supper."

The blue silk of her dress shimmered in the moonlight. The diamond in her cap sparkled as bright as any of the stars crossing the heavens. He could fancy her a goddess . . . a moon goddess.

His goddess. "I'll risk his wrath."

"Mr. Ferrington, please——"

"I only wanted one dance," he said quietly.

"Only one dance?" She shook her head. "Are you saying your needs have changed from yesterday when you offered me *carte blanche?*"

James pushed away from the door and stood up straight, eager to convince her of his sincerity. "I'm saying that I was wrong. I shouldn't have jumped to the conclusions that I did, and I beg you to accept my apology for insulting you."

For a long moment, she studied him in the darkness. At last, she spoke. "Your apology is accepted, Mr. Ferrington. Minerva told me the complete story. She said she encouraged you to make such a proposal. I believe you've gathered by now that my aunt is——" She paused for a word and smiled as she said, "Eccentric."

"Colorful is the word I would have chosen," he said lightly, relieved that she accepted his apology.

"Yes, that would also be a good choice . . . I care for her very much."

"I can understand why." He meant the words.

She placed a hand on the stone balustrade and drew a deep breath. Her next words surprised him. "And my own behavior the previous night could easily be called into question." She looked up at him, the moonlight reflected in her eyes. "For that evening, and what happened between us, I apologize to you."

James placed his hand as close as he dared next to hers on the balustrade. "Caro—Lady Pearson, please know I hold you in the highest regard. The truth is, I've never felt for another woman what I feel for you."

Her lips parted and she pulled back in surprise at his statement.

James cursed himself for his lack of subtlety, especially when she didn't speak. He took a step away from her and stared out into the darkness. "I shouldn't have declared myself. Forgive me."

Still she didn't speak. He turned to her and found her eyes wide and watchful. The silence felt awkward to James. Daniel was right; he'd turned into a fool since the day he'd met Caroline Pearson. If he was wise, he'd turn on his heel and leave her on this balcony.

Instead he asked, "Do you ever look up at the stars and dream?"

She appeared startled by the question. "I don't . . ." Her voice trailed off.

"I do," he said. "I always have, and whenever I really want something, I wish for it on a star." He shot a self-conscious glance at her. "Sounds silly, doesn't it? But it works. I've done it for years. The stars have never failed me."

She tilted her head. "Not ever?" she whispered.

"Not ever," he replied solemnly.

She lifted her eyes to look up at the hundreds of stars hanging in the midnight sky. "What have you wished for?"

"The world."

"The world?"

"Yes." He leaned against the balustrade, enjoying the beauty of the night and the woman beside him. "I knew at a very early age that I wouldn't stay in Kent and be a farmer like my father and his father before him."

"Didn't you like farming?"

"Oh, well enough, but I wanted something more. My parents always said I was a reckless fellow. I enjoy the challenge of a risk, the thrill of a dare. Of course, now that I'm older, I find myself looking to take chances in a new arena."

"Such as London?"

He nodded. "I'm looking forward to tweaking the nose of the East India Company. I may lose my fortune in the attempt, but it gives me great pleasure to see them scramble. And what of you, Lady Pearson? Do you enjoy a challenge?"

She laughed lightly, as if struck by the whimsy of such an idea. "No, Mr. Ferrington, I assure you I'm not one for taking a risk."

"Why do you say that?"

"Because I've always done what I was told to do. I suppose that would make me the most complacent of souls. Before I married, I did as my parents instructed. Then after my marriage, I was under the rule of my husband."

"Was that not to your liking?" he asked cautiously, broaching the topic of the one man whom he considered his rival for her affections, her deceased husband, the man for whom she'd worn black long after the required mourning period had passed.

Her body went tense. She lowered her eyes. He watched the sweep of her long lashes against her cheek, and found he held his breath, waiting for her answer. At last she turned to him. "I knew no other way. I really didn't start to think about myself and what I wanted until after his death." She shook her head, a small furrow forming between her eyes. "And there are times of late when I don't think I've been as wise as I should have been. Perhaps, I should have been more bold, more daring . . . like you."

Like you! Had she just paid him a compliment?

"But it is easier for men," she added, her voice quiet. "They naturally assume their lives have meaning and purpose. A woman struggles with that question every day of her life." She leaned one hip against the balustrade and tilted her head. "How did you find the courage to venture out into the world? I mean, you left Kent, your family, and all that was safe and known to you. How does someone discover that kind of courage?"

"He dreams it, Lady Pearson."

She arched one eyebrow. "Do you expect me to believe that all you are, and all of your great fortune, started with nothing more than a dream?"

"My desire to see as much of the world as I could started with these stars." He nodded to the sky above their heads. "Growing up, my brothers and I would wait until my parents had gone to bed for the night, and then we would sneak out of the house and sleep in the fields." He smiled at the memory. "I loved to lie out in a hayfield and watch the stars. My brothers would go to sleep, but I would dream. These stars over our heads are the same bodies of light that guided Marco Polo on his adventures in China, and showed Columbus the way to a new world. Even before I was sent off to school, I knew I wanted to follow the stars. To me, stars represent adventure, danger, challenges. They've witnessed the death of Christ, the battles

of the Crusaders, and the victories of Charle-
magne. I feel insignificant in their presence."

"I could never imagine you as insignificant, Mr.
Ferrington." There was a hint of smile in her voice.
"It's not a word that comes to mind when I think of
you."

James turned to her. "And do you think of me
often?"

Her eyes opened wide at the directness of his
question. She astonished him by admitting, "More
than I should."

The blood pounded in James's veins. He would
have reached for her, taken her hand, but her next
words stopped him.

"Still, I can offer you nothing, sir, but my friendship."

"Why do you say this?" he demanded, as she
had no doubt known he would.

Caroline was starting to understand James Ferrington, and she knew if he wanted something, he
would not stop until he had it. But he couldn't have
her. She was flawed, a barren woman. No man
wanted a woman who could not bear his children.

Caroline closed her eyes, praying for the courage
to walk away from this man. "I must return to the
ballroom. I have an apology to make to Lord
Wamsley."

"No! Not until you explain. I want to understand. Whatever I've done, I'll apologize. I'll make
it right."

She held up a hand for silence, unable to let him
blame himself. "It's not you. It is I. Mr. Ferrington,
my answer would be the same for any man who
wished to pay his addresses to me. I shouldn't have
come to Elizabeth's ball tonight, and yet I have no

regrets. Tonight has been special. It's like the Irish stories of fairies and having wishes granted, but it's not real. It's not even like your stars. I'm sorry."

She lifted her skirts and started for the door, but he boldly took hold of her hand and pulled her back. "Mr. Ferrington—"

"You haven't made your wish."

"My wish?" she repeated.

"On a star," he said. "If you believe in the Irish stories, then you must know that on a night as magical as this, any wish you make will be granted."

He pulled her gently back to the stone balustrade. "Look at them," he ordered. "All of those stars are waiting. You can't leave. Not yet."

His voice was hypnotic. Caroline didn't have the will to resist, not when he stood so close. She looked up, and lost herself in the brightness of the stars and the velvety dark autumn night. A full moon hung high in the sky, but its light was no match for the brilliance of the stars.

"Make a wish," he encouraged. He stood directly behind her, so close she could feel the heat of his body. A small shiver raced through her, more from the sudden direction of her thoughts than the cool night air.

As if to warm her, Ferrington brought his arms around her protectively. The temptation to lean back against his chest and relax was almost overwhelming.

Caroline straightened her shoulders. "What about you? Are you going to make a wish?"

"We'll wish together," he said, his voice near her ear. "Choose a star."

She looked up at the hundreds of choices and

saw one that burned brighter than the others. "That one," she said, pointing.

"That's a good choice. It's the North Star and always guides wanderers on the right path. Now, keep your eyes on that star and when I count to three, we'll wish. Are you ready?"

Caroline nodded.

"One. Two. Three."

Caroline made her wish. She wished she could tell James Ferrington that she could not have children. She wished her barrenness would not matter.

"What wish did you make?" he asked.

She forced herself to laugh. "I can't tell you my wish. If I tell, then it won't come true."

"Is that another Irish story?"

"Then tell me what wish you made," she countered.

He sobered immediately. His eyes dark and serious, he said, "I wished you would trust me." He lifted her hand to his lips and kissed it.

Caroline felt the force of the small kiss through every fiber of her being. More than anything else in this world, she wanted to give him that trust. She wanted to believe a man could love her and accept her even if she couldn't give him children.

Passion, real and powerful, sizzled between them. He lowered his head, the movement gradual, questioning. In silent answer, Caroline parted her lips, wanting to receive him.

The door to the ballroom opened. A man started to emerge and then, startled to see someone already occupying the small balcony, muttered an apology and returned to the ball. His interruption broke the spell between Caroline and James.

"We must go back." She took a step to the door, but again he caught her hand.

Holding her fingers loosely in his, he said, "One dance. It's all I ask."

Caroline looked at him standing in the moonlight. He appeared invincible . . . and irresistible. A breath of night air blew around them, pulling at the light silk of her dress and playing with the plume of her velvet cap. She felt feverish, hot. "Oh, no, Mr. Ferrington, you ask much more."

"I ask you to trust me."

The words hung in the air between them. Through the glass panes of the door, Caroline could hear the musicians begin to play and the muffled laughter of the guests.

If she'd learned one thing from her marriage, it was the pain of placing her faith in the wrong man. She'd flown too close to the flame and been burned—but now, she realized, she wanted to fly again. Wanted to believe James Ferrington wouldn't burn her.

"One dance," she whispered.

His teeth flashed, dazzling white. "Let's join the others then." He didn't release his hold on her hand until they'd stepped back into the ballroom, and then he placed it on his arm.

Dancers were taking their places for the next set. Mr. Ferrington started to lead her to an open place, but Caroline felt a stab of guilt. She stopped. "I must find Lord Wamsley and apologize for not letting him lead me to supper."

Mr. Ferrington made an impatient sound. "It's not necessary." He looked around the room. "I don't even see him here. He may have found another partner or left for the evening."

"James," Caroline started with a touch of exasperation, and then caught herself.

His mouth dropped open in surprise; his eyes took on a bright, teasing light. "What did you call me?"

Caroline placed her fingers over her traitorous lips before saying, "I meant *Mr. Ferrington.*"

"But you said *James!* Furthermore, you did it without my having to coerce or tease or beg you."

"This is nonsense—"

"No, it's not. I've been waiting from the moment I met you to hear my name on your lips. Now, admit it, Caroline. It felt right and natural." He didn't wait for an answer but took her hand and placed it back on his arm. "Come, we'll both apologize to Wamsley. He may run me through for stealing you from him, but I'll die happy. My lady has called me James!"

Before Caroline could reply to that fresh bit of nonsense, he charged off toward the door and she had to take hurry to keep up with his long strides. At the doorway, Elizabeth stepped in their path.

"Mr. Ferrington, Lord Wamsley is not pleased with you at all."

"I'm sure he isn't," James answered. "In fact, we were searching for him to make our apologies."

Elizabeth shook her head. "I don't think he's ready to hear apologies, sir."

"Of course, he is," James said, his voice full of confidence. "I'll talk to him. Where is he?"

"He's downstairs in the supper room, but I don't think—"

"Please don't worry, Lady Andrews," James said. "I will smooth Wamsley's ruffled feathers." He turned to Caroline. "Perhaps you should stay here with Lady Andrews until I've had a moment to speak to him."

"Oh, but I should apologize as well."

Elizabeth laid a hand on Caroline's arm. "Mr. Ferrington is right. Sometimes it is best to let the men settle matters between themselves."

Caroline was undecided, but James removed her hand from his arm. "Wait here. I will only be a few moments, and then you'll have your opportunity to apologize to Wamsley. But not until after our dance," he added, and then had the audacity to wink.

Caroline watched him walk to the stairs. He was so bold, so sure of himself.

"You've a very gallant cousin, Caroline," Elizabeth observed.

Caroline nodded absently, her gaze still following James. He nodded to Lady Dimhurst and another woman, who were coming up the stairs. Lady Dimhurst returned his greeting, but the other woman frowned and turned her head away from him.

With a flick of her wrist, Elizabeth opened her fan and used it to hide her next words to Caroline. "Oh, that's my cousin Vera—Lady Lavenham— coming up the stairs. Please, pretend to be involved in a very deep discussion and perhaps she will pass us without a word."

Caroline happily obliged. She'd paid her respects to Lady Dimhurst earlier in the evening and did not want to spend any more time in the woman's company.

"What shall we talk of?" she asked.

"Anything," Elizabeth replied. "We just need to keep talking."

They laughed like conspirators and Caroline was about to compliment Elizabeth on the success of her party when Lady Lavenham blurted out, "That's the dress!"

"Ignore her," Elizabeth whispered. "She's a bit odd. You should have seen her earlier. I felt she was inspecting my guests."

"You there!" Lady Lavenham said rudely. "Who are you?"

Silence greeted her demand and it took Caroline several seconds before she realized the woman was talking to her. "I beg your pardon?"

Elizabeth stepped protectively between Caroline and Lady Lavenham. "Vera, have you met Lady Pearson?" she asked, her voice slightly anxious. "Caroline, this is my cousin, Lady Lavenham."

Lady Lavenham's mouth fell open. Fearing the woman was having some sort of seizure, Caroline asked, "Lady Lavenham, are you feeling unwell?"

In answer, the woman turned to Lady Dimhurst. "Millie, isn't Caroline Pearson the name of the woman we talked about yesterday, the woman who lives with Minerva Pearson and teaches at that school you want me to help sponsor with a donation?"

Lady Dimhurst cast an anxious glance at the ballroom door, as if she wished to be away from this spot, before admitting reluctantly, "Lady Pearson has been teaching at Miss Elmhart's. However, you're only teaching one class now, is that not correct, Lady Pearson?"

Before Caroline could answer, Lady Lavenham announced, "Even one class is too much. A woman of Lady Pearson's character should have no access to young, impressionable minds!"

Shocked by the attack, Caroline defended herself. "I beg your pardon, madam, but who are you to question my character?"

"That's not true, Vera," Elizabeth added. "I've known Caroline for years. She is everything a lady of quality should be."

Lady Lavenham's face turned ugly with anger. "I fear you've been cleverly gulled, Elizabeth. Lady Pearson is Ferrington's mistress!"

Caroline literally shook with anger at the accusation. Conscious that several of the other guests were beginning to notice the heated exchange, and moving to position themselves so they could best hear what was being said, Caroline struggled for control. When she spoke, she was proud her voice came out dignified and even. "I have just met you, madam, and I don't know what I may have done to make you utter such a terrible lie, but I ask for Elizabeth's sake that we cease this discussion, or take it someplace more private."

Lady Lavenham pulled back. "A lie! I don't lie. Ferrington paid for the rag that is on your back, and I'll wager it's his money that bought that bauble in your hat. Are you going to deny it?"

"I can and will deny it!" Caroline said. Swallowing her pride, she admitted, "I borrowed this dress from Lady Andrews. Please tell her, Elizabeth."

But Elizabeth didn't answer immediately. Puzzled by her silence, Caroline spun to face her. Her friend shook her head, the distress in her eyes genuine. "I didn't send that dress," she whispered. "The one I sent was a shade of yellow."

Caroline's stomach twisted in a knot at Elizabeth's words. James wouldn't have sent her the dress, she told herself. He *couldn't* have! A gentle-woman would never receive such a personal gift!

Elizabeth was speaking softly to Lady Laven-ham. "I'm sure you have it wrong. "Mr. Ferrington and Lady Pearson are cousins—"

"Cousins! In a pig's eye," Lady Lavenham de-clared. "I've made it my business to learn every-thing I can about Minerva Pearson, and since she lives with Lady Caroline Pearson, I've been asking a few questions. Lady Pearson has no living family members. What nonsense is this about Ferrington being her cousin?"

They'd been found out. It didn't make any difference whether or not she had started the lie, Caroline felt culpable, especially when someone as sweet as Elizabeth had been willing to defend her. "We aren't cousins," she said.

Lady Dimhurst gave a loud gasp of indignation and pretended to affect a swoon. The noise at-tracted more attention.

James had come up the stairs and joined the crowd that had gathered around them. She could see him now, pushing his way forward—and then he was there.

She was glad of his presence. She wanted him to tell Lady Lavenham that her accusation about the gown was unfounded. But when he stepped be-tween herself and Lady Lavenham, he looked so grim she knew immediately that the accusation was true.

He'd brought the dress.

"Caroline," he started, but she refused to listen.

She turned her back on him and faced Lady Lavenham. "It seems you're correct, madam. Ap-

parently, Mr. Ferrington did purchase the dress."
Tears threatened, but she would not give way to
them. "Elizabeth, I'm afraid I must take my leave
now. Would you be so good as to ask my chaperone Mirabelle to join me? Tell her I'll be waiting by
the front door."

"Oh, Caroline, I'm so sorry," Elizabeth whispered, before leaving to do as she'd asked.

Caroline nodded. She couldn't speak. A lump
had formed in her throat, making speech difficult.
With as much dignity as she could muster, she
proceeded to the staircase.

James blocked her way. He reached out to her.
"Caroline, I can explain—"

"No!" Aware that everyone was watching them,
her movements slow and deliberate, Caroline removed the velvet cap with its jaunty plume from
her head. For the space of a heartbeat, the diamond
pin seemed to glimmer with a life of its own, and
then Caroline pushed the hat into his hands. "I
don't want anything more to do with you." The
words were so hard to speak! "Please, leave me
alone."

Mirabelle joined her just then. Without another
word, Caroline stepped around James and headed
for the stairs. She had not made it quite halfway
down them when hot tears escaped her eyes. She
ducked her head and kept moving.

James crushed the velvet hat in his hands and
tossed it aside. He couldn't let her walk away, not
now.

Heedless of the other guests, he called out her
name. "Caroline!" He ran to the staircase. She'd
already made it to the foyer. "Caroline, wait!"

She glanced back over her shoulder. For a second, their gazes locked—then she turned away and slipped out the front door held open by a footman.

James charged down the stairs. He had to stop her.

A group of gentlemen returning from the supper room started up the steps and into James's way. He shoved past them, ignoring their comments on his rudeness. He had to reach Caroline.

The footman started to open the door, but he was too slow for James, who reached for the handle himself and threw open the portal. Outside on the front steps, he took a moment to gather his bearings.

He heard the sound of a coachman urging his team to go forward. The coach had to be Caroline's. Without a thought to sound reasoning, James ran along the other coaches lining the Andrews's drive, hoping he might catch the one that was carrying her.

Several minutes passed before he realized he was too late. A coach and pair was already pulling out onto the street. With a flick of his whip, the driver urged his horses to hurry. James came to a halt, but he refused to give up the chase.

Caroline would return to her home. It was the only place she could go. He'd drive over there and try to reason with her. Sooner or later, she had to talk to him. He'd pound on her door all night until she did.

He turned and started walking back up the line of coaches in the drive, when he heard a soft voice call his name. He turned. No one stood there.

The voice called his name again. It seemed to

come from a point between two coaches lined up side by side. Curious, James took several hesitant steps until he stood between them.

No one was there.

His mind must be playing tricks on him, he decided, and turned to go on his way, when a dark canvas hood came down over his head. Strong arms encircled his body while another set of arms captured his kicking feet. He started to shout—but a whack to the head turned his world black.

Chapter 11

⁓ ◦◦◦ ⁓

James's head pounded as if a blacksmith were striking an anvil inside it. The pain told him he was alive.

In stages, his other senses slowly took in his surroundings. He was lying on a cool, hard dirt floor. Instinctively he started to lift a hand to the back of his head, where it hurt the most, when he realized that he couldn't lift his arm.

Alarm broke through his hazy thinking.

Again he tried to lift his arm, to move his feet, and realized that his legs and arms were tied. Startled, he panicked, struggling furiously against the ropes, tightening them, until reason set in.

Stop.

Think. He had to think.

As his heartbeat steadied, he focused on the single candle placed on the hard dirt floor not two feet from him. He stared at it. The rest of the world beyond that candle appeared darker than Satan's hole. The air smelled of—what? Potatoes, onions . . . and heavy perfume.

He was tied up and lying on what must be a warehouse floor. A devil of a fix.

He sensed that it was still night, that not much time had passed since he'd been clubbed on the head. He'd hazard a guess that he was underground. The air felt damp and cool. He heard a slight rustling and a quiet whisper.

Straining to look beyond the candlelight, James felt another stab of panic.

Outside the ring of candlelight stood several hooded and cloaked figures—he counted four of them. They looked like giant haystacks until he realized the figures were wearing black skirts. Were they women?

He closed and opened his eyes. The apparitions remained and then were blocked from his vision by a huge, hulking giant of a man. His face also masked by a hood, the giant entered the ring of flickering light.

"How very good of you to join us," the giant said. He had a French accent and rolled his words, as if relishing his role as spokesman. He crouched on the balls of his feet so that James could see him better.

James didn't like lying here like a fatted calf waiting for the slaughter. He dug in his heels and attempted to right himself. To his frustration, his actions didn't work the way he wanted. He ended up scooting across the floor a few inches.

"Here, let me help," the giant said, and, taking James by the elbow, he pulled him to an upright position. "We don't want you to feel like a worm."

James hated the comparison.

He allowed the man to touch him only for the time it took to right himself from the floor, and then jerked his arm from the giant's helping hand. Sitting up with both his feet and hands tied made balancing difficult, but James would be damned to hell before he'd show any sign of weakness.

He looked into the eyeholes of the back hood and said in his coldest, most arrogant voice, "Who are you, and what do you want of me?"

"They told me you were very direct." James could almost sense the man grinning at him. The giant continued, his accented voice cultured and pleasant, "We want you to be as comfortable as possible, *Monsieur* Ferrington, but we also want you to understand that we mean business."

James let his gaze drift to the hooded women who stood like silent specters of the Inquisition. "Who are you?"

"That is a question we will not answer, *Monsieur* Ferrington. Furthermore, we will make the demands. For once, *monsieur*, you will listen."

For the first time in James's life, he found himself helpless. It was not a feeling he relished. "You are making a fearful mistake," he said softly. "I can be a powerful enemy."

The giant cocked his head, considering his words, then nodded his head to the figures watching from the darkness. "You already have powerful enemies."

There was enough conviction in the giant's words to make James think he might be speaking the truth. And he had only one group of enemies who were ruthless and desperate enough to attempt blackmail—perhaps, even murder. The East India Company. If he and Daniel won their case Friday and received a license to trade, those scoundrels would lose their tight hold over trade throughout India and a monopoly over cargoes valued at millions of pounds annually.

Over the years, James had heard rumors of how far the Company would go to protect its investment. They'd already attempted to bribe his employees and done what they could to stop his rise in Society and discredit him in political circles. Last month, one of his warehouses had been set on fire.

But would they stoop to murder?

The buggers be damned. He wouldn't cry quarter. Pretending a boredom he was far from feeling, he said, "I'm not interested in hearing your demands."

"You will be, *monsieur*, when it hits you heavy enough in your purse. You have a very important meeting scheduled for the day after tomorrow, don't you?"

His words confirmed James's suspicions. He didn't answer.

"If you don't attend that meeting, *Monsieur* Ferrington, you will lose everything you own to satisfy your investors in this venture. Is that not correct?"

"You seem to know a great deal about it," James replied coldly.

Then the man turned James's East India Company theory upside down by saying, "You will not be present at that meeting, *monsieur*, unless you turn over the deed to Lady Pearson's house."

James's mind reeled with this new piece of information, his mouth dropping open in surprise. He closed it. "Did Lady Pearson set you up to do this?"

"No questions, *monsieur*. *Maintenant*, are you ready to turn over the deed, or do you need to sit in this cellar a while longer?"

Caroline was blackmailing him.

He wanted to yank and pull on the ropes, bite through them with his bare teeth if necessary. While he'd been acting like a lovesick fool, she'd schemed to hit him on the head, truss him up like a pig, and threaten his fortune and his business for the deed to her house. She was probably standing over there with the others, waiting for his answer. This was probably the cellar of her cursed little house!

"I don't negotiate with hirelings." James practically spit the words out. "If Lady Pearson wants her deed, she can confront me herself."

The pure venom in his voice appeared to have a dramatic effect on the hooded women beyond the candlelight. There was a rustle of skirts and hushed whispers. James strained to hear, trying to make out Caroline's voice.

The giant rose and joined the group. The whispering grew more furious, angrier. The giant didn't speak or appear to be one of the decision makers. In fact, watching him in the candlelight, James thought he acted almost subservient.

The giant confirmed his suspicions when he returned and knelt beside James. "*Monsieur* Ferrington, my mistress believes it best we leave you alone to think. She asks that you consider carefully what is at stake and agree to trade your freedom and the future of your business empire for the deed to this house."

"You can leave me down here to rot, but I assure you the answer will be the same."

"What answer is that, *monsieur?*"

"That she can go to bloody hell," James said without remorse.

The giant's shoulders sagged slightly. He looked to the waiting women. A tall one—much taller than Caroline—nodded, and the giant turned to him to translate the signal. "You'll feel differently in the morning, *monsieur*."

"Mayhap you'll grow wings and fly," James retorted calmly.

The giant rose solemnly to his feet, picking up the candle. "I hope that a night in the cellar will improve your temper." He started to leave before James's voice stopped him.

"Leave the candle."

A woman spoke in a voice that sounded slightly familiar. "I'm sorry, Mr. Ferrington, but your wishes no longer carry any weight. Not until you are willing to give us the deed to Lady Pearson's home."

He recognized the voice! Minerva Pearson!

With her edict, the giant held up the candle so that the hooded women could see their way before them.

"I can have you locked up," he threatened. "Do you hear me, Caroline? I can have the bloody magistrate here in a trice after you release me, deed or no!"

The women stopped. In quiet whispers they conferred. James gained great satisfaction that he had put a halt to Caroline's little scheme. "Don't think for a second you can blackmail me," he said, pleased that his words gave them all pause. "Not bloody likely! I'll see you in jail—"

The giant handed the candle to one of the women.

James continued, "—even if I have to hunt you down myself. You'll not get away with this."

The giant approached, but James was in full fury. He'd shout the walls of the house down. He'd make Caroline so angry she'd step forward and identify herself instead of hiding behind a mask! "I didn't build my empire with my own hands to have it taken away by a scheming jade of a woman. Do you hear me? Scheming jade. A woman who teases and lies and betrays—"

Without a wasted motion, the giant stuffed a gag in James's mouth. He returned to the women and they left James in the dark, gagged, bound, and angry.

It didn't help matters when he immediately lost his balance, teetered, and fell onto his side.

Lying there in the dark on the cold hard floor, James spent several minutes in a frustrating struggle before his common sense began to prevail. The knots the giant had tied were good and strong.

He hated being bested, especially by a woman.

He had to use his wits. Because no matter how attractive Caroline Pearson was, he would have vengeance. As God was his maker, she'd rue the day she ever thought she could betray James Ferrington and leave him to spend a night on her cellar floor.

He'd outwit her and still attend the meeting. But he wouldn't ever turn over the deed.

Once they'd climbed the cellar stairs and stood in the kitchen, Violetta was the first to remove her hood. "What do you think?" she whispered to the others.

"I think he'll need to cool his heels for a night and think the matter over," Lady Mary announced. She pulled off her hood and sat down heavily in a chair. The hood had mashed her powdered wig to her head.

"Thank you, Pierre," Charlotte said to the giant coachman, who had set the candle down on the kitchen table. She had removed her hood and pushed her artfully arranged hair into place with her fingers. "I do not know about the rest of you, but I am ready for my bed."

"But what about *him?*" Violetta asked.

"What about him?" Charlotte countered. "He isn't going anywhere."

"But he thinks Caroline orchestrated his kidnapping," Violetta pointed out.

"Furthermore, that man down there is livid," Lady Mary said. "Almost to the point of insanity. I'd rather face a line of enemy artillery than go back down in that cellar. He's not going to give up easily, and when he does, he isn't going to be graceful about it."

"You mean he might not turn over the deed?" Violetta asked Lady Mary. "But you said he'd have no choice except to give in to our demands."

Lady Mary harrumphed. "That was before I saw how angry he is. James Ferrington is the type of man who would walk into blazing cannon fire if he was angry enough. Just like my dear departed William."

"Oh dear," Violetta said, her brow wrinkling with worry since walking into cannon fire was how Mad William Dorchester had died.

"What nonsense," Charlotte interjected. "All men are irrational when you threaten their purse. It's the way *le bon Dieu* made them." She reached for her gloves and pulled them on. "No matter what else a man values, he values his gold more. *Monsieur* Ferrington will come around and bargain with us even if it means swallowing his enormous pride. He is a good businessman. He has no choice if he doesn't wish to lose a great deal of money."

"A great deal," Lady Mary reiterated sagely. "But I still don't think he will come around quickly."

"By tomorrow morning he will be willing to negotiate," Charlotte predicted.

"Would you wager ten pounds on it?" Lady Mary countered.

Violetta turned to Minerva, who had been silently listening to the exchange. "What do you think?"

Minerva lit a candle from the one on the table. "I think it is time we all went to bed. The die is cast, Violetta. There is no looking back. It is unfortunate Mr. Ferrington blames Caroline, but I believe that if we put our minds to it, we can think of something to disabuse him of his queer notion."

"Minerva is right. Any woman worth her face powder should be able to outthink a man," Charlotte declared.

"Well, face powder ain't worth much," Lady Mary replied bluntly.

"We can save this argument for the morning," Minerva said.

"Yes, of course you are right," Violetta agreed, gathering her gloves and hat. "Are you sure you will be safe from him?" She gave another worried look toward the cellar door.

"Jasper will take care of us," Minerva assured her.

"And I will leave Pierre here to stand guard," Charlotte added, nodding to the huge manservant, who had removed his hood to reveal a bald head.

"That's not necessary," Minerva started.

"Yes, it is," the three other women said almost in unison, in perfect agreement for the first time this evening.

Charlotte gave Minerva a kiss on each cheek in farewell before an idea struck her. She turned to Violetta and Lady Mary. "You two must come and spend the night with me. That way we will not waste time gathering ourselves in the morning and can be here first thing when *Monsieur* Ferrington meets our demands."

Before the other two women could answer, Minerva said, "No, don't come in the morning. Caroline might be suspicious."

"And if she finds out, she will only be glad of what we've done," Charlotte answered.

Minerva disagreed. "We'll have more to worry about if Caroline finds out than when Mr. Ferrington reacts next."

"Then we shall wait until ten," Charlotte said.

That seemed a good plan, and the women prepared to depart. Pierre took up his duty by sitting on the floor in front of the cellar door. He pulled a copy of Rousseau from a satchel, ready to spend his watch reading. Minerva promised that Jasper would relieve him in the morning.

As they walked up the hall, Minerva said, "Charlotte, where do your servants come from? I can't believe Pierre reads Rousseau. I don't think Jasper knows how to read other than his name."

"It was the Revolution," Charlotte said with a shrug. "It turned every Frenchman into a philosopher. As for myself, I wouldn't think of reading Rousseau unless I had an urge to fall asleep. But Pierre is devoted to his books."

At the front door, the friends lingered a moment over their farewells, and then all was quiet. A candle in her hand, Minerva leaned back against the door, savoring the peace. There had been a time in her life when she'd had many such havey-cavey nights.

But she wouldn't allow herself any doubts about the kidnapping. It nagged at her that Mr. Ferrington believed Caroline was involved. They'd never expected him to implicate her.

"Minerva?" Caroline's voice came from upstairs.

Minerva gave a start and almost dropped the candle. "Caroline? Are you home so soon?" She began climbing the stairs.

"I left the party early. Is someone with you? I thought I heard voices."

"Just Charlotte and the others. They've all gone home now."

"I didn't hear them come in."

"We've been in the kitchen," Minerva said as she reached the top of the stairs. The upstairs hall was short and narrow. Caroline stood in her bedroom doorway. A candle lit the room behind her. With her flowing white cotton flannel nightdress and hair in one long braid down her back she looked more a child than a self-sufficient young woman. Minerva's heart overflowed with protective maternal feelings. She placed a hand on Caroline's shoulder. "Something is bothering you." Caroline nodded. "Do you want to talk?"

"If you don't mind?"

Minerva was flattered by the unusual request. "Of course, dear." She followed her into the bedroom. Caroline sat on her rumpled bed, pulling her legs up beneath her. The bedclothes looked as if Caroline had tried to sleep and failed. Minerva set her candle on a table. A fire burned low in the small fireplace, but was small defense against the drafts in the old house. "What is the matter?"

Caroline made a production of tucking her feet under the hem of her nightdress. Finally, her shoulders hunched in worry, she confessed, "I'm ruined."

"Ruined? Whyever do you say that?"

Huge tears pooled in Caroline's eyes. She blinked them back. Minerva thought her heart would break at the sight. Reaching out, she sat down on the bed and gathered Caroline close in her arms. "Whatever it is, it can't be so terrible."

"Yes, it is."

"Tell me."

"It's Mr. Ferrington. He's a rat. A scoundrel. A . . . a rake!"

Minerva went very still. "What did he do?" she asked, fearing the worst.

"He bought me a dress!"

Minerva took her niece by the shoulders. "Caroline, you aren't making sense. How can he be a scoundrel because he bought a dress for you?"

"The dress I wore tonight to the ball. The blue one. It didn't come from Elizabeth. Mr. Ferrington sent it as if it came from Elizabeth. He tried to trick me. But Lady Lavenham—"

"Lady Lavenham?" Minerva asked, not sure she'd heard correctly. "Do you mean Vera Stanbury, the Countess of Lavenham?"

Caroline nodded.

"What did she do?" Minerva asked apprehensively. She knew all too well the damage and hatred Vera could inspire.

"She saw James—I mean, Mr. Ferrington—purchase the dress, and she created a scene. She told everyone that I was his mistress."

Her sense of foreboding growing stronger, Minerva asked her, "Did Vera mention my name?"

Caroline slid her a guilty look as she admitted, "Yes. Who is she, Minerva? Why did she attack me that way in front of everyone and ruin Elizabeth's ball? She was wretched. Even Lady Dimhurst appeared to be embarrassed by her actions, although she didn't come to my defense."

Minerva hastened to assure her, "Oh, pooh, a little gossip never hurt a ball. Furthermore, you're *not* his mistress. If he is a gentleman, he'll clear the air of that misconception . . ." Her thoughts strayed to the angry man in the cellar. She took a different tact. "Mr. Ferrington may have purchased a dress, but the misunderstanding was not your fault. And certainly there are worse things that could happen."

"Oh, Minerva, you don't understand or you've forgotten how unforgiving the *ton* is. They dissect every nuance, every mistake, every action that could discredit a person—and people are always doubly suspicious of a widow. There are women in the Charity League who act as if they can't wait for me to kick up my heels and start chasing men. What am I going to do once Miss Elmhart hears about this? Lady Dimhurst has already convinced her to cut back the classes I teach to one a week. Miss Elmhart told me Monday morning that she planned to increase my classes again, once she smoothed a few matters over with Lady Dimhurst. But now it appears that she will be forced to turn me off completely."

"She won't do that, Caroline. You are one of her best teachers."

"She can and she will, especially if Lady Dimhurst becomes involved. Lady Lavenham practically shouted tonight that I wasn't a fit person to be around children. It was so embarrassing. Scores of people were listening. My mother always said that a woman has only one thing of value, and that is her reputation."

"Caroline—"

"—And now I've lost mine."

"Listen to me and mark my words well. There will be those who believe the worst of you because it is in their nature to do so. And there are others who will understand and forgive this stumble."

"Is that what happened to you, Minerva? Did you stumble?"

The question caught Minerva completely off guard. "You mean you don't know," she said, her voice cautious. "I'd assumed my self-righteous family would have told you the story."

"They didn't talk about you. The first time I knew of your existence was when you returned from Italy shortly before Trumbull died."

Minerva took Caroline's hand and held it a moment. When she'd arrived from Italy, grieving over Bernardo, it had been a godsend to have this niece whom she barely knew welcome her with open arms. No questions. No expectations. Only the respect and inclusion of family. And Minerva had been happy to have that. She'd needed it.

Now she realized that she didn't want to say anything that would make her less than perfect in Caroline's eyes. But how could she hide the truth?

"I didn't stumble. I ran."

"Why? What made you run?"

"I understand what you are saying, Caroline, about the gossips and the harsh rules of society. Years ago, I broke those rules. I eloped with a man who was promised to another. On the way to the Scottish border, our coach was involved in a horrible accident. He died."

For several seconds, Minerva couldn't speak. She felt the anguish and loss, as if the accident had happened only yesterday instead of thirty years earlier.

Her grief must have shown in her face because Caroline placed a comforting arm around her shoulders. "I'm sorry."

"I am too. All I suffered in the accident were broken bones. In both legs. That's why I feel such pain when the weather turns."

"Who was he?"

"Robert Edwards. His father was the Marquess St. Just. Robert gave up his inheritance for me . . ." She shifted. "Robert and I spent one night together on the road. Although he respected my virtue and didn't touch me, my reputation was ruined. I wasn't a grand heiress who could offer a suitor money to look past an indiscretion. My father, Trumbull's grandfather, told me I was unmarriageable. He wanted to send me away to serve as governess for one of his friends. But I didn't want to be a governess," she said to Caroline with a smile. "And I refused to be docile. I defied my father. I dared him to turn me out, until finally one day he did. I went through a wild period of my life. I didn't care about my background, my upbringing . . . my reputation. I wanted to destroy myself." She shook her head. "Oh, Caroline, so many nights I used to lie awake and beg God to take me, to just strike me dead with a clap of thunder or a bolt of lightning. I couldn't understand how He could take Robert from my life, and expect me to continue."

"What happened to you?"

"I met Charlotte." Minerva smiled. "I don't think Charlotte would be flattered to know she was the answer to my prayers, do you? She took me in hand." Minerva rolled her eyes at the memory. "We met here in London. Charlotte's baron had died, leaving her virtually penniless. She was only eighteen and had been married to him for three years. I was being passed from gentleman to gentleman."

Minerva forced herself to look at her niece as she said, "It was a hard life, Caroline, and Charlotte knew I wasn't bred for it. She gave me her friendship, and she taught me to respect myself. Charlotte believes there is a huge world out there full of all sorts of exciting things, places, and people . . . and lovers," she added ruefully. "Then I met Bernardo, and my life became quite normal with him. Things between us were as they should be betwixt two people who care for each other. He made me very happy."

Caroline's eyebrows came together as she considered Minerva's words. Finally, she said, "Minerva, I have a confession to make, and I'm afraid it is going to make me sound like a hypocrite."

"Caroline, I can't imagine you doing anything

hypocritical, but please trust me. I would never betray your confidence."

"I've been thinking that perhaps it wouldn't be so bad to . . . stumble with Mr. Ferrington."

Minerva almost fell off the bed.

"He makes me feel—" Caroline appeared to search for a word and then said, "Hot . . . and cold, crazy and sane, giddy and frightened all at the same time." She rose from the bed and began pacing the length of the room, her braid swinging with her movements. "When I'm away from him, I can't think of anything but him, and when I'm with him, no matter how much I harden my resolve against him, he slips past my defenses. I don't even think about the *deed* when I'm around him. I should have asked him for it this evening, and I didn't. I wasn't even angry . . . I was actually glad to see him." She shook her head, her cheeks turning a becoming shade of pink as she confided, "I dream about him, and when I wake I feel so restless, I can't go back to sleep. I haven't felt well rested since I met him!"

"Caroline, I could have sworn that you hated the man. This afternoon, you acted as if he were your worst enemy."

She skidded to an abrupt halt. "That's the hypocritical part of it all. Yes, I want my house back, but if he hands me the deed, I may never see him again. I don't know if I could bear that."

Minerva felt confused. "Caroline, are you saying you want to see Mr. Ferrington? That you aren't furious with him?"

"Yes, I'm furious with him! He shouldn't have purchased the dress, and yes, he did compromise my reputation. But a part of me wants to forgive him." She covered her face with her hands before asking, "When did I lose my common sense? Tell me, Minerva, that I should put him completely out of my mind."

Caroline didn't wait for an answer but charged forward with her thoughts. "This evening, he begged me to trust him. But how can I trust him after what he did with the dress?"

"Caroline, did he lie to you about the dress?"

She crossed her arms before she answered. "No. But he didn't tell me he'd done it."

"Well, then, I don't consider that lying."

Caroline uncrossed her arms in exasperation. "But he should have known his actions would compromise me."

"Sometimes, Caroline, men don't think beyond the moment. What he did may not have been the best thing, but it certainly wasn't the worst."

Caroline pulled her braid over her shoulder, running her hand up and down its silky length before she said, "The last man I felt this way about was Trumbull, and that turned out to be less than what I had hoped. I don't want to make that mistake again."

"James Ferrington is not Trumbull Pearson," Minerva declared firmly. "Trumbull was like his father, selfish and weak. Don't close yourself away from love because you've had one bad experience. You're older and wiser now, Caroline. You can protect yourself from another Trumbull."

Caroline pushed the braid back over her shoulder and stood up straight. "I believe you are right. I will contact Mr. Ferrington tomorrow and ask for the deed . . . and perhaps we'll talk of other things."

The wistful tone of her voice caught and held Minerva. "Are you serious, Caroline? Are you saying that you want to build a relationship with Mr. Ferrington?"

"Is it wrong of me?"

"No, it is not wrong of you, *cara.* In fact, nothing could be more right. However, I think you should also know that if you are serious about building a relationship with Mr. Ferrington, you must hurry."

"Why do you say that?"

"Because he's tied up in the cellar and not in the best of moods."

Caroline stared at Minerva as if she had just spoken gibberish. "What did you say?"

Minerva sighed. "Lady Mary, Violetta, Charlotte, and I kidnapped Mr. Ferrington this evening on his way home from the ball and are holding him down in our cellar until he either gives you the deed to this house or misses an important meeting he has scheduled for the day after tomorrow." Struck by a sudden thought, she checked the watch hanging on a long chain around her neck before amending, "Make that by tomorrow. It is already after one this morning."

She spoke to thin air. Caroline had already run to rescue Mr. Ferrington.

Chapter 12

$\mathbf{C}$aroline charged down into the pitch-black cellar, her bare feet making little noise on the narrow, wooden steps. She raised the lantern she'd taken from Pierre. Roughly twelve feet by twelve feet, the cellar was used to store potatoes and onions and a few pieces of broken furniture left over from some of the house's previous owners.

She let out a small cry when she spied Mr. Ferrington. To think that her aunt had done this . . . and then left him for the night! He lay on his side on the filthy floor, his hands bound behind him, his legs tied together at the ankles, and a piece of cloth stuffed in his mouth. His eyes glittered with fury.

Minerva's warning that Mr. Ferrington wasn't in the best of moods took on a more vivid meaning. Caroline approached him with caution.

"Mr. Ferrington, I am so sorry," she said as she set the lantern down and knelt beside him. Using all her strength, she pulled him to a sitting position. Mr. Ferrington jerked his shoulder away from her and almost toppled over but regained his balance. "I understand why you are upset, and I don't blame you," she hastened to add, "but please try and understand that my aunt thought she was acting in my best interests."

He glared at her, his expression ridiculous with the gag stuffed in his mouth.

"Please be reasonable, Mr. Ferrington. I must have your promise that you won't do anything to my aunt before I can remove the gag and untie you. Will you give me your word of honor?"

Mr. Ferrington's eyes narrowed, as if her ultimatum didn't sit well with him. Caroline reasoned that he had no choice but to give his pledge, and a moment later he confirmed her thoughts with a curt nod of his head.

She almost sighed with relief. "Thank you, sir. I can't tell you how alarmed I am that this has happened. Your understanding is greatly appreciated."

He said something, the sound muffled by the gag, letting her know he wished she'd get on with it.

"Oh, yes, I'm sorry. Let me remove it before I work on the knots in the ropes." Caroline pulled out the gag. Mr. Ferrington coughed, the sound dry and pained.

"I'll run and get you a drink for your throat—and a knife," she added under her breath as she realized that she would need one to cut through the ropes.

She started to rise from the floor but Mr. Ferrington said something, the sound hoarse.

Caroline leaned closer. "What did you say, sir? I didn't hear you."

He swallowed several times before promising vehemently, "I'll have your head on a platter."

Caroline sat back on her heels in shock at the intensity of his anger. "Mr. Ferrington—"

"You think you can blackmail me? That you can hire henchmen and make me do your will? Well, you have the wrong man, Lady Pearson. When I get out of here, you won't be able to run far enough away from me. I will hound you to the ends of the earth if necessary."

The controlled and reasonable James Ferrington she had come to know had disappeared, replaced by this angry, growling gentleman. "You promised," she said. "You gave your word that you wouldn't harm us."

"I was forced to give my word. A promise made under coercion is not recognized by the law, Lady Pearson! But don't worry. I'll leave your aunt alone. It is you I want. You will pay for this!"

Caroline rose to her feet. "Me? What did I do to you other than come down here and try to free you?"

"Do you think me still a fool? Well, why not?" he asked, as if chastising himself. "I am one. A bloody big one." He narrowed his eyes on Caroline; she could almost feel the passion of his anger. "Tell me, Jezebel, how did it feel to have me practically kissing the ground you walked on and knowing all the time you were going to betray me?"

"Jezebel? Mr. Ferrington—"

"And what is this new trick?" His hard gaze dropped from her face down to the soft flannel of her nightdress and centered on her breasts. The expression in his eyes changed to something even more dangerous.

Suddenly Caroline felt very vulnerable. She should have thrown on a dressing gown, should have thought before she'd charged willy-nilly down to rescue him.

The muscles in his jaw tensed. "Have you decided to play me for more of a fool, madam?" His voice had gone hoarse again, but Caroline didn't think it was caused by the gag.

No, this was something else. Something that she recognized. "I don't think you are a fool—"

"Oh, yes I am, madam," he said, his voice bitter. "I'm seven different kinds of fool because I was stupid enough to fall in love with a woman such as you!"

In love? The words scrambled Caroline's brain. She sat back, staring at him, waiting for him to disavow them. But he didn't. Instead, he looked as if he'd stopped breathing. Her ears must be playing tricks on her.

In love? James couldn't believe he had said those words. He didn't believe in love. Love was a fantasy, an illusion that poets used to justify writing about flowers, birds, and other nonsense. It wasn't based in cold, hard facts, ideas that James understood.

Slowly, he released his breath, his gaze never leaving her—and realized the worst. She had said nothing. She was staring at him, her eyes as wide as saucers, her body still, completely unmoved by his words.

She didn't return his affection! She was rejecting him, James Ferrington, a man who conquered all he saw.

Anger, embarrassment, and hurt roiled up inside him in one ball of rage.

"That's the irony," he said stiffly, unwilling to let her know how deeply her silence had wounded him. "You could have had my thousands to spend and not just your paltry little deed to this ramshackle house. Now you'll receive nothing but a chance to rot in gaol—"

"Mr. Ferrington, you don't understand." She came down on her knees again, reaching out to untie him.

James jerked his shoulder away, as if her touch offended him. "Truly, madam? Do you mean that I'm not lying here on your cellar floor with my hands bound? That you haven't just threatened to blackmail me?"

"I never threatened to blackmail you. I can explain. My aunt and her friends were only trying to help. You had taken the deed to my house and refused to give it back, even though it is rightfully mine—"

"Then why didn't you turn the matter over to a solicitor instead of tying me up in the cellar? I'd advise you to turn to a solicitor now, madam. I'll see your name dragged through every court in this land. When I'm finished, you won't be able to hold your head up high in a farmer's pigsty."

Caroline's control over her temper broke. She came to her feet. "That's enough! I came down to free you, but it is obvious that you don't want any of my explanations. You are perfectly happy with your half-baked conclusions."

He relished her anger. It gave him the excuse to allow his own temper free rein. "Am I not tied up, madam?" he mocked her. "Is my head not still pounding with the headache from being knocked out cold tonight? These are facts, madam, not half-baked conclusions."

Caroline clenched her fists, her whole being quivering with outrage. "You are the most infuriating, overbearing, unreasonable man I've ever met—"

"What credit do I give to the opinion of a harpie—"

"Mr. Ferrington," Caroline started, the warning tone of her voice letting him know he was accomplishing his goal.

"Jezebel," he said, jutting his chin out in defiance.

"Stop it," she snapped.

"Delilah." He rolled the syllables.

"I won't take—"

"Shrew."

Caroline stormed away from him. He thought she was leaving, but then, she swung around and confronted him, the fire blazing from her eyes making her look like an angry young goddess—his moon goddess.

It struck him, perverse creature that he was, that she'd never looked more magnificent, with her hair spilling down over her shoulder in one long braid and her nightdress flowing around her—

Nightdress. Immediately James's body reacted with something other than anger. It didn't matter that she was covered from her neck to her toes. Her bare toes.

Caroline was wearing nothing beneath the nightdress. Nothing. Now he could see the soft way the fabric draped over her breasts. He could make out their fullness, and the idea of feeling their weight . . .

Hot, heavy desire stabbed through him with a force he hadn't felt since he was fourteen and one of the upstairs maids teased him by wearing her blouse low to show her cleavage. The headiness. The damnable *need*. Every part of him ached with the wild yearning.

He stared at her lips, at her small perfect teeth, and remembered the night in the coach. Having her under him. Responding to her.

Why the devil were they fighting? Who cared if she didn't love him? He didn't care about anything in this world except assuaging this savage desire beating through his veins like native war drums.

Dear God, he wanted her.

Slowly, as if through a haze, he realized she was speaking to him. Her words formed and made an impression in his mind.

". . . you are selfish, sir! Mercenary, even. I understand now how you built your fortune—by taking what belongs to others and keeping it. Well, I am one woman you can't have or keep. You call me names? Well, I have a few fine ones for you. You're . . . you're . . . a rakehell!" She said the word as if it was the worst she could think to call him.

Dear, wonderful Caroline. Amazing how radiant she looked when she was so angry—and he smiled at her.

The smile was a mistake.

"You laugh at me?" she said, fury weighing her words. "I'm telling you exactly what I think of you and *you are laughing?*" She bit out each word. Suddenly she whirled, and walked away from him, as if needing to put space between them. James watched, fascinated, as she visibly struggled to bring her anger under control.

Experience had taught him that women fell into two categories: they were either creatures of passion or of common sense. But Caroline was a delightful mix of both. He knew it. He sensed it. No wonder he loved her.

He loved her! This time the words didn't embarrass him. They sang through him.

Holding her head as high as a queen, she was saying in a cold, distant voice, "No, I won't come down to your level. Nor can you have everything you want, Mr. Ferrington. In this case, I shall win. You may stay in this cellar until you're old and feeble or turn over the deed." Without waiting for a reply, she turned on her heel and marched out of the ring of lamplight and into the darkness. James listened to her bare feet flounce up the cellar steps. The door slammed.

At least she'd left the lantern, although he was aware that he'd lost a great deal of ground with her. Furthermore, she obviously didn't feel what he was feeling. He would have to change her mind.

A new thought struck him. Caroline Pearson couldn't ignore him now. He would have her undivided attention, and he would use that attention to make her fall completely and madly in love with him.

He could do it. If he had the power to convince sultans to open trade lanes to him, he should be able to win a woman's heart. He'd never tried before, but it couldn't be that difficult.

A few minutes later the cellar door opened again. Heavier footsteps descended the stairs and the giant stepped out of the darkness. James watched warily as the man leaned forward and flipped a thin mattress, the sort found in the servants' quarters, on to the ground.

"*Madame* Pearson told me to make you comfortable. She fears you will be in her cellar for a long time." So saying, the giant heaved James up by the shoulders and dragged him over to the mattress. He turned and left.

Well, this was a start, James decided. He had a mattress, he had light, and with any luck at all, he'd have a chance to woo Caroline. For the first time in days, James fell into a deep, untroubled sleep, his dreams laced with visions of Caroline in white nightdresses.

Caroline didn't fall asleep until shortly before dawn. The thought that James was here under her roof was strangely unsettling. Part of her derived an almost-deep comfort in knowing he was so close, while another part of her felt excited and uneasy. At least he was down in the cellar and out of sight.

She didn't rise to greet the day until noon. Anxious to go downstairs, she reached in her wardrobe for one of her black day dresses, and stopped. The evening dress hung on a hook. For a second, she ran her fingers over the blue silk. It was the most beautiful dress she'd ever owned.

Almost ruthlessly, Caroline pushed it aside and pulled out one of her black mourning gowns. She dressed quickly and went down to the kitchen, where she discovered Lady Mary, Mrs. Mills, the Baroness, Minerva, and Jasper. They'd gathered around the open cellar door, listening.

"What are you all doing?" asked Caroline, who was never in the best of moods early in the morning.

Mrs. Mills shushed her, and the others ignored her. Curious, Caroline moved closer to the door. A man's clear baritone could be heard singing in the cellar.

Caroline pulled back. "He's singing?" She'd recognized the tune, a popular ballad about true love lost and won.

"Yes," Mrs. Mills said. "I love hearing a man's full-bodied voice. He could sing in a choir with that voice."

The Baroness raised a knowing eyebrow. "You know what they say about a man who can sing well."

"No, what do they say?" Lady Mary asked.

"That a man who sings well also makes love well."

"I've never heard that." Mrs. Mills blinked in surprise. "Is it true?"

Caroline made a sound of annoyance. "Look at all of you. This man is our prisoner. He's not supposed to be singing ballads and enjoying himself." As if to add credence to her words, Mr. Ferrington broke out into a sea shanty at the top of his lungs. Caroline frowned. "Instead of praising him as if he were a tenor with the opera, we should tell him to stop that caterwauling."

Minerva turned around to look at Caroline. "You didn't sleep well. Even from my room, I heard you tossing and turning most of the night."

The kitchen suddenly felt too close for Caroline, and Minerva's eyes too sharp. "He and I had words last night. He isn't going to give us the deed."

Mrs. Mills waved a dismissive hand. "Last night he was still feeling the effects of Pierre's blow to his head. This morning he has been in the best of moods. Did you know he speaks Russian?"

"You've already been down to the cellar to see him this morning?" Caroline asked.

Minerva nodded. "We all broke our fast with him." She closed her eyes as if savoring the memory. "A man like that could sweep a woman off her feet."

"And into his bed," the Baroness added.

Caroline needed to sit down. This about-face from Minerva and the others was too abrupt for her. But there were no chairs in the kitchen. "Where are the chairs? Where is the kitchen worktable?"

"We had Pierre carry them downstairs," the Baroness answered. "How else were we going to join him for breakfast?"

Caroline took several steps around the now almost-empty kitchen. "I can't believe this. I'm starting to think we should all be locked up in Bedlam."

"Whatever for?" Lady Mary asked. "Because we like to hear him sing?"

"Because you knocked him over the head and kidnapped him," Caroline said, her voice low and intense. "Because if he ever gets out of the cellar, he'll have us all locked up in prison. And most of all, because you all keep visiting him and ogling him!"

Minerva tapped Jasper's arm. "I think you'd better see to Caroline's tea. You know she isn't at her best until she's had her tea."

"We weren't ogling him," Lady Mary declared,

her chin coming up in indignation. "We were admiring him."

Mrs. Mills smiled. "Yes, admiring him."

"*I* was ogling him," the Baroness answered.

Caroline gritted her teeth. Maybe *she* was ready for Bedlam.

Minerva crossed to Caroline. "My dear, he'd like to see you."

Caroline gratefully took the cup and saucer Jasper offered and swallowed a life-affirming sip of tea before she answered, "No."

"He has confessed that some things he said to you last night were less than gallant," Minerva replied. "Of course, I can understand if he was a wee bit upset at the time."

Conscious that all eyes were on her, Caroline made a show of placing the teacup on the heavy four-legged cutting block before saying tersely, "I have nothing to say to him."

"But he wants to talk to you. Perhaps he wishes to apologize," said Mrs. Mills, ever the romantic, her voice light with hope.

"If he wishes to apologize," Caroline said, "then all he needs to do is turn over the deed. That is apology enough."

"But he says if you want the deed, you must talk to him first," Minerva answered.

Caroline felt her temper grow perilously close to the breaking point. "Then we're at a deadlock, aren't we? I hope he enjoys my cellar."

For a long second, silence reigned in the kitchen—except for the sound of Mr. Ferrington singing a rousing military tune. He really did have a good voice, Caroline admitted crossly, and wished he would shut up. She sipped her tea.

The Baroness's accented voice broke the silence. "I fear we have a dilemma." She looked from one woman to the other before asking, "What shall we do if he doesn't turn over the deed?"

"We could boil him in oil," Caroline suggested. She was ignored.

Mrs. Mills said softly, "Maybe we should release him. I like him too much to ruin him."

"In a pig's eye," Caroline said. She confronted the small group of conspirators. "Oh, I'll grant you he can be charming when he is moved to be so— but so can the devil. That man in the cellar threatened me and took outrageous advantage of me—"

"Advantage of you!" the Baroness said, her eyes bright with delight. "When?"

"The first night I met him," Caroline answered.

The Baroness nodded in sudden understanding. "Ah, yes, the whisker burn. Did you fight him so hard, *chérie?*"

Caroline glared at her.

Mrs. Mills interrupted them. "Oh, listen. He's singing my favorite hymn."

The women and Jasper all paused to listen.

Mrs. Mills closed her eyes and sighed in appreciation. "I'm so glad we kidnapped him."

Caroline said, "I'm not! But now that we have him, we're not going to let him go until he turns over that deed and *if he doesn't,* his business can go to—to—" She searched for a word. "To Hades before I'll give a care." To add extra emphasis to her words, she marched over to the place in the floor that was directly over Mr. Ferrington's head and stamped her foot.

A lock of her hair came unpinned from her

chignon. Her behavior was foolish, immature, un-
befitting a woman of her station, but Caroline was
beyond reason. She gave another stomp for good
measure!

And then Freddie Pearson's voice returned her to
reality. "You've done *what?*"

Caroline tucked her hair back up in her chignon
as she turned toward the kitchen door. "Freddie,
what a surprise!" She shot a nervous glance at
Minerva and the others before adding, "We
weren't expecting you."

Freddie handed his hat to Jasper. "Mother insisted I come. We've heard some distressing rumors about you, Caroline."

"From whom?" Caroline demanded, afraid of
the answer.

Freddie ignored her. "Now whom have you
kidnapped?"

"No one," Caroline said.

"Mr. Ferrington," Minerva answered without
hesitation. "He's tied up down in the cellar."

Caroline whirled on her, shocked to hear her
blurt out the truth.

"Is that a joke?" Freddie asked Minerva. He
waited, but when no one laughed, he said, his
voice uncertain, "You're not joking?"

"No, we're not," Lady Mary said, almost glee-
fully. "We trussed him up like a proper pigeon."

"Trussed him up!" Freddie rounded on Caroline.
"Whatever made you do such an outrageous thing?
So help me, Caroline, if you ruin my reputation,
I'll—" He never finished his promise, but let his
red face and bulging eyes speak louder than mere
words.

Caroline stood her ground, her head held high.

"I'm trying to get my deed back. Remember? The one *you* lost to him?"

"Caroline, the deed is his. He won it in a game of cards." He stopped speaking and narrowed his eyes. "You don't understand, do you?" he said, his tone chiding, as if he spoke to a child. "I don't know why I waste my breath." He started for the cellar door.

Caroline stepped in his way. "Where do you think you are going?"

"I'm going to set Ferrington free."

Her anger turned to panic. "You can't release him, Freddie. He'll have Minerva and me before the magistrate. He promised to do so last night. You must help us with this situation."

For only a fraction of a moment, Freddie appeared to consider that possibility and the complications that might result. "I cannot let you implicate Mother and me. Furthermore, you are the one who insists she is free to make her own choices. Well, I believe now you will have to pay the price." He charged down the steps into the cellar.

Chapter 13

Shocked by the chain of events, Caroline turned on Minerva. "How could you tell him the truth?"

Minerva pressed her lips together. "Because I thought it best."

"You thought it best?" Caroline repeated in disbelief. She placed her hands on her hips. "Well, what do you think it is best for us to do *now?*"

Before Minerva could frame a response, a woman's imperial voice called down the hall, "Lady Pearson. Are you here? The door was open. We let ourselves in."

"Oh, no," Caroline whispered.

"Who is that?" Lady Mary asked.

Caroline motioned for Jasper to hurry out to the hall and see to the new visitors. "It's Miss Elmhart."

"Miss Elmhart?" Lady Mary repeated. Apparently the name wasn't to her liking.

"She owns the school where Caroline teaches," Minerva explained.

"Oh," said Lady Mary. "I thought it was someone important."

"Like the magistrate?" Caroline asked, letting sarcasm color her tone. "Please, Lady Mary, Mrs. Mills, Baroness, please go home and let Minerva and me contact you as soon as the dust has settled here."

"And leave all this excitement?" Mrs. Mills asked. "Oh dear, no."

"Absolutely not," Lady Mary chimed in.

"We'll stay until the end," the Baroness vowed.

Tears welled in Minerva's eyes. She hugged each of her friends. "Aren't they dear friends, Caroline? Such loyalty. Such honor."

"Such silliness," Caroline said under her breath.

"What did you say, dear?" Minerva asked, but Caroline was saved from making a comment by the appearance of Jasper in the kitchen doorway.

"Miss Elmhart and the Reverend Tilton are here to see you, Lady Pearson. They say they must see you on a matter of some urgency. I left them in the parlor."

Caroline didn't want to leave the kitchen. She wanted to be there when Mr. Ferrington and Freddie emerged from the cellar. Still, she could not ignore Miss Elmhart.

"Minerva, I need you to keep Mr. Ferrington in the kitchen until I have Miss Elmhart and the Reverend out the door. Whatever you do, do not let either Freddie or Mr. Ferrington leave until Miss Elmhart is gone. Do you feel you can accomplish that task?"

"I'll do my best," Minerva said.

Caroline could ask no more of her. She forced

a confident smile. "Come then, Jasper, let us see to our guests."

She was almost out the kitchen door when Minerva's voice stopped her. "I don't think he will betray us," she said.

"Who?" Caroline asked.

"Mr. Ferrington. He won't betray us." The other women nodded solemnly.

Caroline had no comment.

She found Miss Elmhart and the Reverend Tilton standing in the middle of her parlor in hushed discussion. Vases of fresh flowers still decorated tables, desk, and mantelpiece, giving the room a festive look and filling it with fragrance. Caroline discreetly cleared her throat. Her guests turned as if they'd been caught in a guilty secret.

"Miss Elmhart, Reverend Tilton, how nice of you to visit," Caroline said, coming in the room and offering them her hands.

The Reverend, to date her only suitor, looked ready to take her proffered hand, but one stern look from Miss Elmhart and he backed off, mumbling something incoherent. He tended to be ruddy-cheeked, but now his face was a bright, beety red. He pushed his gold-framed spectacles up his nose.

Miss Elmhart, a tall, raw-boned woman who looked every inch the governess, crossed her hands in front of her and said in very clear, clipped tones, "Actually, Reverend Tilton and I didn't plan on presenting ourselves to you together but we discovered, on your front step, that we were each prompted to pay a visit by the same grave matter."

Thankful for her widow's black, which made her

look as moral and pious as a Quaker, Caroline smiled with a serenity she was far from feeling. "Oh? I am sorry to hear that. Unfortunately, I am unable to visit right now—especially about a grave matter. Is it possible for me to return your visits later in the day?" Boldly she took the Reverend Tilton's and Miss Elmhart's arms and started leading them toward the door.

Miss Elmhart balked, digging in her heels. "There has been talk," she said without preamble.

"Yes," the Reverend Tilton added nervously. "Lady Dimhurst paid a call on me this morning—"

"And on me," Miss Elmhart said.

"She is most upset," the Reverend Tilton finished.

Caroline opened her eyes wide in feigned innocence. "Upset? Whatever could have upset her—?"

Freddie's demanding voice coming from the back of the house cut her off. "Caroline? Caroline, where the blazes are you?"

"Who is that?" Miss Elmhart demanded, her nose pointing up to sniff the air like a bloodhound.

"My brother-in-law," Caroline said, her pleasant voice coming from between clenched teeth. She could hear Minerva talking to him, their voices carrying down the hallway. She didn't have a moment to waste. Putting one hand on the Reverend Tilton's back and the other on Miss Elmhart's, she steered them toward the door, her words coming out in a rush. "I'm terribly sorry to hurry you on your way, but now is not the best time for a visit—"

"I will not be put off," Miss Elmhart said, attempting to pull away.

Caroline could hear Freddie charging down the

hall. She grabbed their arms and made an about-face with her charges. The parlor, she had to keep them in the parlor—and close the door. She released her hold just as Miss Elmhart started to pull away again. With a cry, the woman stumbled back against the writing desk, her elbow catching a vase of flowers and overturning it, which in turn knocked over the inkstand. Ink spilled all over the desk and blotter.

Horrified, Caroline said, "Miss Elmhart, are you all right?"

"The inkstand," the woman sputtered. "There's ink and water everywhere."

"It's on your hand," Reverend Tilton pointed out. "You're smearing it on your dress. Careful now."

Miss Elmhart practically roared with outrage. "Where did all these flowers come from? A person can barely think sensibly in a room full of floriculture!"

"Here, let me hurry and get something for the stain before it sets," Caroline offered, and turned on one heel to do exactly that. But she never took a step.

Freddie stood in the doorway, wild-eyed and red-faced.

Caroline drew back, her arms going out as if she could hide the sight of him from the Reverend Tilton and Miss Elmhart. Freddie stared at them. Then, as if just recognizing his sister-in-law, he said in a strident voice, "Do you know what he said to me?"

Caroline didn't need to ask who "he" was.

Freddie frowned, his expression so exaggerated it appeared almost comical. "That damn Ferrington told me that if I untied him, he'd knock my teeth down my throat. Said I was less than a man. Said I wasn't fit to have a title." Freddie's eyes were practically bugging out of his head with outrage. "When I told him I should call him out for that insult, he dared me to do so!"

Jasper had appeared with Freddie's hat. So angry his hands were shaking, Freddie smashed the hat on his head. "The man can rot in your cellar for all I care. Bloody upstart! Who the bloody hell does he think he is?" Freddie paused dramatically before pulling himself up to his full height and declaring, "I'm Lord Freddie Pearson. Let him sit on his arse down there and reflect about that!" And with an almost-savage snarl, he charged out of Caroline's house.

Caroline felt as if a whirlwind had just swept through the room. A second later, she was surrounded by Minerva, Mrs. Mills, Lady Mary, and the Baroness, all speaking at once.

"We tried to stop him," Mrs. Mills said.

"He is the most unreasonable man," Minerva declared.

"I don't remember ever being more entertained," the Baroness said, laughing.

"My William would have thrown the man out, just like Ferrington did," Lady Mary boasted.

And then, Miss Elmhart's well-honed voice cut through the chatter. "You have a man tied up in your cellar?"

Caroline froze. Minerva's eyes met hers, and together they turned to face their visitors.

"Please," Mrs. Mills said, "don't blame Caroline. We kidnapped him."

"Mrs. Mills!" Caroline said in dismay.

"Kidnapped?" Miss Elmhart looked close to having an apoplectic fit. "You kidnapped someone?"

Mrs. Mills started to nod her head, but Minerva said quickly, "Violetta, let Caroline deal with this."

"Violetta." The Reverend Tilton said her name as if it was the missing piece to a puzzle he couldn't solve. "Violetta Mills!"

Mrs. Mills regarded him with interest. "Do I know you, sir?"

The Reverend Tilton jumped back as if Mrs. Mills had pointed an evil eye in his direction. "No! But I know you." He pointed an accusing finger. "I was in the church the day you ran away with your—your . . ." His voice trailed off when he couldn't bring himself to speak the word.

The Baroness supplied it for him, "Paramour?" Her accent gave the word a deeper, more exotic meaning.

The Reverend Tilton shrank back, intimidated by the tall Frenchwoman, but the Baroness wasn't done with him. She stalked him, her bearing majestic and proud. "Tell me, is there something wrong with a woman having a lover? Something that frightens you?" She emphasized the word "frightens" and the vicar practically jumped behind Miss Elmhart to get away from her.

Mrs. Mills placed a hand on her arm. "Charlotte, please leave him alone."

"He insulted you, *chérie*."

"Because he doesn't know the full story—"

The Baroness cut Mrs. Mills off. "Ha! A man like him will not understand what it is to live with a man who mistreated you, who abused you—"

"The Reverend Mills is a good man," the Reverend Tilton said stoutly from his hiding place behind Miss Elmhart.

"He should have been horsewhipped!" Lady Mary declared.

"He's a man of the cloth—" the Reverend countered, and found himself immediately embroiled in an argument with all three women.

Miss Elmhart's voice rang through the uproar. "I want to know why that man is tied up in Lady Pearson's cellar. Lady Dimhurst expects an answer today!"

Mrs. Mills told her, "If Mr. Ferrington had been reasonable, we wouldn't have had to hit him over the head."

"You hit Mr. Ferrington over the head?" Miss Elmhart repeated. "Mr. *James* Ferrington, the man who has donated one thousand pounds to my school? Lady Pearson, how could you—?"

"Lady Pearson didn't do anything—" Mrs. Mills said.

Caroline lifted the vase, now empty of flowers and water, from her desk, and dropped it on the hardwood floor. The crash brought the room to quiet. All eyes turned to her.

"Out," Caroline said, surprised at how calm her voice sounded.

"Caroline?" Minerva asked, as if scarce believing her ears.

"Yes, you too," Caroline said. "Visit the Baroness—and take Jasper with you. I want *all of you* to leave."

"Caroline," Minerva started, but Caroline held up a hand, warning her back.

"Please, Minerva, I need to do this alone."

"Do what?" Minerva asked anxiously.

"Deal with Mr. Ferrington."

"I don't think Lady Dimhurst is going to like this," the Reverend Tilton said. Miss Elmhart nodded her agreement.

"I don't care what Lady Dimhurst thinks," Caroline answered. "Not now, not ever, and if she believes the worst of me, then I don't want to work on her charitable committees doing those endless little jobs she and her friends find too distasteful to do themselves." She took his hat from Jasper and handed it to him. "Good day to you, sir, and also to you, Miss Elmhart, and to you, Mrs. Mills." She herded them all to the front door as she spoke. "Baroness, I wish both you and Minerva a lovely afternoon. Lady Mary, farewell, it has been so nice having you visit. Such an adventure. And Jasper, take the day off!"

So saying, she maneuvered everyone out onto the front step, their expressions studies in mild shock, and shut the door in their faces.

She turned the key in the lock. And for the first time since she'd gotten up that morning, she relished a few moments of peace. She leaned her back against the door. Silence. Glorious silence.

She closed her eyes and relaxed.

And then, from a distance, came the muffled sound of a man's voice singing a bawdy drinking song about a buxom young maiden with a great appetite!

Slowly Caroline walked back to the kitchen. The cellar door was still wide-open, and Mr. Ferrington's baritone carried through the kitchen.

What was she going to do with him?

There was only one thing to do. Caroline pulled a knife from a drawer and crossed to the cellar door. She paused for a moment, listening, thinking that no man, no person had ever created more havoc in her life than James Ferrington.

And last night he said he loved you.

For once, she let herself wonder what it would be like if this man really did love her. His song changed. He began to sing in Italian, a lovely song of a lonely shepherd missing the woman he loved. It was a song full of wistful longing, of need, of passion.

It moved her.

Just as it had moved her when she'd heard it sung in the opera several months ago, she told herself. Still, she hadn't imagined it a song the arrogant, commanding Mr. Ferrington would admire enough to learn. Or to sing as if the emotion came from his very soul.

She'd learned the hard way not to trust her heart. Love was an illusion. What was it someone had told her shortly after she'd married Trumbull? That men don't feel as intensely as women. That love for men was a business arrangement, an alliance.

And then her captive sang the words of the song describing how the shepherd's heart breaks and he dies from the loneliness of love lost. The deep emotion of the music washed through her and Caroline felt tears in her eyes—not for the shepherd and his shepherdess, but because for one shining moment, she wanted to believe that such a love existed.

She pressed the tears away with the back of her hand. "You're a fool, Caroline," she said softly, and then started down the cellar steps.

Even at this hour of the day, the cellar was dark. At some point, the women had untied James's legs. He sat in one of several chairs around the kitchen table. Next to the small lantern on the table were a bowl of fruit, a small plate, and a glass of wine.

His strong masculine voice brought the song to a close as she stepped into the small circle of candlelight. He rose to his feet. The notes of the aria vibrated in the air between them.

He stood before her, proud, roguishly handsome, a model of everything that could be admired in a man.

"I've come to free you," she said, and showed him the knife. She forced herself to meet his eyes. Even in the shadowy light of the candle, she could feel their power, their strength, their intensity. Unable to face such scrutiny, she dropped her gaze to the knife in her hand. "I realize that you are completely in your rights to call the magistrate. You may apprehend me, but I ask that you spare Minerva and the others."

"Caroline, I'm not going to call the magistrate."

His voice reached deep within her—and left her feeling empty and sad. A lump formed in her throat. Painful. Tight. She wouldn't be seeing him any longer.

In measured steps, he crossed the space between them until he stood directly in front of her. "Caroline, look at me."

She shook her head. She wouldn't, couldn't. He started to reach for her, but she took a step back.

"Let me cut through the ropes." *This is hard enough. Let me be done with it.* She raised the knife, but this time, he pulled back.

He dropped his hands to his waist. "I don't want to be free."

Caroline fought a near-hysterical bubble of laughter. "I thought Minerva had gone daft when she told me they had kidnapped you. Now, I fear it is you who has lost his wits."

"No, I've lost my heart."

Her gaze shot up to his face.

He was so close. Her mind flashed on moments between them. Of him holding her in a room filled with flowers, or wishing with her on a star . . . or laughing with her when champagne bubbles tickled her nose . . . or kissing her, holding her, whispering her name.

She'd fallen in love with James Ferrington.

"Caroline," he said. In his voice she heard a need that mirrored her own.

"I don't," she started, and then stopped, almost not trusting herself to speak.

"You don't what?" he asked, pulling her into the aura around him that attracted her without his even so much as touching her.

But she felt touched. She felt marked. Never again would she meet another soul who called to her as deeply as he did. The most criminal act she could imagine would be never to see the laughter in the green depths of his eyes, or watch them change from an emerald sparkle to the serious quiet of a deep green forest.

"I don't want to feel this way," she said, sounding desperate.

"But you feel it, don't you?"

She was afraid to answer.

"Caroline, I've already declared myself to you—"

She turned away, afraid to feel so much, afraid to be so needy for what he offered. She would have run, too. Up the stairs, through the house, and as far away from him as possible—except that his bound hands reached out and took her arm, holding her fast, pulling her closer.

"Caroline, I love you."

She attempted to pull away. "Please. Please let me go."

"Trust me."

She ceased her struggles. "I don't know if I'm able to trust."

"Let me help you. You can't continue living your life wrapped up in black. You are a woman of passion and fire. A woman who believes that coaches can float like bubbles in the air . . . who returns my kisses with wild abandon—"

"I shouldn't have—"

"Don't say that! Nothing was ever more right than holding you in my arms. Caroline, I want you."

She wanted him too. But what would come of it? She couldn't marry him. He wouldn't want her once he learned she couldn't give him children, and just as in the song of the shepherd and shepherdess, her heart would break when he left her.

"There can never be anything between us," Caroline said, and started sawing at the ropes with the knife in her hand.

"Caroline?" he said. He tried to yank his hands from her, but she placed her hand on his to hold him in place. Touching him was a mistake. His hands felt strong, capable. James was right; she did want someone to trust. She needed to believe a man could love her with the same honesty and devotion she felt for him.

But could she trust after Trumbull? Could she put her faith in love again?

"Caroline, you may cut through these ropes, but I won't walk out of your life."

The knife slipped, but she tightened her hold before whispering, "You must."

"I can't. Don't you understand? I don't want to live without you."

His words hit their mark.

The carefully constructed shell she'd used to protect herself all these years began to melt. She was tired of being alone. More than the loneliness drove her; she wanted James Ferrington.

For the first time, she faced the force of her desire without fear, and it came down to a simple statement—she loved him. She loved him enough to trust him, to believe he wouldn't leave her once she had enough courage to tell him she was barren.

The rope pieces fell to the floor. He was free. But instead of turning to run, Caroline tilted her head to gaze into his eyes.

"Caroline, I'm not going to leave," he said, the unconquerable spirit that she knew and loved coming through in the firm set of his mouth. "And you're just going to have to accept that fact."

In answer, she reached up, slipped her hands around his neck, and brought his lips down on hers.

Chapter 14

J ames's mouth parted in surprise. Then she felt his arms come around her and he kissed her back.

With a soft sigh, Caroline melted into the kiss. The focus of her being centered on his kiss, his touch, his taste. It hadn't been just the champagne that night . . . or the countless fantasies of several sleepless nights.

His kiss held magic. It filled her senses and left her craving more.

The kiss deepened. He became bolder, more demanding. Her legs no longer seemed capable of supporting her. She wrapped her arms around his shoulders and embraced him, reveling in his hard body against hers, the broad strength in his shoulders beneath her hands, and his very obvious state of arousal pressed firmly against her—

In a flash Caroline realized that the soft yearning moans she heard were hers. She tried to come to her senses. She really tried. She broke the kiss off, gasping for air as if she'd been underwater for a very long time. James pressed his lips against the pulse point of her throat.

Caroline thought she would ignite from the heat of it. "Mr. Ferrington—"

"James," he interrupted her, his deep voice as husky and breathless as her own. He kissed a trail up to her ear before he ordered softly, "Say it. Say James."

Caroline shook her head, feeling a sudden shyness. He effortlessly lifted her until she was seated on the edge of the table. He leaned toward her until they looked into each other's eyes.

"Say it," he said quietly. Caroline watched his lips move with his words and curve into a smile. Such a beautiful mouth. Firm, full, sensual. She wanted him to kiss her again, and then his lips sounded out silently, "James."

Her own lips curved into a smile of their own.

Caroline hesitated and then whispered, "James."

How right and wonderful his name felt to her. She said it again, marveling at its strength and the wealth of pleasure it gave her. "James."

He'd pressed his lips against her forehead, and she felt his smile. "I never want to hear you call me Mr. Ferrington again. Do you understand, Caroline? Never again."

She raised a hand and placed it against the side of his face. "You shaved."

The gleam in his eyes turned sure and knowing. "But of course." His accent mimicked the Baroness's. "Jasper shaved me. The ladies said they didn't want you to suffer whisker burn. They assured me you would come around, if I kept singing."

His comment sparked a joyful bubble of laughter in her. His arms tightened. She hugged him back, and they laughed together until he'd done with laughter and kissed her again.

And oh, what a kiss. Or was it that Caroline no longer worried about Reverend Tilton, Miss Elmhart, or the rigid Lady Dimhurst? Old inhibitions faded and died as she met James with every spark of fervor in her being. She was so occupied that she barely realized until he'd reached the small of her back that his nimble fingers had unbuttoned her dress. "James—" she began.

He pulled away and was now intently pulling the pins from her hair.

"James," Caroline said again, her hands coming up to hold her dress in place. "You shouldn't." He pulled out the last pin and her heavy hair tumbled down around her shoulders.

James stroked her hair in place until it covered her shoulders evenly. He pulled a strand between two fingers. "So silky and fine." His eyes met hers, and there was no laughter in them now. "You are the most beautiful woman I've ever met, and not because of your looks but because of your strength, your spirit . . . the way you make me feel when I'm around you."

With one long finger, he slipped the shoulder of her chemise down her shoulder. He bent and placed a kiss in the hollow where her neck met her shoulder.

Caroline couldn't think. She could barely gasp for air. Shocked, surprised, delighted, she put her hands around his shoulders for support. Her fingers insinuated their way into his thick hair, pulling his head closer to her.

He nibbled now, his teeth nudging the edge of her chemise lower and lower, his lips coming closer and closer to her heart. Caroline thought she would die from the pleasure of it. She wanted to make love to his man. Feelings she'd long thought dormant came rushing through her. The need. The hot, sweet desire. The ache for fulfillment.

Caroline bent her head and playfully nipped James on the earlobe before kissing the same spot.

His response was immediate and intense. His mouth came up to capture hers. He kissed her, possessively and completely, while leaning her back on the table. She heard the wineglass and the bowl of fruit fall off the table with a clatter as he swept them out of his way. And then he was kissing her again, and she could think of nothing else.

Her legs brushed the outside of his and pressed close around him. His lips came down between her breasts, over their crests. A surprise—a very pleasant surprise, she thought on a sigh—as he bent her back and his mouth covered one nipple. Intense pleasure built inside her, starting at the breast he coaxed and teased, and shot straight to where her legs cradled him. His other hand had already raised her skirts, removing the barrier of clothing so that she could get closer to him.

That's when it struck her that she was about to be tumbled on her kitchen table in the cellar. "James?" He moved his head to tease and play with her other breast, an action that stole all common sense from her until she felt him caress the curve of her buttock. "James," she repeated, with more force. He kissed his way up her neck.

Caroline grabbed hold of his head with both hands and raised him up to face her.

"James, we can't make love on the table."

His eyes dark with passion, his expression heart-stoppingly wanton, he said, "Yes, we can."

Caroline caught herself laughing. "No, we can't."

His smile turned flat. "Caroline, don't tell me no. I'm almost past reason." To emphasize his words, he pressed himself against her where they would be joined most intimately.

He was indeed well past reason.

The need to take him inside her almost made Caroline cry. She wanted this man. Wanted him in a way that she'd never wanted any other. He was right. There was something between them. Something inexplicable, mysterious, demanding.

"We can go upstairs," she whispered, "to my bedroom."

"Upstairs?"

She nodded.

"What about your aunt and all the others?"

"I threw them out and locked the front door."

"Where's the key?"

"In my pocket."

He scooped her up in his arms. "James, what are you doing? Wait, you'll hurt yourself." She threw her arms around his neck.

He grinned. The arms holding her were sure and strong. "Where are the bedrooms?"

"All the way upstairs—"

"Grab the lantern."

Caroline lifted the lantern handle and held it high to light their way through the gloom. "This isn't a good idea," she said as he started moving toward the cellar stairs. "You're going to drop me."

"Do you think so?" James murmured, and then made a pretense of dropping her.

Caroline gave a cry of alarm and hugged him with one arm while balancing the lantern. Her cheek was pressed against his neck and she could feel him laughing—and the excited beating of his heart. A beating that matched her own.

He easily took her up the steps. At the top, he set her on her feet, took the lantern from her, and, blowing out the candle inside, set it on the floor beside the door.

Afternoon sun filled the kitchen. In the bright light of day, Caroline suddenly realized what a momentous step she was about to take. James must have sensed her indecision.

He put his arms around her. "We don't have to do this."

Caroline let his words work their way through her. Her cheek rested against the still-starchy folds of his shirt. He meant what he said. The evidence of how much he wanted this joining was still evident—but he meant what he said. If she changed her mind, he would respect her wishes.

The image of one night when she'd changed her mind with Trumbull rose swift and ugly in her head. A shudder ran through her.

"Caroline?"

He started to move away but Caroline pulled on his arm. "The bedroom is this way." She turned and started to move swiftly through the kitchen and down the hall. James had other ideas.

He stepped on the dragging hem of her dress. The front that she held modestly in place with both hands slid dangerously lower. Caroline reached back and pulled the hem out from under his foot, hearing his low chuckle behind her.

A moment later, he tugged at her hair like a disobedient schoolboy. This time when she turned to slap his hand away, he turned her around and kissed her. He kept kissing her all the way up the hallway until he backed her into the newel-post at the foot of the staircase.

Caroline's arms went up around his neck. "My dress is falling," she whispered when they finally came up for air.

"Let it fall," he challenged her. His suggestion shocked and excited her. She took his dare, holding out her arms and letting the dress slide to the floor. Caroline stepped over the material that lay in a heap at her feet.

The gleam in his eye turned predatory. Untying and pulling his neckcloth from around his neck, he stalked her. Caroline laughed, daring him to follow as she backed up the steps.

James took off his jacket, his actions slow and deliberate. He threw the jacket over the side of the stair railing to the hallway floor. "Isn't there something else you want to take off?"

"Like what?" she asked, enjoying the game.

"Like these shoes." He reached out and captured one ankle. Caroline gave a soft cry of surprise and then laughed as he carefully toppled her. She landed on her rear on the steps. He slipped one shoe off, and then another, carelessly tossing them over his shoulder before saying, "Or these stockings."

"Stockings?" Caroline repeated, and then lost all rational thought as he lowered his head and used his teeth to untie the garter ribbons securing her stockings. She reached for him, her fingers curling into his hair as his lips trailed the path of the stocking down her leg and over her ankle. He turned his head to do the other, but Caroline knew she wouldn't make it up the stairs if she let him proceed. "James." He looked up, his hair mussed.

Caroline slid down a step so that her face was level with his. "I love you." She kissed him with all the passion swirling in her being. Her hands now did the undressing. She tugged the tail of his shirt from his trousers and brought it up his back.

He helped her pull the shirt off over his head. They tried to do it without breaking the kiss, an action that got them both hopelessly tangled in the folds. They laughed, as free and joyous as children.

And then their laughter stopped. For a long breathless moment they sat, looking into each other's eyes.

He held his hand up. Solemnly Caroline laced her fingers through his before rising and leading him up the few remaining stairs and into her bedroom.

This was all hers. Here were the white bed-clothes and simple furniture whose beauty gave her pleasure. Here were the muslin curtains she loved to watch dancing in the breeze from the window, which looked out at the huge elm tree, its leaves golden in the autumn sun. And she saw that James noticed and approved.

Hesitant at first, then bolder, Caroline laid her hand against his chest, feeling the warm strength of his muscle, the pulsing beat of his heart beneath her palm. His fingers came up to trace the curve of her cheek, the line of her jaw before he slowly, almost reverently lowered his head and kissed her.

In the cellar, their kisses had been full of passion and unspoken need. On the stairs, they'd been playful, greedy. But here in the private sanctuary of her bedroom, their kisses took on a reverence—and still she doubted.

Caroline wanted to believe. To put her faith in someone and know that her love would be treated as the gift it was.

"James?"

He answered her with an "Ummmm?" too busy kissing her neck.

"Will we have regrets?"

He raised his head to look in her eyes, his expression serious. "Caroline, I'll never have regrets. But if you wish to stop . . ."

She shook her head, certain now. "No."

His teeth flashed wide and perfect in his sudden smile, like a ray of sunshine escaping a bank of clouds. With a glad "Whoop," he swung her up in his arms and threw her on the bed.

Giddy, excited, flushed, Caroline laughed. And he laughed too. Laughter in lovemaking—she'd never thought of it before, but now it seemed completely right.

They wasted no time undressing each other. The time for leisure was past, and suddenly this became serious business. Hurry, haste, desire mingled together. Caroline pulled off his boots as he attempted to untie her corset.

"I don't know why you wear this," he grumbled.

"For the same reason you wear unmentionables," she answered pertly, and then gasped as she undid the buttons and realized that he didn't wear a thing beneath his thigh-hugging trousers.

He laughed at her surprise and pulled his trousers down. Caroline sobered at the sight of his strong male body. She'd never seen Trumbull naked, not fully. He'd always come to her in the dark or in a long nightshirt. The idea of making love during the middle of the day would have struck him as being outside the natural order of things. James Ferrington looked beautiful, handsome, strong, and masculine lying on her bed in the afternoon light. . . .

"Caroline? Is there someone else in the room with us?"

She looked around, shocked by his question. No one had entered the room. He corrected softly, "Were you thinking of your husband?" His ability to read her thoughts caught her tongue-tied. "You must have loved him very much," he continued, his voice sober.

Had she ever loved Trumbull? At one time she'd felt affection for him—but she realized she'd never known what love was. "No."

James frowned. "Then why is he here?"

"He's not," she denied vehemently.

"All these years you've worn black. You've honored his memory."

Caroline shook her head. "Because I didn't want to forget."

"Forget what?" He drew her onto the bed beside him, sheltering her in the safe haven of his arms.

For the second time that week, she found herself speaking about her marriage. This time, it wasn't as difficult as it had been when she'd talked to Minerva. In fact, speaking of what had happened made the memories easier to accept. She began thinking of Trumbull without the deep-seated anger that had burned inside her for so long.

James listened as she told him about being kept prisoner in her own home, the petty humiliations, the violent murder of her dog Wags.

"Weren't you the mistress of the house?"

"No, my mother-in-law would never give up that control, and my husband let her keep it. I felt worthless. I could have died and it wouldn't have mattered to anyone—"

The words stopped abruptly. She rolled onto her side to face him. "I don't want to forget."

"I'm not Trumbull."

"I know that—now."

James didn't speak. He gathered her in his arms and held her close. Comforting her. Loving her. The beauty of it brought tears to her eyes.

She sat up slowly. Shyly, she dropped the straps of her chemise and slid the garment over her breasts, over the curve of her hips and down her legs until she was as gloriously naked as he was.

"You're beautiful." He meant those words. She could see it in his eyes, in the soft set of his mouth.

"You are, too," she said, and then laughed because before she'd met him, she never would have risked those words without fear of disapproval, restrictions, taboos.

She touched him now, boldly, the way a woman touches a man when she knows she is loved, when she knows she can trust. He lay back on the pillows and let her explore the warmth and textures of his body, his soft words encouraging her. She lowered her head and kissed him as he had kissed her, tasting his body at the pulse point of the neck, the nipple, the tender inside of his thigh. And when she wantonly kissed the hardened length of him, he gasped her name, his body quivering with need.

James reached for her, pulling her up to him, and kissed her with all the passion and force of his being. She could taste his desire—and something else. In the possessiveness of his kiss was a promise more sacred than words. She was his. He claimed her.

He rolled her over on the bed, his body strong and powerful over hers. Slowly, he entered her, his green-gold eyes watching her intently until he'd buried himself deep within her. For a long moment they stayed unmoving until he said hoarsely, "We are one."

The miracle of his words raced through her. "Yes," she said, her words solemn with promise, and pulled him in deeper.

They made love.

She discovered she'd never made love before. With Trumbull, the marriage bed had been disappointing and then, later in their marriage, a duty.

With James, making love was more than a mere physical act. He took his time. He teased her, stroked her, caressed her while whispering words of promise, of love. And Caroline responded. She barely recognized herself in her soft cries of pleasure and encouragement. Her hands loved him; her lips worshiped him.

And then something unexpected happened. Something she'd never experienced before. It was like the flames of the sun growing hotter and hotter inside her, making her want to reach deeper, to pull tighter, and then that same wondrous sun seemed to burst into millions of sparkling stars falling through her, with her, in her.

She cried out at the wonder of it and heard his own cry mingle with hers as he buried himself and shudder after shudder of life-giving force ran from his body into hers.

They lay together afterward, arms and legs entwined, too awestruck for words.

James broke the silence first. "Has it ever been like that for you?"

Caroline wanted to laugh at the ludicrousness of the question. Instead she shook her head, still too humbled to find her voice. He laughed proudly, as if she'd shouted from the rooftops what she felt, and hugged her close to his chest, whispering, "It's never been that way for me either."

In that fashion they fell asleep.

Caroline woke to find James watching her. He brushed the hair out of her eyes. "Good evening, sleepyhead."

She sat up, no longer shy with him, and looked out the window. Clouds had formed and threatened rain, but she sensed that it was early evening.

"Hungry?" he asked.

"A bit," Caroline answered even as her stomach growled. He laughed. In her defense she said, "I haven't eaten anything today. I had other things on my mind, like a man in my cellar."

He kissed her forehead. "Don't worry, I'll find us something to eat."

"No, you don't have to. I'll go to the kitchen—"

He pressed her back on the bed. "I'll find something to eat. It's what men do—we hunt and forage. We've been doing it since time began."

"I hope you don't have to plunder the country-side," Caroline teased.

He nuzzled her breast. "I hope so too. I don't want to be gone too long from you."

Her stomach growled again.

"I'm going," he said and walked naked down to the kitchen. He brought back a round of cheese, a bottle of red wine, and a loaf of bread left from breakfast that morning. They sat cross-legged in the middle of the bed and shared the simple repast.

Each moment, she felt herself fall deeper and deeper in love. But instead of frightening her, the knowledge gave her strength. Enough strength to say, "I love you."

His eyes blazed with pride. "I love you, too," he whispered, and leaned over to steal a quick kiss.

The movement on the bed caused Caroline to nearly spill her glass. Several drops of wine splashed on her. She was glad it didn't hit the sheets, but her relief turned to a new, wilder emotion when James bent over and licked the drops up off her body, his tongue running slowly up her thigh.

This time, their lovemaking was heated and quick.

And just as soul-satisfying.

"I feel I can tell you anything." Caroline sat cross-legged on the bed, watching their reflection in the mirror. James sat with her cradled between his legs as he brushed her long straight hair out and down around her shoulders. They were both naked, having yet to find a use for clothes. The light from several candles made the room seem small and intimate. Caroline ran a possessive hand along the firm, muscular strength of his thighs.

He ran the brush through her hair, then slid his fingers along the silky texture. "You can. I would never betray you."

Her eyes met his in the looking glass. "I know."

He smiled. She loved the way he looked when he smiled. Not serious and intense but relaxed, masculine.

"I thought you were terribly arrogant when I first met you," she said.

"I still am . . . and I snore."

Caroline laughed, giving his thigh a playful squeeze. "I've already found that out."

James lifted the heavy curtain of her hair and placed a kiss below her ear. Caroline stirred, her back arching in response. His hand cupped her breast.

In the looking glass, Caroline saw their reflection and felt a quickening inside her.

"So tell me," he said, his voice low and husky in her ear. "What are your secrets?"

I'm barren. "I have no secrets," she answered.

He nibbled her neck before asking, "Then what do you wish for more than anything else in the world?"

Caroline leaned back against his chest. She could almost believe she had everything she ever wanted in the world. To love and be loved. Still . . . "A baby."

His head came up. Again, their eyes met in the looking glass. He smiled happily. "That's my wish, too."

Suddenly, Caroline didn't feel so sure of herself. "It is?"

"Aye." He tossed aside the brush and wrapped his arms protectively around her. "An heir. An heir to turn my businesses over to someday. A lad to raise to manhood just as my father raised me and my brothers. Or a daughter. I'd love a daughter just as much."

Caroline sat very still. For a second, she forgot to breathe. She struggled to find her voice. "That would be it? That's all you've ever wanted?"

He laughed, and began rubbing her neck, his strong fingers massaging the muscles. "That, and you." The hard evidence of his desire pressed against her backside, beckoning her.

She should tell him she was barren. She wanted to tell him. But then, his hand covered her breast with more strength of purpose than a simple caress. His leg pressed her back on the bed. Gratefully, Caroline ignored her doubts, her conscience. This time, she turned the aggressor. James loved it. His response was more intense than ever before and Caroline told herself that even if she could not give him a baby, he could have her.

Oh, yes, he could have her.

Minerva paced the floor of Charlotte's house.

When she hadn't received word from Caroline by half past nine that evening, she'd decided she must return home. Charlotte wanted to accompany her, but Minerva insisted she go alone. She'd already failed Caroline once that day. She could not do so again.

The sight of the dark house made her uneasy. Turning her key in the lock, Minerva chastised herself for not having returned home sooner. There wasn't a light on in the house, not even in the bedroom windows.

Fearing the worst, Minerva opened the door and felt her way in the dark for the table by the door, which held a supply of candles and lucifers. A moment later, a sulfur flame hissed and then steadied. Minerva lit a candle. Quietly, she signaled to Charlotte's coachman Pierre to wait a few minutes more.

Minerva was about to call out when her foot hit something. She raised the candle and saw she'd almost tripped over a lady's slipper. The flame highlighted a pile of dark material at the foot of the stairs. She lifted the material and recognized Caroline's dress. Beside it lay a man's neckcloth. And over by the hallway chair was a man's jacket, the sleeves inside out.

Minerva started up the stairs, where she found a lady's stocking and a man's shirt draped artistically. She moved silently up the steps, uncertain whether to be worried or pleased.

The door to Caroline's room was open. Shielding the candleflame with her hand, Minerva peeked into the room.

There on the bed lay James Ferrington and Caroline, sound asleep among tousled bedclothes modestly pulled up to cover their nakedness. Her head rested on his chest. His arms hugged her protectively.

All was right with the world at last, Minerva thought. She whispered a soft benediction on the lovers and blew out the candle. She retraced her steps easily in the dark, glad now that she'd had Pierre wait. Charlotte wouldn't mind having her as a guest for the night.

James woke up slowly at first. It had to be shortly before dawn. He was ready to roll back to sleep next to Caroline—when he realized, it was Friday.

His meeting!

He had to leave. Daniel and his other investors expected him to lead them in the meeting with the Board of Control and the East India Company. Quietly, he went around the house collecting their clothing.

He was doing a ham-handed job of tying his neckcloth when he caught sight of Caroline's reflection in the looking glass. She slept peacefully among the rumpled bed linens, her thick, shining hair hanging over one side of the bed. She was beautiful.

Then he heard a very soft, completely feminine snore and almost burst out laughing. Joyful laughter—the kind that celebrated life and the pleasure of living it to its fullest.

Crossing over to the bed, he woke her with a kiss.

She smiled when she recognized him, her lazy smile as smug as a satisfied cat's, until she saw he was dressed. Her brows came together. "You're leaving."

He sat on the edge of the bed. "Only for a few hours. I have that meeting with the bankers."

She gave a small laugh. "The important meeting?"

"The very important meeting," he agreed amicably. He brushed a few stray strands of hair from her face. "I'll see you later?"

"Like this?" she teased.

He laughed and kissed her nose. "Exactly like this." He rose from the bed but stopped before leaving the room, leaning on the doorjamb. "I love you."

She smiled, sleepy and content. "I love you, too." She shut her eyes. He watched her drift off to sleep before finally taking his leave.

Caroline woke up several hours later. Looking out the window, she could swear she'd never seen a day so sunny. A beautiful day. She sat up and caught sight of herself naked in the looking glass, but her nakedness didn't embarrass her. She'd be like Eve and never wear clothing. Maybe she and James could create their own Garden of Eden.

For the first time in her life she felt complete and whole.

For the first time in several days, she felt well rested.

And she wasn't going to wear black. She'd wear the blue ball gown if she had to, but she wouldn't wear black. Fortunately, in the recesses of her wardrobe, she found a lavender cambric day dress Minerva had purchased for her years ago. The time had come to wear it. And maybe today, she'd go to the drapery shop and see about material for more dresses. Brightly colored dresses. Dresses in every shade of the rainbow.

It took Caroline the better part of an hour to get dressed, to make the bed, to tidy the room. She kept pausing in her work and remembering the night before.

He'd said he would see her later. She didn't know when, she didn't know what it would mean—but suddenly the world was full of possibilities. What had been insurmountable problems, now appeared small and insignificant against the one unalterable truth that ruled her life.

She loved James Ferrington.

She heard a sound behind her. Caroline turned to see Minerva standing in her bedroom doorway. Her aunt didn't look herself. She looked fragile and pale, as if she'd received distressing news. "Is something the matter? Are you feeling well?"

The stricken expression on Minerva's face didn't change as she held out a copy of the *Morning Post*. Caroline crossed the room and took the newspaper from her. Minerva turned away.

Alarmed, Caroline's eyes quickly scanned the columns. The *Post* was turned to the society pages. There appeared to be nothing that pertained to her . . . until her eyes caught the name of James Ferrington.

She turned the paper to the window, the better to read and digest every word. It was an announcement. An engagement announcement for the daughter of the Earl and Countess of Lavenham to one James Ferrington.

She sat down on the bed. Five times she read the announcement, thinking there must be a mistake. She'd misunderstood. It couldn't be her James. Not the man she'd made love with, the man who'd declared he loved her.

Each time the announcement read the same.

"Caroline?" Minerva's worried voice came from the doorway.

She'd trusted him. A cold hardness stole around Caroline's heart.

"Are you all right?" Minerva asked.

Caroline heard her aunt's voice as if from a great distance. "Yes. I'll be all right," she whispered. The pain of his betrayal sliced through her. For a moment, she couldn't speak, couldn't even breathe . . . she crumpled the newspaper in her hand. "I'll survive," she promised. "I don't need him. And I'm going to make certain he understands that fact."

Chapter 15

W here have you been?"

James looked up from the papers spread across his desk to his partner standing in the study doorway. "Good morning, Daniel. It's good to see you, too." Then he stared. "Daniel, you should see your tailor. You look as if you've slept in your clothes or crawled through every hellhole in London.'"

Daniel stopped at the edge of his desk and started untying his limp and soiled neckcloth. "I did! Looking for you. I don't suppose it would do any good to ask you where you've been for the last twenty-four hours."

James didn't even look up from the report he was studying as he answered. "Not very much good, no."

"I've spent the last day and night looking for you. In between getting those reports done," Daniel declared, ignoring him.

"And a good job you've done, too." James flipped over a page. It was important that he commit as many facts to memory as possible. Over the past decade, the Crown had not been entirely pleased with the East India Company's aggressive policies in Mauritius and Java. Since his first day in London, James had petitioned Parliament to consider a new system of handling the India trade—the issuance of licenses for ships of a certain tonnage. This system would give the Board of Control more complete supervision over the Company's finances and had caught the interest of many in Parliament who wished to see the Company's wings clipped.

"I didn't know but what your body might show up floating in the Thames," Daniel said, still grumbling. He turned and marched toward the door. "I have a clean shirt upstairs. I'll be right down. Don't go anywhere." With that last command, he left James to push facts and figures into his brain in preparation for the presentation this morning.

James wasn't worried. This morning he felt as if he could conquer the world.

Because of Caroline.

The information he'd been trying to memorize fled his brain and was replaced by a picture of Caroline as he'd last seen her that morning, naked in bed, her body rosy from lovemaking.

He sat there daydreaming until Daniel charged into the room. "There are a number of new developments I have to tell you about," he said, his hands tying a fresh, starched neckcloth. "Collins from the bank is riding with us to the meeting. He's just returned from Java and is willing to give testimony to what the Company is doing there. They've set up their own government, even going against the wishes of their own directors. The Company directors had wanted native rule."

Daniel rubbed his hands together in anticipation. "I can't wait until Waitley, that Company bastard, sees us walk in with Collins." He referred to the East India Company agent who had so far successfully thwarted their efforts. "Yesterday, he tried to cancel the meeting twice. I think he'd heard word you were missing." Daniel shot James a dark look.

James smiled back, unrepentant. He pulled out his watch. It was close to nine. "Shouldn't we be leaving?" A rush of confidence and anticipation made him anxious to get started. This was it. The moment he'd dreamed of since the day he'd left to seek his fortune in the lucrative Orient trade.

"As soon as Collins appears—"

At that moment, Calleo appeared at the doorway. "*Sahib*, Mr. Collins waits for you in the receiving room." He bowed respectfully.

James's gaze met Daniel's. "Don't worry," he said, coming to his feet and stacking the ledger sheets on his desk in a single neat pile. "I've been at these since sunrise. You did a good job, Daniel. I think I've got it."

"Lavenham contacted me yesterday and said he is publicly throwing in his lot with us."

That was good news. James started for the door. "Then today is only a formality."

"James, I think there is something you should know—"

"Is it more important than this meeting?" James started down the hallway to the receiving room with purpose in his stride.

Following at his heels, Daniel looked surprised

for a moment before admitting, "Nothing is more important than this meeting."

"Then let me concentrate on what we are about to do. Now, don't look so worried. We will not lose."

Calleo held open the door to the receiving room, and James entered without breaking his step. He held his hand out. "Collins! Good of you to come with us this morning."

"I understand congratulations are in order. Lavenham's decision bodes well."

"Lavenham knows a good opportunity when he sees one," James answered. "But hold your congratulations until after the meeting. The East India Company is a crafty lot. They still have time to get our license request rejected."

"Not with Lavenham on your side," Mr. Collins said.

Calleo announced, "*Sahib*, your coach is waiting."

James took his hat from the servant and directed Mr. Collins to leave ahead of him.

The day was bright and sunny. Riding in his burled wood coach, James remembered the last time he'd ridden in it, the night he'd met Caroline. Consequently, he arrived at the Bank of England, the agreed-upon location, in even higher spirits.

Many of the key players had already arrived for the meeting. Gathered in the bank's Court Room were Sir Charles Chaney and Sir Victor Francis, both well-respected bankers; Lord Handley and his compatriot on the Board of Control, Lord Monleith; and representatives of the East India Company. Each group had its own assortment of clerks to take notes and do their bidding.

Waitley stood off to one side with two other men, who had the look of solicitors. They were surrounded by a bevy of junior men. James laughed as Daniel practically growled at the Company men.

James knew he would win, but he was surprised the others knew it too. The bankers and Parliament men were already wishing him well.

"Congratulations, Ferrington," Lord Handley said in greeting.

"I say, congratulations, Ferrington," Sir Charles said.

The well-wishes came from every important player in this meeting—except for the Company men.

The premature congratulations bewildered James. He considered it rather unorthodox for the gentlemen to be so free with their preferences before the hearing, but he took their good wishes in stride, especially since they made Waitley turn dour and glum.

He couldn't wait to tell Caroline about his victory.

Lord Handley directed the assembly to take their seats around the long mahogany table in the center of the room. Sir Charles called the meeting to order.

As Daniel and James had anticipated, the Company was not going to lie down and let them walk out with the license. They put up a damn good fight. The Company men stated their case eloquently. They'd done their research. They had documents and testimony to James's character, his business relationships, every fact and figure about his company. They showed him in the worst possible light. James wondered how much it had cost them to gather the information.

The two Parliament men who represented the Board of Control listened intently. Both men were close personal friends of the Earl of Lavenham.

James leaned toward Daniel and said in a low voice, "You are sure they support us?"

Daniel gave a sharp half laugh under his breath. "Absolutely."

James sat back.

When it came James's turn to speak, he quickly and deftly settled all counts against him, then easily relayed the information he'd memorized only that morning. James's business was his pride and joy. He knew it better than anyone else, including Daniel, and his confidence helped swing opinion in his favor.

After Mr. Collins's testimony of abuses of power that even the Company's own directors had not authorized, the Board of Control wasted little time in coming to a decision. James could have the license for a period of five years, upon which time the situation would be reviewed. The action ended the East India Company's two-hundred-year-old monopoly over the India trade.

Jubilant, James shook Daniel's hand. He shook the hands of the bankers and the men from the Board of Control. He almost shook "that bastard" Waitley's hand, except the Company men stormed off, angry. Daniel watched them go before turning to James and, with a lift of one brow, drawled, "I'm afraid that bastard Waitley's about to get sacked." Then he laughed, as happy as James.

The bankers, Mr. Collins, Sir Charles, and Sir Victor approached. "I'll see to the drawing up of the necessary paperwork," Mr. Collins said. He made as if to withdraw.

James wanted to leave immediately to see Caroline, but he understood the dictates of protocol. "No, come celebrate with me at my club." He turned to Lord Handley and Lord Montleith. "Please join me. I insist."

No one refused, and James soon herded the group toward White's. He wanted all of London to know he'd secured his license, that James Ferrington had reached the pinnacle of success. Today marked a turning point. No longer was he a small trader, albeit a wealthy one. In receiving the license and securing his investors, his fortune had tripled in worth in a matter of hours. By the end of the next decade, provided he played his cards right, he could be the richest man in London, in England. In two decades, who knew? Maybe the world.

And White's was the place to go to make sure that everybody who was important in government and society knew he'd scored a victory.

Raggett, the owner, met him the moment he shepherded his guests through the front door. Last year, when James had just arrived from India, Raggett hadn't known his name. Today, he bowed and said, "It's good to have you with us today, Mr. Ferrington. Congratulations."

"Thank you," James said, handing a footman his hat. He said to Daniel in an undervoice, "It's surprising how quickly the news has spread. I would not have thought it possible."

Daniel caught James up short. While the others were busy handing over their hats, he pulled James over to the side. "James, what exactly do you think they are all congratulating you about?"

Puzzled, James shrugged. "For being appointed a license to trade, of course."

Daniel laughed, shaking his head. "No, that's not it at all. They're congratulating you on your engagement to Lavenham's daughter."

"*What!*" James felt as if the floor had opened up under his feet. He grabbed the lapels of Daniel's coat and pulled him closer. "What are you saying?"

Daniel removed James's hands and pulled him into an alcove to one side, away from prying ears. "I told you this morning Lavenham threw his lot in with us. He came to me yesterday, ready to make the match. That's the other reason I was searching for you. For some reason that Lavenham can't even explain, his wife has decided to give her blessing to your engagement to her daughter Lena. She is positively thrilled with the idea."

"I'm to marry Lavenham's daughter?" The words sank in slowly.

"James, it is what you wanted. I tried to find you yesterday, but you were nowhere to be found. Lavenham was anxious to get the announcement in the papers before Lady Lavenham changed her mind. Did you know he uses moneylenders all the time? The poor old chap must be up to his ears in debt."

"Everyone is congratulating me for my engagement?" James asked in quiet disbelief.

"However, I agree with you now." Daniel clapped James on the back. "It's a very good match, even if you have to live with Lena's lisp. Between your business knowledge and Lavenham's contacts, no one will be able to stop us. Look how easily we won our case today."

"How do people know I'm engaged?" James almost feared the answer.

"Have you grown stupid?" Daniel asked irreverently. "I just said Lavenham wanted the announcement printed immediately, and I knew you would want the word out before the meeting. I placed the announcement in all the papers. It was to be in the *Post* this morning and the *Gazette*. I imagine everyone in town will know by the end of the day."

Everyone in town.

James turned on his heel and started toward the door. The servant scrambled to open it while the footman who'd taken his hat hurried to give it back. James grabbed it and stalked out the door.

Daniel chased him. "James, where are you going?"

"I've got to get to Caroline."

"Caroline?"

James dismissed him with an angry wave.

Still Daniel followed. "What about the bankers? Your guests?" Daniel pulled at his arm.

James shook him off angrily. "You deal with them."

"I can't do that! Not without you."

James stopped abruptly and turned to his partner. "You must."

For a second, Daniel stared at him as if truly seeing and understanding for the first time. His arms dropped to his side. "Will I see you later?"

"Maybe," James said shortly. He hurried up the street before adding to himself, "If I'm still alive."

James didn't stop until he reached Caroline's doorstep. He took the steps up to her house in one leap and rapped on the door.

A moment later, her aged butler opened the door. He looked James up and down, his wig shifting on his bald head with the motion, and then lifted his brows in clear disapproval of what he saw. "May I help you?" he asked with stiff formality.

"I'm here to see Lady Pearson."

"May I have your name?"

"You know damn well what my name is, just as I know your name is Jasper! You had breakfast with me yesterday morning after I spent a night in the cellar."

Jasper raised his eyebrows in shock at James's angry tone, but he didn't budge.

"Ferrington," James snarled. "Mr. James Ferrington."

"One moment, sir, and I'll see if Lady Pearson is at home to you." Jasper shut the door in James's face.

James wasn't accustomed to cooling his heels on anyone's steps—but he did so for Caroline. She must have seen the announcement. Nothing else could explain her servant's rudeness. His mind conjured up her reaction. She would be shocked, hurt. Maybe even angry. He had to get to her, assure her that his love for her was constant and true.

Just when he was about to lose patience and knock again, the door opened. Jasper bowed, almost losing his wig. "This way, sir."

James stepped in and handed his hat to the butler.

"She is in the parlor." Jasper nodded to the closed door.

James walked over to the door and started to lose

his nerve. All the times he'd been in this house, he'd never seen this door shut. "Tell me," he said to the butler, who was already on his way down the short hall, "has Lady Pearson read the papers today?"

Jasper looked at him with haughty disdain, which was almost comical in someone so short. "Lady Pearson takes all the London papers," he replied, before turning on his heel and proceeding down the hall. The butler's announcement didn't bode well for James. Suddenly, he wasn't overanxious for the confrontation with Caroline.

Meanwhile, Jasper had gone only a few more steps when Minerva's head popped out of the back room, which was used as a reading room and office. "Announce him," she hissed in an undervoice.

Startled, the confused manservant turned back toward the parlor. "Announce him! Of course. Of course!"

Minerva's head disappeared back behind a closed door as her butler hurriedly retraced his steps.

Minerva quickly tiptoed over to the wall between the parlor and the reading room. Charlotte, Violetta, and Lady Mary were already there with crystal glasses held up to the wall in an attempt to hear everything that was going on in the next room.

"It's a pity your walls are so thick," Violetta whispered.

"Yes, a pity." Minerva agreed, and picked up her glass. She crouched next to Lady Mary.

James stood outside the closed parlor door, taking a moment to straighten the knot in his neckcloth. He squared his shoulders and was reaching for the door handle when Jasper reappeared and put his hand on the handle first.

"I'll announce you, sir," he said with a glower. He started to turn the door handle when he realized he still held James's hat in his hand. For a moment, he seemed puzzled as to what to do with it before he turned and tossed it onto the staircase newel-post.

Satisfied, Jasper opened the door, stepped into the room, and drawled out in sonorous tones fit for a ballroom, "Mr. James Ferrington."

Jasper bowed for James to enter.

But James didn't enter. He stared slack-jawed at the scene in front of him. Caroline was sitting on the settee, the flowers that he'd purchased still on every available table space—but this was not *his* Caroline who wore widow's black and did charity work.

In fact, he wasn't entirely sure this luscious creature was Caroline at all.

Her hair had been pulled back and curled so that it fell in charming disarray around her bare shoulders. A lush red velvet dress, cut low over her breasts, molded her figure as if it had been painted on her body. When she looked up to see who had entered the room, she drew a breath and James found himself holding his, sure that she would overflow the almost-nonexistent bodice.

But what truly riveted his attention was the man on his knees at her bare feet, painting her toenails. And the two other fellows who leaned over the settee as if they, too, expected her to pop out of her dress and could barely wait for the moment.

"James!" she said gaily, her eyes bright. "Come join us." She patted a place next to her on the settee and started laughing as the man on the floor ran his finger along the arch of her foot. She squirmed, and the men leaning over the back of the small couch held their breath, their eyes on her cleavage.

She was using cosmetics. To great advantage, James thought angrily, as she captured her tickling attacker by cupping his chin in her hands, her rubied lips pouting slightly before she chastised him with a shake of her head. "No, no," she teased—and then kissed him on the nose!

James's blood began a slow boil.

The man she'd kissed threw himself dramatically down on the ground, clutching his heart as if struck by her kiss. Caroline giggled, the sound warm and delighted.

James had never seen such complete foolishness, and he was about to grumpily tell her so when he recognized the man on the floor. "Devon Marshall!" The most notorious rake in London! The man had bastard children scattered from London to Edinburgh and not a shilling to his name. If it moved, and "it" was female, he seduced it. And he was a charming enough scamp to get away with it.

"Get up, man. You're making a bloody fool of yourself!" James practically spit the words out.

Lord Marshall raised his head, the effect almost comical, except James wasn't laughing. "Is that you, Ferrington? Bloody jolly to see you."

James sat stiffly on the edge of the settee and crossed his arms. "Don't bloody swear in front of a lady."

"I didn't swear—"

"You did too. You said 'bloody.'" James frowned.

"You said 'bloody,' too."

"I did not."

"You did too."

"Did not!"

"You did, Ferrington," said one of the gentlemen behind the couch. "I heard you."

James turned and looked at the fellow. He was a young one with deep blue eyes and curly dark hair. The kind of man women swooned over. "Who are you?"

Caroline laughed, the sound enchanting. "This is Alex—I mean, the Viscount Thierry." She leaned over and placed her hand on the arm of the soulful-looking young—very young—man with blond hair and liquid brown eyes who was leaning over the settee. "And this is Bannastre Lynnford. He is a friend of Alex's and brought me this marvelous spray of roses."

For the first time, James realized that not all the flowers in the room were the ones he'd purchased.

Caroline reached back to the vase of roses on a nearby table and pulled out one perfect, creamy pink long-stemmed rose. She held it up to her nose. "The fragrance is heavenly." She stretched, as languid as a cat on a sunny afternoon. "How did you know I adore roses, Bannastre?"

The thought shot through James that he hadn't known she liked roses. He would have bought her dozens and dozens if he'd known she liked them.

"I love their fragrance . . . and their texture." She smiled and began waving the rose lightly back and forth. "So fresh, so smooth, so seductive." The rose touched the full mound of one breast swelling high over her bodice, and then the other to emphasize her words.

The men's heads bounced back and forth with the movement of the rose even as Caroline ran the flower up her breast, along the curve of her collarbone, and along her neck to rest against her cheek—a path that James had followed the night before with his lips. His mouth went dry. His body tensed, hot desire thrumming through his veins.

Apparently he wasn't the only one reacting in such a manner.

"I feel a poem forming inside me," the young Bannastre said, his voice husky with a need James recognized all too well.

Caroline turned to the young pup. "To me?"

"To your roses," Bannastre declared fervently—and James knew he wasn't talking about roses! "Where are paper and pen?"

Caroline smiled. "Over in the secretary." She nodded to the small desk where James had cornered her only the other day. A sudden vision danced before his mind's eye of Bannastre cornering his Caroline there and making wild, passionate love to her on top of sheets of poetry.

James couldn't write poetry.

He hated poetry.

He hated poets.

"And what about me?" Lord Marshall said. He sat on the floor, one knee up, looking roguishly elegant in top boots and thigh-hugging trousers. "I'm a slave at your feet. Mortally wounded. Kiss me, Caroline. I beg you."

Kiss me, Caroline. Hadn't James said those words last night when he'd held her in his arms and brought her to passion. He couldn't stand the thought of another man knowing what a passionate, giving creature she was between the sheets, or anywhere else.

He was about to growl at Marshall when Caroline laughed. "I can't kiss you," she said.

"Why not?" Marshall asked, his charming smile turning to a frown of disappointment.

"Because you haven't finished painting the nails on my other foot," Caroline said sweetly.

Marshall came up to his knees in one fluid movement. "Then let me, my lady. Let me worship at your feet. I will paint your nails with my tongue—"

"Your tongue?" James barked out, unable to contain himself any longer.

At that moment the puppy Bannastre cleared his throat and read from a hastily scribbled upon piece of paper. "The Breath of a Rose Upon My Lady's Breast—"

"That's ridiculous." James crossed his arms. "Roses don't breathe!"

"James," Caroline chastised mildly, "he's taking poetic license."

James barely heard her. Instead, his attention was captured by Marshall, who was on his hands and knees dipping a small brush into a pot of paint. He took Caroline's foot in his hands, much as James had taken the same foot the night before on the staircase, and lifted it to his lips.

Jealousy shot through James. He clenched his fists. "Caroline, I need to talk to you. Alone. In private."

He didn't bother to keep his voice low. He itched

to throw out the whole lot of them. Marshall smiled good-naturedly at the couple on the couch. "You can't have her all to yourself, Ferrington."

"And why not?" James asked rudely.

"I'd challenge you for her. Caroline is truly quite extraordinary." Marshall emphasized his words by lightly biting the arch of her foot.

James shot up from his seat on the couch, ready for a fight. He'd rip the man's head off!

Marshall also rose to his feet to meet the unspoken challenge. The room vibrated with tension.

Caroline came to her feet as well and stood between the two men. "James. Devon. Please, there is no need for this." Her sparkling eyes, brimming with—of all things—laughter, looked up at him. "Let me settle this fairly. Devon painted the nails on one foot. Now it is James's turn."

The viscount gave a soft sigh. "I was hoping you would let me do it, Caroline."

She considered for a moment. "Well, if James does not wish to exercise his turn, I would be glad to give it to you."

The poet called out, "Are you ready for the first verse?"

"Why, is it finished already?" Caroline asked.

Bannastre crushed the paper to his chest. "With such beauty as yours to inspire me, it does not take a day to write a poem. Not even so much as an hour."

Caroline laughed, apparently flattered by the idiot's nonsense. Then she turned to James. "So, are you going to paint my toenails, James, or shall my precious viscount have the honor?"

Until that moment, James had considered "seeing red" an expression. He prided himself on control, sharpness of mind and planned, carefully well-thought-out moves:

But he saw red now, even as he swung Caroline up in his arms and marched with her out of the parlor, across the hallway, and into the small dining room. He unceremoniously set her on her feet, kicked the door shut, and, turning to face her, growled out, "Now we will talk."

Chapter 16

"T alk about what?" Caroline turned and faced him, the hem of her skirts swirling around her ankles.

Dear Lord, he couldn't bear the thought of losing her.

"My engagement."

Caroline shrugged one elegant shoulder. "Oh. Are you engaged? I'm sorry, I hadn't heard."

"You don't lie well."

"Unfortunately, you do."

Her point hit its mark. James took a step back, suddenly unsure of himself. "Caroline—"

"You don't owe me an explanation—"

"Yes, I do."

"No, you don't." She moved away from him, as if feeling the need to put distance between them. "Nor do I want to hear one. What you *do* owe me is the deed to my house."

"I'll send you the deed."

"Yes? Well, that's very thoughtful of you," she said dryly. "Now, if you will excuse me, I have guests."

James stepped in front of her, blocking her way to the door. "My marriage is a business arrangement, nothing more, nothing less—"

Her hand came up, cutting him off. "No." For a brief second, he saw in her clear eyes the pain he'd caused her. She blinked and it disappeared, replaced by an icy coldness. "We are done."

"Please, don't say that."

"Why not? It's true, isn't it? Or did you think I would agree to be your mistress? Is that what last night was? A test of sorts?"

"Last night had nothing to do with what is happening now. When I saw Lady Lavenham at the ball, she all but informed me that she would refuse my marriage offer."

"She's obviously changed her mind," Caroline answered, her voice brittle.

"But I didn't know that. Caroline, I've been with you since the ball. It wasn't until today that I found out I was officially betrothed."

"Why didn't you tell me of the offer? You've had ample opportunity to say, 'Caroline, I've already asked for the hand of another woman.' You could have given me some warning."

She was right. He could have said something. "I didn't think." The excuse sounded lame to his own ears, but it was the truth. "Everything between us has happened so quickly."

Caroline studied him for a moment before shaking her head. "I believe you. I'm still so starry-eyed that I want to believe you. Isn't that ridiculous? I must be in love to be so baffle-brained."

"No, I'm the one who is wrong because I've ruined everything. Caroline, Lena doesn't care for me. She's not even fond of me. I love you. There must be a way we can be together. Lena may have my name, but you would have my love."

"James, do you honestly believe that you could have your wife and me also?"

If God could have granted James Ferrington one wish at that moment, it would have been to answer "no" to her question. To say it truthfully, honestly, and without hesitation. Instead, he whispered, "I don't want to give you up."

She took a slight step back. Her head lifted proudly. "The decision isn't yours. I would never accept the role of paramour. It goes against everything I was taught to believe. Do you think men are the only ones with honor?"

"Caroline—"

"No. I'm going to have my say. Be honest, James. You came running over here this afternoon expecting to find me swooning in female hysterics over your betrayal. Well, I'm not." She straightened her shoulders. "What I did last night may not have been right, but it was what I chose to do. I accept responsibility for what happened between us . . . However, there is no room in my life for you. When I give myself again, it will be to a man who doesn't lie to me."

"Caroline, I didn't lie to you."

"You never told me the truth either. And that counts, James. That counts," she added, her voice soft. She crossed her arms as if warding off the cold and added, her voice strong and sure, "I may not have my position at Miss Elmhart's or be welcome at St. Mark's, but I have my self-respect. And I have friends like Minerva, on whom I can trust and depend. I will survive. What I don't need is you."

She dropped her arms to her sides before finishing,

"And no, I will not share you with your wife. Ever."

From somewhere in the house a clock marked time, but it seemed as if time had lost all meaning. Everything in his life had turned to ash.

"Yes," he said, "I understand." He stepped aside.

Caroline didn't waste a second. She stepped around him and opened the door to reveal a smirking Marshall leaning negligently against the parlor doorframe, waiting for them. Behind him, the two young lords shuffled their feet, embarrassed to be caught eavesdropping.

James struggled with an urge to smash his fist into Marshall's grinning face.

Marshall's smile widened. He looked to Caroline. "Is everything all right, Caroline?"

James couldn't believe his ears. She permitted Marshall to use her Christian name.

"Everything is fine, Devon," she said—and James went wild with jealousy.

Bitter disappointment mingled with outright anger. He wanted to pound something, to vent his rage—and the closest thing at hand was Devon Marshall's smiling countenance. James doubled his fist, took the two steps to bring him toe to toe with the man, and punched Marshall a good one in the jaw.

Marshall's head snapped round and he stumbled back through the doorway onto the floor, landing right at the feet of the two young pups.

Caroline gave a cry of alarm and rushed to Marshall's side. Kneeling beside him, her velvet skirts spread around her, she took Marshall's head in her lap. Marshall made the most of it, groaning as he languished in her arms. James wanted to pull him to his feet and pop him again—especially when the rakish lord rested his head against Caroline's breasts.

The sound of feet running down the hallway surprised James and then Caroline's Aunt Minerva, the Baroness, Mrs. Mills, and Lady Mary rushed into the room. "What happened?" Minerva asked anxiously.

Caroline looked up at James, her gaze burning with accusation. "Mr. Ferrington, I must ask you to leave."

"Caroline," he started, then caught himself. He was a man, damn it, not some mewing courtier. If this was Malacca or Canton, and not a London drawing room, he could have shot the man dead and no one would have raised a challenge!

James straightened his shoulders. The old ladies looked at him with wide-eyed amazement. The two young pups practically shook in their boots while Marshall made groaning noises that sounded so completely feigned, Caroline must realize the man was playacting.

She didn't. Instead, she cradled him closer to her bosom.

And James could do nothing to stop her. He had no right. He was engaged to another woman. In the eyes of society, he was as good as married to Lena. The restraints of social convention tightened around him until he felt he could no longer breathe.

From somewhere the butler appeared and offered James his hat.

James put it on his head and, without a backward glance at Caroline cooing words of comfort to his victim, let himself out of the house.

His coach waited for him on the street. James motioned the coachman aside and took the reins himself, feeling the need to drive, to be in control . . . since he no longer felt in control of his own destiny.

Sitting on top of the coach, he found he had nowhere to go. He should return to White's and the party of men he'd left when he'd run off to find Caroline, but he didn't want company. His success of the morning lost all meaning when compared to the loss of Caroline.

With a snap of the reins, he set the coach in motion, not caring in which direction he drove. Riding through London, he remembered his arrival there a year ago. He'd been confident then that he would conquer this city—and he, a squire's son from Kent, had done exactly that. Every door was open to him. So much so that soon he would be the son-in-law of the Earl of Lavenham. And someday, he could earn, or buy, a title of his own to go with his even greater fortune. There were no limits to how high he could climb.

But he no longer had any desire to reach for those goals.

He'd driven to the outskirts of the city. Tired of aimless wandering, James spied a sign advertising an alehouse. He pulled over and turned the reins over to his coachman. "Take the coach to White's and see if Daniel needs you."

"Do you want me to come back for you, sir?" the coachman asked.

James jumped down to the ground. "No."

"Then how will you be getting home, sir?"

"I'll find my way." James started for the ale-house.

"What shall I tell Mr. Harvey if he asks?"

"Tell him that this time, I don't want to be found," James threw over his shoulder before entering the alehouse.

The minute the door shut behind James, Caroline dropped Marshall's head to the floor, where it landed with a bounce.

"Ow," the rake said.

"How dare you?" Caroline snapped. She rose to her feet.

"Dare he what?" Minerva asked.

Caroline wasn't about to say, "Stick his nose down my bodice" to her aunt, no matter the woman's past. She crossed her arms protectively and moved away from Marshall, who sat up on the floor rubbing the back of his head and the side of his jaw.

"Ferrington can plant a good facer," he admitted cheerfully.

"You can laugh about it?" the viscount said. "He knocked you a foot backwards."

Marshall hopped to his feet. "I've been knocked farther than that." He looked to the younger men. "It's one of the hazards of the chase—especially if the female in question belongs to another man. I had one husband throw me out of a second floor window. That laid me up a bit. But I'm back." He shot a winsome smile in Caroline's direction.

She ignored him. The passion of anger and need for justice that had been carrying her suddenly deserted her. He was gone. Just like that, James Ferrington was out of her life.

Marshall came to her aid. "You look as if you need to sit down." He took her elbow and directed her to a chair. Caroline gratefully sank into the cushions. "Thank you," she whispered. He patted her hand, the rake replaced by a kind man.

Minerva brought her a glass of wine from the decanter on the secretary. "Are you all right?"

"What did he say?" Lady Mary demanded. "We couldn't hear a thing."

"Did you make him grovel?" the Baroness asked.

"Forget that," Lady Mary said with a snort. "What did he say? What did you say?"

Caroline shook her head. The events of the last few minutes were jumbled in her head with feelings of emptiness and regret. She felt as she had felt the day her parents had died, uncertain of the reality and dreading the moment when she did understand. "It's over," she managed to say.

"Oh," Lady Mary said, her disappointment plain.

Minerva came to her rescue. "There is time enough later for all of this. Let us give Caroline a moment or two alone."

"Does that mean we've fulfilled our end of the bargain, Aunt Mary?" the viscount asked from the parlor doorway.

Lady Mary looked up in surprise, as if just discovering that her nephew and his friend were still there. She paused for a moment before dismissing them with a wave of her hand. "Go on, you scamps. You did a good job. My William would have been proud of you."

"You won't forget our bargain, will you?" the viscount said. "Bannastre and I both get a new pair of boots from the bootmaker of our choice. Remember?"

"I remember. I remember," his aunt said. "Run along now and send the bills to me."

"I don't want boots," Bannastre said quietly. He crossed over to Caroline and gave her the paper with the poem written on it. "Mine was not an act, my lady. I mean the words on this paper. I would be deeply in your debt if you would allow me to call upon you again."

His sincerity surprised her. She looked down at the words on the page, the letters blurring. Thoughtfully, Caroline took his hand in hers. "I'm touched by your kindness, Mr. Lynnford . . . but not right now."

His cheeks turned a shade of red. He dropped his hand. "Of course. Cow-handed of me."

Caroline hated embarrassing him but couldn't find it in herself to be more encouraging. And he was young. A pup, as James had called him.

Lady Mary took charge. "Come, both of you." She took Bannastre's and the viscount's arms. "Take me home. I'm in need of a nap. There isn't much going on anymore."

The two young men dutifully did as they were told.

"Are you coming, Violetta?" Lady Mary called over her shoulder.

"Yes, I'll be right there," Mrs. Mills said. She started to follow but stopped in front of Caroline. "I'm sorry it didn't work out. I wish it had." She gave Caroline's hand a light squeeze and left.

"You know the best thing for forgetting a bad romance is to start another," a deep male voice said beside her.

Caroline turned with some surprise and found herself looking into the midnight blue eyes of Devon Marshall. He'd pulled a footstool alongside her chair and lightly ran his hand along her arm. Caroline shivered, unmoved. She shook her head, the rejection unspoken.

Marshall's lopsided grin turned rueful. "Ferrington is a lucky man."

"Was," the Baroness corrected. "Was. Come, *mon cher*, and let us give Caroline a moment of peace. She's not cut of the same cloth as you and I."

Marshall rose. "It's a pity." He lightly touched Caroline's hair. "If you ever need me, tell Charlotte."

"Yes," the Baroness said with a touch of amusement. "He always comes running at my beck and call."

"I did this time, didn't I?" He offered his arm to the older woman.

"Ah, Devon, you are always so gallant. It is a pity not all Englishmen have your dash."

"That's because not all Englishwomen appreciate me as you do."

"Too many already have, *chéri*," came the Baroness's light reply. A moment later they'd left.

Jasper closed the door behind them and appeared in the parlor. "Will there be anything else, Lady Pearson?" He rarely deferred to Caroline if Minerva was present, and it told Caroline that he was as sorry as anyone else that things couldn't be different.

Minerva replied, "That will be all." Caroline was glad. She didn't have the energy to respond.

The manservant bowed and left them alone.

Minerva broke the silence first. "It will get better, Caroline. With time."

Caroline looked at her hands, lying limp in her lap. "Yes."

The long seconds stretched between them. With one breath Caroline wished she'd never met James Ferrington so that she could discover what had been missing in her life; in the next breath, she denied that wish. How terrible it would have been to spend a lifetime without knowing the magic of those too few moments in his arms.

"Isn't there anything that can be done?" Minerva asked. The frustration in her voice echoed in Caroline's own soul.

"No."

"Did you ask him to break the engagement?"

Caroline looked at Minerva for the first time. "I couldn't ask him to do that. A gentleman doesn't break off an engagement. Such an action would ruin James socially. It would be a disgrace . . . not only to him but also to Lavenham's daughter."

"I hate Society, with all its rules."

Minerva had voiced that sentiment before, but for the first time Caroline could agree with her. She stood. "I need to get out of this dress so that we can return it to the Baroness."

"She's not anxious for it. It doesn't have to be done right now. She hasn't worn it for years."

Caroline managed a slight smile. "When she seduced a German prince, right?"

Minerva returned her smile. "German princes are easy to seduce. She wore that one for a Greek king."

"My mistake," Caroline said with a lightness she

didn't feel. "Well, I'd better get out of it. I can barely breathe. And I have to remove this paint from my toes." She made a face at her red-lacquered toenails peeping out from under her skirts. "Where did the Baroness get this paint?"

"A Manchurian warlord."

"Tell me, Minerva, has your life been as adventurous as hers?"

Minerva laughed, the sound genuine and warm. "No. Charlotte is a breed apart."

Caroline nodded and started to leave, but Minerva placed a hand on her arm, stopping her. "Someday there will be someone else in your life."

Caroline drew a deep breath, feeling the seams of the dress ease with her breath. She shook her head. "No. Not like this. I feel as if he took a part of me with him when he walked out the door."

Minerva dropped her hand. Tears welled in her eyes. "My poor child. I wish I could spare you this."

"Were you ever sorry, Minerva, that you chose the life you did?"

Minerva rocked back on her heels, caught by surprise. Slowly, she shook her head. "Years ago, when I was younger and with the other men—but not with my Bernardo. I loved him, Caroline, and he loved me. But there was always something bittersweet about our love. A man who is married can never give you his full love. If I'd had my choice, it would not have happened the way it did."

Caroline pressed her lips together. She felt so shaky inside. She started up to her room, needing to be alone, then stopped on the staircase.

She looked down at Minerva who stood at the

bottom of the stairs. "I know this will sound funny, but I was thinking earlier today how much Trumbull and James are alike."

"Trumbull and James have nothing at all in common!"

Caroline smiled at Minerva's staunch defense of James's character. "Yes, they do. Both men have strong characters. Each likes to have his own way, and each has a touch of arrogance. But in Trumbull those qualities were mean-spirited and hateful. In James, I found them challenging, invigorating. I was never afraid to disagree with him, or to show him my temper. I was *myself* with him." She paused before adding quietly, "I'm going to miss him very much."

Up in her room, she shut the door behind her, unlaced the dress, and slipped into her white nightdress. Sitting on the edge of the bed, Caroline looked out the window at the sheltering branches of the elm tree. Time lost meaning. Minerva knocked once and asked if she wanted a light supper. Caroline didn't answer. Weighed down by grief, she'd lost the will to speak, to think.

Finally, knowing she must move, she slipped under the covers. The sheets smelled of James—warm, masculine, loving. She curled her arms around the pillow and fell into sleep, waiting for tears that refused to come.

Something woke her. Caroline lay in bed for a moment, disoriented—until she heard the sound again. Hail hit the window, then stopped.

Caroline sat straight up in bed. It couldn't have been hail. She could see the moon between the branches of the elm tree.

The windowpanes rattled again as another light barrage assailed them.

Rising from bed, she crossed to the window. No hail. And then the panes rattled again and she realized that something had been thrown at the window. She opened it and looked outside.

"Caroline," a voice hissed in the still calm of the night.

Startled, Caroline looked around and then down through the tree branches. A man stood in her small yard, his white shirt bright in the moonlight.

Not just any man. James Ferrington.

Her heart stopped beating.

"Caroline, I have to talk to you."

She should close the window. Now, with a resounding slam.

Instead, she slid down to the floor and leaned her arms against the window ledge—not wanting to let him go. Not yet.

"Please, Caroline."

She shook her head. Her throat hurt to talk. She didn't want to prolong the pain.

"Wait, Caroline, one moment." A cloud covered the moon, and, a second later, she heard the leaves of the tree begin to shake.

She found her voice. Up on her knees, she leaned out the window. "What are you doing?"

"Climbing up to you," came his huffed reply.

"You're climbing a tree! James, get down now. You'll fall and break your leg, or worse."

He laughed, the sound almost lighthearted. "I climbed trees all the time as a lad, and ship rigging since the day I first stepped aboard one." The cloud passed. With the grace of an acrobat, he swung up into the branch almost level with her window and settled himself, his legs hanging free, his back against the trunk. He'd removed his neckcloth, and his open collar gave him the rakish look of a pirate. "Don't worry. I don't plan on climbing out on the limb." He shot her a quick grin, his teeth flashing white in the darkness. "Unless you encourage me."

Suspicious, Caroline asked, "Are you foxed?"

"A bit," he conceded genially. "Then, I realized that I wouldn't find what I wanted in the bottom of a bottle." His grin faded to a look of sober contemplation. "Caroline, I'm sorry."

She pulled back, defensive. "To say that, you could have come in through the front door."

"Would you have let me enter if I had?"

"No."

"Then I made the right choice."

Caroline leaned her arms on the ledge, suddenly needing this moment alone with him. "Possibly," she said slowly, "but it doesn't matter."

"Yes, it does. Don't ever say it doesn't matter."

She drew in a deep breath. "Then I'll say it matters too much."

"Yes."

For a long second they stared at each other in the night. He said quietly, "I needed to see you again. I have to tell you—"

"James, it's not necessary," Caroline cut in, suddenly afraid of what he might say . . . what she might do if he asked.

"Yes, it is. At first when I left I was angry, hurt. And wildly jealous. Then I realized the nonsense with Marshall and the others was a performance for my benefit. It was, wasn't it?"

Her back stiffened. "Of course not," she started to deny, then stopped. "Yes. But how did you know?"

He shook his head. "It was so completely out of character for you."

"You can't see me as a paramour?"

"I can see you all too well as a paramour, but I know your favors aren't easily given. I acted like an ass this afternoon." He leaned toward her. "Caroline, I made the offer to Lavenham's daughter months before I met you—"

"James—"

"No, don't deny me this, Caroline. I've never loved a woman before." He paused before adding softly, "Losing you is almost unbearable."

She heard his pain in every word—and felt it, since it mirrored her own heart.

"It was business, Caroline. Business and nothing more. I made the offer to win Lavenham's support for my license. But from the moment I met you, I forgot Lena . . . I forgot everything."

"And will this marriage give you everything you wanted?" she asked, her voice cold as she searched for an opportunity to hate him.

"Yes," he said simply. "Lavenham's name helped me secure the license for the shipping rights." He laughed, the sound bitter. "You see, Caroline, I've turned a new leaf. I tell nothing but the truth from now on. I am a man who doesn't lie. This marriage will give me everything I've ever dreamed of wanting." He stretched out on the tree limb toward her before adding, "But I've discovered that it means nothing without you."

She couldn't speak. Instead, she reached out, taking hold of the tip of the branch on which he lay as if she could reach him. "How simple we were before we first met. Two people who felt complete, alone and unto ourselves."

"But were you happier?"

"No."

"Caroline, run away with me."

His words shocked her.

"We'll leave London and marry on our way to the coast," he said.

"James—"

"Please. This afternoon, I realized how empty my life is without you. And in my heart, I'm married to you. I can't take vows before God to marry another woman."

For a moment, she was tempted. And then reality set in. "We can't."

"It's the only way. I saw Lavenham this evening. He'll let me buy my way out of the marriage agreement, but the countess refuses to release me from my promise. Suddenly, she's decided that I am the only son-in-law she wants. Caroline, we have no choice, not if we are to be happy. We can be gone by morning."

"And where would we go?"

"To the Americas. To the Spice Islands. Anywhere as long as we can be together. I built one fortune. I can build another."

He sounded so eager, so sure of himself. "You'd give up everything for me?" she asked.

"Yes."

Caroline sat back on her heels and slowly shook her head. "No. We can't. You'd be giving up a decade of dreams. I can't let you do that."

"The dreams don't matter anymore."

"Yes, they do, and if you don't try and follow

your dreams, James, then you wouldn't be the man you are." Caroline traced the window ledge with one finger before saying thoughtfully, "The reason Minerva's family disowned her is because she ran away, and it led to a tragic accident for both her and her lover. I asked her this afternoon after you'd left if she'd ever regretted the decisions she made. And, yes, she has regrets." Caroline leaned against the window ledge. "I think, James, that if we ran away, if you gave up everything for me, someday you might regret it."

He started to deny it, but she shook her head. "I know what you say now, but I would always wonder. . . . So, no, James, I will not run off with you."

"Then we'll stay here."

"And face the scandal down?"

"We can do it."

He was so full of hope, but she had a clear-eyed view of the price they would be forced to pay. "You would be ruined. You don't know how vicious Society can be. Not only will we be condemned, but the reputation of an innocent young girl will be drawn into the scandal. There is no honorable way out, darling, other than Lavenham's releasing you from your promise."

"I never meant to hurt you," he said, his expression bleak, his voice hoarse with pent-up emotion. "I'll never be complete again."

Neither would she. Without him in her life, there would be no other.

She loved him.

And because she loved him, she would give him her trust, and a chance to realize how wise he was to be rid of her. "It's best this way—"

"No."

"Yes." She reached out her hand until it touched the branch he sat on. "James, I can't have children. I'm barren. I couldn't have given you what you truly wanted. I couldn't have given you a baby."

"How do you know this?" he demanded.

"Trumbull and I tried. He wanted an heir. But I never became pregnant." Her cheeks burned with her admission.

He was silent a moment. Then he leaned forward on the branch, his arm stretching out until the tips of his fingers brushed hers. Caroline closed her eyes, rocked by the power of his touch.

His words came to her through the night. "Caroline, I want you more than I want to sire a child. You're a part of me."

And she believed him.

She had to let him go, but she couldn't—not yet. *Please, God, forgive me.* "James, come to me."

He didn't need a second invitation. With the agility of a cat, he slipped from the limb and through the open window. Caroline took him in her arms. Their lips met.

Here, sheltered by the night, they could be as one.

Caroline watched the first light of dawn spread across the sky. Lying beside him, she traced a heart on his chest. He caught her hand and reverently placed a kiss on the tips of her fingers, drawing her closer.

"You must leave," she warned.

"Caroline—"

She placed her finger to his lips to stop the flow

of words. "Please, no more. We've made our decision. Let's not make it harder."

He leaned up to look down at her. Gently, he pushed her hair from her face. "If I could have been honored to call you my wife, there isn't a day that would have passed that I would not have thanked God for my good fortune. I don't love easily, Caroline. I love you."

Caroline wrapped her arms around his neck, hugging him, needing to remember the feel of his body next to hers, the smell of his skin, the beat of his heart. "I don't know if I'll be able to live without you," she whispered against his neck. "I wish time would stop. I wish I could command it to stay right here in this moment."

"We can still run away. Will you come with me?"

Caroline shook her head. "I can't."

She knew it wasn't the answer he wanted.

He looked as if he would say something else, and then thought better of it. Quietly, he rose from the bed and began dressing. Caroline rolled herself in the sheets on the side of the bed still warm from his body.

They'd never be alone again, never like this— and suddenly the years ahead stretched long and empty before her. But she had no regrets. She'd never regret loving James Ferrington.

A second later, the mattress gave as he sat down on the bed beside her. She sat up, holding the sheet with one hand to hide her nakedness and faced him.

He smiled, the expression heart-stoppingly dear to her. She traced his lips with the tips of her fingers. "I've always loved your smile."

"One last hug, darling," he said.

She threw her arms around him and squeezed him as if she would never let him go—and then she did let him go, pushing him away before she lost all self-control.

He drew in a deep, steadying breath. "If you ever need me," he said, *"for anything,* send a message and I will be by your side as quickly as humanly possible. Promise me you'll remember that."

She couldn't promise him. She couldn't speak as she swallowed back tears. She nodded her head.

"Good night, my love," he whispered. He gave her a quick kiss. For the briefest of moments, his hand cupped the back of her head, and then he went to the window. He swung outside and into the elm's massive branches. A moment later, she heard him hit the ground. His footsteps hurried across the yard, the gate creaked as he opened it and then . . . she could hear him no more.

Caroline lay down on the bed, pulling the sheets up and over her head. "No regrets," she whispered.

At last the tears came.

In her room next to Caroline's, Minerva sat in a chair by the window. She'd overheard the whispered conversation between the lovers in the middle of the night. That conversation reminded her so much of another, decades ago, between herself and Robert, a man very similar to James Ferrington. A man she had loved.

Now she listened to the soft, muffled sounds of weeping, knowing that in a few hours, Caroline would present herself at the breakfast table as cool and poised as ever. She would never admit in the light of day that her heart had been broken.

Something had to be done to stop Ferrington's marriage to the Countess of Lavenham's daughter. Minerva no longer doubted that James loved Caroline. No man could speak from his heart in such a manner and not understand the loss of love.

That is exactly what she said to Lady Mary, Charlotte, and Violetta, later that morning when she relayed the conversation to them.

"Caroline is right. Running away isn't an answer," Violetta said, dabbing a handkerchief against the tears on her cheeks.

"But what can we do?" Lady Mary asked.

"Not 'we,'" Minerva corrected her. "This is something I, and only I, can do. Charlotte, may I borrow your coach?"

"Certainly, *chérie*, but first you must tell me what you plan."

"I'm going to pay a call, my friends, on the only person who can stop this farce of a marriage," Minerva said.

"And who is that?" Violetta asked.

Minerva pulled on her gloves. "The Countess of Lavenham."

Chapter 17

⌒◯◯⌒

The Earl and Countess of Lavenham lived on a palatial estate in one of the oldest, most prestigious sections of London.

Minerva's gaze took in the long graceful lines of the curving staircase, up to the high ceiling with its requisite forest scene of cherubs and nonsense that showed signs of being freshly painted. Minerva smiled. Vera Forbes Stanbury's taste had not improved with age.

The butler, dressed in a very undignified rose silk livery, came down the steps. "Lady Lavenham will see you. Please follow me."

He didn't offer to take her hat and shawl and his manner was as cold as the mansion's stone facade. His rudeness had no effect on Minerva. She had no desire to ingratiate herself with Vera or her ill-mannered servants.

Following the butler through a maze of hallways, Minerva noticed that once they'd gone past the formal section of the house to the private family quarters, the carpet became threadbare and the walls showed signs of ill repair. Darker rectangles of paint showed where pictures had once hung and the paint had faded around them.

The butler turned a corner and entered another wing of the house. Again, the decor changed. In this section, the carpet was deep and thick, the art on the walls amateurish and new. This had to be Vera's wing.

The butler stopped before a large white-and-gilt double door guarded by a footman dressed in a livery of the same outrageous rose silk. The butler rapped politely.

The door was opened by a lady's maid dressed in more bright rose.

"Lady Minerva—" the butler stated in a somber voice.

"Miss Minerva Pearson," Minerva corrected him.

"Miss Minerva Pearson," he intoned without missing a beat.

"Miss Minerva?" came a querulous voice from inside the room. "My, how the mighty have fallen."

Minerva took that as her cue to enter. She wasn't intimidated by servants or trappings, and Vera would soon find out she wasn't intimidated by her either.

In the dim light of the overheated room, Vera Forbes, now Vera Stanbury, Countess of Lavenham, lay in studied repose on a tufted divan made of the same rose silk as her livery. Even the drapes, closed to the late morning sun, were of the same shade, so that the whole room was bathed in a rose tint. Two bright-eyed spaniels sat on the countess's lap, their ears done up with rose silk ribbons that matched the silk ribbons in Vera's fussy lace day cap and dressing gown. A large white Persian cat with a rose silk bow around its neck lounged on a chair next to the divan.

"Minerva, what a surprise," Vera said. She took a sweetmeat off a tray beside the couch, pinched it in half, and fed it to her dogs. "Do you always come calling so early?"

"This isn't a social call, Vera."

She dismissed the servants with a negligent wave of her hand. "I didn't assume it would be."

Vera waited until they were alone before offering, "Do you wish to have a chair? Oh, I'm sorry. My cat is already sitting there. Too bad." She popped one of the sweetmeats into her own mouth.

"You haven't changed, have you?" Minerva said without heat. "Over thirty years have passed and look at you. You haven't changed at all."

Vera sat up, pushing the dogs off her lap. "Oh, I've changed since we last met. I have a husband and the respect and admiration of family and friends. Whereas you have no one. I'm a leader of Society and you are a nobody, a disgrace." The words seemed to give her pleasure. "I thank God I have lived to see this day."

"Am I the reason you've agreed to the match between your daughter and Mr. Ferrington? Did you discover his interest in my niece?"

Vera scratched one of the dog's ears. "I think he'll make an excellent son-in-law. So rich . . . handsome . . . well connected. Lavenham says Ferrington will become richer still." She kissed the dog on the nose. "Lavenham worries too much about money, but he says that with Ferrington in the family, our fortune is made."

She smiled at Minerva. "Do you worry about money, Minerva? It must be hard living without the comfort of a man's money and respectability for protection. Life must have been a great trial for you."

Rage filled Minerva. "How dare you interfere with two people's happiness for no other reason than your own petty need for revenge!"

"Petty? Oh, no," Vera said. "I've lived for this day. I've waited for it. Dreamed of it. And to think that it fell into my lap, the perfect way to repay you in kind for what you did to me years ago."

Minerva refused to back down. "I did nothing to you."

Vera's eyes narrowed. "Yes, you did!"

"Robert wasn't yours." Minerva enunciated each word distinctly.

"He was promised to me. Everyone knew it."

"Everyone assumed that you were promised because that's what you led them to believe, Vera. He'd made no promises to you."

"He should have done what was right—"

"But he *loved* me. And that is what really torments you, isn't it? He chose me."

"No!" The countess came to her feet, her fingers curling into fists. "He felt a mad infatuation for you. Love had nothing to do with it."

"Oh, love had everything to do with it," Minerva shot back. She stepped back, letting herself remember the man she had once loved, years ago when she'd been the toast of the London Season. "I gave up everything for him—and I would do so again in a heartbeat, even today. He loved me, and

I loved him. If fate hadn't intervened, we would have been married."

Vera's face turned a bright angry red. "No! He would have made an offer to me if you hadn't appeared on the scene. He was mine first. Everyone knew it. He danced with me twice at the Duchess of Stirling's ball. Our parents had spoken!"

"Those events happened before me." Minerva shook her head. "Vera, people don't own people. Robert and I couldn't have stopped what happened between us if we had wanted to. From the moment we first met, we were destined to be together."

Vera lunged toward her. "He kept company with me. Everyone assumed he was mine until you came along and broke the rules."

"There are no rules in love, Vera—"

"You made him forget his promise!"

"The promise his father made, not Robert!" Minerva snapped her fingers, feeling her own anger rise to the surface. She moved away, leaning more heavily than usual on her walking stick. She turned to face her rival. "What happened was a very long time ago, Vera. I know you cared for Robert . . . but he didn't return your regard."

"You destroyed him! You killed him!"

"Robert died in a coaching accident—"

"Which you caused!"

"If anyone caused it, you did!" Minerva said, finally shouting her down. The cat, frightened by the commotion, jumped down from the chair and hid under the divan. "You! With your wild accusations and selfish ways. You're the one who refused to release him from his parents' promise."

The countess sat on the edge of the divan. "You destroyed my life."

"No, I didn't, Vera. Nor was I responsible for Robert's death." Minerva leaned forward on her walking stick. "You know, for many years, I did believe that I was the cause of his death. My pain and guilt drove me to leave London."

Vera shot a spiteful look in her direction. "You left London because no one would receive you after I got through telling them what you did. All doors were closed to you—and they will remain closed as long as I'm alive."

Minerva shook her head. "You can't hurt me, Vera . . . because you can't change the truth. No matter what you say, or whom you say it to, we both know that Robert chose me."

"And he died for you!"

"He died in an accident." Minerva squared her shoulders. This wasn't a story she liked remembering. "But it's true, we were eloping when the accident occurred. I held him in my arms as he drew his last breath. And do you know what his last words were, Vera? His last words were, 'I love you.'"

The tears flowed freely down the countess's face. She sat down on the divan and turned her head. "I don't want to hear this. I don't believe you."

"It doesn't matter what you believe anymore, Vera, because you have no power over me. Years ago, you chased me off, but you can't do it again. You'll never be able to destroy me. I've loved too well in my life. Can you say the same?"

"Loved well?" the countess said with sarcasm. Her beribboned lace cap bounced as she shook her head. "I know exactly what you've been doing with your life. I've made it my business to know."

"But of course," Minerva said with a small smile. "I would expect nothing less of you."

Vera's eyes flashed with contempt. "You were living in Italy with your lover, a married man. Don't put on airs with me, Minerva Pearson. I know you for the strumpet you are."

Minerva drew in a deep breath, then released it with a light, sad laugh.

"What's so funny?" Vera asked.

"You. I can't believe that with your husband, your house, and your children, you've had no better way to spend your time than nursing your hatred for me. I don't know whether to be honored or humiliated!"

As if she were a judge delivering a sentence Vera said, "You shouldn't have survived. You should have *died* in that accident. You, not my Robert."

Minerva nodded. "I thought my world had come to an end with Robert's death, and no one blamed me more than I did myself. And all that blame was foolish. I told myself that if I'd agreed immediately to the elopement, we would have left the night before, but I was silly. I worried about what my friends and family would think of me. Just imagine, Vera, if we'd eloped the night before, he'd be alive today."

For a second, hot tears threatened. Minerva blinked them back. Her grief was private. "It took me years to realize that I have no control over fate. What I do regret is that I let you and others chase me out of London. Even my own family turned its back on me." She gripped the carved head of her walking stick, forcing herself to be honest in front of her enemy and admit, "There are even some things I did during those years that I am not proud of. But then, I met Bernardo Danesi, and I began to live again. Yes, I was his mistress. His parents had arranged a marriage for him when he was only seventeen. He and his wife grew to hate each other. That could have been your life, Vera, marriage to a man who didn't love you and couldn't stand to be in the same room with you."

Vera pulled her two spaniels to her protectively. "Robert loved me until he met you."

"So you keep telling me. But look at yourself now, Vera. You sit there up to your neck in lace and sweetmeats, lavishing your love on dogs. Would Robert love you now? Do you truly believe that he was the kind of man who would be proud of you for scheming against me?"

That well-aimed barb struck home. The countess practically quivered with outrage. "I am a good wife. I am well respected. Everyone admires me. My children care for me."

"And you care for your children so much you are willing to sell your daughter into a loveless marriage!" Suppressed fury etched Minerva's words.

"Lena adores Mr. Ferrington!" The room echoed with her words.

Minerva took a step back. Years ago, Minerva had felt no remorse when Robert rejected Vera, but now she saw in full what fruit that rejection had borne.

She had no desire to see history repeat itself.

Minerva chose her words carefully. "I'm sorry to hear that. He does not love her. Vera, if you had married Robert, you would have been more disappointed and angry than you are now. We cannot choose whom we love. The poets are right. Sometimes there is no rhyme or reason. If there were, Robert would have married you. You were prettier, wealthier . . . had so much more to offer than I did. But please, if you care for your daughter and her happiness, don't let what happened years ago dictate what is happening today. A loveless marriage is a prison."

For a moment, Minerva thought she was going to win. Vera's expression softened, her limpid eyes looked misty, and then, her head snapped up on her neck. Her eyes hardened. She hugged one of her pets to her chin. "You know, Minerva, the Italians are right."

"About what?" Minerva asked sharply, knowing the battle was lost.

"Revenge is a dish best served cold." She leaned forward, her eyes alight with the need for vengeance. "No. I won't release Mr. Ferrington from his promise."

Minerva lifted her chin proudly. "I won't stand idle and let you hurt my niece, not as long as I'm drawing breath."

Vera gave a shout of laughter. "There's nothing you can do to prevent this marriage. The announcement was printed in *all* the papers yesterday. And don't think that Ferrington and your niece can elope. It would be a terrible insult to my husband, who would stop at nothing to see that Ferrington lost everything."

"We'll see," Minerva said, unwilling to admit defeat. She turned and walked to the door. Vera's voice stopped her before she turned the handle.

"And, Minerva, don't ever come to my door

again." When Minerva didn't react, she added, "If you do, I'll set the dogs on you."

Minerva paused and looked back. Vera, her color high and her face streaked with tears, hugged her pets so tightly they struggled to be free. "You're a bitter woman, Vera. But remember, there's still time to change. Don't force James Ferrington to marry your daughter."

Not waiting for an answer, she opened the door and left, shutting the door on Vera's screamed "Never!" and the shattering sound of the sweet-meat tray striking against the door.

The footman guarding the door jumped. Quickly recovering himself, he looked at Minerva with a new sense of respect. "May I see you to the door, madam?"

Minerva started to say "Yes," when a maid hurried up to them.

"Please, ma'am, may I show you the way out?"

The footman frowned. "I don't think it's the wise thing."

The maid placed her hand on his arm. "Lester, just this once. There's no harm in it."

"There will be if she finds out." He nodded toward Lady Lavenham's door.

"She won't unless you tell her," the maid said.

At that moment a bell started ringing from inside the room. "You see?" the maid said. "She's calling for you. I'll see this fine lady out."

The footman looked undecided until the ringing started up again. He shrugged and waved them on.

Leaning heavily on her walking stick, the arthritis in her knee paining her, Minerva followed the young maid but her thoughts weren't on where they were going. Instead, she allowed herself to be swept up in the emotions of decades ago, of that first all-important love. Robert. Bold, self-confident Robert. How much she needed his strength now.

"What are we going to do, Robert? We can't let them end up like we did," she said softly.

"Excuse me?" the maid asked.

Minerva shook her head. "Just an old woman musing." She looked at the hallway. Here again the carpet was threadbare, but this was not a hall the butler had used when he'd taken Minerva up to see Vera. "Excuse me, but are we going a different way back to the door?"

The maid bobbed a small curtsy. "Please, ma'am, just a moment longer."

Curious, Minerva followed and then the maid stopped in front of a door and rapped a code—one knock, a beat, then two knocks—before opening the door. "Please, enter, ma'am," the maid said. She held the door open.

Minerva entered a bedroom done up in the same rose Vera favored, but toned down with touches of yellow to create a very pleasant effect. And then she stopped dead in her tracks as a young woman stepped forward. A woman who, with her blond hair and round blue eyes, was the complete image of Vera Forbes in her youth.

"Please," she said with a slight lisp that made the word sound like "pleath." "I didn't mean to startle you. I need just a moment of your time." She nodded and the maid closed the door on the three of them. "I'm Lena Stanbury."

The daughter. "Oh," Minerva said, already dreading the interview.

As if reading her mind, Lena hastened to explain, her lisp slurring the words. "Yes, I did hear what you said to my mother. This house was built during the Restoration and there are many priest holes and secret rooms. I was hiding in one of them off Mama's room."

"I think I need to sit down, if you please," Minerva said calmly while her mind raced with the worry of what she was going to do now.

The maid and Lady Lena moved a chair over to Minerva, who gratefully sat. Lady Lena knelt on the floor beside her. "I've upset you, Miss Pearson, and that wasn't my intent. Truly it wasn't."

"Then what do you wish of me?" Minerva asked. "You heard what was said in your mother's room?"

"Everything."

Minerva placed her hand against Lady Lena's cheek. "I am so sorry. Those words weren't meant for your ears. If I had known you were there, I would never have spoken so plainly."

Lady Lena shook her head impatiently. "No, I'm glad you said what you did. I don't want to marry Mr. Ferrington."

"You *what?*" Minerva said, caught by surprise.

"He's old," Lady Lena confessed candidly. "I don't want to marry an old man."

Minerva stared Lady Lena in the eyes. "You don't want to marry Mr. Ferrington?" she repeated dumbly.

Lady Lena shook her head. "I love Roger Thampson."

"Thampson?"

The young woman rolled her eyes with exasperation and said clearly with effort, "Sampson."

"And who is he?"

"A captain in the Guard. He's the youngest son of the Duke of Allvery," she explained. "Do you know about the feud between the earls of Lavenham and the dukes of Allvery?"

Minerva shook her head.

Lady Lena moved closer to share her secret. "Well, a hundred fifty-three years ago, the Sampsons were like the Stanburys, mere earls. However, right before the Battle of Naseby, the Earl of Lavenham performed an important service for Charles I. But his loyalty went unrewarded because Cromwell won the day and Charles was beheaded."

"What was the service the earl performed?" Minerva asked.

"I don't know," Lady Lena answered, "and Roger doesn't know either. In fact, we doubt anyone in either family can remember. What happened, though, is that when Charles II was restored to the throne, the Sampsons took the credit for the service and were given a dukedom as a reward. Since that day, the Stanburys have hated the Sampsons and the Sampsons have hated us in return . . . until I met Roger." She smiled as she said his name. A moment later, Minerva was surprised when tears brimmed in the young woman's eyes.

"Lady Lena, what is it?" Minerva asked a mere second before Lena buried her face in Minerva's lap and sobbed as if her heart were breaking.

Looking up in surprised shock, Minerva discovered that the maid, too, was crying, big, fat tears that rolled silently down her cheeks.

Minerva placed her hand on Lena's shoulder.

"Please, please, my dear. I don't know what the matter is, but certainly it is not that bad."

Lady Lena lifted her head. "Yes, it is," she lisped and hiccuped. "Miss Pearson, I have done a terrible thing."

Minerva patted the girl's hand comfortingly. "You're too young to have done anything so very terrible. Come now. Dry your tears and tell me what concerns you so."

The younger woman's chin quivered as she tried to stop the flow of tears. The maid scurried to take two handkerchiefs out of a drawer. She handed one to her mistress and used another for herself.

Lady Lena swiped at the tears, struggling for composure. Finally she sat back on her heels.

"Now take a deep breath," Minerva instructed, "and release it slowly."

Lady Lena pulled her shoulders back and did as instructed.

"There," Minerva said soothingly. "Don't you feel better?"

"Yes," Lena said, leaning her head back and drawing in another deep breath, and then another which she released with a sigh. Finally, she said, "I married Roger Sampson four months ago, while I was visiting my cousin in Aylesbury."

Minerva practically fell out of the chair. "You *what?*"

Once again Lady Lena's chin began to tremble and Minerva immediately regretted her outburst. She put her arm around the girl's shoulder. "Please, you must pardon me. It is such a surprise. How did you marry him?"

"He took out a special license and my cousin

helped us while I was visiting her. We told my aunt that we were going to take a ride over to some old ruins that everyone likes to visit and have a picnic. Actually, what we did was ride over to Waddesdon, and there we were married. Oh, Miss Pearson, it was so romantic. He'd taken a room at a small inn and, well . . ." She smiled and shrugged.

"I think I understand," Minerva said slowly.

Lady Lena grasped hold of Minerva's hand. "He is the most dashing, handsome, brave man in the world."

"Excuse me, dear, but if your families are such great enemies, how did you get together?"

"Through the same aunt I was visiting. Aunt Jane thinks the feud is ridiculous. Her son Stephen is in the same battalion as Roger and they became great friends. The summer before last, Stephen brought Roger home with him and I was there visiting." She shrugged her shoulders. "We fell in love. We didn't mean for it to happen."

"One never does, dear," Minerva said, her voice soft with irony.

Lady Lena pushed away and rose to her feet. "But the marriage isn't legal because we lied and told the vicar that I was one and twenty. I couldn't ask my parents for permission. They would never have given it!"

"Then how did you ever believe that they would agree to the marriage?" Minerva asked.

"Well, Mama doesn't think that Roger is a terrible person just because he is a Sampson. Plus, I thought I had time to get Papa and Mama used to the idea because Mama swore only last week I'd never marry someone untitled like Mr. Ferrington."

"Hmmm. But I don't think she'd approve of your captain either, would she?"

"She might," Lady Lena said hopefully. "Granted he's the youngest son, but if his five older brothers die, he would be duke."

"Charming thought," Minerva murmured.

"And then yesterday morning, Mama called me to her room and said she had changed her mind. She said I had to marry Mr. Ferrington. Now I know why." Tears welled up in her eyes.

Minerva picked up the handkerchief that had fallen to the floor and, rising, handed it to Lena. "Please, Lady Lena, don't cry. Not yet. There may still be hope."

"No, there is no hope. Mr. Ferrington tried to buy his way out of the engagement, but Mama wouldn't hear of it."

"How do you know this?"

"I was listening. There's another priest hole behind the wall in my father's study."

"Ah, of course."

"But it is worse, Miss Pearson. If Mama had agreed, Papa would have allowed Mr. Ferrington to buy his way out of the marriage contract. However, Roger read the announcement in the papers and confronted my papa last night after Mr. Ferrington left. He told Papa we were already married. Papa got angry and shouted at him that the marriage will be annulled because I'm under age. What's worse, Roger's father agrees with my father! The duke himself arrived last night while Roger was here. There was so much shouting going on. Roger's father has disowned him!"

She dried her tears with the handkerchief. "I'm confined to the house until I marry Mr. Ferrington, but Roger got a note through to me and says that he can't stay and watch me wed another man. He's taking orders for a company in India. He leaves London in two days and will sail to India at the end of this month." Fresh tears rolled down her cheeks. "I'll never see him again."

"And all for a woman's revenge," Minerva muttered under her breath.

"Miss Pearson, what am I to do? I love Roger so much. I'd run away if I could think of a way to sneak out of the house, but my parents have warned all the servants that I am not to leave. The only one who will help me is my maid Molly."

Minerva stooped to pick up her walking stick that had fallen to the floor. She paced the length of the room. "We must think of some way to outsmart them."

"We must do it soon—"

"Yes, before he leaves for India," Minerva agreed absently, working through the problem.

"And because I think I'm carrying Roger's baby."

Minerva almost walked into the bedpost. "Are you certain?"

It was Molly who answered. "She has all the signs, ma'am."

Minerva sat down slowly in a chair by the bed. She'd come to this house seeking a solution to Caroline's dilemma, and here was one being handed to her. Of course, Mr. Ferrington would not have to marry Lena Stansbury if she was pregnant and already married. All she would have to do is make that information public.

But at what cost?

The wide-eyed girl stood before her, anxiously

twisting the handkerchief in her hands . . . and Minerva knew she didn't have the heart to betray this child's trust. *Oh, Robert, there has to be another way*, she said silently to herself—and could almost imagine the two men she'd loved most in her life, Robert and Bernardo, laughing at this strange twist of fate.

"Please help me," Lena whispered in her soft lisp. "I think I'll die if I can't be with my Roger."

And then Minerva had an idea.

It was quite simple actually. A slow smile spread across her face. "Here now, no more tears. I think I have a plan that just might work."

Lena stopped crying and gave a hiccup before asking, "What are we going to do?"

"You're going to be kidnapped."

Chapter 18

A t the mention of the word "kidnapped," Lena's eyes turned as wide and round as an owl's. "You can't possibly kidnap me," she whispered. "Mama and Papa have given orders that I am not to leave the house for any reason."

Minerva frowned, resting her hands on the head of her cane, while she considered the matter. Finally, she asked, "You haven't told your parents that you are expecting Roger's child?"

Lena's face drained of all color. "I've dared not breathe a word of it to another soul, other than Molly. I have no idea what my parents would do if they found out."

"So, not even Roger knows."

Lena shook her head. "I was waiting until I was certain, but now they won't even allow me to post a letter. One of the other officers got Roger's message through to Molly, telling me he is leaving England, and that is the last I've heard."

"Through Molly, hmmm?" Minerva narrowed her gaze thoughtfully on the maid—and then the

idea hit her. It could work. Molly and her mistress
were of the same height and build, although
Molly's hair was carroty red. Still . . . if Lena
pulled Molly's mobcap down low over her head
. . . and since her costume was in that horrid rose
that Vera favored . . . "Molly, take off your dress."

The maid's eyes widened. "I beg pardon,
ma'am."

"And you, Lady Lena, you need to undress,
too."

Neither woman moved.

With an impatient sound, Minerva said, "Now,
don't stare at me as if I've grown horns and a tail.
You're going to trade places with your maid,
and we are going to walk out the door as boldly
as a vicar takes the pulpit to deliver a Sunday
sermon."

"Are you mad?" Lena asked.

"No. I'm quite sane." Minerva leaned forward
on her walking stick. "No one pays attention to the
servants in a huge house like this. Not even the
other servants notice the comings and goings of
everyone. In your maid's dress, you're going to
escort me right out the front door without anyone
being the wiser. Molly's mobcap will hide your
hair. And you, Molly, are going to have to help us
pretend that Lady Lena is here in her room."

"Why, yes, ma'am," Molly said.

"No. Absolutely not." Lena turned to the maid.
"If Mama or Papa finds out that you helped me,
they'll turn you off without references."

"But what else are you going to do, my lady? If I
don't help you, then your husband will leave for
India without ever knowing of the babe you're
carrying," Molly answered.

"Molly is right," Minerva said. "You don't have many choices. When is your husband leaving?"

"He said immediately," Lena answered, and again tears welled in her eyes.

"Please don't shed another tear," Minerva said firmly. "Crying won't help. Furthermore, if the British army continues true to form, 'immediately' can mean tomorrow or two years from tomorrow. Now, are we going to try my plan or not?"

"It will never work," Lena said. "We'll be caught before we make it down the stairs."

"Do you have a better idea?" Minerva asked.

Lena shook her head.

Molly took her hand. "Please try, my lady. If you don't catch your husband before he leaves, think of what will happen to you when your parents find out about the babe."

Lena trembled at the thought. "All right. We'll do it."

"Then quickly, out of your clothes," Minerva said.

The young women exchanged outfits.

They were unsure the plan would work until they stood before the looking glass and saw how complete the transformation was. Minerva walked over to the two young women and completed Lena's costume by placing the mobcap on her head.

"It's amazing," Lena lisped.

"I wouldn't believe it if I didn't see it," Molly whispered.

"Not even Mama would recognize me," Lena said.

"And, I should hope, not the butler," Minerva answered. She turned to Molly. "We haven't a moment to spare. Will you be all right in this room?"

Molly nodded. "I can stay here until suppertime and then sneak upstairs to my quarters. The housekeeper keeps extra uniforms in a wardrobe in her room. When she is down in the kitchen, helping with the serving, I'll put on one of the extras and then deliver the message that Lady Lena isn't feeling well and wishes a tray in her room."

"Which is what I have been saying ever since my parents confined me to the house," Lena added.

"Very good. That's perfect," Minerva said.

"But it isn't going to work," Lena said. She looked at herself in the mirror. "Someone will recognize me—"

"Not if you keep up your courage!" Minerva interrupted her impatiently. "You must believe that you will win, my dear. Trust me, there have been times in my life when I've been very afraid, but I never let anyone see it. Furthermore, Molly's sacrifice will be in vain if you lose courage before we even begin. Now, let us go forward boldly and not think of failure."

Lena nodded, but didn't move. Minerva took her hand and dragged her to the door. "Courage," she whispered. Lena straightened her shoulders. Minerva turned to the maid, who looked like a young lady of quality. "Good luck."

Molly bobbed a quick curtsy. "And to you, too, ma'am. Don't worry yourself none, Lady Lena. I'll make a noise or two in here so they'll think you are still in your room moping. You can depend on me."

Lena turned on her heel and ran back to the maid. Impulsively she kissed and hugged her. "Thank you, Molly. I'll make it up to you, if I can."

"Good luck," Molly whispered.

The young gentlewoman turned to face the door. The tears were gone, and in their place was firm resolution. "Shall we go? I believe it best that I lead the way since I'm the servant."

"Exactly right," Minerva said approvingly.

Lena opened the door, and it was as if she became a different person. Gone was the straight back and practiced poise of a debutante and in its place was a head-bobbing, foot-shuffling serving girl seeing a visitor to the front door. "This way, Miss Pearson," Lena said, dropping a quick curtsy.

"You must enjoy charades and playacting," Minerva said.

"Mama says I have a talent for it."

"Here, let me lean on one of your arms so that everyone will think I have trouble walking. Then no one will question why you are walking me to my coach."

"Very good idea," Lena said, and took Minerva's arm as if she were an invalid—or a broken woman. Wouldn't Vera enjoy that image!

Lena carefully guided them to the intersection of two hallways, making sure no one saw them. "Well, here we go."

"Yes," Minerva agreed. "And may luck be with us."

They actually had very little trouble. They met only servants, who lowered their gazes when they passed Minerva and didn't seem to give a second's notice to the little maid in a mobcap showing her to the door. Even the butler didn't recognize his mistress. Conscious that Minerva was a visitor held in disgrace, he averted his eyes when she passed, snapping for a footman to hold the front door open for them instead of opening it himself. Minerva gave him her sweetest smile.

They'd made it! At the foot of the mansion's stone front steps, Charlotte's coach waited. "This will be the tricky part," Minerva whispered to Lena. "You must make as if to pass the coach and then duck around the other side and crawl in by yourself. I'll pretend to drop my walking stick so that anyone watching will look at me and not see you. Can you do it?"

"I didn't think we'd get this far," Lena whispered back.

"Believe you can," Minerva instructed her. "Believe."

Lena nodded.

Pierre hopped down from the coachman's perch and started to come up the steps to help before Minerva waved at him to stay. Puzzled, he returned to the coach and opened the door, waiting for them to descend.

Minerva took her time going down the steps. She didn't want to make any sudden move that would alert the Lavenham servants before the right moment. Just as she came to the last step, she dropped her walking stick with a soft cry. She shook off Lena and grabbed her back. "Oh, dear. Pierre! Help me. Something has gone wrong. Help me."

She made as if to fall to the stone drive just as Pierre jumped forward to catch her. Minerva let herself relax in his arms, praying that Lena would seize the opportunity. She made as if to stand, and then collapsed again—just to give the young woman a little extra time.

"What is going on here!" a woman's voice cried

out—a voice that sounded suspiciously like Charlotte's.

Minerva peeped around Pierre's shoulder. Charlotte had already descended from the coach. Violetta and Lady Mary both hovered anxiously inside. Minerva brought her head up sharply. "What are you doing here?" she demanded of them.

"What? You think we would let you do this alone?" Charlotte shot back. "We drove over in Lady Mary's coach—and it is a good thing we're here, too. Pierre, put Minerva in the coach."

Before Minerva could protest, Pierre picked her up and carried her the last few steps to the door. Lady Mary and Violetta started to sit back in their seats and then froze.

The coach door on the other side was open and Lena stood as if helpless to know what to do.

"Let her in. Let her in," Minerva ordered as Pierre set her in the coach. When everyone still stared at each other in surprise, Minerva leaned across Violetta and took Lena by the front of her dress and pulled her into the coach. The girl landed on the floor between the older women. "Shut the door," Minerva ordered Violetta.

Charlotte handed Minerva her walking stick and was about to step in with Pierre's help when she caught sight of Lena. "Who is that?" she asked with a disdainful expression.

"Lady Lena," Minerva said. "Now get in here and be quick about it." She looked out the coach door and what she saw made her heart pound faster.

The butler and one footman had come out on

the porch, apparently very interested in all the activity around the coach. "Hurry and get in," she snapped at Charlotte.

Charlotte did not have to be told twice. *"Vite!"* she told Pierre as she pulled the door shut and fell back into the seat next to Lady Mary, who dropped the coach window curtains. The four of them were snug as caterpillars sharing the same cocoon while Lena was forced to sit among their feet.

The coach took off with a groan.

"Stay down," Minerva told her.

"I couldn't get up if I wished," Lena whispered in response.

"Will someone tell me what this is about?" Charlotte demanded, "and why we are all whispering?"

Minerva obliged by asking bluntly in her normal tone, "What were you all doing there anyway? I told you to wait for me at Charlotte's, and where is Lady Mary's coach?"

"We didn't want to wait at Charlotte's," Lady Mary said.

"Or miss any of the fun," Violetta added. "After we followed you, we decided it would be best to wait for you in the coach you arrived in, and we sent Lady Mary's coach home. We're here because we knew you would need us."

It was on the tip of Minerva's tongue to say, no, she didn't, when Charlotte asked, "Now, why are we kidnapping Lady Lena? And why is she dressed in the Countess of Lavenham's livery." She looked down at Lena with a frown. "The color is atrocious."

"It's Mama's favorite," Lena lisped.

"Then your *maman* has bad taste."

"Really?" Lady Lena looked down at the costume. "I rather like it."

"Then *you* have bad—" Charlotte started to say, but Minerva cut her off.

"Lady Lena, I would like you to make the acquaintance of my friends. This is the Baroness de Severin-Fortier. Across from me is Lady Mary Dorchester, wife of the late Colonel Sir William Dorchester, and next to her is Mrs. Violetta Mills. My friends, this is Lady Lena—" She paused a moment before adding, "Sampson. Lady Sampson."

Lena reached up and gave Minerva's hand a quick squeeze of appreciation.

Minerva continued. "Now that the introductions have been dispensed with, let us move on to business. We must hide Lady Sampson."

"Yes," Lady Mary said. "I've been wondering. What is the story?"

Minerva was about to tell them when suddenly they heard Pierre shout for the horses to stop. The wheels creaked as the brake was applied. Minerva lifted the curtain and shot a glance outside.

"What's happening?" Charlotte asked.

Minerva shook her head. "I don't know, but we are only at the end of the Lavenhams' drive."

"They've caught us," Lena squeaked.

"Not yet!" Minerva said. She dropped the curtain. "Quick, Violetta, cover Lena with your shawl." Outside the coach, a man said something to Pierre.

Violetta spread out the shawl, just as a knock sounded on the door.

Everyone inside the coach went very still.

Minerva cleared her voice. "Yes?" she asked, using her haughtiest tone.

"It's James Ferrington," came the voice from the other side. "May I have a word with you?"

Minerva immediately brought her hand up to her chest in relief. "Mr. Ferrington, you can't imagine how glad I am to see you."

"Mr. Ferrington!" a voice squeaked from the floor.

"Lena, it's all right," Minerva whispered to the woman shaking under the shawl. "Trust me." She didn't wait for an answer but threw back the curtain and lowered the coach window. For a second, she almost didn't recognize James. The forcefulness and confidence that seemed so much a part of his personality appeared to have vanished, leaving only a shell of the former man behind. He nodded to Charlotte and the others, but didn't seem to notice the quaking shawl between their knees.

"How's Caroline?" he asked.

"Much like you," Minerva answered. He'd laid his hand on the window ledge and she touched it. "You know, Mr. Ferrington, I want you to think of me as a friend."

He raised her gloved hand to his lips and placed a kiss on the tips of her fingers. "I appreciate that, Miss Pearson. And if you or," he paused before saying, "Lady Pearson," his voice softened on her name, "ever need me, you have only to call."

Minerva leaned forward, squeezing his hand. "Please take heart. Matters are not as dark as they seem."

"I can scarce imagine that at this moment. I'm up

to see Lavenham to formalize our arrangement and sign the papers for the marriage contract." He tightened his gloved fist resting on the door. "The deed is as good as done."

"No!" a voice cried out.

Mr. Ferrington looked with mild surprise at Lady Mary, Violetta, and Charlotte. They all sat as if turned to stone.

The shawl shifted and moved and a pink-mobcapped head popped out. "No!" Lena said again. "I don't want to marry you!"

Mr. Ferrington's eyes had grown wide with surprise. "Lady Lena?"

The young woman nodded her head unhappily, and then looked away, as if barely able to stand the sight of him.

James slid a sly look at the four women sitting in the coach. "Are you all *kidnapping* again?"

"Mr. Ferrington," Minerva said, "it will be a terrible squeeze, but perhaps you'd better join us in the coach, and I wouldn't worry about your appointment with Lavenham until after you've heard Lady Sampson's story."

"Sampson?" he asked.

"I'm married, Mr. Ferrington, and I have no wish to marry you," Lena stated bluntly.

James stared at her for a second, and then a slow, delighted grin spread across his face. "I'd love to join you in the coach, Miss Pearson."

Caroline's first letter of the day arrived shortly after nine. It was from Miss Elmhart.

Apparently, after Caroline had forcibly shown Miss Elmhart to the door, Minerva and the others had explained that they, and they alone, had kidnapped Mr. Ferrington and tied him up in the cellar. However, as Miss Elmhart explained in the letter, since the man was in Caroline's cellar, Caroline must bear some responsibility, and in short, ". . . Lady Dimhurst and I are agreed that kidnappers do not make good schoolteachers." Caroline had been discharged from her duties at the school, effective immediately.

The second letter came on the heels of the first. It was from Freddie. He wrote that Caroline could either move in with his mother or else. The Pearson coffers were empty and Freddie himself was leaving for the Americas the minute he posted this letter.

Caroline crumpled the missive in her hands and threw it on the fire. It was just like Freddie to run. Heaven forbid that he should try and work out his financial difficulties or, horror of all horrors, work for his living as she'd been forced to do.

She was expecting a letter from the Reverend Tilton when someone knocked on the door. Jasper hurried to answer it. A moment later, Caroline heard the Reverend Tilton's voice.

Well, at least he had enough courage to confront her face-to-face.

She met him at the door. "Reverend Tilton, how pleasant to see you."

His gaze met hers briefly before he looked away. "May I have a moment of your time, Lady Pearson?"

The thought crossed Caroline's mind that she was about to be sacked by the church—and it made her angry.

"Certainly," she answered, her tone clipped and impersonal. "Jasper, please take the Reverend's hat and scarf." Once he'd removed his outer wear, she led him into the parlor. "Do you care to sit?"

He looked indecisive for a moment, then said, "Yes, I rather think I will."

With a nod, Caroline indicated the sofa, while she took the chair across from him. The Reverend Tilton politely waited until she sat before taking his own seat. She noticed he was dressed in the black superfine tailcoat and lace-edged neckcloth he usually saved for Sundays.

She folded her hands in her lap, and waited.

He drew a deep breath, folded his hands in his lap, and stared into the fire. He said nothing.

He was drawing his third deep breath in the same number of minutes when Caroline asked, anxious to see this interview to its conclusion, "Did you have something to say, Reverend?"

He looked up from the fire as if surprised that she'd spoken. He pushed his glasses back up his nose.

But he didn't say anything.

Finally Caroline had had enough. "Reverend Tilton, you obviously came here for some reason. I wish you would kindly say what you wish to say and be done with it. I understand that you are reluctant, sir, but, trust me, the words will not grow easier to say with time."

Her directness startled him. Slowly his face turned red, as if his collar had grown too tight.

She couldn't help but feel sorry for him. She was about to grant him clemency and announce that she would no longer be able to continue her work with the Ladies Charity League when he fell to his knees on the floor between them.

"Lady Pearson, would you pay me the great honor of becoming my wife?"

Caroline stared at him as if he'd babbled in tongues. It took her a full minute to recover her wits. "Reverend Tilton, I'm surprised. I don't know what to say."

"Say yes," he pleaded, scooting closer to her.

Caroline leaned back in her chair. He'd been proposing every week for the last six months, but none of his proposals had been so dramatic. She looked around before asking him the question that was foremost on her mind. "Why?"

His watery blue eyes blinked. "Why what?"

"Why are you still asking me?" She bent down toward him. "Yesterday you indicated you'd heard complaints about me from Lady Dimhurst. Today you propose marriage. I would think that after hearing what Lady Dimhurst had to say, you would think me a singularly poor candidate for a vicar's wife. Am I not correct?"

The Reverend Tilton sat back on his heels. "Lady Dimhurst might be a touch upset."

"A touch," she agreed. "Not to mention the other women in the Ladies Charity League. I don't think they'd find me a good choice of partner for you either."

The Reverend Tilton took off his glasses. "I don't listen to rumor, if that is what you are suggesting. And I know that sometimes it appears that I let the women of the Ladies Charity League dictate to me, but I can stand up to them. I've just not had reason to do so since my wife died. It's been easier to go along with their demands and their wishes, but I wouldn't let them harm you."

Caroline was touched by his sincerity. Deeply touched. She knew that for all his brave words, he was a man who did not enjoy conflict. "Why are you really doing this?" she asked softly.

He frowned. "You don't mind if I get up and sit back in the chair, do you?"

"Not at all," she assured him.

He rose and sat uneasily on the edge of the sofa. Pulling a piece of cloth from his pocket, he cleaned the lenses of his glasses before speaking. "I can talk to you."

"To me?"

He nodded and set his glasses back on his nose. "I know most people wouldn't understand this, but running a parish is a lonely business." He looked down at his hands in his lap, his cheeks turning redder, before adding, "You've always been kind and sympathetic. Proposing to you every week has given me the opportunity to spend time with you, alone."

"I always imagined that you were relieved every time I refused your offer."

"I was, a bit," he admitted candidly. "However, since Lady Dimhurst came to see me this morning with a group of other ladies from the Charity League and insisted that I ask you to tender your resignation, I find the thought of not seeing you ever again deeply distressing. Today, my proposal is made with my most heartfelt sincerity."

"Reverend Tilton, I . . . I don't know what to say. I mean, you've asked every week but still . . ."

"You won't accept me?"

"I don't think of you that way, the way two people should feel about each other when they marry." The way she felt about James Ferrington.

"I wouldn't expect us to live as man and wife," he hastened to assure her. "At least, not until we knew each other better."

Caroline rose to her feet and crossed to the fireplace. She watched the flames lick at a log while she considered his proposal. "I have my husband's aunt, who lives with me."

"Miss Pearson would be welcome to live with us . . . although she may have to change some of her more flamboyant ways."

Could Minerva change, especially to what Lady Dimhurst and the other matrons would deem acceptable? And what about herself? How would she fit in that same mold?

On the other hand, she and Minerva would have a roof over their heads and the gentility that came with respectability.

But it would be a marriage without passion.

She closed her eyes, allowing herself to savor the feelings of last night, of holding her lover in her arms and giving him both her love and her passion.

She opened her eyes and turned to him. "I'm sorry, Reverend Tilton, but I must refuse your very kind offer."

"Lady Pearson, please reconsider—"

The front door flew open. Minerva, the Baroness, Lady Mary, and Mrs. Mills bustled in. A step behind them, James entered—carrying in his arms a rather attractive young woman dressed in a bright rose dress. Her blond hair tumbled down her back and she looked very young and innocent.

Sharp jealousy shot through Caroline, especially when the woman looked up at James as if he were her savior.

Minerva clapped her hands. "Caroline, we have

the most wonderful news. You are going to be so happy." She came to a halt. "Why, hello, Reverend Tilton. How fortunate you are here at this very moment."

"Fortunate?" Reverend Tilton said unhappily.

Caroline barely registered Minerva's words. She watched James carry the woman into the parlor and deposit her on the sofa as if she were made of fine china. "Thank you, James," she said, batting limpid blue eyes up at him.

"Who is this?" Caroline asked Minerva in a low aside.

"This is Lady Lena! Lena, I wish you to make the acquaintance of my niece Caroline Pearson."

Lady Lena. Caroline faced her rival. Minerva hurried toward the young girl. "Never mind her outfit. Her mother has terrible taste—but that is another story. What is important, Caroline, is that Lena is having a baby!"

If the earth had opened up beneath her feet, Caroline could not have been more shocked. It didn't help matters when Lena took James's hand and declared in a very pronounced lisp, "And James is the finest man imaginable!"

Chapter 19

Stunned, Caroline whirled to face Minerva. It couldn't be true. "There must be a mistake."

"There's no mistake! Is this not the most wonderful news?" Minerva asked.

The Baroness sat down on the sofa next to Lady Lena and pulled off her gloves. "What we need is champagne to celebrate. Jasper, go fetch Pierre. I will send him to my home for champagne."

"A party! Yes, we need a party," Lady Mary declared, the plumes of her wide-brimmed hat nodding with her head. "Right now, in celebration."

"If you'll permit me, Baroness, I will provide the champagne," James said gallantly. "After all, it is my good fortune we're celebrating."

Caroline stared at them. Lady Lena still hadn't relinquished her hold on James's hand. She looked so happy, so content.

"Reverend, I am glad you are here," James was saying to Reverend Tilton. "We are going to need your good advice and perhaps, even your services."

Caroline clenched her hands into fists, struggling to ignore the flickers of light around her eyes and the drumming in her ears. It seemed she kept breathing only through strength of will and she wished, by some strange magic, to disappear, never to live through this moment in time.

"I'd be happy to be of service to you, sir. I'm sorry, I didn't hear your name?" Reverend Tilton said.

"Ferrington. James Ferrington." James finally shook off Lady Lena and held out his hand to the vicar.

While they were exchanging pleasantries, Minerva hovered over Lady Lena. "We must get you something to drink, dear. You've already done far more than you should have in your delicate condition."

Delicate condition. Caroline dug her nails into her palms. *I will not faint. I refuse to faint. Not yet. Please, not yet.*

It was Mrs. Mills who noticed. "Caroline, is something wrong? Your face looks absolutely white. You're not taking ill, are you?"

Caroline felt all eyes in the room turn to her—including James's.

His eyebrows came together in concern. "Caroline?" he asked, his tone uncertain.

She shook her head. She couldn't stay in this room a second longer, not with Lady Lena beaming with happiness. Ducking her head, she ran to the door—but James stepped into her path.

"Please," she managed to say, trying to push past him.

"Caroline, what is the matter?"

"The matter?" she asked, finding her voice, the words practically choking her. "You announce that your betrothed is carrying your child and then ask me what is the matter? Have you lost all consideration for my feelings?"

For a second, her questions were met with stunned silence. Then, everyone in the room except Reverend Tilton burst into laughter. Caroline's confusion turned to anger.

She started to walk out of the room, but James wouldn't let her. He placed his hands on her arms, his eyes sparkling with good humor. "Caro—" he started, and then Caroline cut off any further conversation. She kicked him.

He released her.

She didn't wait to see if he was all right. Judging by the way the wind left him and how he doubled up, she had a feeling he wasn't! She ran out of the room, threw open the front door, and charged out into the street.

She didn't know where she was going. She didn't care. Behind her she heard Minerva call her name. Caroline lifted her skirts and started running. She turned the corner at the end of a block and then turned another and, finally, afraid that they would give chase, she ducked down an alley, needing to be alone.

Clouds covered the sky and the air was cold and damp. Caroline wished she'd thought to take her hat or shawl, but she wouldn't go back. She'd never go back. She pushed back a loose lock of her hair, tucking it behind her ear, then stopped.

What was she doing? She had nowhere to go; no one to turn to—except her former mother-in-law. She shuddered at the thought.

She didn't even have Minerva.

A deep male voice interrupted her thoughts. "This time you were easier to find."

James.

Caroline turned to face him. He stood at the end of the alley, a tall imposing figure in polished boots and a greatcoat with seven capes. So bold. So handsome.

He'd never be hers.

"We have nothing to say to each other, James. I want to be alone. Go back to the woman who is going to have your baby."

"Do you have such little faith in my character that you believe I would bring a woman carrying my child to your doorstep?"

His words cut right to her heart. "I don't know what to believe. Not anymore."

He began walking toward her, his steps deliberate. "Then believe in my love for you. Believe that I would never intentionally harm you, that my sole purpose in life is to love, honor, and protect you."

I don't care, she wanted to shout, but it would be a lie. Instead, she felt rooted to the earth as she helplessly watched him come closer and closer until, finally, he stood before her.

Even now her traitorous body wanted to melt into him. She wanted to throw her arms around him and beg him to tell her it wasn't true—

"The baby's not mine."

Caroline stared up into his handsome face, his eyes dark and serious. She couldn't have heard him correctly.

His green eyes lit up with laughter. He waved a hand in front of her face. "Hello? Did you hear me?"

Caroline blinked, coming out of a trance. "Did you say the baby isn't yours?"

He nodded.

Caroline walked several steps down the alley, digesting this information, and then came rushing back. "If the baby's not yours, then whose is it?"

He laughed and looked heavenward. "Finally she's starting to understand." He smiled down at her. "The baby is her husband's."

The words seemed to hang between them until their meaning slowly sank into Caroline's consciousness. "James, she's already married? I'm not certain I understand."

"I'm not surprised. It took me a telling or two to grasp the full story, but apparently Lady Lena ran off several months ago and married a young military man. Of course, she did it without the permission of her parents, but the marriage has been consummated. Her parents don't know about the baby—yet."

"Then, you can't marry her," Caroline said, slowly beginning to understand.

"Lady Lena is going to cry off," he said, his arms coming around her, before he whispered in her hair, "so that I can be with the woman I love."

At first, she didn't think she'd heard him correctly . . . then it was as if the heavens had opened and granted her one and only wish. The day was no longer cold and chilly, but fresh and full of possibilities. Caroline laughed, feeling lighter and happier than she had in years. She could have danced, right there in the alley.

A thought struck her. "But why were you carrying her into the house?"

He smiled. "Suspicious, aren't you? She rode with us on the floor of the coach and her leg had fallen asleep. It hurt for her to walk, and I carried her in because I couldn't wait to tell you the good news."

"But she looked at you as if you were her savior."

"I am. I've promised to see that she and her husband can be together. In fact, Daniel is over at the War Office working on that right now. I'm certain Captain Sampson is still in London. And later today, Daniel and I will confront the Earl and Countess of Lavenham and make them recognize the marriage."

"Why would they not?"

"The Earl of Lavenham and Sampson's father, the Duke of Allvery, are involved in a feud that has gone on for generations. However, I will have Lavenham's consent before nightfall."

"How are you going to accomplish that?"

"I can be persuasive." His arms tightened around her until their bodies were pressed thigh to thigh and nestled together as close as spoons. She could even feel his heart beat, its rhythm matching her own. Tilting her head back, her chin against his chest, she looked into his face, at those laughing green eyes full of love and at his lips only inches from hers . . .

"Caroline, will you marry me?"

Yes! her heart wanted to shout, but another, deeper, fear made her say, "James, no. We can't.

He frowned down at her. "Why not?"

"Because I can't have children."

"Caroline, whether or not we have children is in

God's hands, not ours. Don't refuse me for something over which we have no control. I don't want to live without you."

"But, James—"

His mouth came down on hers, cutting off her protest. He kissed her thoroughly, soundly, and possessively until Caroline couldn't stand on her own, let alone think.

They broke for air. "Have I convinced you yet to be my wife, or will it take another kiss?" he asked.

"Oh yes," she said, embracing him with all of her heart. "I'll be your wife . . . and yes, I'll take another kiss."

Epilogue

The Earl of Lavenham and the Duke of Allvery refused to set aside their feud for the sake of their children.

It didn't matter. Captain Roger Sampson was overjoyed at the news that he was to be a father. James liked him immediately and offered to assist the young couple in any way he could. The two decided that since they didn't have the approval of their parents, they would go to India as a couple. James owned several properties close to the military headquarters in Calcutta and offered one of them as a wedding gift.

James gave Caroline the deed to her house as an engagement present. He'd wanted to marry her with all the pomp and ceremony his money could buy, but she convinced him that she would prefer a less ostentatious wedding. He agreed but made a sizable donation to impress St. Mark's Ladies Charity League. The donation was so impressive that Lady Dimhurst was wild with jealousy, especially when some of the members suggested it might be time for her to step aside and let someone new lead the group . . . such as Caroline Pearson Ferrington. The Reverend Tilton wrote a gracious note thanking them for the donation but declined to officiate at the wedding since he planned on being out of town on that date. Lucinda Pearson, Caroline's mother-in-law, also refused to attend.

However, no one else felt the same way. Their wedding was *the* event of the new year.

And so it was that on the morning of January 24, 1814, in St. Mark's Church, Caroline and James were married, with Daniel Harvey serving as groomsman. The bride was beautiful and serene, the groom anxious and proud—just as it should be at weddings, everyone said.

Of course, the real talk amongst the guests was that the wedding breakfast was being hosted by the infamous Baroness de Severin-Fortier. It was her gift to the wedding couple. And several people noticed that standing next to the Baroness was Miss Minerva Pearson. People wondered if she was the same Minerva Pearson whom they had heard was disowned by the Pearson family—or was it Lord Freddie who had been disowned? Many decided it must be Freddie, who hadn't been seen since he fled London to avoid his creditors.

The other person to incite comment was Mrs. Violetta Mills, who stood next to Lady Mary Dorchester, wife of the late "Mad William" Dorchester. Mrs. Mills was such a mousy creature, it was hard to believe the stories about her were true. And it was so good to see Lady Mary out and about again, although she fell asleep halfway through the ceremony.

What really puzzled the guests was the wrong

turn Ferrington's burled wood coach made after the wedding ceremony. At first, the other coachmen slowed down, uncertain whether to follow Ferrington's coach or take the most direct route to the Baroness's.

The Baroness solved the problem. She and Miss Minerva Pearson leaned out of the windows of the Baroness's coach and signaled for the guests to follow them on the more direct route. Since they didn't seem disturbed that the bridal couple were going in the wrong direction, the guests decided they wouldn't worry either and soon found themselves drinking iced champagne in the Baroness's huge and lovely home.

In fact, the guests had time to enjoy several glasses before the bride and groom, their eyes bright with love, made an appearance almost an hour later. Several people wondered if the bride was feeling well. Her face definitely appeared flushed.

Someone asked Miss Minerva Pearson if the bride suffered from a rash.

"It's not a rash," Miss Pearson said as she handed champagne from a servant's tray to the Baroness, Lady Mary, and Mrs. Mills. "It's whisker burn." The four friends clinked their glasses together.

And that is why no one who attended the wedding was surprised when nine months later, almost to the day, James and Caroline became the proud parents of a healthy baby girl. They named her Diana, after the Greek goddess of the moon, and no two parents could have rejoiced more in a birth.

Avon Romantic Treasures

*Unforgettable, enthralling love stories,
sparkling with passion and adventure
from Romance's bestselling authors*

LADY OF SUMMER *by Emma Merritt*
77984-6/$5.50 US/$7.50 Can

HEARTS RUN WILD *by Shelly Thacker*
78119-0/$5.99 US/$7.99 Can

JUST ONE KISS *by Samantha James*
77549-2/$5.99 US/$7.99 Can

SUNDANCER'S WOMAN *by Judith E. French*
77706-1/$5.99 US/$7.99 Can

RED SKY WARRIOR *by Genell Dellin*
77526-3/ $5.50 US/ $7.50 Can

KISSED *by Tanya Anne Crosby*
77681-2/$5.50 US/$7.50 Can

MY RUNAWAY HEART *by Miriam Minger*
78301-0/ $5.50 US/ $7.50 Can

RUNAWAY TIME *by Deborah Gordon*
77759-2/ $5.50 US/ $7.50 Can